LOVE
it's complicated

JEANNINE COLETTE

Copyright © 2023 by Jeannine Colette
All rights reserved.

Visit my website at jeanninecolette.com
Cover Design by Sarah Hansen, Okay Creations,
www.okaycreations.com
Editor: Jovana Shirley, Unforeseen Editing,
www.unforeseenediting.com
Proofreader: Courtney DeLollis
Proofreader: Virginia Tesey Carey

No part of this book may be reproduced or transmitted in any form or by any means, electronic or mechanical, including photocopying, recording, or by any information storage and retrieval system without the written permission of the author, except for the use of brief quotations in a book review.

This book is a work of fiction. Names, characters, places, and incidents either are products of the author's imagination or are used fictitiously. Any resemblance to actual persons, living or dead, events, or locales is entirely coincidental.

ISBN-13: 9798376500934

For Marissa Jones and Lauren Costa.

one

"JONES. MELISSA."

My name being called from the other side of the thick steel bars has me rising from the cold bench and wiping my hands on my jeans.

An officer stands at the far end of the room, looking at me—the lone inmate in a holding cell at the Valor County Jail. He's probably wondering why a thirty-four-year-old wedding designer with a nice home and two young children broke into a salon in the middle of the night. A high-end luxury salon in the nearby snobbish town of Greenwood Village, of all places. I scratch my head and wonder why myself. I suppose I could blame the wine. There was a vast amount of Whispering Angel Rosé involved in the events preceding the alleged break-in.

"Mrs. Jones, I have a couple of questions for you." His deep baritone echoes from across the room, where he remains, seemingly in the shadows. His voice is commanding in that tone police officers use on TV to intimidate people.

For the record … it's working.

This moment is quite theatrical really. Me, a frazzled woman, alone in a cell, while the man in dark navy appraises my every move. It's like I'm being interrogated, a convict in the spotlight as she's probed for information. It has my spine standing up straight and a chill radiating up my back as I take a long, quivering breath.

I grip the bars tight, my hands clenched into fists as I shout toward him, "This is all wrong! I'm a good woman, for Pete's sake."

"Ma'am, please calm down."

"Calm down?" My question is exclaimed. "You don't understand. I'm not a criminal. Yes, I understand you must hear that sort of thing a lot, but I can explain. I tried to tell your friend, Officer I Just Want to Arrest Innocent Women." I point toward the cinder block wall and not at the officer I'm referring to because *that* man, the one who handcuffed me about two hours ago, isn't actually in the room.

"When the cops showed up to Bella Boutique Spa, the officer didn't let me explain my purpose for being there as he read me my rights and cuffed me." The thought has my chest clenching. "*Oh my God*, I've been read Miranda rights. And handcuffed," I cry out as I rub my wrists where the metal cinched my skin. "I'm a vagrant. A criminal in the eyes of the law. Did they really need to take a mug shot? I hope it's more Nina Dobrev than Reese Witherspoon because Nina looked adorable in hers. Granted, she was only twenty. Reese's was cute, too, but she wasn't even looking at the camera. As long as I don't look like Heather Locklear … or Lindsay Lohan …" My ramblings cease, and my eyes widen as the gravity of the situation comes into focus. "I'm a convict. Fucking Tyler!"

With a swift push, I shove off from the bars and start to pace the cell. It's pretty forgiving in size, and I'm the only one here, so I have plenty of room to walk in a circle as my hands run through my hair.

"It's bad enough he got the house and the kids on the weekends. Every single weekend. That's so excessive, don't you think? It's what I get for trying to do the *right thing*. Did you know he cheated?" I ask the officer, who shakes his head and takes a step closer.

"No, ma'am."

"With Maisie freakin' Mirlicourtois. I mean, I couldn't come up with a sexier name for his mistress if I conjured one up myself. I probably would have envisioned *Debbie Dicksalot* or *Bonnie Bendover*, but, no, he had to bed Maisie Mirlicourtois, the only woman in a hundred-mile radius who can do my color."

His head tilts. "She colors?"

I lift a strand of my orange hair. Yes, brassy orange highlights by someone who clearly can't do color like Maisie.

LOVE ... IT'S COMPLICATED

"She's the best hair artist in the state and the only one who has the formula to do my hair the perfect shade of blonde without looking fake, which I haven't seen since she stole my husband. So, now, not only does Tyler get to keep my entire life, but he also has my hairstylist. And before you assume I care more about my hair than my ex-husband, the answer is yes." I pause and stare at him for dramatic effect because it's true. "She can have him. He's a lying, cheating bastard of a man. I just want my hair back!"

Moisture builds behind my eyes as they well up with a heaviness behind them. I hate Tyler more than I could hate any man. Yet why does the mention of him make me so damn sad? Oh, that's right—because he was my husband and I loved him something fierce before he went and stuck it to Maisie, the hair goddess.

The anger from the reminder of his illicit affair brings a surge of adrenaline that has me slamming my fist into the cinder block wall.

"Damn it, that hurt!"

As I clutch my now-bruised fist to my chest, I take a seat back on the cold bench and hunch over. I have a wedding to set up tomorrow, and an injured hand is not ideal when you have to hang fifty yards of tulle over an altar to create an ethereal effect. That is, if I ever make it out of here.

The officer takes a few steps closer to the bars. His footsteps heavy against the concrete as he draws near.

"Are you okay?" He sounds sincere.

"I actually liked Maisie. Every six weeks, I sat in her chair and told her my secrets. It should be criminal for a hairdresser to use your thoughts against you. It should be like violating attorney-client privilege or HIPAA."

My comment earns me a deep chuckle from the officer.

"You should hear what's said in the barber shop. There's an unspoken code of what's said in the chair, stays in the chair."

I sit up, press my back against the cinder block, and laugh lightly. "Seriously. Instead, I bet she took every morsel and used it to woo him. Not that it was hard. We were quasi-separated. Smart woman to swoop in when she did. I'm such a fool.

"You know what hurts the most? My son, he loves her. Thinks she's so cool, and he's right. Maisie's so damn cool. And beautiful and successful. A catch. A total upgrade." I sigh, not in a *woe is me* way, although there's plenty of that going on. I sigh because it's true. Maisie is a total catch. "At least Izzy doesn't see it that way. She hates

Maisie. She hates Tyler too … and me for that matter, so I guess that doesn't count for much."

"You entered Ms. Mirlicourtois's salon at eleven thirty in the evening for—"

"My hair color card." I stand up again, holding my fist, and start my pacing again, this time a little closer than before. "I blame the wine. And my best friend, Tara. She got me all excited, and, well, after a bottle … and a half … I thought, *You know what? Enough is enough.* That witch has my house and my kids on the weekends, and she wore my robe and used my waffle iron while making *my* kids breakfast in *my* gourmet kitchen, and I was so damn tired of her having everything."

"So, you—"

"Went to the salon and used the back door while the cleaning crew was there. It's not breaking and entering if the door is literally open."

"Mrs. Jones, I have to stop you before you say any more."

His use of the married abbreviation halts my steps. "It's *Miss* Jones. Thank you for not calling me ma'am again. It makes me feel so old. There should be a rule you can't call a woman ma'am until she's older than forty, which I am nowhere near."

"You're thirty-four," he states with a smile as he comes up to the bars, out of the shadows and into the light that my cell provides.

I stand up straighter as my heart freezes.

My chest rises as he closes in, and I have to clear my throat.

"I know," I stammer rather breathlessly. While I am a little worked up from the pacing, fist punching, and overall self-deprecation, I'm mostly taken aback by how handsome he is.

Tall, broad shoulders, square jaw, and a killer grin. Officers shouldn't have grins like this—the kind that gives a mischievous wink of the eye, which are both hazel and piercing. The kind that gives him divots in his cheeks and makes a woman weak in the knees. I'd confess to murder if he smiled at me like that because I'd be so hypnotized that I wouldn't realize what I was saying.

He places a key in the cell lock. "I have to stop you there because I spoke with your ex-husband, Tyler Landish, and Miss Mirlicourtois. He said he gave you permission to be in the salon, and she is not pressing charges."

The lock clicks, and the door opens. As the steel moves away, he holds it and gestures for me to step out.

LOVE ... IT'S COMPLICATED

"Oh." I feel a little embarrassed. I just poured my heart out to this man, and for no reason, as he's clearly releasing me. "So, I'm good to go?"

"Yes, ma—" He pauses, as if catching himself before saying ma'am. "Ms. Jones. You are free to go, so long as you can confirm that what Mr. Landish and Ms. Mirlicourtois said is correct."

"Yes!" My shoulders are squared, and my chin is held high. "That's what happened."

"Then, you're free to go."

He closes the cell door behind me, and I look up at him.

When he was standing on the other side of the room, he felt imposing, and I can see why. His tall height, paired with his lean yet muscular frame in that fitted uniform, is quite impressive. White teeth, tan skin, and a jawline that could slice granite, he could be a poster boy for the police department. It would make me join the academy.

I look back at the cell and think about all the things I said in there. "Is there any form of officer-felon privilege?"

His eyes widen, and it looks like he's going to choke on his own air. I stare at him in confusion until it dawns on me that what I said sounded way worse than what I intended.

"Oh God. No! Not that kind of privilege. I mean, like what we were saying. Like the barber shop. What's said behind the bars, stays behind the bars. Because some of the things I said in there, while true, aren't exactly—"

"You're good." He gives that damn winky smile again.

"Thank you," I say with a shaky breath and glance at the tag on his uniform.

W. Bronson.

He leads me out of the room and into the main room of the police station. In a quiet place like Valor County, there isn't a ton of criminal activity. A few officers are at desks, including my arresting officer. I give him a sneer as we pass and follow Officer Bronson to the front of the room, where my ex-husband, Tyler, is seated in a wooden chair.

As we approach, Tyler stands.

I blink at him a few times and then look at Officer Bronson and back to Tyler. My eyebrows squish together. "Why are you here?"

My ex looks at me with a mixture of exhaustion and annoyance. "Maisie came down here to give a statement, and then we had to switch because someone needs to watch the children. It's way too late for a woman, especially one who's possibly still drunk, to take an Uber alone. So, unless you want me to wake your father up to come down here to drive you home, I suggest you let me give you a lift."

The problem with dating someone since you were fifteen is that they know everything about you and your family. My father, Gavin Jones, would be far more ornery than usual if we woke him up for a reason other than the fact that someone was lying dead in a ditch.

"Fine. Let's go." I'm about to walk out when a warm, strong hand touches my arm. I turn to see Officer Bronson pulling me back.

"Your belongings. You need to sign for them."

I nod, having completely forgotten I had a purse. I leave Tyler unhappy to be waiting longer. I understand his grievance. It's now two in the morning, and we could all use a good night's sleep.

Bronson walks me over to a counter, where a female officer has my bag in a large Ziplock. We go through the contents, and then I look inside my purse, signing a form to confirm everything I had with me tonight is accounted for.

When I'm done, I'm about to walk back to Tyler, who is impatiently tapping his foot by the front door, when Officer Bronson halts me. Those light eyes look down, slightly unsure, before he looks straight into my eyes. I take a deep breath, which seems to be a habit when he stares at me. It's the smolder. The man has a look that burns slowly, melting you on the spot. I wonder if it has anything to do with the uniform. Like how Tim McGraw looks hot with the cowboy hat, but not so much without it. I don't think the intense gaze of Officer Bronson would be as powerful if he were wearing pajama pants and a hoodie.

I tilt my head at him, wondering what it is that has us standing here.

His lips purse for a moment. "Are you okay, going home with him?"

"Tyler?" I ask incredulously. "He's harmless."

"You had a lot to say about how he hurt you. I need to make sure you're emotionally okay, being alone with him." His words are purposeful and laced with concern.

I let out a breath, enlightening this man's understanding of my feelings. I look down at his hand and don't see a ring on his finger. "Do you have kids?"

LOVE ... IT'S COMPLICATED

He shakes his head.

I shrug my shoulders and sigh. "Divorce sucks. You expect to love each other forever, and when that doesn't happen, you end up fighting over property and pensions and who gets the fine china. It's an exhausting process that leaves you feeling very bitter, very alone, and suddenly very, very single. But when you have children with that person, that *until death do you part* promise comes into play. I might hate that man, but he's still the father of my children, and for at least the next thirteen years, until my son goes to college, I'm stuck with tolerating him. And despite his flaws, he did me a solid tonight."

He squints his eyes and gives a sly grin. "Are you confessing that you did indeed break into Bella Boutique Spa in order to obtain your hair color card?"

Yes, actually, I did break into the salon because I was frantic and drunk, but that's beside the point.

I scrunch my face and raise a finger at him. He's slick, but not that slick. "Nice try."

I walk away from the handsome officer and to my scoundrel of an ex, who rises again from his seat and holds his hands out, as if saying, *Are you ready?*

With an air of sarcasm, I grunt at him. "Jeez, Tyler. Can we please get out of here now? I've been waiting on you for hours."

He lets out a groan as I brush past him and out to his brand-new Mercedes-Benz. I'll have to remember this new car when he complains about the upcoming cost of Izzy's braces.

I slide onto the soft leather and close the door. Tyler climbs in on his side and starts the car. He's wearing jeans and a sweater—something he must have thrown on quickly to look presentable at the station. He drives through the streets of Greenwood Village, the radio turned off.

He runs a hand down the side of his face. We make it about seven blocks before the silence is broken.

"Lyss, if you need money, just tell me. Robbing the salon is not the answer."

My back hits the side of the door as I stare back at him, incredulous, hoping he's joking with that comment. The way his brows lower and he looks at me with pity has me barking out a laugh.

"I wasn't there to rob the salon."

"Then, what were you doing? Maisie got an alert on her phone that the security cameras went off in the back room, and the cleaning crew never goes in there, so when she looked at the camera feed and saw you, she called the cops."

"Maisie is the one who called the cops? I thought it was the cleaning crew. Jesus, Tyler. You two really think I was there for her money? What business owner keeps money in a store at night anyway? You're supposed to take it home with you at the end of the day. Besides, most of her clients pay with credit cards."

"You know an awful lot about her salon."

If my eyes could shoot daggers, I'd let them. "I know a lot about running a business because I run one myself."

"Party planning isn't a cash operation."

"Go to hell, Tyler."

He slams his head against his seat. "Fine. You're not gonna be straight with me. Just promise you won't go near Maisie's business or any of her things again."

"That's a good idea. Then, maybe you should tell her to stop wearing my robe. I didn't even realize I'd left it there until the kids mentioned she was wearing a white robe with the initials *MJL* on the breast pocket."

"She forgot hers at home and found yours tucked into the back of the guest room closet. As you and I agreed, she still sleeps in the spare room when the kids are there. She didn't want to come downstairs in the morning, looking inappropriate."

"I heard Maisie is moving in with you. Doubt she's gonna stay sleeping in the guest room."

His face pales slightly, and he scrunches his eyes. "I was going to tell you when I dropped the kids off on Sunday."

"I should have been the first person to know."

The rest of the thirty-minute drive to Newbury is in silence. We pass the woods that surround the town on two sides, a place we used to go for hikes in as a young family.

He pulls over in front of the neighbor's house. It's an old habit from our teenage dating years, when he'd have to let me out at the house two doors down from my parents' so they didn't hear the car door close in the middle of the night and wake up.

When the car is parked, he turns to me with a hand stretched out on the back of my seat. I remember when he used to park here and put his arm on my seat this way. It was a different time, when we had different feelings for each other.

LOVE ... IT'S COMPLICATED

"It's been two years—"

I hold my hand up to stop him. "No, Tyler. Don't wax poetic about what we were and what we are now. Believe it or not, what happened tonight had nothing to do with unrequited feelings I have for you. Because there are none. I just had too much wine and a really bad idea, which led to me being handcuffed and arrested for the first time in my life, having my mug shot taken, sitting in a cell for far longer than I ever planned on, and being questioned by an impossibly handsome police officer."

Tyler raises a brow at that last comment. "Handsome?"

I clear my throat. "Yeah, wasn't planning on saying that out loud. It just came out."

He lets out an incorrigible laugh. "You'll never change."

Now, it's my turn to raise a brow at him. "Is that a good thing or a bad thing?"

"Both. Definitely both." He unlocks the car door. "You owe Maisie a thank-you for tonight."

"Yeah, well, she owes me an apology for stealing my husband, so let's call it even."

He shakes his head with a sigh. "Good night, Lyss."

"Night, Ty."

I slam the door and start walking down the quiet suburban street I grew up on, trying to figure out how my ladies' night with Tara went haywire. While I should be condemning myself for the wicked behavior, I can't help but replay a certain grin in my head. A brooding smile with a smolder that could torch a small city. I could go for a little fire lighting. It's been a long time since I've felt the heat of a man's touch.

Little did I know one night of bad decisions would awaken something inside of me.

A man is the last thing I need in my life and the furthest thing from what I'll allow. Still, it's nice to know I'm not entirely dead inside. Just the thought of Officer Bronson gives me a small shiver. A quake. A very nice feminine quake.

"Maybe I *am* still drunk," I say to myself.

Yes, nice smiles on handsome men are fun to think about. I'm an adult woman—and a feral one at that. That is, until I stand on the front path of my childhood home and see the bedroom light of my father's room on, and suddenly, I feel like a sullen teenager, about to get in trouble for sneaking into the house late at night.

JEANNINE COLETTE

Divorce sucks.

So does growing up, even when you're a divorced mother of two.

two

"I THOUGHT MY DAYS of seeing Tyler Landish drive you home were long over," Dad comments with eyes on the *Valor County Gazette* as he sits at the kitchen table, drinking his coffee.

He's sipping from the mug that reads, *Smells like freshly signed divorce papers*. It was a gift from Tara when I was declared legally single by the state this summer.

I walk over to the coffeepot on the counter and fill a tall Yeti thermos. With only five hours of sleep last night, I need the caffeine.

"And I thought your days of spying out the window were long over." I give him a kiss on his head and watch his eyes lift over the top of his reading glasses.

"Does this mean a reconciliation is in the works?" he asks as I take a seat at the table.

"Absolutely not. I found myself without a ride, and he happened to be at the same place, so he gave me a lift home." My ability to lie to my father has always come way too easily.

He gives a grimace. "I don't like to put my nose where it doesn't belong, but if there were something happening between the two of you, I'd like you to think about it seriously. What you went through—"

"Dad, it's not that at all." I place a hand on his arm and give a reassuring smile. "In fact, Maisie is moving in with him. He's very happy with her, and I'm happy with you."

I tap his nose, and he gives a low harrumph from inside his throat as he shakes out the paper to read another article.

I run my hand over the grain of the oak table, one he made for my mother thirty-five years ago, when they moved into this house. It's a good table. Strong, sturdy … just like their marriage. When Tyler and I moved, I bought a cheap yet attractive table the kids could destroy and figured I'd buy a better one when they were older. Perhaps I should have upgraded to the Thomasville.

"Not that I was watching you come in and out of the house all night," he states. "I just happened to be up at that hour."

"You can admit it, old man; you still care. It doesn't matter how old your children get; you worry about them when they leave the house at night. Soon, I'll be the old lady peering out the window, waiting for Izzy and Hunter to come home."

"Who are you calling old?"

"You." I yawn and stretch my arms out wide, letting my back arch into the back of the wooden chair.

Dad pats his stomach, which is very taut for a man in his late sixties. "Old in age, but not in spirit. I'm up to two hundred and fifty crunches a day."

"Damn. Maybe I should join you in the garage."

My dad's home gym is in our garage—something he set up after Mom died. It's one of the many ways he fills up his days, which were once blessed with dinners, dancing, and casual nights of watching *Family Feud* and crime shows with his bride. In the years since she's passed, he's kept quite the regimented schedule with a trip to the home gym being first each morning.

"More than welcome if you need a trainer. You're looking a little wimpy these days."

I swat him in the arm and stick my tongue out. "I kickbox twice a week. Although Tara thinks I should get in there more."

"Could be good for you. Help you blow off some steam."

"When do I have the time? Some of us still work for a living and are single parents during the week."

LOVE ... IT'S COMPLICATED

"Never underestimate the need for a good workout to get your mind off things you don't want to think about. Maybe you can pretend the bag is Tyler's face when you kick it."

I laugh with a nod and brush down my pant leg, making sure there's no lint on my black ponte pants. It might be a weekend, but since Tyler has the kids so much, I'm either setting up a wedding or hosting appointments with new clients. Guess I'm filling up my days in a different way from my dad. A loss is a loss and all.

"How's the new office coming along?" He places the newspaper down and looks up at me.

"Slowly. Jillian hopes we'll have the keys next week."

"You sure you need the expense of an office? You've been doing very well, operating without one, and the overhead is going to—"

"Dad, it's time. We're ready to expand, and an office space is the professional thing to do. I'm tired of using the coffee shop as my office. I'll miss the lattes and coffeehouse music, but I will certainly not miss the nosy patrons on each side of me."

When Jillian and I started our wedding planning company, we operated out of her home office and rented a storage space to keep supplies. Two years later, we have a steady flow of business and a well-curated office space to help us showcase our talents better and bring in more high-end clientele.

"Don't listen to me. I'm just a retired gym teacher."

Dad's comment causes me to roll my eyes.

I stand up to start heading out when the open newspaper on the table catches my eye. In the far-right column is a picture of a man in uniform—a wickedly attractive officer with hazel eyes and a concern for divorced women leaving precincts with their ex-husbands. Officer Bronson's photo is showcased, his handsome face looking stoic and professional.

"I know him." Leaning forward, I read the headline.

HERO OFFICER RETURNS TO FORCE

Dad clears his throat and adjusts his glasses to read the article. "Oh, this is the officer who was shot this summer when he stopped that robbery."

I glance down and read some of the article.

JEANNINE COLETTE

Officer William Bronson of Valor County Police Department was injured in June when he arrived at the scene of a robbery turned hostage situation at Nick's Convenience Store in Castleton. According to the Connecticut Police Department, Officer Bronson was off duty when he disarmed the robber and was shot in the chest during the altercation. All five patrons in the store, including clerk Terrence Houssein, were unarmed. Bronson returns after a three-month leave.

If I didn't already think Officer Bronson was a fine specimen of a man, knowing he took down an armed robber, using his bare hands and sheer will, just pushed him up a few notches.

Dad takes off his glasses and looks up at me. "How do you know him?"

"Just ... from around."

I hide my expression with the thermos and take a very large sip of coffee. It's scalding hot, so my eyes bug out as I swallow and injure my throat by being an idiot who can't just tell her father how exactly she knows the hero officer on the inside pages of the paper.

"Damn, that's hot," I say after the swallow and have to breathe in cold air to cool my injured larynx. "See you for dinner tonight?" I sling my purse over my shoulder.

He clears his throat and then goes back to reading the paper, his eyes avoiding mine, and I already know what he's going to say. "Anna and I are going out to dinner."

I inhale deep and hold it, then nod my head. "Great. Have fun." I spin on my heels and rush out the front door.

Anna is my father's girlfriend and someone he started dating soon after Mom died. She's nice and all, but she's a poor replacement for my vibrant and wonderful mother.

I let out an exasperated breath as I close the front door and head to my car.

While my desire to be around Anna or even hear stories about her is limited and my father knows my feelings on the matter, I try not to voice my opinion. Gavin Jones is good man, a great father, and an even better grandfather. He deserves to be happy. It's just ... I wish I could explain it. So, I don't. I avoid. It's not the best course of action, but it's a dance we've been doing for quite some time.

LOVE ... IT'S COMPLICATED

As I drive toward the wedding venue where Jillian and I are setting up today, I plug in my phone and call the kids. Even though Tyler has them, I need to talk to my children at least twice a day. I dial Tyler's house number and wait for someone to pick up.

"Hi, Mommy!" Hunter's sweet voice fills my car, and my shoulders relax. I'm thankful *he* picked up and not one of the adults in the house.

"Good morning, my *son*-shine!"

"I miss you. Can you come here?"

"No, baby. I'm sorry. I have to work, but when you come home, we'll play some games before dinner."

My kid is not only cute as hell—brown hair, brown eyes, and the sweetest cherub face on the planet—but he's also the happiest kid. Seriously, nothing gets him down. He loves everyone he meets and has the best view on life because, as he says, each moment is an adventure.

"Mom, you are not going to believe this. We had French toast for breakfast, and—get this—Maisie put chocolate chips and strawberries on them, and it was so good. And then we went outside because we have a new bounce house. We get to keep it in the garage and use it in the backyard whenever we want!"

"French toast *and* a bounce, all before nine a.m.? You're having the best morning, my baby!" I say in an overly excited voice.

"Yep, and later, we're going to the petting zoo. We were going to go early, but Daddy's still sleeping. He didn't sleep well last night, so we're gonna go to the zoo later."

"Yeah. Daddy needs to sleep."

"Maisie said I can wake him up at noon. I'm gonna jump on the bed and sing a song really, really loud."

"That's a fantastic idea."

"Did you know there's a magic trick where you can lift someone off the ground? I saw it on YouTube, and it looks so cool. I asked Daddy to teach me, but he doesn't like magic."

"Not his favorite thing, no."

"Can you teach me?"

"I don't know how to levitate someone, but I can try."

I smile, knowing this is gonna take some serious Googling. Making a promise to a five-year-old is like selling your soul. They forget nothing and will ignite a hellish fire around you if you don't live up to your word.

"You can't lift someone off the ground, Hunter. It's fake." I hear Isabella's sharp tone in the background.

Oh, my Izzy. You're too young to be so angry about everything.

"Hunter, can you put your sister on?" I ask sweetly.

"Yep! Izzy, Mommy wants you."

"Why?" Her groan sounds more like a sixteen-year-old than a child who's only eleven.

"Because she just does." Hunter, on the other hand, is easy-breezy and silly.

I hear the sounds of the phone being passed over and his padded footsteps scampering away on the hardwood.

"Hello?" Izzy answers with an annoyed huff.

"Good morning, Isabella."

"Hi."

I might not be able to see her, but I can picture her curled on the couch with her knees up to her chest. Her strawberry-blonde hair unruly from her waking not too long ago. Her mouth pinched with her bottom lip out. She gets her full mouth from her father. He's always had great lips.

"Did you have fun in the bounce house this morning?"

"It's okay. It's small and for little kids."

"It's something new to do."

"I'd rather be on Roblox, but Maisie and Dad have a *no iPad* rule when it's nice outside."

"That's a great rule."

"It's stupid because there's nothing to do here."

"That's why they bought you a bounce house. Plus, they're taking you out."

"The zoo's boring."

I clench my jaw. "Izzy, the attitude is really uncalled for. Daddy bends over backward for you. Don't be ungrateful."

"I'm not ungrateful."

"Stop saying everything's boring!"

There's a small pause, and I rub my fingers against my brow. Izzy breathes into the receiver.

"When can I go home?" Her voice is low, as if she doesn't want anyone to hear her talking. That annoyed preteen tone is swapped with one of a little girl.

I sigh at the sound. "Tomorrow."

"I wish I had a phone. I could call you whenever I wanted."

"You can call me on Dad's phone. You just want a phone so you can play games and talk to your friends."

"You moved me away from all my friends, and I don't get to talk to them like I used to. Dad won't let me see them while I'm here because he says it's his time with me and he doesn't want to share. At least if I had a phone, I could talk to them. This is so unfair, Mom!"

"Your father and I discussed this. You're not getting a phone until high school."

"You're not even a couple anymore. Why do you have to do everything Dad says?"

"It's *my* rule."

"I hate your rule!"

I grip the steering wheel and fight the urge to scream at her. I remember being a sullen teenager. It didn't hit until years later, when I was actually a teen, but I also didn't have to go through my parents' divorce and a new woman in my dad's life. Hell, I'm a grown woman, and I'm having a hard time with my own father moving on.

I try to cut Izzy some slack. "I'll talk to Dad about letting you have some playdates on the weekends. He just misses you. So do I. I love you, Izzy. I love you very much."

She takes a beat before answering. I can picture her looking down at the blanket, picking at the fuzz and furrowing her brow. "I love you too."

"Kisses. Call me after the zoo. I want to hear all about it."

"Fine."

A woman's voice chimes in the background, "Is that your mom? I want to talk to her."

"Love you, Iz. Bye!" I hang up quickly before Maisie can get her paws on the phone and talk to me. I'm not in any shape mentally to have a conversation with her.

Despite my cheery disposition when talking to the kids, I'm tired and internally cranky as fuck. I feel like I have no control over anything. Not my kids, my life's path, my emotions. Everything is so far out of reach, and I'm spiraling into a downward shift.

Just as I emotionally hit rock bottom, I pick myself back up, slap on some lip gloss, and be the fabulous me that I am.

Because that's how you get through the day.

It's hard, adulting, sometimes.

three

"I CAN'T BELIEVE YOU were in the clink last night! You should've called me." Tara waves her beer in the air from her place at our table at Lone Tavern.

It's been a long day. Normally, I'd head home after a wedding like the one Jillian and I worked today. Once I mentioned my incarceration to Tara while on the phone this afternoon, she guilted me into coming out tonight so she could get the full story.

I shake my head at her. "As I recall, you drank just as much wine as I did, which means once your head hit the pillow, you were dead to the world."

"You could have rung *me*," Jillian, my friend and business partner, chimes in. "I would have bailed you out in a heartbeat."

I place my hand on her arm. "We had a wedding to put together today. One of us had to be cognizant of our responsibilities. Besides, Tyler showed up and took care of everything."

"That bastard. I can't believe he had the nerve to play hero." Tara takes a long swig of her Heineken.

Jillian places her lowball glass on the table. "Okay, we did not get a chance to properly discuss this today at work. What exactly happened last night?"

Before I can answer, Tara is answering for me. "What happened was, Melissa found out Tyler is moving Maisie into their honeymoon cottage. The one they bought together after Izzy was born. What a creep!"

I look at Jillian as I point at Tara, our fiery, loud-mouthed friend. "This is why I make bad decisions."

Tara scoffs, brushing her curly, dark tendrils off her shoulder. "A bad decision would have been burning down the salon. Had I known you were on your way there last night instead of going home, I would have accompanied you and happily torched the place." Her toothy grin is silly despite her harsh rhetoric.

Jillian tilts her head. "Tara, we're supposed to be keeping Melissa levelheaded. She's a mother, and she owns a business, might I remind you. Arson doesn't exactly bode well for either."

Tara and Jillian are two of the best women I've ever met, and they're complete opposites.

Jillian is a career event planner, who left a large event company to open her own boutique firm and asked me to join her. She's thirty-one with long auburn hair, skin that looks porcelain, and a wardrobe to die for. Single with one child, she's a pillar of strength and professionalism.

Tara is my best friend. An accountant and kickboxing aficionado who never left the town we grew up in and still acts like it's senior year of high school. She's funny and courageous, and she has your back, no questions asked. Seriously. When I told her Tyler was cheating on me, she showed up with a bottle of wine and shovel, stating I had to pick one and she was down for either choice.

I should have chosen the shovel.

I sigh. "Quick version of the story is that Tara and I went out to dinner last night after Tyler picked the kids up. I was a little down because I had just learned about the Maisie situation. After five glasses of rosé, it was after ten, and we were solving the world's problems, politics and religion be damned!"

"As all women do when we drink wine," Jillian says as she and Tara clink glasses. "We seriously need a good woman president."

Tara replies, "Yes, with that eye-patch guy as vice president. He's crazy hot!"

I roll my eyes at them and continue, "And then Tara made a comment about my hair."

"Why did you bring up the hair? It's not *that* bad," Jillian chastises Tara.

"Stop being the kind friend. It's horrible. Melissa always had gorgeous blonde locks. She looks like Brassy Barbie," Tara states with flailed hands. She accidentally hits someone behind her, who gives her the stink eye and she gives one back.

"Enough talk about negative stuff. You two dragged me here when I should be catching up on some much-needed sleep." I yawn as I look around the bar that's not our usual hangout. "Why are we here exactly?"

Lone Tavern is a rustic-themed country music bar with an eclectic crowd. I haven't been here since my early twenties, and even then, I wasn't too keen on the place. It's loud, it smells like day-old beer, and it's filled with young twenty-somethings, wearing crocheted crop tops.

I glance down at my tank top, skinny jeans, and heels. This used to be a hot outfit to wear on a Saturday night. Now, I need wide-legged jeans with holes in them to fit in.

"There's this guy I met online who mentioned he was coming here tonight, and I couldn't show up alone." Tara's looking around the room, presumably for the man she's here to see. Disappointed he hasn't arrived, she looks back at our table and swivels toward Jillian. "I'm surprised *you* came out tonight. This isn't exactly your cup of tea."

"I would much prefer a refined restaurant in Greenwood Village, but Melissa here looked like hell today at work, and I thought she could use a friend to keep her out of trouble. We don't want any more arrests tonight."

I give Jillian the finger and laugh. "Trust me, I won't be doing anything salacious like that again. Besides, I kicked ass today despite last night's happenings. That altar I created was ethereal, and every aspect of today's event went off without a hitch ... despite the best man showing up drunk and the flower girl spilling her Shirley Temple all over the seating chart display. I re-created that in a heartbeat."

"Best calligrapher in the state!" Jillian and I high-five each other. "We really are a great team."

"Ooh! There he is!" Tara chants as she bolts up from her seat, then sits back down quickly and starts reapplying her lip gloss. "Do I have anything in my teeth?" she asks Jillian, who evaluates her and shakes her head. "His name is Kent, and he's a sergeant. How hot is that?"

"Which one is he?" I look over the crowd of people toward the front, where she's gazing.

"Brown hair, trimmed beard. Wearing the T-shirt with a buck on it. I bet he hunts. I love a rugged man." With a ruffle of her curls, she stands and then adjusts her jeans. "Wish me luck!"

Jillian holds her hands up as to stop Tara. "You're going over to him? He just got here."

"Girl, I'm over thirty and single, and I have been in the game long enough to know that if I don't get over there right now and sink my talons into that man, some other girl is going to get him first. It's a game of availability, and I, Tara Parsons, am very available. Now, if you'll excuse me, ladies, I have a sergeant to see."

She grabs her bag, drains the last of her beer, and saunters off in the direction of her man. I know better than to say anything. I would never call her desperate or overbearing because I've never been in her shoes. I've been married and had my babies, while Tara is still waiting for the fairy tale.

I lift my now-empty glass and look over at the bar. "I'm getting a refill. Want anything?"

Jillian rises, smoothing out her linen pants. "I'm calling it a night. I have to get Ainsley from my parents' place, and then I plan to binge some *Bridgerton* on Netflix. Plus, I have my cousin's baby shower tomorrow. You want to head out with me?"

"Nah. I'll stay for one more drink and make sure Tara's good solo before I leave. I won't be long. I'm meeting with a prospective client tomorrow."

"Don't tell me it's the one who keeps on canceling? Allison Lalayne?"

"Fourth time's a charm."

"I wouldn't give her the time of day."

"She begged, and I'm a sucker for a desperate bride. Plus, she's taking me to brunch at Mountain View Bistro."

"You do love a good brunch. Let me know how tomorrow goes. I can't wait until we get the keys to our new office. It's gonna be a game changer when it comes to these meetings," Jillian says, and we hug good night, promising to text each other when we get home. "Don't stay out too late."

I smile as Jillian walks through the crowd and out the door.

Not wanting to occupy a table for four all by myself, I make my way over to the bar, shimmying myself between coeds. There's a country song playing overhead and a line dance happening on the dance floor. It looks like fun, albeit a little silly. People dancing in sync is not my thing.

"Vodka soda with a lime." I speak loudly so the bartender can hear me over the music.

He slides my drink to me. I slip a ten across the bar and turn around, only to collide with the strong chest of a man.

Navy tee that hugs his torso, light jeans that cling to strong thighs, and boots—construction, not cowboy.

"Excuse me," I say as I go to scoot around him, but when my eyes travel north, I inhale sharply.

"Ms. Jones," he croons, and I nearly collapse at the smolder of Officer Bronson standing before me, gleaming down with that wicked smile.

Damn, he's attractive. His face structure alone is impossible to keep your attention off of. He even has a cleft in his chin, which makes him look masculine and refined. His arms are on display, and they're thick and veiny, the kind that can lift things—heavy things. I stop myself from envisioning all the things he could lift. Namely me, up against a wall, as he does salacious things with his mouth.

I thought it was the uniform that made this man hot, but in jeans and a tee, he still looks drop-dead sexy, which just confirms that he's indeed ... beautiful.

Maybe it's the boots. I always have had a thing for a man in construction boots.

four

"You," I say and swallow.

"Me," he responds.

I squeeze my eyes in embarrassment and shake my head. "Sorry. I wasn't expecting to see you here."

As I open my eyes, I lean back against the bar, feeling the curved wood dig into my lower back, and take a deep breath. My reaction to him is silly. He's just a guy. A man. A person. Albeit the same person who unlocked me from a jail cell not even twenty-four hours ago, but a human nonetheless.

"Same. Never seen you here before."

"Here? No. Not my scene." I close my eyes yet again, and bite my lip in embarrassment. "Not that there is anything wrong with this place. It's cute. And fun. I just haven't been here in a really, *really* long time."

He laughs. "No offense taken. I can see how it's not everyone's style. I like it because it's no frills. You can just come out, listen to good music, dance, and play darts."

"Makes sense. I shouldn't rag on your place. We used to go to this place called Dempsey's in Newbury—small bar, filled with locals—and we ran that place like we owned it."

His tilted nod is one of remembrance. "That place closed down a couple of years ago. I went there a time or two. Definitely didn't see you there."

"When you have your first baby at twenty-three, your bar nights become nonexistent."

"You were a baby, having babies."

"Didn't feel like that at the time. Now, I feel ancient. A lot of the girls I went to high school with have newborns, not an eleven- and a five-year-old." I wave the air between us. "Sorry. I tend to talk about my kids a lot. I'm sure it's not something a guy in his twenties comes to the bar to talk about."

He smiles. "You're fine. I like talking about kids. I have eleven nieces and nephews, so I can chime in. You said you have an eleven-year-old? Wait until thirteen. My sister is ready to pull her hair out when it comes to her daughter, Mia."

"Thanks," I grumble, having heard that advice before.

"And for the record, I'm thirty, and from what I hear, that means I'm capable of less superficial conversation and something deeper and more worldly."

Someone bumps into me, and I'm launched into William, my hand hitting him in the chest. He doesn't flinch, but as soon as I do so, I immediately apologize, "I'm so sorry. Your injury!"

A slow smile builds on his lips. "Reading up about me?"

I narrow my eyes at his cocky assumption. "You were in the *Valor County Gazette* this morning. I wasn't looking you up or anything."

He lifts his chin. "Really?"

"It was in the paper."

"What's my name?"

"William Bronson."

He smiles again, and his eyes twinkle with that damn crinkle.

"It was in the paper!"

He crosses his arms and leans back on his heels. "Call me Will."

I raise my drink to my lips and take a swig. "It's nice to officially meet you, Will. I don't want to take up too much of your time. You said you're here with a friend?"

With a nod toward my glass, he asks, "No wine tonight?"

My head tilts, and then my shoulders fall with his words. He's recalling my diatribe from last night.

"That was so not me."

LOVE ... IT'S COMPLICATED

"Unless it was another woman with a habit of pacing and oversharing, then it was definitely you. I'm not judging. At all. I just remember you saying you drank quite a bit of wine last night. I know you're a good girl. I saw your record."

My smile is smug. "Who's the one looking up who now?"

"It's my job."

"Sure," I say sarcastically.

"Seriously, I have to look up your past when you enter the precinct."

"Where do I live?"

"Twenty Thompson Str—" His hands fall to his hips, and he lowers his forehead and glances up at me. "You're clever."

I giggle. *Oh God, I'm giggling.* And flirting. I can't believe I'm in a bar, flirting with a younger guy who happens to be a hero cop and smoking hot, and I'm having a good time. I haven't flirted with anyone since I was fifteen years old.

"I have a photographic memory," he defends.

I think he's flirting with me too.

"Call me Lyss."

I don't know why I said that. Only one person calls me Lyss.

I instantly regret telling him to do it. It must register on my face because he takes a step forward and says, "If it's okay, I'd prefer to call you Melissa. It's a beautiful name. Unless, of course, you prefer I call you ma'am."

I laugh loudly. "Please no! That is the kiss of death to any sense of confidence a woman has."

"Melissa it is." He looks around the bar briefly and then brings his attention back to me. "I'm here with my friend, but I think he's meeting a woman. Online dating. I'll never understand the appeal."

"Your friend wouldn't happen to be a sergeant named Kent who's meeting an accountant named Tara who loves kickboxing, crafting, and wine out of the box?"

He raises a finger to his cleft and narrows his eyes. "Either you're clairvoyant or your friend is most definitely meeting my friend. And if I know *his* dating profile correctly, it says, *I solemnly swear I am up to no good. And by no good, I mean, I want to eat Chinese food on the couch and binge Apple TV.*"

My back hunches over with my laugh, and I spill a little of my drink on the floor. "That definitely sounds like the kind of guy Tara would go for. She saw him when he came in and went in for the kill.

Since they're missing in action, I take it, they're getting along, and you are on your own."

"The wingman never gets enough credit."

"Try being a wingwoman. We don't even get a cool name. Just a revision of what you guys are."

"Yes, wingman is kind of sexist, but wingperson is just lame." He takes the space next to me and leans against the bar. "What should we call you?"

"Paramour?"

"You'd have to be lovers. Sidekick?"

"Too comic bookish. Copilot in love?"

"Matchmaker."

I lift a finger as it comes to me and smile. "Fairy god-homie."

Will turns to me, leaning his elbow on the bar, and nods. "Fairy god-homie. I like it."

I raise my chin in acceptance of his compliment. When I turn to him, our faces are much closer than they were when he was standing in front of me. The crowd around us sends a wave of pressure, forcing us closer in proximity. His strong chest rises with a deep inhale, and I catch his gaze lingering on my mouth.

My teeth graze my lip.

It's been nearly two decades since I've done this, and I'm not even sure what *this* is. I'm definitely flirting, but his intentions are completely lost on me. Is he just making nice conversation with the woman he met last night? Is he biding his time until Kent decides he likes his curly-haired vixen? Is he desperately wondering what's the best way to exit this conversation without insulting me?

I have so many questions running through my head. I have to stop looking at his face and getting lost in the heat that radiates from a single look because when those eyes lift to mine, I feel a zing down my entire chest.

I clear my throat and look at his arms. A tattoo peeking out of his sleeve catches my attention. I lift the cotton from his arm and see the bottom of what appears to be an elaborate tattoo of a vicious and sinister-looking snake being pierced with a sword.

Will places his large hand on top of mine and moves the shirt up, taking my hand along with his. I leave my hand there a beat too long, feeling the warm strength of his palm over my hand. Slowly, I drag my fingers away from under his hand and glide my nails down his arm, tracing the outline of the intricate design of his tattoo.

LOVE ... IT'S COMPLICATED

I was wrong. The tattoo is not vicious.

It's glorious.

Taking over his entire bicep is an angel, who looks like a gladiator, with large wings that span from one side of his bicep to the other. In the angel's hand is a shield with a sword in the other, piercing the snake in death. The look on the angel's face is one of anger, determination, and triumph. The curves of muscle on the angel's body and the hair flowing in the wind are expertly crafted.

I'm still touching his tattoo, marveling at the artwork, when I pull back suddenly. I blink and realize I've been too handsy with this man I barely know.

"It's okay. I like how enamored you are with it."

"It's stunning," I breathe.

When I look up, he's staring at me with an intensity that causes me to take a step back and count backward.

Will lowers his shirt and smiles. "It's Saint Michael. Patron saint of police and military. If it were anything else, my mother would have disowned me for getting it."

"I could see her being upset for tarnishing your perfect body with something permanent." My eyes widen because I just called his body perfect, but then I laugh. "Fuck it. I'm not embarrassed. You know you're good-looking. And you clearly go to the gym every day."

"Clearly." He smiles.

I take another drink and realize my glass is empty. I've been sipping it without realizing, needing something to do with my hands. "Are you not drinking?"

"Wasn't going to. Unless it makes you uncomfortable to drink alone? I can order a beer—"

"No! Don't order a drink just for my sake. We're not here together or anything. You don't have to do anything for me. I was just asking. No big deal."

I look up at him. His eyes are narrowed slightly, and that grin is raised on only one side.

"What?"

"You ramble. It's cute."

I lift my eyes to the ceiling. Never has my rambling ever been considered *cute*.

The band starts playing a new song, a slower melody, and I look to the dance floor. The line dancing has ceased. People are dancing rather intimately with couples swinging each other around and grinding against one another. It's kind of sexy, which is not something I associate with country music.

"Do you dance?" Will asks, mistaking my interest in watching others dance for a willingness to be out there myself.

"Thought all country was line dancing."

"They don't look like they're line dancing."

"I can see that. And, no, I don't dance."

"Ever?"

"I dance. Just not to country. I like pop and rock. Stuff like that."

"Have you ever tried to dance to country?"

I shake my head. Will takes my drink from my hand and places it on the bar. I turn to him with a scowl on my brow. Next, he takes my hand and pulls me toward the dance floor.

"I said, I don't dance."

He ignores me as he guides me to the dance floor and speaks over his shoulder. "Never having tried something doesn't mean you don't do it." When we reach the near center of the floor, he turns around and faces me. "It just means you've never tried it."

I blow out a large breath and shake my head in refusal.

He grins in response and my knees have now become too jellylike to walk away.

Will snakes a hand around my waist and pulls me toward him. Our torsos touch, making our hips and groins press against one another. I knew this man was a rock of a specimen, but I didn't know he felt as hard as he looked. I want to glide my palms along him just to feel every divot and curve of his physique, but I don't because that would be inappropriate … but I want to. So bad.

He sways his hips, and I follow suit until I'm quickly swung away from him with his arm over mine, and then he's twirling me back into his arms.

We're face-to-face, and our lips nearly touch.

"Not terrible," he says, seemingly impressed with the fact that I managed a simple spin move into his arms. "Let's see what else you got."

He swings me away again, and I follow along. I'm not a horrible dancer. I can keep a beat. Yet there is something about the way *he* dances, as if from his core, not just his legs, that makes it easy for my body to follow.

LOVE ... IT'S COMPLICATED

When he spins me, he flicks his wrist, and our connection is broken as I twirl back in. His free hand lands low on my waist, gliding me back into him, and I land firmer against his chest.

Closer.

Intimate.

We stay like this for a few sways. His breath hits against my cheek, and the pulse of the music hums through his chest. When he releases me, I not only make my way back into his arms, but his hand also rests against my hip, guiding me down into a dip until my back is resting against his knee. My leg instinctually rises in the air, and my hair falls like a waterfall toward the dance floor.

I feel feminine and light, free and sensual as he leans down and brings us up together.

I'm like a rag doll, and he's my master, bending and moving me as I succumb to his every silent whim.

Will can dance. Not just dance. He can command his body. My body. The whole dynamic is controlled through simple movements. I've never danced with a man like this before, and it's addictive. I could dance with him forever.

I laugh and smile the entire time as we enter into a second dance and then a third. I'm becoming comfortable with my ability. Brazen even. He twirls me and starts to show off himself with his own rotations, catching my hand to twirl me again and again, and before I know it, his hand catches me by the back of my neck in a reverse choke hold, as I'm now dangling in the air in a backward dip.

Slowly, ever ... so ... slowly ... he raises us to a standing position, and we're face-to-face.

Breaths ragged.

Eyes glued to one another.

Our mouths inches apart.

His hazel eyes and that damn smolder are not only heat, but they're also intense fire. My entire body is ignited with electricity piping throughout, making my head light, my breasts heavy, and my core tight. I lick my lips to cool myself down, but it's no use.

His hands are still on my neck and hip, gripping tightly and molding us together.

It's erotic as hell.

Turns out, I've been dancing to the wrong music my entire life.

Will's breathing is harsh. He silently stares at me with somewhat of a frown. Whatever power the dance had on us has now dissipated from the air. "I have to go."

His hand lowers from my throat, and I nod.

"Oh. Okay. Yeah. Me too. I have a meeting in the morning."

Will and I find Tara and Kent talking at a table on the far side of the room, close to the entrance. She gives me the nod that all is good while simultaneously waggling her brows at the sight of Will. I give her a face that lets her know there is nothing going on between me and the handsome man at my side.

Kent also looks at me, standing here beside Will, curiously and a bit concerned. He must be wondering how his friend and Tara's wound up sweaty from dancing. It *is* quite the coincidence.

"Do you have a ride home? I can order you an Uber," Will asks.

"My car is in the lot."

"Mine too. I'll walk you."

Inside the bar, Will and I were practically glued at the hip from the moment he discovered me ordering my cocktail. Outside, it feels like he can't get far enough away from me.

Did I do something wrong? Perhaps I came off too strong or made a face that freaked him out while we were dancing. Our faces were *really* close. I would have kissed him if he had given me the impression that he wanted me to. He must have seen it on my face how badly I wanted to kiss him. I'm such a dork sometimes.

This is what happens when you haven't dated someone new in sixteen years. You meet a handsome man and have three good dances, and suddenly, you think he wants to kiss you back. No one wants to kiss you, Melissa.

"Are you okay?" His deep voice pulls me out of my thoughts.

"Huh?"

"You were mumbling to yourself. Something about kisses?"

I slam my palm on my forehead. "I am such a lost cause!" I scurry toward my hatchback and take my keys out of my bag. "This is me. Thanks for walking me safely to the lot. Have a good night."

I open the door and hit myself with the door before opening it properly.

"Melissa."

Embarrassed, I turn around to face him. He's about five feet away. His hands are in his pockets as he leans back and looks down at the pavement. There's a pause, as if he's collecting his thoughts. I'm dying to fill the silence. It's what I do best. Instead, I just stand here. Waiting for him to … something. When he looks up at me, his gaze steady, his thoughts gathered, I brace myself for what he's about to say.

"You're amazing. Beautiful. Cool." He takes a breath. "A catch. A total upgrade."

A catch.

A total upgrade.

Those are the words I said about Maisie last night.

"Good night, Melissa."

He turns and starts walking to the other side of the parking lot. This gorgeous hero of a man, who is funny and clever and knows how to dance, just told me I was a total upgrade. It's been a long time since I've desired someone. Nearly as long as I've felt worthy of such desire. Is it possible I'm not a throwaway? More than second best?

I might not have done this dating thing in years, but I know when a guy likes a girl. These bones still felt the tingle in my spine when his hand dropped a little too low on my hip and felt the way his heart was beating when my palm grazed his chest. I felt his breath on my skin, hot and ragged. And I saw desire in his eyes.

Tara says if a good man walks in, you go to him before someone else swoops in and takes him.

"Fuck it," I say out loud.

Will must have heard me because he turns around just in time to see me close the distance.

I kiss him.

I wrap my hands around his neck and press my lips to his, taking his mouth in mine. A groan escapes his mouth, and I swallow it whole. His lips part, and his hot and greedy mouth takes over our kiss.

His tongue circles mine, and my hands rise to his hair, tugging and pulling as he grips my waist and pulls me in. Not only have I not kissed a man in a long time, but I also haven't made out with someone in years, let alone in a parking lot, like teenagers in heat.

It's a heady kiss, and it ends as abruptly as it started when he pulls away from me quickly and with a jerky push.

My hand rises to my swollen lips. "I ambushed you. I don't know what got into me."

"Fuck," he says in response.

"Is that a good fuck or a bad fuck?" I giggle in embarrassment, but he's incredibly too serious for the situation.

"Both. Mostly bad."

His hand rises to the back of his neck and rubs it rather violently. Not exactly the reaction you want after an incredible kiss that still has your heart racing and toes curling.

Will opens my door and escorts me—nay, shoves me—into my car. "You sure you're okay to drive home?"

After a kiss like that, I don't think I'm good enough to walk home, but I'll do so anyway because staying here is clearly out of the question. A girl knows when she's not wanted.

"Yeah, I'm fine."

Will closes my door. His hands are still on the roof of my car as he peers inside the glass and continues to stare at me with a severely pinched brow as he swallows hard. I stare back at him. It's impossible not to when he looks so pained.

Fuck, he says silently.

I can't hear him through the closed door, but I see his lips move. That's probably the one word in the English language you can hear, even without a sound.

When he finally moves from the car, I start the engine. Driving away, I try to keep my eyes on the road and not in the rearview mirror and the lone man standing in the parking lot of Lone Tavern, watching this lone girl go home to her lone bed with her lone thoughts of the lone kiss that just made her and crushed her in the same instant.

five

I ARRIVE AT MOUNTAIN View Bistro, early for my brunch with Allison Lalayne, a prospective bride who has canceled on us thrice.

One time was in advance. It was the day before we were set to meet. She said her fiancé didn't think they needed help designing the wedding. We exchanged pleasantries with Jillian wishing her congratulations, and we parted ways.

It was a surprise when Allison called a few weeks later and asked to set up another meeting. I was sitting in Beans and Leaves, a coffee shop in town, waiting for her, when she called and said her fiancé was busy at work and asked to reschedule.

Yesterday was the third time. Not wanting to take any more time out of our schedule, Jillian and I told her she could swing by the wedding venue as we were setting up and discuss options for her own event while we showcased what we could do. She called ten minutes before she was set to arrive and asked to reschedule.

I was concerned she didn't really want a designer for her wedding because brides typically don't cancel twice, let alone three times. So, when she called to reschedule, I declined, but she pleaded, stating my style was exactly what she wants for her event and promised she wouldn't cancel this time. She offered to meet at Mountain View Bistro for brunch, and I caved because I love brunch. If she cancels, I'm staying for the food and sending her the bill.

To my surprise, Allison arrives on time.

She's a sweet-looking thing with long brown hair and big eyes. She has on a floral dress, paired with a simple heart necklace.

"I'm so excited we are meeting today. I want to have my bridal shower here because the food is amazing and the view is so pretty," she gushes as she takes her seat at the finely set table.

The restaurant sits atop a hill on the far edge of Valor County, overlooking the fall foliage. It's a decent drive from my house, about forty-five minutes, but lovely and worth traveling to.

"I think your guests will love it. Is your family hosting your shower?" I ask as I look at the menu.

They have crab and avocado eggs Benedict with maple syrup bacon. My mouth savors just thinking about it.

"My mother is throwing me a *surprise* shower—wink-wink. I think she's more excited than me for this wedding. She gave me my grandmother's ring when I got engaged. I can't get over how perfect it fits! Totally meant to be."

I look at the solitaire diamond on a gold band. It's elegant. Understated yet exquisite. "A family heirloom is better than any Harry Winston or Tiffany solitaire out there. The sentimental value alone is priceless. You're very fortunate."

She beams, stretching out her hand and appraising the ring. "I'm thinking about resetting it."

"There's something special about knowing this exact band sat on your grandmother's hand. If it were me, I wouldn't. It's perfect just as it is. Think about getting an elaborate wedding ring."

"I love that idea. This is exactly why I want to work with Lavish Events!"

My chin falls into my palm as I gaze at her. She's adorable and sweet. This is the kind of girl I adore planning weddings for. Hopeful, starry-eyed, and I'm sure wildly in love with her beau.

"Can I get you anything to drink?" the waiter asks when he approaches our table. "Mimosas and Bloody Marys are included with the menu today."

Allison and I look at each other and nod, stating in unison, "Mimosas!"

LOVE ... IT'S COMPLICATED

I take my iPad out of my tote bag and turn it on. "I don't know how far you've gotten into the wedding planning process, but I wanted to show you a few venues my partner and I—"

"No need to show me. I follow you on Pinterest and Instagram. I've seen all your work, and I'm sold. You did my cousin's wedding. Nicole and Victor Talini. They married at Wolfson Manor last year."

"I remember. They were wonderful to work with. How are they?"

"Expecting a bundle of joy due any minute."

"Please send our heartfelt congratulations." I place the iPad on the table and fold my hands. "Usually, Jillian and I meet with the bride and groom, and we get a feel for what you want and decide if we mesh well together before signing a contract. Your wedding is an intimate experience, and nothing should keep you from enjoying it."

"Absolutely. I am ready to start, and I know this is going to work out."

"Okay. Great. I'll email the contract over for you and your fiancé to sign. Why don't you tell me what you're looking for? I'll put together a vision board and proposal this week. Will you be needing wedding planning services as well or design only?"

"The whole shebang. I will go bananas if I have to make sure everything stays on schedule. Can we start with the design first?"

I nod, and she claps her hands together at the thought. This is the best and worst part of the experience. The telling of the dream wedding. Every girl has a vision of what she wants. From the venue to the flowers, music, food, decor, favors, it all comes together to make a magical day. It also adds up fast with costs that are often astronomical.

Since Jillian and I started planning weddings together, we've met couples who have two hundred thousand dollars to spend and others with twenty. We pride ourselves on working with all budgets, but some are hard to make the dream happen with.

"Mimosas." The waiter appears with our drinks.

Allison and I clink our glasses and take a sip.

"Are you ready to order?"

"Is your fiancé coming?" I ask her before I begin to order.

"Yes, but he's running late, and I don't want to hold you up," she says as she orders two vegetable and egg white frittatas, one for each of them.

I almost hold off on the rather fattening eggs Benedict but order it anyway because I've made a lot of bad decisions this weekend and I'm not going to stop by depriving myself a good meal.

The waiter walks away, and Allison gets right to discussing her dream wedding.

"The Local, the old bank on Main Street, is high on my list of dream venues. It's so unique. I want something modern and chic with a clean look. Everything has to be white. The linens, flowers, you name it, everything crisp white. I want a photo booth ... and a DJ, not a band."

Allison continues on with her checklist of wants for the event. I don't have to write down a thing. Everything is pretty standard as far as weddings goes. Nothing unique or special. For a girl who's wearing her grandmother's heirloom ring, I'm surprised there isn't something special on her list—an ode to a family member who passed or a nod to a family tradition. Everything about the event she wants sounds gorgeous. It also seems impersonal.

I give her some ideas to flow with the kind of event she wants. Crystal chandeliers, draped from the ceiling to add some elegance. A mixture of high centerpieces to draw the eye across the room, paired with cascading rose arrangements low on every other table for a romantic effect. I suggest bringing in a live entertainer for a portion of the event, perhaps dinner.

Each of my ideas has her nodding her head with vigor. I'm almost nervous to ask what kind of budget she's working with because she has yet to say no to anything I've suggested. Nothing is too extravagant for her taste.

She's currently telling me about a particular stairwell flower arrangement she saw me build online when I'm distracted by a man.

A very specific man with a soul-piercing smolder.

William Bronson. A man I only met days ago, yet it's the third day in a row I'm seeing him. What are the odds? Really, what are the freaking odds he would be in this restaurant, five towns away, on a Sunday afternoon? The odds must be good because he's here. Not only is he here, but he's also walking toward me and stopping at my table.

I don't know what to say to the man I leaped at and kissed last night and who stopped said kiss abruptly and put me in my car as fast as lightning. I can't immediately speak because while my mind is reeling at seeing this handsome man, his face looks anything but excited to see me.

"You're early!" Allison beams as she stands up and kisses his cheek.

Early?

I didn't even know he was supposed to be here. If she's saying he's early and she's excited he's here then …

Fuck.

"Melissa, this is my fiancé, William. Babe, this is the wedding designer I've been trying to get you to meet."

Allison has her arm around Will's as he stares at me, dumbfounded. We must have matching expressions because I am equally as confused as to why he's here with his fiancée. Yes, the man I kissed last night has a fiancée. I think I'm going to be sick.

"You're a wedding planner?" he asks, that deep voice so damn low and disappointed that it rattles my gut.

My head slowly rises and falls at his question. "Wedding *designer*. My partner is the wedding planner."

I never told him what I did for a living. If I did, maybe the fact that he had a *fiancée* would have come up.

Will rubs his hand along his jaw as he turns sharply to Allison, forcing her to remove her hand from his arm. "I didn't know we were meeting with a wedding designer today."

"You've been so busy, so when I finally got you to agree to brunch, I figured it was the best time."

He lowers his head to her ear. "We need to talk privately about this. You can't ambush me to pick a date."

"Maybe if you picked a date, I wouldn't have to ambush you with a wedding planner." She talks back in an equally hushed tone despite the wide, forced smile on her face. "Take a seat. I ordered you the frittata."

For a man as physically commanding as William is, he takes the seat. He doesn't look pleased at being told what to do. That, or he's having serious man guilt. He should. *Bastard.*

Allison takes her seat beside him, scoots her chair close to the table, then grabs his hand and gives it a squeeze. "Babe, Melissa and I worked out a dream wedding for us. Melissa, why don't you tell him some of your ideas?"

William's eyes rise to mine, and it's hard not to notice how uncomfortable he is, sitting here. His lips are pursed, making them look small and not as full as they did last night.

Those lips were on mine. I can still taste his tongue gliding along my bottom lip and feel his hands as they gripped the fabric of my clothing so tight that I think I still have indentations of his fingers on my ass.

I take a drink of my champagne and orange juice. I might need a few more of these to get through this meal.

"Well, Allison was talking about having a modern event. All white with a DJ, a photo booth, and a rose arch behind the dais. She suggested a venue, but I have a few I'd like you to consider. I am going to see what dates are available for each and work up a proposal for the event design based on availability, and we'll work from there."

Usually, I'd be more conversational with a prospective groom, but I can't this time. I no longer want to talk about their magical wedding. Not when the groom is the man who, just yesterday, I thought was funny and a great dancer and who, for the first time in two years, I actually let my guard down for. I hadn't realized I had a guard up, but now that I let it down, I know for a fact that I did, and it's back up, never coming down again.

I'm such a fool.

I down my mimosa and place it on the table in a rather unladylike way. "Weddings are crazy expensive, and if you're gonna spend the money, you have to make sure it's what you want."

"Exactly. That's why we want to do this right from the beginning. Right, babe?" Allison grabs his hand again, which I assume he let go of while I was talking, and places it on her lap.

She looks so hopeful. A woman on the verge of the rest of her life while the man next to her is dancing with other women and kissing them back in parking lots. Sure, I'm the one who initiated it, and he pushed me away ... but he kissed me back. I know I'm not crazy. Maybe I am. Maybe Tyler ruined me for good.

Men. They're all scoundrels.

"It's one day," I say. "The entire experience is eight hours, max. Everyone says it, but no one listens. They plan detail after detail, as if this perfect day is going to dictate the next fifty years of their lives.

"Next thing you know, you're pregnant. You have a kid, then another, and a mortgage, and that's when the fights over whose turn it is to take the trash out and why men never have to clean the toilet, start. He leaves the empty orange juice container on the counter and his laundry on the ground, like you're the maid who has to pick it up. So, you hire a cleaning girl to help out, but it's never enough.

"He gets resentful because you spend more time with the kids than him—and he's not wrong. You genuinely like the kids more than you like him. And you fight all ... the ... time ... and then your mom gets sick and that little time you did have for one another—you know, after work, and kids, and life—is now taxed to the point that you don't even speak until you separate and he ends up in bed with another woman."

A woman walks around with a pitcher and refills my mimosa. I take a drink.

"That's all very"—Allison sits with raised brows and a slack jaw—"intense."

"It is intense. We're sitting here, talking about the difference between ice white and snow-white linens when you should be discussing the possibility that this might not work out. You should figure that out before year ten because that's when the pensions get shared and there's the 401(k) and the stocks you dabbled in on Ameritrade."

I swivel my glass in the air as I continue, "The house, the cars, the kids ... everything is up for grabs, and before you know it, you're paying a mediation law firm twenty thousand dollars to end up exactly where you started, except the attorney has a nice big check in his pocket and you two are both screwed. All the while, he's screwing the hairdresser, and you're left with bad hair!"

"Who ordered the crab and avocado eggs Benedict?" the waiter asks with a tray of three plates in his hand.

Allison is looking at me, bewildered, while Will just ... stares at me.

I lift a finger and watch as I'm served my dish, and then I waste no time in taking a bite because the best way to end a weekend of very bad decisions is to eat my damn eggs Benedict with a bride and the fiancé I made out with last night.

"Do you have any hot sauce?" Yeah, my mouth could go for a good scolding too.

six

"Mommy!" Hunter runs up the front steps with his arms wide open.

I lean down and grab my baby boy, hugging and kissing him, drinking in his delicious little boy smell ... even when it currently smells like Cheetos and apple juice.

"I missed you. I love you. Can we snuggle on the couch? I want to show you my new comic book I got."

This new routine of Tyler having the kids every weekend is going to take serious getting used to. We might have separated two years ago, but the divorce papers still have fresh ink. It took a while for me to agree to the weekends at his house, only because I want my children with me. His argument was that I work long hours on the weekends, sometimes past midnight. Plus, the kids want to be with their father too. They love him while I often hate him. It's a double-edged sword.

Izzy comes up the steps with her backpack slung on her shoulder. She's wearing the denim jeans and long-sleeved shirt she went to his house in on Friday night. Tyler thinks it's best if the kids have wardrobes at each house that shouldn't leave. Apparently, after a decade of cleaning his underwear, I can't be trusted with basic laundry.

Hunter's still in my arms as I greet Izzy. "Hey, sweetie. Did you study with Dad for your social studies test tomorrow?"

Her blue eyes roll up to me in annoyance. "No."

My mouth pinches. "Why not?"

"We were really busy." She shrugs defiantly and walks into the house.

Tyler closes his car door and carries Hunter's backpack to the front door. "Mr. Snuggles and iPad are both inside. We had a good time today, right, champ?" He ruffles Hunter's hair, and our boy smiles.

"Daddy let us have ice cream on our waffles, and then we went in the pool one more time before they closed it."

I tilt my head in confusion. "It's a little cool in the season for the pool. You weren't cold?"

"Daddy installed a heater! It was so warm. Like a hot tub."

Of course he installed a heater in the pool.

"Let me guess. Maisie wanted it."

Tyler places his hands on his hips and sighs. "Hunter, do you mind going inside while I talk to your mom for a few minutes?"

I put Hunter on the ground, and he turns to give Tyler a huge hug. "I love you, Daddy."

Tyler lifts Hunter and holds him tight. They're carbon copies of each other with their big brown eyes and wide smiles. Tyler might be a scoundrel, but he's a good-looking scoundrel who gave us a beautiful son. When Hunter laughs, I see and hear every bit of Tyler.

Hunter grips his dad's face, smooshing his cheeks together, and lines up their eyes. "Tell Maisie I said good-bye and that she's the best."

Yep, like father, like son.

Tyler speaks through his smooshed mouth. "Yes, sir."

They kiss on the lips, and then Hunter scurries into the house, leaving Tyler and me alone on the front porch.

I remember when he used to pick me up for dates on this porch. He was a teenager with a goofy grin and curly hair that flipped up from his baseball cap, long before that hairstyle was cool.

His hair is much shorter now yet just as full. There're no signs of gray, nor does the man have a single permanent wrinkle. He's aging well—not that thirty-four is old, but I've already started seeing signs of my own demise on my skin. A line on my forehead is wondering when it's time to start Botox, and my boobs don't naturally sit as high on my chest, thanks to breastfeeding two babies.

A cool breeze blows as we stand here on a crisp autumn day and stare at one another as I wait for Tyler to say whatever it is he wants to talk about.

"How are you doing?" he eventually asks.

"Okay," I answer, surprised by his question.

"I'm worried about you, Lyss. Friday night was so unlike you. If you weren't at the salon for money, then it has to be to get back at Maisie and me—"

"I'm not trying to be vindictive toward Maisie. Believe it or not, this had nothing to do with her. It's me, Ty. All me."

"I just don't understand."

"I'm trying my best to be brutally honest, but I don't know how to explain myself. It was a stupid thing to do. Believe me when I say, I wish no harm on Maisie or anything bad on her business."

He looks down and nods. "I know you don't. She wishes you'd talk to her."

"We chatted at Hunter's pre-K graduation in June."

"She said you looked really pretty that day. I agreed."

"Thanks. So, as you can see, we're all good here. You are I are killing it with this co-parenting thing. We put Gwyneth and Chris to shame."

When he looks up at me, his eyes are soft. "I really do worry about you. You're going through a lot. Leaving the house, moving back in with your dad, surrounded by reminders of your mother ... it's a lot on you and the kids. I don't take for granted what you guys are going through."

This is why I can't totally hate Tyler. He might do idiotic things sometimes, but he's a decent guy. Not the best, but decent.

"I'm actually doing really great, so thank you for the concern, but everything is great."

He lifts a brow. "Great, huh?" With a nod, he grimaces. "Suppose you were having a good time Friday night to be as drunk as you were."

"I was out with Tara Friday night. We went out on Saturday night too."

Tyler's brows rise in interest. "Two nights out in a row with your single friend? Knowing Tara, she's hooking you up with all kinds of guys. I guess you're ready to date then."

I won't lie to myself. Tyler's seemingly displeased reaction with my dating again leaves a slight smirk on my face.

"Yeah. Turns out I like country swing dancing."

"You? Swing dancing? Huh. Must have found yourself a good dance partner."

Tyler doesn't need to know he already met that handsome dance partner at the police station in the wee hours of Saturday morning … or the fact that my dance partner is engaged to marry someone else and I spent a good portion of my day having an internal freak-out because life is just so damn cruel sometimes.

For the purpose of this conversation, all he needs to know is, "He was pretty spectacular. He did this thing when his palm wrapped around my throat, and he slowly dragged me up to his chest, leaving us in a sensual embrace. It was very sexy. Looking forward to doing it again."

His eyes rise to the sky as he shakes his head before looking back at me with a grin. "And there's my girl, busting chops, like always. Glad to see you're still you, Lyss."

"Sad to see you're not the old you, Ty."

My comment makes his grin fall.

"I'll see you Tuesday when I pick the kids up for dinner." He walks down the porch steps and stops after opening his car door. "Easy on the drinking."

I point toward the house. "Sure. I'll stop as soon as I finish the handle of Tito's I opened this morning. I think there're a few drops left."

He runs his hand over the top of his head. He and I both know I don't drink when the kids are home. I never liked it, never will.

I wave him off as Dad comes outside just as Tyler pulls away from the curb.

"Surprised you didn't come outside to say hello," I say to him as we watch the taillights disappear down the street.

"Why do that when I can eavesdrop perfectly from behind the door?"

I rub his back and give it a pat. "Hear anything good?"

"Just enough to know that I'm raising a teenager again."

"Izzy's only eleven."

"Not her. You. Feels like you're in high school all over again. If you don't watch it, that boy is gonna fall in love with you again, and I'll allow it over my dead body."

LOVE ... IT'S COMPLICATED

"No, Dad. Tyler chose Maisie."

"He once chose you."

"You know the expression, *There's a lid for every pot?* Sometimes, the lid fits on two different pots. It's a perfectly good lid, and it's currently sitting on another pot, where it belongs."

"There's also an ass for every seat," he grumbles and starts walking back into the house. "Just make sure that ass stays where he belongs!"

I laugh. If I learned how to bust chops, it was clearly from the best.

The week goes by as seemingly normal as possible. The kids go to school, I go to work, and Dad sticks to his routine. As I pick the kids up from school, I watch as Hunter waves to his friends and carries conversations, even as he's walking away. His eagerness to chat with his new classmates is adorable.

The contrast to Izzy's sullen walk to the car makes my heart sink.

When Tyler and I made the decision to move the kids to the school in our old hometown of Newbury, the place I was moving back to, we thought it would be easy because this is where we grew up. We have fond memories of this building and thought the transition would be easy.

I hadn't planned on Izzy taking this long to adapt. Starting a new school in the fifth grade must be tough, but being that the middle school here starts in the fifth grade, it should be easier than this. A lot of the kids are new, and the classes rotate, so there's plenty of opportunity to make friends.

Izzy doesn't wave good-bye to a single child. She hasn't exchanged numbers with anyone new, nor does she talk about kids from school. It's great she has her old friends in Greenwood Village and still keeps in touch. I hope she makes at least one new friend here.

"I'm gonna be in the talent show!" Hunter shoves a flyer in my face that he pulled out of his backpack.

I lean down and grab the now-open backpack to keep everything from falling out as I simultaneously take the flyer from his hand. "That's awesome. Are kindergarteners allowed to perform?"

"Yes! I want to do magic."

I let out a ragged breath as I buckle him into his booster seat. He can do it on his own, but it's a habit I haven't broken yet. "Honey, we don't know any magic. When is this show?"

I place his backpack on the floor and close the door. Looking down at the flyer, I see it's in a few weeks. I suppose I could help him put *something* together for an elementary school performance.

As I slide into the driver's side, I look at Izzy, who is seated in the back on the passenger side. She's gripping her backpack to her chest and looking out the window.

"What about you? Do you want to perform in the talent show?"

"It's for the lower school only. The middle school doesn't have one. Even if they did, I wouldn't be in it. I don't have a talent," she replies.

"You have a ton of talent. Art, for one. You make beautiful sketches. Plus, you cook. Better than I ever did as a kid."

"A monkey can make pancakes," she states matter-of-factly as she fidgets with the tag on her backpack. She's quiet for a moment before asking, "Do you really think I'm good at art?"

"Yes! You might not think it's anything more than a hobby, but you have real talent."

Izzy shrugs and looks out the window. "I guess so."

"There's an art studio in downtown Newbury. I could look into getting you some classes. Maybe you can make friends there with similar interests?"

"I already have friends, Mom. They live near Dad. Not that he lets me see them because he and Maisie always have something 'fun' planned." She uses air quotes for the word *fun*. "Why do they try so hard? Hunter and I don't need to be entertained every second."

Hunter chimes in, "Speak for yourself. Dad says he's taking us out on ATVs this weekend."

I look at them through the rearview mirror with horror. "ATVs? This is the first I'm hearing of this."

"There's this place with a super-cool track. I have to ride with Dad though. Izzy's tall enough to ride alone."

"See? Tries way too hard." Izzy folds her arms over her chest and falls further into her seat.

"I'm sure it'll slow down once winter starts and it's too cold to do anything."

LOVE ... IT'S COMPLICATED

"We're going skiing!" Hunter shouts, causing Izzy to cover her ears.
"Maisie is a black diamond skier," she says to me in explanation.
"Why would I have ever thought otherwise?" I sigh and pull out of the parking lot. "Hey, what do you say we go to Target? We'll look for a magic kit for Hunter, and, Iz, you can pick out some new art supplies."
"Look who's trying too hard now."
I narrow my eyes at Izzy's comment. *Touché, kid.*
I'd be more annoyed with her than I am, but it's hard when Isabella Landish is the carbon copy of her mother. I was once the moody, sarcastic one, and I didn't have to move out of the only home I'd ever known.
I cut her some slack, as I always do.
I just hope she snaps out of it soon.
We head into Target, and like all trips to this store, we leave with more things than we planned to purchase. Izzy picked out a new sketchpad and colored pencils, plus these paint pens that I'd coerced her into trying. The only magic kit Hunter and I could find was a wooden set that cost more than I had hoped to spend but has enough tricks in there for us to come up with something exciting for his show. My side of the cart was packed with new body wash, a loofah, and shampoo. I even bought some new throw pillows for the living room, a blanket, and some fall decorations.
Due to recent shopping cart thefts in the area, our shopping center no longer allows you to take your cart farther than the storefront. Magnetic locks kick in when you enter the parking lot, so the kids and I load up our hands with bags holding our new purchases.
Hunter is taking his magic kit out of the sack because he insists on carrying it to the car when, out the corner of my eye, I see the one man I don't want to see.
William Bronson.
He's hard to miss. There aren't many gloriously tall men like him walking around the Target shopping center these days. There aren't any men like him walking around ... anywhere. Even in October, he has golden skin. That, or he visits the tanning salon, which I highly doubt. If he did, I'd feel better. No one should glow this naturally.
"Let me help you with that," he says as he approaches the cart and our full hands.

"We're good. Thanks," I say, not looking at him.

Izzy eyes Will curiously. "We don't talk to strangers."

I groan. "It's okay. I know him. He's a potential client of mine. He and his fiancée, Allison, are looking to get married sometime next year."

"We're not getting married next year," Will says to Izzy.

"Or the year after. I have to work up the numbers. I'm sorry I haven't given those to you yet."

I'm grabbing the last of the bags when Will places a hand on mine.

"Let me help you. You have a ton of stuff."

"It's fine. We got them," I proclaim as I make a show of grabbing the handles of the gray bags in the most haphazard way, struggling to get the one with the throw pillows out of the cart because it's sandwiched next to another bag.

"Here," Izzy says, extending her hand and giving a bag to Will. "You can carry this one."

He smiles at Izzy and takes the offered bag. "Thanks. I'm William."

One look at my daughter and the pink in her cheeks, and I can see the smolder has worked on her. Poor girl.

"I'm Isabella, and that's Hunter."

Hunter lifts his hand. "Hi."

Will looks down at the box in Hunter's arms. "Magic, huh?"

"I'm going to perform an entire act for the school talent show!"

"I don't know about an entire act. Let's see what's in the box when we get home." I nod toward my car parked at the far end of the lot. "We're parked over there."

Will takes the bags out of my hands, and before I can complain, he's walking toward my car. I take Hunter's free hand, and Izzy stays close as we follow.

"I know a few magic tricks myself." Will talks over his shoulder as he strides through the lot.

"Can you levitate a person?" Hunter asks with an excited beam.

"What great magician can't?" Will says, approaching the car.

I hit the unlock button, and Will stands near the hatchback. Hunter and Izzy get in the backseat while I lift the tailgate for Will.

As he puts the bags in the car, Hunter leans over the backseat and talks to Will. "Can you show me how to levitate someone?"

"No," I answer for Will. "Officer Bronson has a lot to do."

LOVE ... IT'S COMPLICATED

"You're a cop?" Izzy asks, seeming impressed. She, too, is now in the backseat with her brother, on her knees and peering out the trunk. "Have you ever shot someone?"

"Izzy!" I scold, but Will places a hand on my arm. For a moment, I enjoy the feeling of his hand on my skin—until I realize I shouldn't like it there. I move away.

"It's okay. She can ask. Unfortunately, Isabella, I have fired my weapon."

"Have you killed someone?" she asks.

Will looks at me briefly, and his brows furrow.

I answer for him. "Officer Bronson saved a lot of lives not too long ago. He even took a bullet in the chest and is recently back from medical leave. He's a hero."

"Wow." Hunter gapes.

"That's so cool," Izzy says, wide-eyed. It's the most engaged I've seen her in anything in months.

"It's just my job," Will says.

His modesty is endearing. As is his charm. Then, I remember he's engaged, and I snap out of the Bronson voodoo.

"As you can see, Officer Bronson is very busy with saving lives and wedding planning and can't be teaching little boys how to levitate."

I close the tailgate and walk toward the driver's side, but Will is blocking me.

"Melissa, we need to talk."

"Did you follow me here?" I ask incredulously.

"No. Absolutely not. I have to buy a gift for my nephew, and you're here. It feels like fate. Melissa, I've been dying to talk to you."

I try to walk around him to the left, but he moves in sync and doesn't let me pass.

"I'll have those estimates ready for you by the end of the week."

"I haven't been able to sleep."

"The turnaround time at Lavish Events can be as long as three weeks."

"There are things I have to tell you, and I don't want to do this in front of your kids. Can we meet sometime for coffee?" he asks as I try to pass him on the right.

"I'm still waiting for one of the venues to get back to me. As soon as they do, I'll email the numbers right over to you."

"Melissa, stop."

He gently lays a hand on my shoulder, and I back away, raising my hand to push his arm off of me. The action startles him.

"What the hell, Will? You should have told me you were engaged to be married."

He runs his hand up his jaw and up into his hair. "You're right. I should have. It didn't come up. I just ... we were having a good time and talking. I don't know why it didn't come up."

"I've been racking my brain, trying to think about what I did and didn't say that night, and I keep coming back to the fact that you were flirting with me. I know it. And that dance. It was ... I never would have thrown myself at you if I hadn't felt that attraction."

"I'm sorry if I gave the wrong impression."

"You kissed me back. You cheated on your fiancée when you kissed me back, and it's made me feel terrible. For the first time, I'm the other woman, and it's a horrible position to be in. Because I liked you, Will. I liked you so much, and I didn't want to like someone. I wasn't ready, but you just swooped in, and then you brought me to the lowest place I could ever be. I know what it's like to be on the other side of that heartache, to have someone you love be with someone else. So, yeah, you might want to talk, but there's nothing—absolutely nothing—you can say that would make me feel any less like scum."

"Melissa, please—"

"Stop. No pleading. If you're worried I'll tell Allison what happened, I won't. I threw myself at you. You pushed me away. That's all that matters."

I try to pass him again, but he lays his arm on the car, creating a blockade. It forces me to look up at him—really look at him and that soul-searing gaze. If I had thought he wasn't affected by what was going on, I was wrong. Just one glance, and I can see he's been going through hell—dark circles under his eyes, frown lines around his mouth, and a pout that weakens his smolder.

I cross my arms in front of my chest and tilt my head at him, begging for him to say something to make this right.

"I kissed you back," he whispers, and it screams down to my toes.

"You shouldn't have."

"I know," he breathes.

LOVE ... IT'S COMPLICATED

My chest caves with this horrible feeling of jealousy, sadness, disappointment, and elation. It's a feeling I can't explain. I weave my body around his.

He doesn't follow me. His head is still down, hand on the roof, look of defeat shadowed on his profile, as I open my door.

"Thank you for your help with our bags, Officer Bronson."

I'm in the car, and I close the door as quickly as possible. Will steps to the side so I can back out of the parking spot. I try not to look at him as I drive past him. If I do, I might crumble.

"I like him," Izzy says as we exit the Target parking lot.

Great. The first time my daughter shows interest in anything in months, and it's in the man I'm dying not to be interested in.

seven

"I CAN'T BELIEVE WE finally have our own office space!" I gush as I walk through the modest three-room office suite we are renting in Greenwood Village.

Yes, it's the same town as Maisie's salon and Tyler's house, but we carefully chose a location on the opposite side of town to avoid them as much as possible. It makes sense because it's close to where Jillian lives and the clientele in this area is who we're attracting.

The office is on the second floor of a three-story building, just above a wedding dress boutique. I glance out the window and down at Main Street, which is lit with gas lanterns and has cobblestone walkways.

I fell in love with this town the first time Tyler and I drove through. It's why we bought our home here. It's the smallest house in the neighborhood. but we chose quality over quantity. Living in this town was more important than purchasing any large, center hall Colonial we could afford in Newbury, the town where we grew up and where I'm currently living. It's funny how things work out.

"Our lease doesn't technically start until next week, but the last tenant moved out early. All we have to do is pick out colors, and I have a painter lined up to get it completed over the weekend."

She holds up some swatches, and we giggle.

We're sharing the smaller single office and using the other office as a storage room. The front main room, where you walk in, will mostly be prep space with a table to the side for meeting with clients since it's the largest room.

"I like the cream colors. It'll brighten up the room and make it feel larger," I suggest.

"What do you think of doing some textured walls, using wood slats? It'll give some character and help us define the creation stations from the meeting area."

"My father would love to do that for us. I'll see if he can get the pieces cut before the painters come. Maybe add some shiplap in the bathroom and kitchen area. It's small, but we can brighten it up."

We walk around the office like we would any new event space and talk about how we'll decorate it, including glossy prints of some of our most impressive weddings.

We're currently measuring the office walls for the wood texture elements we plan to add when the buzzer rings. We haven't opened up shop, so we both jump a little in surprise that anyone is here.

Jillian walks over to the intercom. "Lavish Events."

I laugh. It's a funny way to answer an intercom. She could have just said hello.

"I want them to know who we are since they're probably here to see Bob's Accounting or whoever was here before us," she says to me as we wait for the person on the other end to speak.

"Hi. This is Allison Lalayne. I'm here to see Melissa."

The inside of my stomach drops to my feet.

Jillian hits the button to buzz her up. "Were you expecting a client?"

"No. I sent her the wedding proposals but haven't heard from her." Realization hits me as I say, "I put the new office address on the proposal. It looked better than the PO Box we had on the old forms."

Jillian nods as she holds the door open, waiting for Allison to walk up the stairs and come into the office.

Allison appears in jeans and a blouse today. Her hair is perfectly combed, but her face looks puffy, like she's been crying.

"Are you okay?" I ask, fidgeting with my hands as she walks in.

"I'm sorry for just showing up, unannounced, but you took all that time to sit with me and William last week and then did all that work on the proposals, which were perfect, by the way." She rubs at her red nose. "I wanted to let you know that we won't be needing your services after all."

"Oh." It's all I can say because I'm a mixture of relieved for not having to plan Will's wedding and sad for how terrible she looks. How terrible she must feel. "You didn't have to go through the trouble of coming down here. I totally understand if you don't want to use our services. We have brides cancel on us all the time."

Jillian makes a face at me for the lie. While we've had a few people decide they weren't going to use our services, it's barely considered *all the time*.

I widen my eyes at her and open my hands in a *what the hell am I supposed to say to this crying girl* way.

Jillian's brows shoot up, and I shrug.

Allison is still wiping her nose. "We don't need your services because William called off the engagement."

"Oh," I say again because, now, I really don't know what to say.

Allison collapses on my shoulder and starts to sob uncontrollably. I pat her awkwardly and look to Jillian for help. There's nowhere to sit, so she looks around aimlessly. Jillian opens a closet and finds a bucket. She flips it upside down, and I move Allison over and usher her to take a seat.

I rummage through my bag that's sitting on the windowsill and grab a packet of wet wipes I keep on hand for Hunter, handing her the entire pack.

"Thank you," she says as she takes out two and blows her nose.

Jillian and I stand in front of the brokenhearted bride sitting on a neon-orange Home Depot bucket in an un-vacuumed, unpainted, vacant office space. In the two years we've been planning events together, this is most definitely a first.

"You met him, albeit only that one time, but did you get the vibe that he was unhappy? He was happy that day, right?"

"Well ..." I think back to that lunch. I was trying very hard not to look at him, for fear I'd melt into a pile of adultery goo. "He was pretty quiet for a groom. You and I had already gone over all the details that you wanted, and he just showed up for the frittata."

"I never even asked him what he wanted in a wedding. I didn't think he cared. The wedding planning wasn't really his thing." Allison lifts the wet wipe and starts to sob again.

"We are so sorry about your wedding being called off. If there was anything we could do for you, we would, but unfortunately, I think this is a situation best resolved with your friends and family," Jillian says.

"My mother is devastated, and my girlfriends are ready to castrate him. My dad thinks there's another woman."

I nearly choke on my own saliva. My eyes close, and my hands shake lightly.

She's right.

There was another woman.

It was me, but it was just a kiss. A single kiss that meant absolutely nothing.

I have so many things I want to say to her. If I had known he was engaged, I never ever would have flung myself at him. I wouldn't have desired him.

I also want to tell her that he pushed me away. He knew it was wrong, and he probably called off the wedding out of an insane amount of guilt.

I can't say any of those things though. None of it will make her feel better.

I kneel by her side and go to grab her hand yet pull pack and lay my hand on my thigh. "Allison, I am so sorry that you are going through this. I don't know why Will called off your engagement, but you're better off finding out now that the man who you love isn't the one for you. I understand the heartache of your whole life plan just evaporating before your eyes. This is a heartbreak that will linger for a while, but you *will* get through it."

"I think I was pushy. I tried too hard."

Jillian takes a step forward. "You can't do that to yourself. Don't go into the what-ifs of life. Sometimes, things don't work out. And sometimes, they do. Maybe it's just a case of cold feet, and he's going to come back and beg for your hand. It wouldn't be the first time a man panicked before making the biggest commitment of his life."

"I'm nothing now. I was supposed to get married, and now, I'm a sham," she cries.

"You are beautiful and very sweet, and from what I understand, you have an amazing family. A million girls would envy you, and yet you're hurting. You can't define your self-worth based on who loves you. I'm sorry we can't help you," I say.

She sniffs and takes a few long breaths, nodding and looking over at me. "Actually, there is one thing you can do. So, part of me thinks maybe you're the reason he got cold feet."

My insides plummet to the bottom of my gut. "Me?"

"Well, you probably should refrain from talking to future grooms the way you did to Will."

"It was just conversation and a dance or three." My voice cracks.

"Dance? Oh, did you mention that? I just remember you talking about divorce and pensions and whose turn it was to take the garbage out. I mean, I'm sure they're all valid things we should discuss before walking down the aisle, but I don't think he was prepared to have that conversation with the wedding designer."

Jillian's head flinches back slightly. "You talked about pensions?"

"I might have lost a moment of clarity during that brunch," I explain and then turn back to Allison. "I shouldn't have brought my divorce status to the table, but I don't know how I can help now."

"You should talk to him. Tell him all the good things about being married and how amazing weddings are."

"That sounds like a terrible idea," I say, and she wails again. It's loud, and it sounds like a siren of bridal despair. "Of course … anything's worth a try. I'll *try*, but I don't think he wants to hear from me, a stranger."

"Thank you. I just don't know what else to do. I think William needs a push, you know. If everyone keeps telling him how happy he'll be once we're married, he'll do it. He just has to get to the altar, is all."

"Coercion. Brilliant plan. Let's help you up," Jillian states rather matter-of-factly as we each place a hand under Allison's arms and raise her from the bucket. "Melissa will talk to … what's his name?"

"William," she mutters as we walk her to the door.

"Yes. Hopefully, it all works out," Jillian says. "You need to know that no man is worth feeling this terrible over. There might be someone far better waiting for you in the future, and if not, there's nothing you can't accomplish without a man. God created dildos and sperm banks for a reason."

"Thank you both," she says, and I think she wants to say even more, but Jillian slowly yet forcefully closes the door after waving and wishing Allison the best of luck in the future.

With her gone, Jillian and I stare at each other for a beat.

"That was weird," Jillian states, rubbing her temple.

"Yeah. Especially since, only a week ago, I was making out with her fiancé in the parking lot of Lone Tavern."

Jillian's jaw drops. "Girl, you'd better start explaining."

eight

"YOU MADE OUT WITH a guy and didn't tell me or Jillian!" Tara says we wait in line for our espressos.

Her schedule as an accountant gets hectic during her second busy season, which is attributed to business clients who applied for six-month extensions on their taxes. Because of said busy schedule, I haven't been able to fully digest the Will scenario with her.

Here we are, on a Sunday, meeting for coffee before I head to the supermarket. Who said your thirties aren't glamorous?

"It was embarrassing, so I chose not to divulge. Then, he showed up for lunch the next day, and honestly, I just want to forget all of it."

"Apple crisp, oat milk macchiato," the barista calls out, and I take a step forward to grab the drink and leave a tip in the mason jar on the counter.

"You still gave her a proposal for her wedding." Tara leans into me, still trying to comprehend my recent drama.

"I'm a professional."

"Iced, shaken brown sugar espresso." Tara's order is called out, so she grabs it and turns away from the counter, still not done with our conversation.

"You should have told her the fiancé was a cheating manwhore!" Tara explains.

A fellow patron gives Tara a cautious look, clearly frightened of my friend with the mop of dark curls, who is chanting about infidelity in a coffee shop. Tara doesn't seem to notice.

"We should cut his balls off. Better yet, make Wanted posters and put them on every corner in Valor County." Her hands spread out like she's showcasing a marquee. "*Wanted: creepy philanderer who follows innocent women into parking lots and shoves his tongue down their throats!*"

"Yeah, well, that's not at all how it happened. In this case, I would be the creep who shoved her tongue in *his* mouth. I'm still having a bit of an internal war in my head regarding the whole thing."

The entire situation has really messed with my emotions. As if I didn't have a zillion things going on in my life with Tyler, the kids, Dad, the business, being infatuated with a man who is … *was* … engaged and the drama that comes along with it is not something I am mentally prepared to deal with.

"You're probably better off. Bad enough that your ex-husband is a complete dipshit. You don't need another undeserving asshat in your life."

"Tell me how you really feel."

She pushes her tendrils from her face and smiles. "Everyone needs a friend like me in their life."

"I couldn't agree more."

Women have a superpower. They can build each other up and knock another down with a single comment. I've been blessed with an incredible group of women by my side. When Tyler and I started having marital problems, Tara was always available to listen to my tales of woe. She never rolled her eyes or told me I should just be lucky to have a husband and children, as other single women might say. She always encouraged me to expect more from my relationship because I deserved it. When I chose to fight for my marriage, she never looked down on me or said I was a fool. I've had her full support, no matter what.

This is why I can confide in her about everything. I hope she feels the same way.

"Any updates on Kent?" I ask when we walk outside.

"Three dates in. I'd say it's going in the right direction. He's kind of prudish though. I don't know if that's a good or bad thing."

"Given your track record, I'd say slow is a good thing. Enjoy the *getting to know you* stage. Try not to overthink it."

LOVE ... IT'S COMPLICATED

"Great advice from the queen of overthinking. Have you gone out at all in the last two weekends? I know this cop messed with your head, but don't let him get you down. Not all men are cheaters."

I scoff. "Leave it to me to have only kissed two men in my life, and they both put their lips on someone other than their betrothed."

"Look at it as a win. At least you know you're ready to get back out there."

With a groan, I take a sip of my drink and head toward her car, which is parked closer than mine.

While Tara heads off to go do whatever it is single ladies do on a Sunday, I'm off to do the most exciting thing there is for a divorced mother of two to do on a weekend—grocery shop. It might seem like sarcasm, but grocery shopping without a husband to itemize your grocery list is a godsend.

Sugary snacks for the kids? *Into the cart!*

Honeycrisp apples that are double the price of Empire apples? *Let's do this.*

Life's too short to have someone always questioning why you're getting what you're buying. And I am living my best life in aisle four.

Family-size jar of Nutella? *Yes, please.*

It's for the best that my short-lived crush on hot cop Bronson didn't pan out. I'm just getting used to living by my own rules. Who knows if I'll be able to become accustomed to someone else's?

Maybe I'm blowing this whole situation out of proportion. I'd like to say I'm not a dramatic person, but that would be a lie.

I used to be a girl who thrived off of losing control.

As a teenager, I got into so much trouble that I'm sure my parents were thankful they only had one kid. Then, I met Tyler, and my fifteen-year-old heart exploded and landed around him. I spent every moment following him around Newbury. To his football games, the pizzeria on Central Avenue, the last row of the movie theater ... the backseat of his car parked in a small wooded area on the outskirts of town, where no one could see us.

Tyler went to a state college, and I stayed close to home. We saw each other every weekend, and he proposed at his graduation party. We married young, and were pregnant right away.

To say our families weren't constantly chasing us with shouts of, "Slow down. You have your whole life ahead of you," is an understatement.

There were so many arguments back then, but we didn't care. We went with the motions, and soon, we were the couple who people looked up to. By the time Hunter was born, no one could imagine life not happening just as it did.

Then mom got sick.

I grab a can of tuna fish off the shelf. The Best By date is five years from now. This is why it's a good buy. You don't have to use it right away. It's an item you can place on the shelf and come back to next year and eat it. Hell, I can open this when Izzy's in high school and serve her a sandwich. Good, dependable tuna fish. That is, until you go for it on year six and realize time past by when you thought you had more time. So much more.

I put the can of tuna fish back on the shelf.

I've never liked it anyway.

I grab a bunch of bananas. These babies warn you when their time is about to be up.

I like them more.

Somewhere along the line, I went from the girl who thrives off losing control to the one who craves it more than anything.

I drive home and pull into my parents' driveway. I've been living here for six months and still call it my parents' house. While Tyler and I figured out our divorce agreement, I lived in our old home, and he stayed with Maisie. When the papers were signed, I moved out of the house, and he moved back in.

Years ago, as I set out to take over the world with Tyler in our dream town of Greenwood Village, I never thought I'd be back in Newbury, let alone sleeping in my old bedroom.

Taking my grocery bags out of the trunk, I walk over to the back door that leads to the kitchen. The handle is unlocked, so I turn the knob and walk inside.

"Oh my God!"

Those words are spoken by me. Shouted really as I drop the bags in my hands and use one hand to cover my eyes while I back up and knock into the door as it careens with the wall.

Dad and Anna are making out in the kitchen up against the center island, where I serve my children breakfast. If I'm correct, his hand was on her boob.

"Would you stop acting so theatrical?" Dad says, but I don't see him because my hand is covering my face.

LOVE ... IT'S COMPLICATED

I move my fingers to take a peek through them and spy Dad and Anna standing, fully clothed. Anna is running a hand down her short brown hair to make sure it's in place, while Dad is glaring at me with his lips pressed into a white slash.

"Put a tie on the doorknob next time," I grumble.

Anna looks bashful. "It was nice seeing you, Melissa. Gavin, I'll call you tomorrow."

Thankfully, she grabs her purse from the counter and leaves without a good-bye kiss.

With her gone, I move to collect the dropped bags from the floor. Dad has already started to gather the items that rolled across the beige tiles. It's an attractive tile. One my mother picked out when they redid the kitchen ten years ago. It matches the countertop. The one her husband was just groping the neighborhood cat lady against.

With everything now on the counter, Dad places his hands on his hips and looks down. Eye contact in these situations is not his strong suit.

"Didn't realize you'd be home this early."

"Tyler is dropping the kids off soon. He and Maisie have a lovers' getaway planned."

"He told you that?"

"Not in so many words. Said they're going to the Cape for a few days. I read between the lines."

His forehead is down as he grabs a can of corn from the pile of recovered grocery items. I stare at his head of full hair—something he takes pride in, considering many of his friends have lost theirs by now. My father really is a good-looking guy. He's not vain, but he takes care of himself, and he should be proud of that. It's no wonder women are throwing themselves at him.

"Anna didn't have to go," I say, more to be cordial than anything.

He clears his throat. "She has her grandson's basketball game tonight. Just swung by to have a cup of coffee."

I look at the unused coffeepot and give a closed-mouth smile. I hate that he has to lie for my benefit, yet I'm too much of an insecure child to tell him he doesn't have to.

He starts putting items in the cabinets while I take the produce and place them in the refrigerator.

"How does pappardelle pasta with sausage and spinach sound?"

"Hunter's gonna hate it," he says.

"I know, but the kid has to start eating healthy. He can't live on chicken nuggets and hot dogs forever."

Dad smirks. "Do you remember what your mother said when Izzy wouldn't eat anything other than pasta with butter or macaroni and cheese?"

I do, so I do my best impersonation of my mother as I say, "So, you mean she eats exactly what's on a kid's menu at every restaurant in the country?"

"Exactly. The restaurants offer kids what they want to eat. I was always on your mother to get you to eat better. You grew up on tater tots and corn dogs and turned out just fine."

"You were the broccoli drill sergeant."

He looks over at me. "You sound like your mother when you impersonate her. You sound like her, even when you're not trying. You have a lot of her in you."

"I don't know about that. I feel like she'd have a better head for all the changes happening."

"Don't be so sure. Your mother had great advice, gave the best of anyone I've ever met. Yet when it came to matters of the heart for herself, she could be a little irrational."

"Then, maybe I do take after her."

Dad moves his hands to the countertop and leans against it. With a deep, heavy sigh, he nods and then looks up at me. "So, about Anna. What you walked in on was just us embracing."

My eyes widen as I swallow and start aimlessly opening cabinets, looking for ... *something*. "Yeah."

"If it's okay with you, I'd like to invite her over for dinner with us and the kids."

With my back to him, I close my eyes, thankful he can't see how uncomfortable I am with this conversation. "Sure. Maybe after the holidays. I have a ton of weddings, and the kids have studying and school events. Maybe after the new year?"

My ask is selfish, I know. My mother's been gone for two years, yet it feels like an instant. I'm happy my father has found peace in her passing, but I'm still getting over the fact that she's not going to walk through the door any minute with her tote bag falling from her shoulder as she immediately starts telling us a story about what just transpired at the post office.

Mom was a great storyteller.

I miss her so much.

LOVE ... IT'S COMPLICATED

I spin around and see Dad standing in the kitchen with a small nod.

"Yes. After the new year. That sounds like a good time. I'll be in the garage if you need me."

"Working out?" I ask, surprised because he usually does his cardio in the morning.

"I think I'll putter around at my woodworking table for a bit. How did those wooden slats work out for your office wall?"

"Great, Dad. They were perfect. Thank you."

"Now, if only the neighbors would let me fix that death trap next door, I'll be happy."

I look out the window at the tree house in the nearest yard. It's been in an oak since I was a kid, and it was a place I used to sneak into at night when I was a teenager, up to no good. It hasn't been used in years. Shame since it was a great hideout.

"Maybe you can do a covert operation and repair it at night."

"Risk falling off that old ladder in the dark? I'll stay right here on firm ground."

With a tap on the wall, Dad disappears into the garage, and I start on dinner. I sauté the sausage and add the spinach. I'm adding the pasta to the pot of boiling water when the door opens and I hear a car door close.

Knowing my babies are home, I run to the front porch and hold out my arms. Hunter comes barreling up the stairs. His hair is an unruly mess, and he has dirt on his cheeks.

"Mommy! Daddy took us riding on ATVs today!"

My head shoots up to Tyler, who is carrying the kids' bags up the stairs. "We said we'd discuss this. I told you I wasn't comfortable with them on those death traps."

"They loved it." He beams, completely ignoring my body in a *what the fuck, Tyler* pose.

My scowl alone should be indication enough that I'm pissed, but I state it clearly, "I'm pissed."

"You're overreacting. Isn't she, Iz?"

Izzy ignores Tyler as she walks up the front steps with headphones on her ears.

"She had a blast and doesn't want to show it," Tyler explains calmly, but I'm still reeling.

"Mom, I was going so fast! They let me ride on one all by myself. I was flying!" Hunter's elation is adorable, if not unnecessary.

"Of course you loved it. It was dangerous and not appropriate for a five-year-old."

Tyler drags his hand through his hair. "You're overreacting."

"I asked you for one thing." My tone is one I use for scolding the children, and in this case, he is the child because he can't follow basic directions, like *don't put our children on death traps.*

"They're my kids, Lyss, and if I want to take my kids to a safe and reputable ATV track, then I will. Hunter loved it."

"He also loves magic, but I don't see you taking him to see a show."

"Magic? Lyss, come on. It's …" He pauses, realizing tiny, almost six-year-old ears are listening. "ATVs are cooler."

I tap my foot. "Hunter, go inside. I want to talk to Daddy."

Tyler holds up a finger and starts to back away. "As much as I'd love to have this conversation, I have to run. Maisie is waiting for me, so we can leave."

"A disappearing act. Who says you don't like magic?" I'm oozing sarcasm.

"You should see what I can do with a rabbit and a hat." He winks with devilish charm, and I stomp my foot so damn hard against the stone porch that I hit nerve in my heel and feel a zing up the back of my foot.

"Shit, that stings."

Tyler is hastily running down the stairs as I call out, "I'm not done reprimanding you!"

"Didn't think you were," he shouts over his shoulder as he rounds his car.

Hunter and I wave Tyler off—me using only one finger instead of an entire hand.

"Okay, so let me tell you all about the ATV track!" Hunter grabs my hand and walks me inside.

For the next four hours, he talks about his weekend with his father nonstop. He talks through dinner, in between the grumbles and protests about eating spinach, and he continues through bath time and even as I'm putting on his pajamas. I love hearing the joy in my son's voice, yet I'm still annoyed it's about something I asked Tyler not to do.

Once he's in bed, I check on Izzy. She's on her bed, reading a book. I stop in and take a seat on her bed. My hands comb her long hair, and then I run a thumb along her soft cheek.

LOVE ... IT'S COMPLICATED

"How was your weekend?" I ask her now that the two of us have some one-on-one time.

"Fine."

"That's all? If you enjoyed the ATVs, you can tell me. Lord knows, Hunter has been talking about it all night."

"I know you hate it, Mom. Just say it. And you hate Dad. And Maisie. And this whole situation. You can say it to us." Her cheeks are red as she spits her words out like they've been held inside her for too long.

She's right.

I do hate Tyler and ATVs and this whole situation, but I made a vow a long time ago that I would never ever get my kids involved in our disagreements. It's not good for them, and if I start now, then what the hell did I go through two years of agony for?

When I don't say anything, she rolls over and pulls the covers with her, hiding her face from me. "Turn the light off when you leave."

The cold shoulder is practically freezing when it's iced by an eleven-year-old who you love more than you can breathe.

With the two of them in bed, I head downstairs to make myself a cup of tea.

I'm mad. I'm sad. I'm aggravated and just so damn tired.

And then I'm panicking.

Hunter's scream from his bedroom sends my heart racing and my feet scurrying up the stairs. I run into his room as fast as I can, swinging open the door and panting. Hunter is standing in the middle of the room in his pajamas and looking at his bed, sobbing uncontrollably and completely distraught.

"Mr. Snuggles! I forgot him at Daddy's house!"

My shoulders fall as I let out a huge breath. "That stinks. Are you sure?"

"Yes. He's not in my bag."

Izzy comes to the door, seeming as concerned as Hunter is. "Hunter, you never sleep without Mr. Snuggles."

"Where is he?" Hunter asks in desperation.

I kneel next to him. "Maybe he's in Daddy's car."

Hunter wipes his cheeks as tears fall down them. "That means he's in Superman's cape."

It takes me a second to realize what he's talking about. "No, baby, Daddy is in Cape Cod. Big difference. If Mr. Snuggles is in his car, then he's too far to get."

Izzy walks into the room. "Mr. Snuggles wasn't in the car. Dad would have taken him out with our bags. I think Hunter left his bear in the kitchen. Remember, Hunter, you had him in your hand when Maisie asked if you wanted to help her water the plants before we left for the track?"

His little face lights up in remembrance. "Yeah. And then we went in the car. Daddy must have forgotten to grab him."

"Okay. We'll get him when Daddy comes back. My new office isn't too far from his house. I can go there and get him."

"No! I need Mr. Snuggles tonight! I can't sleep without him."

"What about Woody?"

I grab the *Toy Story* character off the nightstand, followed by his Squishmallow and seven other stuffed animals that he could easily sleep with, but none seem to calm him down. Instead, he becomes more frantic with each replacement toy I offer.

"Hunter, you have to pick someone else to sleep with because Mr. Snuggles isn't here."

"But I love him. Nana Mary gave him to me." His sweet words are spoken through uncontrollable sobs.

Nana Mary. *My mom.*

She gave him that blue bear the day he was born. It was fat and fluffy and had a satin ribbon around the neck. Now, he's a bit deflated, and his fur is like hard cotton from being thrown in the wash on the wrong spin cycle.

Mom was so excited to have her first grandson. She was by my side when he entered the world and cherished him until the day she died. She cherished both my babies, and now, all we're left with are the memories and a rag of a bear. I'm thankful for that ugly stuffed toy because, until this moment, I wasn't sure if Hunter even remembered my mom. He was so young when she died.

"Mommy's gonna get Mr. Snuggles back."

nine

"JONES. MELISSA."

There are many things a woman hopes she'll do twice in a lifetime. Travel to a foreign place, have a child, purchase a home, land a dream job, meet a celebrity.

Being arrested is not one of them.

Well, not for me at least.

I swat the air in front of me as I try to figure out exactly how I went from being Mom of the Year to *America's Most Wanted* in the same hour.

I'm in the Valor County Jail, the same cell where, just weeks ago, I was pacing along the cinder block and pacing like a loon. The frightened feeling I had from being in this cell last time is replaced by sheer annoyance.

How can, I, Melissa Jones, have been arrested ... again?

An officer stands by the door, calling my name. I look over at him. The same shadows are cast in the doorway, but I know it's not *my* officer. This man's shoulders are narrow, his stature shorter, and the tone of his voice is mellow. My shoulders droop, and then I kick myself because I'm not supposed to be downhearted that Officer Bronson isn't here.

I stand and fold my arms against my chest, my fingers tapping rapidly along my bicep as I clench my jaw.

"I'd like to make a phone call," I state with my head held high. I'm sober this time, and I know my rights. I won't go nefariously admitting to crimes like I did last time, although I really want to explain that, once again, I was not breaking and entering, like they claim. "My children are probably worried sick."

"In a few minutes. I've been instructed to have you wait here while we sort the paperwork."

"You can't withhold my phone call! It's my constitutional right to make a call within three hours of my arrest!"

The officer laughs lightly. This action irritates me further.

"What are you snickering about?"

"He said you were a wild one. Just sit back and wait." The officer's demeanor is very calm. He stares at me for a beat, probably taking in the fact that I'm wearing pajama pants, loafers, and a sweatshirt that says, *Good Moms Say Bad Words*. "Can I get you anything? A bottle of water?" he asks.

I blink at him. My arms drop to my sides as I glare at him. "Is that normal for a cop to ask an inmate?"

"Nothing about this is normal, ma'am. And you're not an inmate."

"Please don't call me ma'am."

"Yes, ma'am."

I growl at him as he walks out the door.

I fall to the bench with a sigh and roll my head back, rubbing the cords twanging in my neck.

"Not an inmate," he says. I don't know what else you'd call me, caged in a cell like an animal.

Animals have nicer holding pens than this.

This entire room is made of stone. The floors are concrete; the walls and ceiling are made of cinder block. I can't imagine this is any more than a twenty-four-hour holding cell. I'm surprised they don't just make the rooms out of Sheetrock. Couldn't kill them to bring in the cozy feeling, considering people have to spend the night here. Not like someone's gonna Shawshank their way out of this place.

It's also very cold. The rosé might have kept my body temperature warm last time because, tonight, I am chilled to the bone. Scooting into a corner, I pull my knees to my chest and curl into a ball for warmth, tucking my nose inside my sweatshirt. Maybe if I lay my head against the wall, I can fall asleep and wake up to find this was all a bad dream. It would be nice to wake up in my bed to learn I hallucinated this entire evening.

I do as I suggested and close my eyes, hoping I can sleep this horrible experience away, when the loud click of a door, followed by the loud bang of a metal door slamming shut, demands my attention.

I open an eye and glance through the steel bars to the other side of the room.

There's a figure of a man. It's not the same as the thinner, shorter officer from before. No, this man has a towering frame, brawny build, and commanding manner. I could pick that body out in a lineup.

With furrowed brows, I watch as Officer Bronson saunters toward the jail cell. He's not in uniform. Instead, he has on jeans, a sweatshirt, and those construction boots from the night we danced. I like those boots on a man. They look particularly good on *this* man.

Stupid boots.

He grabs a chair from a desk on his side of the room and lifts it easily, placing it gently on the floor in front of the bars. There's a coffee cup in his hand. Bastard has the audacity to stroll in here, all casual, sipping on some java and looking at me with that smolder. His ability to access his molten sexuality with a simple look of his eyes is infuriating, especially when I'm sitting here with a messy bun and pajama bottoms with little cappuccino cups on them.

I sit up straight. "What are you doing here?"

"Heard you got yourself into quite the pickle tonight."

Pickle. It's an adorable word. I love that word.

"By pickle, if you mean I went to my house to get my son's teddy bear, then, yes, I got into a pickle."

His mouth twists as he tilts his head. "*Your* house?"

"My ex's house. Semantics. It was mine for nearly ten years. How about this? It's my child's house, and as his legal guardian, I have the right to access my son's home."

I imagine the look on my face is very smug because that's how I feel with that answer.

"That's an impressive argument, Miss Jones."

Will takes a step forward and breathes heavily, making his chest rise and his lips part. Goose bumps run down my arms, so I rub them fiercely.

His eyes narrow. "You're freezing."

"An area rug would do wonders to warm up the place."

He holds out his hand, bearing the coffee cup. "I brought this for you. Heard you were jittery."

"You thought coffee would help calm my nerves?"

"I brought you hot cocoa."

"You keep hot chocolate in the break room?"

"Break room? No. The bottom left drawer of my desk? Yes. I happen to have a thing for Swiss Miss. Milk chocolate, not dark."

"Tiny marshmallows?" I ask skeptically.

The side of his mouth lifts. "They dissolve too quickly. Like to add my own." He weaves his hand through the bars and holds out the cup. "For you."

I really don't want to take anything from this man, but the steam coming out of the lid's opening is too inviting. Deciding the least he can do is bring me a cup of cocoa, I stand and take it rather eagerly. As I drink, I'm thankful it's not too hot that I burn myself. It's just hot enough. The kind of hot that warms my bones the second it passes through my body. I hold the cup tightly and let that warmth simmer into my palms.

With a small grin on his face, William relaxes into the chair on the other side of the bars. I take a seat on the bench again, this time closer to the bars than I was before.

I lean forward. "I need to call my father. I left God knows how long ago and never came back. He's probably sick with worry. Especially Hunter."

Will places his hand in his pocket and produces his cell phone and a pair of AirPods. He hands me an earpiece. "Call your father. Tell him you'll be home in an hour."

I don't ask how he knows exactly when I'll be out of here. My mind is only on the immediate task at hand, and that's letting my family know why I haven't come back. I tell William the number so he can dial it. The phone rings once before Dad picks up.

"Who is this?" he asks in a gruff yet concerned tone.

"Dad, it's me. I'm sorry I didn't come back. Something came up. It's a long story. I'll explain as soon as I get back in an hour. How are the kids?"

"The kids are asleep in their beds."

"Even Hunter? He needs Mr. Snuggles."

"A cop showed up and brought the bear. Said not to worry and you'd be back at the house before midnight. You're not in trouble with the law, are you?"

"Absolutely not. There was a small problem with the house alarm."

"Whose number is this?"

"A friend. I left my phone in the car. Go to sleep, and I'll be home very soon." I say my good-byes, and William ends the call.

"I have to call Tara to drive me to my car after I have Tyler clear this misunderstanding."

"Nope." He places the phone in his pocket and holds his hand out for the AirPod.

"I only get one phone call?"

"Technically, you're entitled to three."

"Then, give me my three! If every detainee is entitled to three phone calls, then I want mine."

"You're not a detainee," he says matter-of-factly.

"Then, why am I here? Why are *you* here? And why aren't you wearing a uniform?"

He leans back in the chair with his legs spread wide and his hands on the tops of his thighs. He looks like he could lounge here all night.

"I was home, enjoying a quiet evening when my police scanner alerted me of a potential breaking and entering on Lowerington Drive. I remembered the address as your ex-husband's."

"You remember that from taking down his address for his statement?"

He taps his temple. "Photographic memory, remember?"

I roll my eyes. "You went to Tyler's house when you were off duty to save him?"

"The call said a woman, approximately five foot six with brassy blonde hair, was caught snooping around the house for what the neighbors assumed was a key."

My jaw drops. "They said my hair was brassy?"

He smirks. "No. I added that to rile you up. Actually, they said a drop-dead gorgeous woman was found at the scene."

"Really?"

"No."

"You're infuriating!" Launching from my seat, I shoot daggers at him and then walk up to the bars to declare my side of the story. "I went to Tyler's house because Hunter had left Mr. Snuggles there and he can't sleep without that bear. I told him to let it go, but then he brought up my mom, and honestly, it was like a piercing to my heart because I hadn't even known that Hunter remembered her. He was so young when she died. But he brought her up, and I realized his attachment to that ball of fur was because it was a piece of her. I'd never thought of that before, so when he said it, my entire heart exploded and shattered at the same time. I got in the car, determined to get my little boy's bear. Would you believe Tyler changed the damn locks?"

"Probably thought someone might use the old key to break in."

"I wasn't breaking in! It was my house once. My kids' house now. I was just getting his bear. I know he kept a key outside somewhere. It used to be under a planter, but the bastard moved it."

"A neighbor called and said someone suspicious was lurking in the dark."

"I found the damn key. He put it in the grill. How generic."

"Certainly not as cryptic as the planter."

I growl at him, and he raises his brows.

"I let myself inside, and then the house alarm went off."

"Let me guess. He changed the code too."

"It used to be my birthday. Figuring he changed it to his, I tried that, but it wouldn't turn off. Then, I tried the kids'. Fail and fail. Finally, I tried Maisie's, and it turned off. I started my frantic search for Mr. Snuggles, who wasn't in the kitchen, like Izzy had thought." I pause my pacing and explain, "Mr. Snuggles was in the bathroom. On the floor. Wedged between the toilet and the wall. By the time I was ready to leave, there was a police car outside the home. Apparently, after three failed attempts, they send over a police car to check the premises. I tried to tell them the story, but they didn't listen, and since my ID didn't have the address as the residence and I couldn't prove I lived there, I was breaking and entering. They took me away in a police car … again. Handcuffs and all. Thankfully, they didn't take my mug shot. Why didn't they take my mug shot?"

"Because no one is pressing charges."

My arms rise and fall in pure exasperation, but I'm careful not to spill my cocoa. "Why the hell am I here?"

"I asked them to keep you."

"I'm so confused."

Will leans forward, places his elbows on his knees, and looks up at me. The look in his eyes is one of earnest, as is his tone. "Melissa, please, take a seat."

I stomp my foot while I huff.

"Please?" he asks again gently.

I have to look away from him, for that puppy-dog look is completely disarming. My heart is racing, my arms tingling, and yet there's something coursing through my veins, warm and soothing. One would think I was drinking magical, calming hot chocolate, but that's not it. It's his voice. Will has this deep, soothing voice. Like whipped cream, it's thick and sweet.

"Fine." I take a seat. "But only because I want to get out of here and you're holding me hostage."

Seeming relieved, he watches as I get settled in. As soon as my back hits the wall, I shiver.

"Wear this."

Will stands and grabs the hem of his sweatshirt, lifting it over his torso. A sliver of abdomen is exposed, and I stare at the taut muscle. It's quickly covered by a T-shirt that falls back into place as he fully removes his sweatshirt and then holds it through the bars in offering.

"You're freezing. Put this over your sweatshirt."

I place my cup on the floor and take his sweatshirt, sliding it over mine. It smells of vanilla cologne and a woodsy, manly scent.

"Speak, Bronson." I take my seat and lift my cup, taking a long sip.

Will sits down again, making us eye-level. "I called the officer on the scene. He explained the situation. I asked him to bring you here and had another officer escort Mr. Snuggles to your home. I came straight here and called Tyler to confirm he would not press charges, and then I made you a cup of cocoa."

"That's the most insane thing I ever heard."

"It is."

"If Tyler's not pressing charges and I'm not in trouble for anything, why the hell am I behind bars?"

"How else was I supposed to get you to hear me out?"

My eyes widen. "You're out of your mind."

"Honestly, when it comes to you, I am."

"William! What were you thinking?"

"I'm thinking that I met this amazing woman a few weeks ago, we had a great night out and shared an amazing kiss, and now, she won't talk to me."

"Because you were engaged."

"*Was*. Past tense. I called off the engagement."

I nod at the news. "Allison was in my office, wallowing in tears on a Home Depot bucket. She thinks something I said at brunch scared you off. If it did, I apologize. I shouldn't have laid my shit on the two of you. My divorce was a really low time in my life, and I think I'm still getting over it."

He leans forward. "I thought your meltdown at brunch was because you were shocked that I was sitting across from you with my fiancée."

"That too." *That only.*

Tyler did a number on me, but that outburst was purely about William.

"Please don't call off your wedding because I said some very off-color things at brunch. Marriage is beautiful and joyous. Sure, there are ups and downs. That's why people say marriage is work—a quote I despise, by the way—but I get it. It's not easy, but the good outweighs the bad. I promise."

"I was going to end it for good with Allison at brunch. I didn't know she'd hired a wedding designer, let alone you. The end of the engagement had nothing to do with what you said at brunch."

"So, it was the kiss? Please don't say it was the kiss." I bend forward with my head in my hand. "Damn it, Will, why didn't you tell me you were engaged?" I shoot up to a standing position and point at him in accusation. "Don't say *it didn't come up.* Or you *don't know.* That's not good enough."

"I'll tell you, but you have to sit down, sip your cocoa, and give me a few minutes of uninterrupted time to talk. When you do, I promise I'll let you out of here."

I drop to the bench. "Fine."

"Good." He runs his hands over his face. His pained, confused, chiseled-with-anguish face. "Fuck. I don't know where to start."

"The beginning is a good place."

He steeples his fingers and rests them under his chin and nods. "I've known Allison since high school. We went to junior prom together but just as dates. We weren't a couple. I was enrolling in the police academy, and she was going to go to college out west. We reconnected almost two years ago at a bar on St. Patrick's Day. She'd moved back to town after living in Chicago, and the attraction was stronger as adults than it was when we were teenagers. We dated, casually at first. Soon, my friends were hanging with her friends, and the social circles entwined, where everyone we knew was a couple or

LOVE ... IT'S COMPLICATED

friends with each other. My cousin married her best friend. My friend is engaged to her old roommate. Our moms even know each other from their days of working at the middle school together. Everything with Allison was ... easy. Us as a couple, being together, it just made sense. When you're with someone, you don't just commit to them. You commit to this lifestyle. If you end one relationship, it spirals to everything else. Don't get me wrong; she's beautiful, smart, and caring. Everything a man should want in a woman. Still, something was holding me back."

He places a hand over his heart, and mine feels like it's pressing against my chest.

"Then, the comments started. *When are you going to propose? She isn't getting any younger.* I loved Allison, but I wasn't ready to get married. I honestly never thought I would be. I put off proposing, and she was a saint for waiting. She told me there was no rush, but a man knows when a woman is miserable. I would see her staring idly at a bride or have a jealous twinge when a couple moved in together. The thought of holding her back from what she wanted in life was a burden I couldn't bear. I broke up with her, and it was awful."

"How did you go from breaking up over getting engaged to actually being engaged?"

His shoulders and eyes fall, as if what he's about to say was his undoing. "Allison showed up at my house with the announcement that she was pregnant." His eyes open, but his gaze remains lowered. "I didn't want to get married, but being a dad ... that didn't freak me out at all. I was on board the second she said it, and she was shocked. My dad was on my case instantly. He said I had to marry Allison. I had to do the right thing, and he was right. I proposed. She was so happy. Delirious even."

He looks away and rubs his eye before continuing, "She lost the baby. It was horrible. The loss was early in the second trimester, yet she was devastated. I stayed by her side. Nursed her while she healed and held her hand as she coped.

"Then, I got shot. They said I died on the table before being revived, and when I came to, Allison was the first person I saw. She was there for every second of my hospital stay. Our family, our friends, this amazing community of ours hovered around, and I was grateful for them. Grateful for her yet so confused. I was alive, yet I didn't feel like I was living. I was engaged to a woman I didn't want to marry, but I'd made a promise to her."

He looks up at me, and I feel like every amount of emotion of his is being sent through the bars and barreling into my chest. "One day, I went to work, and there was this girl in the holding cell, pacing. She was wild and funny without even trying. I thought about her the entire night and was stunned when I saw her at a bar the next day. She kissed me, and I kissed her back.

"So, you asked why I didn't tell you I was engaged. It's because I was confused. I pushed you away. Not because I wanted to. Because I had to. Little did I know that one kiss would awaken more in me in a nanosecond than anything else had in my entire life."

His words are a hymn to my ego. That kiss was life-altering, I agree. Just not the way it was supposed to be.

My stomach sours. "Damn it, Will. You need to be with Allison. Don't let that kiss ruin everything."

"It was over with Allison before you and I even began."

"No. No, no, no. Don't say that. I've been on the other side of that heartache. I can't be the woman who ended your relationship. Oh my God, Will. You made me the *other* woman!"

"You're not understanding. It's not you. It's me."

"That's cliché."

"Believe it or not, you're not my type. At all."

My ego, now bruised, is back to where it's supposed to be. Trampled and lying in the pit of my stomach. "No need to beat a dead horse about it."

He runs his hands through his hair and rises. His jaw is clenched, as if he's annoyed rather than mad. He slides a key out of his pocket, opening the door, and steps inside.

He takes a seat beside me on the bench.

"Our breakup was inevitable. I didn't feel with Allison what a man who is supposed to spend a lifetime with someone is supposed to feel. I finally did what a real man should do, and I ended it."

"This is so messed up."

"Tell me about it. My family isn't talking to me. My mother won't answer my calls. Our friends are all taking her side, and I understand why. I should have ended it a long time ago."

"Why would you even be with her when you didn't *want* to be with her?"

"I loved her. But not enough to spend the rest of my life with her."

"And you realized this when we kissed?"

"I had known before. The kiss confirmed it."

"And I'm not supposed to feel like this is my fault?"

"You didn't know she existed, and I never set out to hook up with you. You and I just got along, and it went too far."

I lean my head back against the wall and sigh as I roll my face toward his. "I hate this."

"Me too." He leans back as well and mimics my body language. "My life is pretty fucked up, huh?"

I laugh lightly. "Everyone's life is chaotic. It's pretending that yours *isn't* is the messed up part. Let's not forget that I'm a woman who has now twice been arrested for breaking and entering into my ex and his new lover's places."

He laughs, and it makes the nerves in my body relax.

The door is open, and I could easily leave, yet ... I don't want to right away. Being here with Will, talking to him and hearing his story, makes me want to stay here a bit longer. We sit in silence for a few minutes until I'm reminded of something he said earlier.

"I'm sorry you lost your baby."

"Thanks." He rolls his head to face mine.

"Your story was laced with regret, but being a father wasn't one."

"No. I really wanted to be a dad."

"You will. Someday. And I'm sorry your parents aren't talking to you."

"My mother is the most strong-willed woman I know. Holds a grudge like no other. She's also my favorite person in the world."

"Moms are amazing," I sigh, recalling my own. "Don't let too much time pass before breaking down her door and making things right. You never know how much time you have until it's over."

"Thanks. I'll keep that in mind."

With a deep breath, I sit up and rub my thighs. "I think you're disillusioned about one thing. What you had with Allison sounds like a marriage. Not every relationship keeps that spark forever."

"Maybe I'm more of a romantic than I thought because when I plan on spending the rest of my life with someone, I want it to be with someone I'm excited to spend forever with. Even if forever ends up being a dud, I can't begin a lifetime, already dreading it."

I nod with a frown. My hands are inside the pocket of his sweatshirt. I look down at them moving through the fabric. "I'm sad for Allison, yet I understand. In my line of work, we have a lot of couples come through who are more excited to plan the party than their lifetime of commitment. We can pretty much call the divorces as we're planning the nuptials. Man, that's a horrible thing to admit."

"It's honest. I get it. In my line of work, I get called on a lot of domestic disturbances. Some people should never be together."

"Those are the extreme."

"More common than you'd think. You'd never believe the seemingly happy couples whose lives are complete turmoil inside the walls of their perfect homes. I don't want a life that appears perfect while everyone's miserable on the inside. I was willing to settle for a life that was headed in that direction. I know it's a gamble, but if I ever get married, it's going to be because I can't wait to run down that altar. Not scared to walk it."

"Maybe your near-death experience put some perspective in your life."

He laughs lightly. His eyes shimmer as he looks at me and then down at the gray floor. "Yeah. That's what it was," he says, yet I'm not convinced he believes his words. With a heavy sigh, he looks back up at me. "You're the first person to acknowledge the fact that I lost a child."

"Fathers are often forgotten when these things happen."

"It's traumatic for the mother. There's no comparison."

"It's not right though." I place a hand on his arm and look up at him. "You hurt, and you deserve a friend acknowledging that."

His gaze is steady on my hand. "Is that what we are now? Friends?"

"Not sure. My friends aren't the kind to purposefully lock me in a cell to have a heart-to-heart."

"You need better friends then." He smiles, and I make a face at him.

"Now that I've heard you out, will you drive me to my car?"

"Only if you promise me one thing," he says, and I look up at him, intrigued. "Clear your schedule for one day next week. During the day, while the kids are in school."

"Why?"

"Just trust me on this."

Trust him?

LOVE ... IT'S COMPLICATED

The man literally kidnapped me tonight and held me against my will. On the other hand, he also called my ex, got my name cleared, and made sure my son had his teddy bear to go to sleep. I suppose I do trust him. Plus, he said he's not attracted to me. I believe the correct phrase was *not his type ... at all*. I'll try to forget how that arrow to my ego is dangling from my chest, but it's for the better. I don't need a man in my life, let alone one who just ended an engagement.

Yet, for all the reasons I shouldn't clear my schedule for this man, I somehow end up saying, "Fine."

He smiles as he slides his hand into his back pocket and produces my car keys. "Good. And I don't have to drive you to your car. I had one of my officers bring it here."

I snag them from his hand. "You're insane."

"Melissa, we already established that, when it comes to you, I'm a bit deranged."

ten

SINCE WILL SAID TO clear my schedule, I spent all week trying not to wonder where I was going. To my surprise, he hasn't said a word. It's infuriating. I refuse to text him because I don't want him to think I care because ... I don't.

Yet I do.

For the record, being nonchalant is mentally exhausting.

I'm dressing and redressing myself for something I don't know how to dress for. I decide on jeans, a sweater, and leather boots. My hair is blown out straight, and my makeup is minimal.

A car door closing outside has me looking out the window to see Will heading up the front path. I take my time walking down the stairs, taking so long that he rings the bell a second time.

With the most casual of movements, I open the door. Will is wearing dark jeans, a leather jacket, and those damn boots. A small shiver runs up my sides, so I shimmy my shoulders a little. A hot cop in leather is what dirty magazines were made for. I'd turn to page twenty to see the centerfold.

Will slides his hands into his jacket pockets and leans back on his heels. "Do I look okay?"

"Yeah. You look good. Why are you asking?"

"Because you're staring." The bastard has the nerve to say that straight-faced.

I ignore his cockiness. "Shouldn't we be talking about if I look okay, considering I don't know where we're going?"

His eyes leave mine, and he takes a quick glance at my attire. "You look fine."

"Couldn't have killed you to throw in a compliment."

I put my coat on, and he grabs my elbow, forcing me to halt and look up at him. The sultry look in his gaze is fluid and sexy.

"That sweater you have on brings out the blue in your eyes. It's actually unfair how intimidating they are—like the ocean before a storm. I could get lost in them and die drowning." His smolder morphs to a wide grin with a wink. "Better?"

If the walls had a stethoscope, they'd hear my pulse pounding.

"Much." With a swallow and a severe clearing of my throat, I grab my purse and follow him to his truck. "I don't understand why I can't drive myself."

"I want to make sure you show up."

"A police escort of my very own. What did I ever do to deserve this?"

"Got yourself locked up twice."

"Oh, that's right. Will I be returning to my residence with a home electronic monitoring device on my ankle?"

"Only if you're lucky."

He closes the door behind me, and we drive toward the highway in the direction of Castleton.

I settle into my seat, admiring the neatness of his car. It beats mine, which has Goldfish remnants and fruit snack wrappers thrown about. I even found an old banana peel under the seat last week.

"Your house is nice," he says.

"My parents' place. Not exactly living the dream."

His mouth twists as he looks straight at the road, and his fingers drum on his thigh.

"You want to ask me something," I state. "Say it."

The side of his mouth rises at my comment as his head tilts to the side. "Why did your ex get the house?"

"Good question. Well, I didn't lose it in the divorce, if that's what you're wondering. In fact, I won the right to live in the residence, but Tyler couldn't afford to pay the mortgage and buy something of his own. To keep it, I had to buy Tyler out, which I couldn't. Even with half a mortgage, the bills were too high for my salary. We were going to sell it and split the profit fifty-fifty, but then what? Tyler would get a condo somewhere in town, and the kids would be sleeping on a couch during their weekend visits. This plan ... was my plan. Tyler bought me out of my share of the house, and the kids and I moved in with my dad. This way, the kids still get to live in their childhood home when they're with their dad, and they're also living at their grandfather's house, a home they know and love, with their mom during the week. It's all familiar and safe. The kids each get to have their own bedroom and get to be around family. Divorce is such a whirlwind of change for kids. I wanted to provide them with as much familiarity as possible."

"That was very unselfish of you."

"Not entirely. I demanded the kids live with me on the weekdays. School nights should be spent in the same bed. If it were up to me, they'd never sleep out, but Hunter can't handle being away from Tyler that long, and Izzy needs a reason to be alone with her dad and bond. She has so much resentment in her young mind."

"Apple doesn't fall far from the tree."

"Izzy's a realist and always thinks so negatively."

"What kind of girl are you?"

"A *go with the flow and let things happen* kind of girl. I'm a wedding designer. I have to believe in unicorns and fairy dust and all that other crap."

"Bigfoot and the Loch Ness Monster too?"

"Absolutely."

He laughs as we listen to the radio while he drives, and he pulls into the parking lot of a strip mall. He points to a hair salon and then gets out of the truck. I lean forward and stare up at the storefront of white stucco and gold metal lettering that reads *Illusion Salon and Spa*.

My door opens, and I turn to see William has walked around the front and opened my door.

"Did you make me clear my day to get my hair done?"

"Yep."

I furrow my brow and look up at him. "That's incredibly presumptuous! A women's hair is a delicate matter that can only be trusted to a limited few. You can't just bring her to any Joe Schmoe establishment and expect her to have blind trust. I need a hair goddess, not a hack."

He takes my hand and escorts me out of the truck. "Last I heard, your hair goddess ran off with your husband, and you've been suffering from brassiness since."

"You had to bring up the brassy."

"You're the one who broke into a salon for your hair color card."

"Are you going to bring that up every time?"

He opens the glass door of the salon and grins. "As long as it gets me what I want."

I narrow my eyes at him as I walk into the salon. Polished marble tiles, white walls, black lacquered stations, and gorgeous oversize black chandeliers on the ceiling. There's club music playing on the speaker of the packed salon. The smell of bleach permeates the room. It's heavenly.

Will slides my coat off my shoulders and hands it to the receptionist at the counter as I remain slightly dumbstruck by the high-end establishment.

"This is Melissa Jones. She has a ten o'clock appointment with Genevieve," he tells the woman.

She points to her computer screen behind the counter. "We have you right here. VIP for full color and highlights. Can I get you a cappuccino, espresso, water, or iced tea?"

"I'll take a water," he states. "Melissa?"

"I'm good," I say with a sigh. I don't get overwhelmed often, but this place is really nice, possibly out of my budget, and Will is acting very laissez-faire.

He leans into me and places a hand on the small of my back, his breath tickling my ear. "Does this constitute as a Joe Schmoe establishment?"

I elbow him in the ribs, and he chuckles—a deep, *arm vibrating down to my toes* chuckle.

"Will!" A woman appears from around the half wall that separates the reception area from the rest of the salon. Her arms are up in the air as she crashes into Will for a long hug. Then, she extends a manicured hand to me. "I'm Genevieve. You must be Melissa. It's nice to meet you."

"Thank you for squeezing me in. I'd imagine it takes weeks to get an appointment here."

Genevieve grins at Will. "I owe this guy a favor. He helped my brother get on the straight and narrow a few years ago. When this man calls—and he rarely does—I always make my chair available."

I smash my lips. "Brought women here before, Officer Bronson?"

"My mother, smart-ass. I bring my mother. Gen has been doing her hair for years."

Genevieve waves me toward her. "Come on back to my chair, and we'll get you settled in."

She starts walking, and I follow until I realize Will isn't behind us. I do an about-face and walk back to him by reception. "Are you waiting here?"

"I'm gonna leave. Gen will text me when you're done."

"Oh. Okay."

"You seem disappointed. I hope you don't mind me ambushing you, but Genevieve is my friend and an incredible colorist. I've seen her work throughout the years, and it's remarkable."

I lift a strand of my hair. "Anything is better than this, I suppose. She seems nice too."

"She's the best." He slides his hands into his pockets and lowers his gaze to me. "I'd never put you in a situation that made you uncomfortable. If you want to leave, we can hightail it out of here."

I gnaw at the inside of my cheek. "Well, you did go out of your way to make this happen. I'd hate to be ungrateful."

"You can thank me later. And don't worry. Genevieve has great chair etiquette. What's said in the chair, stays in the chair."

I hate how much I love the way he remembers our shared moments.

"So, I can gossip about you and your tawdry behavior?"

He lifts a brow. "Maybe skip that part."

I tap him on the nose. "Don't worry. Your secrets are safe with me."

With a salute, I turn around and walk to Genevieve's station. She's standing behind it, waiting for me to be seated. An assistant has a black cape that she puts around my neck as soon as I take a seat.

Genevieve's hands are on my shoulders as she assesses my look. "The color is definitely a result of overcorrecting. We're going to use the formula your color specialist used, but if you're okay with it, I'd like to soften your base first with a warm ashy blonde. I'll paint the pieces onto the hair in between your highlights."

"This isn't from my colorist. I was the perfect shade of light blonde without being bleached."

Genevieve takes an index card out of her pocket. "Yes, straight bleach was all she used. Your hair must lift nicely on its own because she didn't use toner. The new place must have used a toner and left it on too long, and then you went into a spiral of trying to fix the mess."

I stare at the card through the mirror. With a twist, I take it from her hand and read the handwriting on it. "This is Maisie's. How did you get it?"

"From Will. He said he got it from your old salon."

"Will went to my old salon and got my color card?" I ask, dumbfounded.

"Surprised he didn't tell you." She crosses her arms in front of her body. "Have you known each other long?"

I swivel my chair in her direction and lay it on her straight. "If you're inferring that Will and I—"

"Listen, the last thing I'm gonna do is gossip about my friend. All I'll say is, things have been dramatic in the world of William lately, so when he called with a favor, I was glad to help. The man has been getting mentally beaten up by everyone in his life, especially his mother. The less I know, the better."

"I promise there is nothing to know. We're just friends, if you can even call us that. I'm still on the fence on if I think he's a really good guy or a moderately deranged."

"How did you meet?"

"He helped me out when I was trying to drunkenly get back at my ex."

"Badass. I can appreciate that, and I do love a good story. So … how about you tell me about it while I get you looking like you again?"

"Please!"

***

For seven years, I considered Maisie Mirlicourtois to be the hair goddess who gave me a golden glow. Today, Genevieve has taken that title.

Light-blonde hair with highlights that shimmer. The color of my hair makes me appear brighter, happier, and shall I say … sexier?

After singing her praises and realizing the time is way later than I thought, I bid Genevieve good-bye, and I scurry toward the front of the salon, snaking my phone out of my purse and looking for

Will's number. I'm just about to hit Send when I approach the reception desk and see him standing in a waiting room, surrounded by women's magazines and bottles of beauty products.

He's looking down at his cell phone and laughing. I peer over and see what he's watching.

"*Family Feud* reels?"

Will fumbles with his phone and stands up straight. As he does so, his expression morphs from relaxed to a more serious gaze. His lips part as he lifts his chin. Those eyes roam over my face, and then his brows lift, and his mouth curves in appreciation.

"Wow. You look incredible."

I do a little spin for dramatic flair. "Your friend is a genius. I am now praying at the hair coloring altar of Genevieve for the rest of my life. But first, I have to pay, and you need to get me home because my kids need to be picked up, and I was not planning on this taking so long."

"Let's go then." He nods toward the door.

I motion for the receptionist. "I have to pay."

The receptionist looks at my credit card in hand, and waves me off. "Your boyfriend took care of it already."

I turn to Will with a frown as he places a hand on my shoulder and motions me toward the door.

"We have to pick up your kids."

"You can't pay for me!"

"Not the place to argue, and you don't have the time." He holds my coat out for me.

I growl and then do an about-face as I take two twenties and a ten out of my wallet and lay it on the counter. "Please get that to Genevieve and the ten to her assistant and say *thank you from Melissa*."

As I walk out of the salon—well, more like be strongly guided toward his truck—I'm still talking as Will opens the passenger door, and I slide in.

"How much do I owe you? Was it two hundred? Two fifty?"

He closes the door and walks around the vehicle. When he gets in, I turn to him with my hands out in question.

"Oh my God, was it one of the places that charges five hundred dollars for color? I mean, I love how I look, but I can't afford to fall in love with a color artist I can't afford. Then again, I've tried the inexpensive route, and that got me nowhere."

He leans over the center console. "You want to do that seat belt, or should I strap you in myself?"

"I can strap myself in, thank you very much. And you're not answering my question."

With a grin, he turns the truck on, places an arm on the back of my seat, and backs out of the lot.

"I didn't know I was going to be ambushed with a spa day. I'm lucky I had enough for a tip. Do you take Venmo? I can Zelle too. Just tell me what it was. You know, I can just call the place and ask. Maybe that's what I'll do." I take out my cell phone and start to look up the salon when a thought hits me. "Unless you and Genevieve have a thing going on and she did this for you on the house?"

"A thing?" His brows pinch as he drives back toward the woods of Newbury.

"A sexual thing. Maybe a rendezvous was had. A tryst!"

Will shifts in his seat, seeming uncomfortable. There's a stillness in the air. A feeling of tension as Will's jaw clenches. Before I know it, the truck is pulled over rather forcefully to the shoulder of the road, and he puts it in park.

His expression is pensive, a molten intensity of seriousness. His voice is like gravel as he says, "Melissa, I know we met under extraordinary circumstances, and my behavior wasn't ideal, but I need you to understand something very important. I did not cheat. I am not a man who has rendezvous or trysts, as you call it. Until that night at the club, I never so much as looked at another woman during my relationship with Allison. It is very important to me that you understand that."

"Yeah. Okay."

He doesn't appear convinced that I'm convinced. "Today was about a man wanting to do something nice for a woman who he felt deserved it. You *deserved* a day to be pampered. I hope you know that. And I hope you know that it gave me great pleasure to treat you. Some people enjoy doing nice things for other people. You have hundreds of hair appointments in the future to pay for yourself. For now, let me have this one."

I nod slowly and close my eyes because his words are too potent for my heart. A woman who has been second best for too long isn't used to being told she deserves anything. It's heartwarming and disheartening at the same time, and that damn way he leans into me,

LOVE ... IT'S COMPLICATED

as if giving me his full attention, his full self, is playing tricks on my brain and my heart.

When I open my eyes, I lift my chin and roll my shoulders back. "If I knew you were going to treat, I would have stayed for a manicure."

His mouth tips. "You should have."

Will moves his body back to driving position and puts his blinker on, then points at the clock. "We'd better hurry."

"Yes. You need to drop me at home so I can get my car."

He shakes his head. "We're not getting your car. We're getting your kids."

eleven

"DON'T YOU HAVE A special pass to park wherever you want?" My knee is bouncing as I look at the time.

The parking lot at Newbury Elementary is less than ideal, which is why I try to get here twenty minutes early.

Will leisurely pulls around the lot, looking for a spot. "I'm off duty. I have to follow the rules, like everyone else."

I roll my eyes. "Such a Boy Scout."

He lifts a brow and turns the wheel, moving us out of the parking lot.

"Why don't you just pull over and I'll run out to get the kids?" I suggest as he hops a curb on the side of the building in a no-standing zone.

He puts his hazard lights on and then turns the truck off. I get out of the passenger side and am surprised to see Will exit as well.

"I'm coming with you," he says as he locks the doors.

"What happened to following the rules like everyone else?"

He pushes his shoulders back as he puts his keys in his jacket pocket. "I left my Boy Scout sash at home." Will brushes past me and starts walking toward the quad of the school, where the three buildings of the elementary, middle, and high school are housed.

There is a mess of parents waiting by the doors. Will and I weave through a few and find a spot in the center, right in front of the doors.

I give a few nods and waves to parents I know. While everyone gives me a friendly smile, I'm getting a few extra stares. I run my fingers through my new hair and grin. With my chin high and chest puffed out, I am feeling extra good today.

As I'm peacocking myself in the middle of the crowd, I follow a particular mom's eyes. She's talking to another mom yet looking in this direction. Except she's not looking at my hair. She's staring at the tall gentleman to my left.

My shoulders deflate as I turn toward Will. He's standing here, all six feet two-ish inches of him, glistening in the damn sunlight. The natural blond highlights in his light-brown hair are even twinkling under the rays as he stands, not noticing a single stare.

Will has his hands in his jacket pockets as he looks toward the entrance. His smile appears as he points to the door. "There's Hunter."

I see my boy coming out of the building with his class. He's waving at me, so I wave back, letting the teacher know I'm here. As Hunter barrels through the crowd, I bend down to scoop him up.

"I got a sticker!" His chubby fist has a star sticker on top. "Only five kids got them because we weren't chatterboxes today. And the teacher gave the whole class pretzels at the end of the day since we did so good on our spelling test."

"That's awesome, baby." I place him on the ground and ruffle his hair as he stares up at Will.

"I know you. You're the magic man."

Will's mouth tilts up. "You remember."

"Yeah. You said you'd help me levitate someone. Are you here to do magic? I have a box, and I want to show you all the tricks I have."

"I'm free today," Will starts, but I shush him.

"Don't feel obligated."

Hunter grabs my shirt and pulls on it as he stares up at me. "Please, Mom! The show is coming up soon, and I need to practice!"

"Give your mom a little breathing room, kiddo," Will says as he takes Hunter's backpack and slides it over his shoulder. "Did you notice anything new about your mom?"

Hunter looks up at me and squints. "No. She's still mom."

"That's a good thing, I guess. I don't want to look like someone else." I'm giving Hunter a kiss on the head when there's a tap on my back. I turn around and see my daughter. "Hey, sweetie. How was school today?"

I'm wise enough to know not to give her a kiss hello in front of her peers. Word has it, that's the ultimate "cringe."

Izzy looks at me with her head tilted at Will. She has a hand on each of her backpack straps. "You're the Target guy. The cop who was shot."

"Nice to see you again, Isabella," Will replies.

She stares at me for a beat longer than usual. "You got your hair done." She gives a curt nod. "It looks good."

Izzy turns around and starts toward the parking lot. I look at Will and shrug. He lifts a shoulder in return, and we follow Izzy out of the quad, me with Hunter's hand in mine and Will with an Avengers backpack on his shoulder.

Will shows Izzy where we parked, and despite her scowl at the illegally parked vehicle, she gets in without a word.

"Shoot!" I state as I open the back door. "Hunter needs a booster seat."

Will opens his truck bed, reaches in, and emerges with a red booster seat in his hand. "I always keep one for emergencies."

I take it from him. "Do you often give emergency rides to young children?"

"Eleven nieces and nephews, remember?"

I tap my head. "Non-photographic memory, remember?"

With Hunter buckled in and secure, I slide into the front seat. Izzy's sitting with her backpack on her lap and looking at Will as he gets in the truck.

"Why did you come with Mom to pick us up?" she asks as he drives.

Opening my mouth to answer for Will, I'm startled when he places his hand on my thigh. While my mind races to understand why he's touching my leg, I soon realize it's because he would like to answer Izzy's question and not have me speak for him.

"I took your mom to see a good friend of mine who colors hair. I knew your mom wouldn't go on her own, so I drove her."

Izzy gives a small nod. There's a thread on the strap of her bag that's unraveled. "That's smart," she says as she pulls lightly on the thread. "Mom's been going to the worst hairdressers. Your friend did a nice job."

Will looks at her through the rearview mirror. "Thank you. I'll tell Genevieve you said that."

He removes his hand from my leg and places it on the steering wheel as he weaves through the side streets before pulling up in front of my parents' house. Will parks his truck, but keeps it running, gets out and opens Izzy's door. I am out and unbuckling Hunter, who starts chattering immediately.

"Are you staying for dinner?"

"Will has other things to do than hang out with us," I explain.

"Not really," Will says as he and Izzy walk around the truck to the sidewalk. "I spent most of the day running errands while I waited for the text to say you were ready. All I did was drop you off."

"Work?" I ask.

"Night shift starts at eight."

"See, Mom, he's free! Can we do magic then?" Hunter jumps up and down.

I move my head from side to side. The last thing he wants to do is come into my chaotic house and watch the homework doing, dinner making, and general unraveling from a long day. He must sense my apprehension of the situation because he takes a step toward Hunter.

"Your mom probably has a ton of work to do since I made her clear her day. Plus, dinner is already planned. There's definitely not enough for me. Full disclaimer: I eat like a horse."

"That's right. We don't have enough food," I agree and help Will with his *get out of jail free* dinner card.

"That's not true," Izzy says. "You bought the family pack of chicken cutlets and said it was enough to feed the four of us for two dinners. Plus, Will, you already said you did all your errands, so you're just gonna be bored at home."

Izzy brushes past us and starts walking up the stairs.

"That settles it. You're staying!" Hunter grabs Will's hand. "I'll show you around. I have a dinosaur collection and a robot that follows you around the house and listens to your every command. Plus, there's a basketball hoop in the driveway. Mom had to lower it so I can reach it, but we can raise it for you. Oh, there's also Netflix, so you can watch anything you want, just don't use Grandpa's profile because he gets really upset when you mess with his shows. I did that once, and he wasn't happy."

Hunter is pulling Will up the stairs as Will turns to me and grins with that backpack still slung over his shoulder. "Looks like I'm staying for dinner. Turn my truck off and get my wallet from the center console."

The two of them disappear up the stairs with Hunter chattering on about the wonders of the house. I turn off Will's truck, and grab the keys and his wallet from the center console. His key ring has several rectangular tabs, each with a different school picture of a young child on each, all with last year's date on them.

I'm smiling when I enter the house. To my surprise, Will and Izzy are at the kitchen table with her books open. He is taking his jacket off and placing it on the chair.

I place his keys and wallet on the table beside him and am rewarded with a wink as he takes a seat.

"Homework?" I ask, to which Izzy glowers at me.

Noting I am not needed, I move over to Hunter, who is sitting at the kitchen island, opening his own schoolbag and taking out his books. I take a seat beside him, a little confused. My children usually like to unwind a little before tackling homework. This obedient, calm homework atmosphere is a little unusual for the Jones household.

"Will said he won't work on my magic show until after I do my homework," Hunter states.

"That explains a lot." I look over at Izzy and Will, then lean in to whisper, "How did he get Izzy to do her work?"

He leans in like he has a big secret. "She asked to see his bullet hole."

I laugh lightly and peer over at Will and Izzy, who are looking over her science homework. They are talking about the elements.

We spend the next hour completing homework with the kids.

Izzy's homework takes that long because she doesn't understand the concept, but Will goes slow with her, the two of them even Googling things when Will seems to have no idea how to explain it. He's sweet and patient with her. Judging by the pink in Izzy's cheeks, I'd say she's a little smitten with the handsome tutor. Can't say I blame her.

Hunter only takes so long because he has the attention of, well, a five-year-old. He drops his pencil seven times, needs three snacks, and complains in the middle of having to write his sight words three times each. I coax him back to the task until we're finally done.

I pack up Hunter's things and send him to go play. Will and Izzy are done with her work when she mentions she has a history project due next week. Will convinces her to get a start on it now, and she doesn't complain.

With those two doing her work, I ask Alexa to play songs by Coldplay, keeping the volume low for background music. It's still early, so I take the free time and open my laptop.

Jillian and I have seven weddings coming up next month, and I have three design proposals to submit to prospective couples. I start making a vision board on my computer of a wedding for clients who want to marry at an old barn in the country. I have a drawing of the tent we'll raise and the room set up in my sketchpad with a slew of images on my digital pin board. As Chris Martin croons about sparks flying, I'm lost in thought, envisioning the couple dancing under the stars and leaving the reception to a walkway of sparklers being lit by their friends and family, wishing them a lifetime of congratulations.

A strong hand glides along my back, snapping me out of my daydream.

Will slides into the seat beside me and leans in to look at my design. "This is how the master creates her vision."

"It's how this *novice* works on her ideas."

"According to Allison, you are the queen of weddings. She raved about you for months. Of course, I didn't know you were *you*." Will must sense my trepidation at the mention of Allison's name, so he clears his throat. "What is this circular thing in the center of your drawing?"

I tilt my head. "That is a chandelier I'd like to have installed inside the barn." There's an open tab on my web browser. I click it, and a website with a chandelier I can rent for five hundred dollars from a vintage marketplace is on display.

"That's amazing. You can install that just for the day?"

"As long as there's electricity and a ladder, I can do pretty much anything."

He holds my gaze for a moment. "I bet you can." His breath is long, deep, and then his eyes flicker to my lips before he jolts back to the computer and taps on the screen. "These are all your designs?"

"Some. Others I took from the internet and know I can re-create it. The wedding is on a farm, so I want to incorporate outdoor elements on the inside. The centerpieces will have soft hues from roses, peonies, and hydrangeas as well as artichokes and pomegranates to make it earthy and warm."

"You could set bowls of figs and plums on the table. So long as they're in season," he suggests, and I laugh out loud at his comment. He widens his eyes. "Are you mocking me?"

I turn and place a hand on his chest. "Absolutely not. I'm sorry. That was the wrong reaction. I'm actually impressed. I laughed because it was, well, unexpected."

What's also unexpected is the feel of his heated chest beneath my hand and his heart thumping beneath the cotton of his shirt.

I move my hand and run it through my hair. "That's a great idea. Any more I might want to add?"

"A signature drink that people actually like. Every wedding has one fruity cocktail of shit alcohol that no one wants."

"What would be a cocktail of your preference?"

"You want earthy, so go with a bourbon."

"That's a cool idea. Though we usually serve the bride and groom's favorite drink as a signature cocktail."

"Well, if it were my wedding, I'd want whiskey."

"Note taken," I state and then click around my laptop, not really looking for anything in particular.

His comment reminded me of the wedding I was going to design yet didn't because it was called off. Scrunching my nose, I lean back in my seat, which only puts me further into his arm.

"I have your wedding notes in my head. White everything. Modern. Clean—"

"Exactly what I didn't want."

"I had a feeling."

"What would you have planned for me?"

A wedding for Will Bronson. I wouldn't know where to begin. I wouldn't know where to end. I have so many things I think I know about him, yet he continues to surprise me with every action.

"Can I get back to you on that?" I ask softly.

"Yeah," he says with a knowing grin and nudges my sketchpad. "Is this something you always wanted to do?"

"I never knew what I wanted to do. I majored in graphic design because it came easily to me. After I graduated, I took a job at a firm in the city, but once Izzy was born, the commute was too much. I stayed home for a few years, was heavily involved in the PTA, and one day, I saw an ad for a party planning assistant and thought, *I could do that and be available for my kids*. So, I interviewed and got the job."

"You were great at it, and the rest is history?"

"Opposite. I was horrible. Planning details and keeping a timeline are not my strong suits. The design part? That I liked. Jillian was a wedding planner there and introduced me to one of her clients as a wedding *designer*. I honestly hadn't even known the job title existed. When Jillian decided to open up Lavish Events, she asked me to come on board as a partner and head designer. It was perfect timing because Tyler had just filed separation papers and I needed cash. Fast. Plus, I really like working with Jillian."

"Must've been hard, planning other people's happily ever afters when yours was falling apart."

"It sucked." I laugh ironically. "It also reminded me that love is real, and whether it lasts or not, it's a beautiful thing to be part of." Realizing I've found myself in a wistful haze, I shake my shoulders and turn to ask him, "Do you believe in happily ever after?"

"I do."

Hunter comes barreling down the stairs. He's changed from his school clothes and into Captain America pajamas and is holding his magic kit. "Can we work now?"

Will runs his hands on his thighs. "A good man keeps his word."

He rises and heads into the den with Hunter and takes a seat on the couch.

I take a look at the clock. It's earlier than I was planning on making dinner, but I should start it so Will isn't here all afternoon. The chicken is out of the refrigerator, and I'm whisking eggs when Izzy comes over. She looks at Will and Hunter through the open door of the den. They're reading instructions and testing a trick.

"Will's cool," she says.

I place a piece of chicken in the egg mixture and hand it to her to place in the breadcrumbs. "You're only saying that because you want to hear about how he got shot."

She puts the breaded cutlet on a plate. "He told me already."

My brow rises as I wonder when he could have told her.

"You were lost in your wedding haze. He told me after we finished my chemistry homework," she explains.

"And?" I hand her another egged piece of chicken and wait for her to tell me the story.

LOVE ... IT'S COMPLICATED

"Not my story to tell."

"That's very mature of you."

Izzy and I cook together and listen to music. I haven't had her help in making dinner in a long time. I want to point it out, but I know better. Instead, I enjoy having my daughter by my side, doing something as simple as frying up chicken cutlets and warming up vegetables.

When the meal is ready, we call Hunter and Will to the kitchen. The two boys set the table while Izzy and I make the plates. We sit down for dinner, and it's ... nice.

The kids ask Will about being a cop. He regales them with stories of arrests and what his training was like at the academy. He keeps his stories kid friendly, as I'm sure there are many dreadful things he's witnessed.

In turn, Will asks the kids questions about themselves and school. Hunter talks about his passion for magic and superheroes, which I'm pretty sure Will already figured out. Izzy slowly and coyly shrugs off her art. Will asks to see it, but she refuses.

The meal is possibly the most interesting we've had in a month. Hunter and Izzy usually eat and run after their meals, eager to get on their iPads or watch television. Tonight, they're taking their time and enjoying the conversation. I'm enjoying it too.

Everything is going nice. Too nice.

That is, until the front door opens, and we're all greeted by a very gruff, very confused, "Who the hell are you?"

twelve

"Dad, I thought you were coming home later. I invited a friend to dinner," I explain as Will stands up and holds out a hand for my father, who approaches the kitchen table cautiously, like he just walked into an armed robbery in progress.

"I know you. You're the man from the paper." Dad appraises him as he takes off his cap.

"Yeah. He was shot!" Hunter exclaims.

Izzy hits him on the arm. "Don't be disrespectful."

"There's a lot of news in that paper." Will brushes off the comment.

"Not many about men who put themselves in front of a gun to save a stranger. What you did was heroic. Glad to see you're back on duty." Dad takes his offered hand. The two shake, and Dad appraises our dinner guest. "You bench?"

"I prefer CrossFit, sir."

I lean forward. "You don't have to call him sir. It's like when you call me ma'am. Very formal."

"He can call me sir," Dad says, and Izzy giggles. "I like a man with respect. What's your name?"

"William Bronson."

"Good name. You married?" Dad asks as he puts his hands on his hips.

"No, sir."

"Ever been?"

"No."

"Why not? What's wrong with you?"

"Haven't met the right woman to settle down with, sir." If Will is annoyed with this interrogation by my father, he is not letting it show.

"What are your intentions with my daughter?"

I lift a hand and halt the conversation. "Will is just joining us for dinner. Not asking for a hand in marriage. In fact, he's not even asking for a date. We're just friends. Just. Friends. Now, sit. I'll make you a plate."

I go to stand, but Dad waves me off to sit back down.

"I already ate. Had a bite with Anna."

I nod and take a bite of my chicken, my mouth too full to respond. Hunter looks down at his plate and moves his food around. Dad strums his fingers along the granite countertop and looks down at the floor in interest.

Will looks around the table, probably feeling the tension that is now dancing in the air like fireflies.

Izzy leans over and explains loudly, "Anna is Grandpa's girlfriend. Mom's uncomfortable with the fact that her dad moved on from her dead mom so soon."

"Izzy!" I scold.

She's not incorrect, but it's rather rude to just air other people's feelings out at a dinner table.

"What? You should try having to quasi-live with your dad's new girlfriend every weekend. They're all kissy and huggy and calling each other baby doll, which is super gross. And you're still alive, and I have to put up with some other lady in Dad's house. If you want to compare shitty *dad's new girlfriend* scenarios, trust me, I win. It sucks ass. Big time."

My jaw is practically on the ceramic of my dinner plate. Dad's eyes look as wide as can be as he fiddles with the cap in his hands. Izzy hasn't been this forthcoming with her feelings in, well, ever. It's good, yet she has terrible timing because she's calling me out on my feelings, and I don't like it.

"That does suck," Will says matter-of-factly. Our gazes shoot to him as he holds a fork full of chicken and declares, "Plus, a grown man being called baby doll is embarrassing."

LOVE ... IT'S COMPLICATED

"Exactly!" Izzy exclaims as she leans her elbow on the table.
There's a small bout of silence.
I take a long, deep breath and then let it out in a total *who gives a fuck anymore* vibe. "It could be something way cooler. Like ... hot stuff."
Izzy looks up at me, as does Will, whose mouth tips up in a crooked grin.
"Lovebug."
"Honeybunny," I add.
"Lamb chop." He builds onto our list of names Maisie and Tyler could call each other.
The kids giggle as they become more ridiculous.
"Pumpkin pie."
"Papa bear."
"Pudding."
"Nugget."
"Butt!" Hunter shouts out, and Izzy chimes in with, "Darling."
The momentary awkwardness is replaced with fits of laughter by the four of us. Dad even fights back a slight quirk of his mouth as he watches the interaction.
"Well, if you ask me, sweetie pie makes me gag," Dad says as he moves into the foyer, where he takes off his shoes and hangs his hat in the closet.
The kids take their giggly bodies to the sink and start cleaning off the table. Will and I are behind them, gathering dishes.
I turn to him and mouth, *Thank you.*
"For what?" he asks as he takes a glass from my hand.
"For just ... being here. Tonight was nice."
And there it is ... *the smolder.* You can't see the flame, but the heat is intense as he fixes his gaze on mine and holds it steady, taking all the energy from the room and igniting it with a single look.
"The night's not over." His voice is deep and low.
I swallow hard. "No?"
"Hunter and I have to show you what we've been working on. Are you ready for a show?"
"Yes. Um, why don't I clean up the kitchen while you two set up your tricks?"
"Tricks? We have a performance. Do you have popcorn?" he asks, and I nod. "Let's start the show then."

While I clean up, Izzy makes the popcorn, and Hunter and Will set up the show. Will asks my dad if he has a hat, which Dad gets.

The dishwasher is on, the counters are clean, and I'm soon being called into the living room.

Hunter and Will are each wearing hats—a wizard hat for Hunter that we got from Disney World and a men's bowler cap for Will. Hunter has a Captain America cape on while Will has Spiderman and Thor ones around his neck. They each have a wooden spoon in their hand as they stand by the fireplace. They look ridiculous and adorable at the same time.

Izzy and I take a seat on the sofa, and Dad sits on the side chair. We each have a small bowl of popcorn in our laps.

"Ladies and gentlemen, welcome to the super-amazing magic show, hosted by me, Will, and the great—"

"Huntino!" my son exclaims as he waves his arms in the air.

They start with a trick from the box. Hunter shows the crowd the red velvet pouch that sits on a round wooden frame with a handle.

"I'm going to put this coin in the pouch and—wait, what do I do?" he asks Will, who leans down and shows Hunter where the tiny lever by the handle is to make a mechanism inside the pouch swoop to push the coin out of view, appearing to have disappeared.

Hunter makes quite the show of moving the mechanism, to the point that Izzy leans over and whispers loudly, "He needs to practice big time if he wants to be in the talent show."

"It's his first try. Give him some time."

Hunter pulls off the trick. Dad, Izzy, and I act like we can't believe the wooden coin disappeared, which makes Hunter smile from ear to ear.

"Now, for my next trick, I need my assistant to help me."

For the next two tricks, Will has to practically do them himself because Hunter has trouble manipulating the toys. With each, the couch audience applauds with great fanfare.

My son looks adorable as he puts on his show, but I can't keep my eyes off Will. It's sweet really. A grown man in a child's capes, helping a little kid do magic in his living room. He doesn't know Hunter. He doesn't really know me, and yet he made today amazing for my entire family. Well, verdict's still out on Dad.

LOVE ... IT'S COMPLICATED

They take their bows, and I let out a loud whistle, then yawn. It's seven o'clock. This day has been incredibly long yet quick at the same time.

Izzy takes the bowls into the kitchen and then retreats upstairs, where she'll probably be for the rest of the night. Hunter gathers his magic kit and puts it away in his room. Dad has made himself scarce, which leaves only Will and me standing in the living room.

"That was quite the show." I slide my hands into the back pockets of my jeans.

He steps around the coffee table and takes a place by me near the couch. "I think magician's assistant could be my backup calling if this law enforcement thing doesn't work out."

"Nice to have a fallback. You're not very good at your job."

He grips his chest in mock offense. "How so?"

"Last I heard, you had a woman imprisoned just so you could talk to her."

"She was caught breaking and entering. Twice. I was just protecting the community."

I bite my lip and look down. "We both seem to be making some stupid mistakes lately."

"Maybe it would have been worse if we *hadn't* made them."

His words have me looking back up at him. There's this thing about Will I can't put my finger on. In one breath, I think he's this knight in shining armor who is here to rescue me. Then, I think about his called-off engagement and our shared moment at Lone Tavern, and I'm reminded that he's not the hero I think he is. But he is a hero since he was literally shot while protecting people. Then, he locked me up just to get me to hear his story, which I'm pretty sure is illegal, although I'm not entirely sure.

"William Bronson, I can't figure you out."

Every reason I give myself for why he's good or bad makes it harder to rationalize why I'm standing here with him in my living room.

Why I'm standing here and liking that he's standing here with me.

"Don't try. Just let me be me." He speaks gently.

"I think I can do that."

He takes a step closer, not too close, but he closes the distance enough that my breath hitches at the sense of his warmth invading my space. It's a spicy vanilla-scented warmth that makes a shiver run down my arms, like he just placed his hands on my skin and ran his fingers down my sides.

"Good, 'cause I like you. You're quirky."

"Not an adjective a woman faints over hearing about herself."

"I like you just the way you are."

"Okay, now, you sound like a bad romantic comedy."

"This isn't a romance."

I scratch my head. "Yeah, what is this exactly?"

Will bends down and makes his eyes level with mine. "Two people who happen to be in each other's life at just the right time."

I look up at him and unfurl my lip from between my teeth.

With a look at his phone, Will takes a walk toward the kitchen table and grabs his jacket. "I should get out of here."

"Are you leaving?" Hunter asks as he barrels down the stairs. "Will you come back and do more tricks with me? I need an assistant for the talent show. You can do it with me. I want to levitate. You never showed me how to levitate."

I pull my precocious five-year-old away from Will. "Tonight was a special treat. It's impossible for Will to take the time needed to do more tricks with you, let alone appear onstage in a show."

"I'll do it."

My head pops up at Will's offer. He doesn't seem affected by the request as he walks toward the front door.

"I go to the schools a lot and discuss school safety, lockdown drills, and even visit the kindergarteners on Career Day. Standing on a stage and doing a super-cool magic show with the great Huntino is part of my job description."

"Yes!" Hunter fists-pumps the air and gives Will a high-five. "It's gonna be the best!"

Hunter runs up the stairs, squealing. I open the front door and walk Will out. Not knowing how to do a good-bye with him, I salute him. He gives a salute back and starts walking down the stairs. He's about five steps away when he turns around.

"In case I didn't tell you, you look really pretty with your new hair."

I blush. Yes, I'm blushing like a teenager who was just told she was pretty by the high school quarterback. My cheeks are warm, and my head has a slight tingle.

Thankfully, he retreats down the stairs and hops into his truck. I don't watch him drive away. Instead, I walk back into the house

LOVE ... IT'S COMPLICATED

and jolt back when my dad, standing in the foyer, shocks me with his presence.

"Officer Bronson is a nice man." Dad's words are baiting. I merely shrug in agreement. "He wouldn't have anything to do with Mr. Snuggles appearing mysteriously the other night."

"That was a favor. It was nothing," I say, and Dad makes a harrumph sound. I mimic him. "What was that for?"

He makes the sound again. "Dinner at five o'clock is early for you. I can't figure out if you like him and needed to find a way to get him to stay or if you fed him early so he'd leave early."

I make that sound but for real this time. Honestly, I have no idea which of Dad's scenarios is right.

My pause is too long because Dad rubs his hands together, his brows pinching.

"Don't be introducing the children to anyone you don't plan on keeping around a long time."

"I doubt we'll ever see him again."

"We'd better. He just promised my grandson he'd do a magic show with him. And if you ask me, that man doesn't like magic as much as he lets on."

"Why would you say that?"

"Because he looked ridiculous in those capes."

thirteen

"I'M GETTING CONFUSED. DO you like the guy or not?" Jillian asks as she gives a right-hook, uppercut-elbow sequence to the freestanding punching bag beside mine.

We're at a kickboxing class together, beating the bags as rock music from the early 2000s blasts through the speakers.

"No." I slam my elbow into the vinyl and then switch stances to do the sequence with my left arm. "It's complicated."

"It's really bad for business."

"He was never a client. They didn't sign a contract." I brush a hair away from my face and grab hold of the top of the bag. "Wait. Do you think I did something unethical? I would never put our business in jeopardy."

She rubs her forearm over her auburn head. "If word got out you're dating a prospective groom, that would be detrimental to our reputation."

"I'm not dating him," I explain, and she gives me the side-eye as she goes back to working out. "I swear. We didn't even hook up."

She gives a more severe side-eye this time as she right-hooks the bag.

"That one time, but it was ... you know what? Doesn't matter since Will and I are not hooking up or dating or anything other than being people who happen to have met."

"Nice hair," she says with a sly grin, mostly because she knows how he surprised me with a trip to the salon.

Tara walks over to where Jillian and I are working out. "Less chitchatting from you hens," Tara says to us. She's the instructor of this class—something she started doing years ago and enjoys as a second job.

"We were just talking about Officer Bronson," Jillian says through huffs. Even sweaty, she looks pristine in her Lululemon ensemble.

"Kent says Will's been pretty miserable the last few months. He thought it was because of the injury, but apparently, Will's been more relaxed lately. Interesting, considering no one in his family seems to be talking to him. Or his friends really. Just Kent."

"How is Kent?" Jillian asks with waggling brows.

Tara grins and then turns down the music. "Okay, class, you have thirty seconds to grab yourselves a sip of water. A sip only. I don't want you upchucking on the mat!"

Jillian and I walk to where we have our water bottles lined up. I grab mine and take more than a sip. I'm hot, sweaty, and parched.

Tara joins us by the wall. "Kent and I went to this sweet little French restaurant last night."

"So, have you two …" I follow it up with a whistle to insinuate *done it*.

"Not yet. If he's not all in, then I'm wasting my time. If he's dating someone else, then he's a jerkface and should have his balls cut off. Speaking of …"

She walks to the front of the room and shows the class how to execute a knee to the groin. We're given a three-step kick sequence to do.

The music kicks on, and we go back to our bags.

Jillian's face is fierce as she slams her knee into the bag and turns into a roundhouse kick. For a reserved girl who doesn't easily show her emotions, she's using today's workout to express whatever it is she's feeling internally. I feel bad for whoever she is imagining the bag to be.

"Anything new going on in your life?" I ask over my shoulder.

"Nope. Same nonsense. Different day."

Her tone is typical of the one gripe she has in her life.

"Your mother starting up again?"

LOVE ... IT'S COMPLICATED

"I think at this point in my life, I'd be surprised if she didn't make a comment about my not knowing who the father of my daughter is."

"Ainsley is three. By now, your mom should be ecstatic she has a grandchild, not caring how she was created."

"Apparently, it's too difficult to explain to her country club friends, or the Historic Society, or whatever group she's decided to chair."

"Most of those people are doctors and lawyers. I think they'd understand a successful single woman who wanted to have a child on her own and used medical advancements to make it happen."

She pummels the bag. "Exactly. They're not the problem." Jillian strikes the bag so hard that she knocks the wind out of herself and has to turn around and lean against the bag to catch her breath.

I move from my bag to hers and place a hand on her shoulder. "Jillian, you can't let your mom do this to you. I don't know what she's saying, but it's the only thing in this world that gets you wound up like this."

"You wouldn't know. Your mom was amazing. Supportive. Kind. Funny. Mine's just a ..." She scrunches her mouth, as if the words are too vile to say so I say it for her.

"A colossal bitch. I think your problem is, you don't say what's on your mind. Trust me, as ridiculous as the things that come out of my mouth are sometimes, it's very therapeutic."

She laughs as she looks up at the ceiling. "You and Tara speak enough for an army. I was raised different. Be seen, not heard. Focus on academics, not fantasy. I've worked my ass off to become a success, opened my own business—"

"And made the selfless decision to bring a child into the world despite societal norms. I'm sorry your mom sucks at accepting that, but you are a badass woman with an amazing kid, kick-ass career, gorgeous face, killer body, wardrobe to die for—"

"Okay, Tony Robbins. The confidence-boosting adjectives are getting a little out of hand." She stands up straight and gives me a slight punch in the arm. "I know what you're trying to say though."

"Good. Now, can we get back to kicking the shit out of these bags? And maybe not thinking that it's your mom?"

She raises her brows in agreement. "Can I pretend it's Tyler?"

I sweep my arm in the air and make a welcoming gesture toward her bag. "By all means."

For anyone to assume any woman has life under control is out of their minds. Whether you're single and looking for love, married with two kids, or riding a wave somewhere in between, you constantly feel like there's another level you should be at. We get angry at things that happened in the past and always look toward this expected happiness that will come in the future. Well, I do at least.

The highs are exhausting to climb, and the downturn is exhilarating, yet as soon as you enjoy it, it's time to start uphill again.

Being a woman is a fucking roller coaster.

After our workout, I run home to do homework with the kids, take a quick shower, change clothes, and kiss them good-bye. Dad is taking Hunter and Izzy out for pizza and ice cream while I head to the middle school for Isabella's parent-teacher night.

When I get to the school, the parking lot is full, so I have to park on the main road and walk an impossibly long distance to the building. Just as I'm approaching the entrance, a familiar Mercedes enters the lot. I see Tyler inside, talking on his speakerphone. I'm about to wave to him to say the lot is full when a car starts backing out of the closest spot near the entrance and Tyler pulls his car in.

Figures the prick would show up right on time and get the closest spot.

I go inside and sign in at the security desk, then follow the hallway to Isabella's History class. We've been asked to follow along with the student's daily schedule and see the teachers in the order our kids have them each day. History is her first class of the day, so I take a seat in a chair in the hallway just outside the room.

The hallway looks the same as when Tyler and I went here. Yellow-tiled walls, white linoleum floors, and fluorescent lighting that's cruel to preteens going through their changes. Even the lockers with their scratched-up metal frames line the walls. You can tell they've been painted since, yet the dents in the steel remain.

The double doors at the end of the hallway open. Tyler struts through, as only he can, with his long gait, shoulders back, and a brow that is furrowed in a serious manner. He's looking down at his phone, yet the seas would part for how his mere presence demands the space before him be cleared. His body is a weapon, used to command a room, and when he lifts a brown eye to his opponent, it's disarming in the best way.

LOVE ... IT'S COMPLICATED

I don't think Tyler ever knew just what kind of presence he had until he started working in finance, taking meetings, making presentations, and closing deals.

As a teenager, he was an athlete, working the field with talent and grace.

As a man, he became serious and persistent. It's a sex appeal that ages well. The arrogance that came with success did not.

"Hey, Lyss. She running late?" He nods to the closed classroom door.

"He. Mr. Adams. I just got here and took a seat."

Tyler knocks on the door. "Is he just sitting there, twiddling his thumbs?"

"He's probably meeting with another parent. Are you in a rush?"

"Dinner plans," he states matter-of-factly, and I widen my mouth and bob my head, unsurprised.

Based on the bright blue button-down he has on—something he never would have worn when we were together—I should have assumed he was going out.

Tyler takes a seat beside me, his legs spread wide, and he looks at me, as if finally realizing that I'm sitting here. "You just shower?"

I touch my damp head. "No. I walked through the car wash on the way here. Thought I'd see what it was like to get slapped around by the bristles for a while."

He grins with a pinched mouth. "Sounds like it hurt."

"Not as much as you did."

"Lyss …" he reprimands with a sigh.

"Ty …" I match his tone. "I'm just joshing you. My hair is wet because I just showered after a long kick boxing session, where I envisioned the bag was your face."

He chuckles as he puts his phone in his pocket. "Now, that I don't doubt."

The door to the classroom opens. A parent exits the room, followed by a man with black hair and matching dark eyes. He has stubble on his chin, and from what I remember, he married at the Wolfson Manor.

"Victor Talini," I say as I stand from the folding chair.

He points at me and squints his eyes, as if trying to remember where he knows me from. "You worked my wedding, right?"

"Yes. I was your wedding designer from Lavish Events. Jillian Hathaway was your wedding planner."

Victor smiles and snaps his fingers. "Right. Nicole handled all the wedding planning. Crazy seeing you here. I was talking about you not too long ago. My cousin, Allison Lalayne. I believe you met with her. She ended her engagement. Terrible situation, but these things happen, I guess."

"Yeah. It's sad when it happens."

"She'll be okay. My wife has her out almost every weekend. She's young and beautiful. A good guy will snatch her up quick. I'll tell her I ran into you."

My brows furrow with uneasiness. "Um ... I didn't recognize your name on the syllabus."

"I took Nicole's. She has all sisters and wants to carry on the family name."

"You took your wife's last name?" Tyler bemuses with a laugh, and I punch him in the face with my stare.

"Do you have a student at Newbury Middle School?" Victor asks.

"Yes. Isabella Landish."

He leans back on his heels and blows out a deep breath, as I'd imagine a surgeon would before giving a bad post-op report. "Yes. Isabella. I was hoping her parents would show up."

"Is there a problem with Izzy?" Tyler asks.

"Why don't we take a seat and discuss?" Victor leads us into the classroom and closes the door behind him.

He motions for us to take a seat at the classroom desks. They're much nicer than the kind we had as kids. Individual tables in the shape of a trapezoid with a seat that's not attached. Tyler and I choose front row seats in front of Mr. Adams's desk.

"Isabella has been in my class since the beginning of the year. I'm her homeroom teacher, and I see her first period for History. We spend quite a bit of time with each other in the morning."

"You don't sound like she's doing well," Tyler implies.

"Academically, she's doing okay. Eighties on her tests. Nothing exceptional, yet no red flags to worry about. She could benefit from additional time studying for tests. It's an adjustment for our middle schoolers. The tests are longer and less frequent. It's more information to study."

"That's Lyss's job. She has the kids during the week."

I bite the inside of my cheek. "Thanks, Tyler. I'll be sure to work harder with Izzy on her studying."

LOVE ... IT'S COMPLICATED

"Actually, our last exam was on a Monday. I gave the kids the full weekend to review."

If I could high-five Victor for that comment, I would.

He folds his hands on his desk and looks at Tyler and me with a grimace. "What concerns me actually is her demeanor. She's very reserved. Not too social with her peers. Eats lunch alone in the cafeteria. She chooses to sit on a bench and draw during free period instead of playing in the gym or even talking with the other students. The adjustment period is over, and most students have formed small cliques. Isabella seems resistant to forming bonds with anyone. Is this typical for her personality?"

Tyler shakes his head. "Not at all. She is our social butterfly. At her last school, she had a ton of friends and played soccer."

"She opted to take a break from sports while she adjusted to the new course schedule of middle school," I add. "She also didn't want to compete against her friends in Greenwood Village. They were a close group."

"Recently divorced?" Victor surmises.

Tyler and I nod. The confirmation has him sighing knowingly.

"It's common for kids who have a dramatic life event in the household to go through a personality adjustment. Does she talk to anyone?"

"She has us. She and my girlfriend, Maisie, talk all the time."

I scrunch my eyes and shake my head. "Izzy talks to Maisie. Since when?"

"They're always huddled together, talking." He turns to Victor. "My girlfriend and Izzy are very close."

Victor gives a closed-mouth smile. "I'm sure they are. What I'm suggesting is a therapist. We have a fantastic social worker on staff—"

"Izzy doesn't need a social worker," Tyler bites out.

Turning to Tyler, I offer, "A therapist doesn't sound so bad."

"It doesn't?"

"Not really. If she's not talking to anyone and she's going through something, maybe she could benefit from one."

"She talks to Maisie."

I clench my fist and hold it at my side as I keep a forced smile on my face. "While I'm sure Maisie's expertise in child psychology is superb, I think finding a professional therapist through our insurance is a better idea."

Tyler's tongue rolls over his back teeth, and he leans back in a huff. "Can we talk about this first?"

Victor intervenes. "It was just a suggestion. Whether Isabella sees someone here at school or at an outside facility, she could benefit from the interaction."

"Is that your professional opinion as a History teacher?" Tyler sneers.

"As an educator and advocate for children, yes, it is."

I rub the pads of my fingers over my forehead and fight the embarrassment that is my ex-husband and try to mentally figure out what the heck is going on with Isabella. I know she's been sullen, but having a teacher broach the subject is a new level of concern. "Thanks, Victor, um … Mr. Adams. We're going to discuss this and see what we can do for Izzy."

"Anything else about her education we need to discuss other than *study more*?" Tyler's sarcasm is as obnoxious as his shirt.

"That's it," Victor replies.

"Thanks." Tyler rises and is quickly out the door while I give a wave to Victor. He's halfway down the hall when I step out of the classroom and storm after him.

"Where are you going? We have to see her English teacher next."

"Dinner," he states and then stops just by the exit doors, spinning to me and waving a hand in the air. "This is bullshit. Therapy for our kid? Is this a school or some namby-pamby feelings bullshit center?"

"Her parents divorced. It's hard on a kid."

He pushes open the door and walks outside toward the lot and his Mercedes. "Next thing you know, she's gonna be walking around with an emotional support ferret because she can't deal with her parents' divorce."

"You're just behaving this way because you feel guilty."

Tyler stops and turns around with raised brows and an open mouth.

I throw my hands up in exasperation. "Don't act like you don't think this isn't your fault."

"We were separated, Lyss. Whether I filed for divorce or not, we were on our way to divorce."

"You filed after you had an affair. You gave up on us, Ty."

LOVE ... IT'S COMPLICATED

His mouth opens and closes, and he switches his stance. His hand is on his hip, and his other palm is up, as if he's going on the defense. "It's not like that, and you know it. I've explained myself. I didn't mean to fall in love with Maisie. I was lost in our marriage when I met her, and we just started talking."

"You talked to her, Tyler. You put yourself in the position to fall in love with someone. A man who is fighting for his family doesn't willingly open himself up to someone else. You did that on purpose."

"Would you have preferred it was an affair of sex and not emotion?"

"Absolutely! Sex is short-lived. But you loved someone else enough to break up our family. And now, Izzy probably has this paralyzing fear that any relationship she forms will end the same way. Abandoned and alone."

"Don't assume things about our daughter. How could you possibly think that?"

"Because that's how I feel!" I yell, and it's followed by a quick gasp of air and the intense, overwhelming sensation that comes when one speaks your truth.

"Lyss—"

"Don't *Lyss* me!" I back away from him, clenching my jaw and willing myself not to cry.

A family is walking through the main entrance, looking at Tyler and me, clearly in a dramatic confrontation.

I give them a forced smile and then lower my voice when I speak to Tyler. "Don't try to tell everyone how they feel and why. You were lost? That means you were bored, and you *will* get bored again. When you do, I hope you're kinder to Maisie than you were to me." Despite my attempts, a tear falls down my face, followed by another. I lift my chin and my shaking jaw. Tyler takes a step forward, but I step back and look away. "Go to dinner, Ty."

He shakes his head, but tightly. "No. I'll stay and meet the rest of the teachers."

"Please don't. You'll just irritate me, and I want to actually focus on what these people have to say. I'll fill you in."

There's a short curb behind him. He's careful not to fall as he walks in a small circle and rubs the back of his neck. More families are walking in, many talking with one another as they pass through the doors. A particular one has brought their daughter with them.

She's hammering on to her parents as she walks beside them. The dad laughs at something she says as he holds the door open for his wife and daughter. They walk inside. It's suddenly very quiet. Too quiet.

Tyler's stopped pacing. His hands are on his hips as he looks up. "If you think Isabella needs help, I'm all for it."

"I think we should try it."

"Great." His mouth is pinched. "Set up whatever you want. Here or private."

"I'll let Izzy decide. She should feel comfortable."

"That's a good idea."

Tyler says he was lost in our marriage. He was, and he still is. He's just as lost as he was the day we brought Izzy home from the hospital, except it's no longer my job to help him find his way.

"Where are you going to dinner?"

He seems surprised by my question. "Lin Chun in Greenwood Village."

I nod, knowing the place well. "They have those spareribs that fall off the bone. So good. They're a choking hazard though."

"That's right. The tiny bone got lodged in my throat that time. Thanks for the reminder." He hits the unlock button on his car, and the headlights turn on with the familiar beep of the horn. He starts walking toward his car.

"Tyler."

He pauses with his hand on the handle. "Yeah?"

"Order the ribs."

A small smile appears on his lips. "Night, Lyss."

Tyler gets in his car, and my chest clenches with that familiar balance of *I hate him* and *I remember how much I once loved him*, pounding from deep within me.

While I hate my ex-husband, I don't actually want him to die.

Although a scare with some serious discomfort and a prayer to Jesus for being a prick … that I'd take.

fourteen

"LAVISH EVENTS," I ANSWER the phone at the new office and listen to the barking cough on the line.

"Don't kill me."

My stomach drops. There's only one reason someone would make that statement as soon as you pick up the phone. I wait for Samantha, the assistant we hired to work with me today, to finish coughing.

"I can't work today."

I fall into my desk chair. Honestly, I have zero business sitting. There are boxes of wedding supplies that have to be loaded into my truck that I need to drive thirty minutes away to the wedding venue my clients are expecting to be transformed into *A Midsummer Night's Dream* banquet.

"My boyfriend bought me every cold medicine under the sun last night, but I woke up, feeling like crap. I just got back from urgent care. Doctor says it's a respiratory infection with pneumonia."

I'm not a cretin. A sick woman needs to rest. It still doesn't keep me from asking, "Is it contagious? Can you do *any* work today? Just a few hours, and I'll whisk you out of there before the bridal party arrives."

Samantha makes a sickly groan. "I'm so sorry, Melissa. I feel like I'm about to die. Just going to the doctor was an ordeal. Plus, if people hear my cough, they're going to freak, thinking it's something much worse and highly contagious. It would look horrible for the business."

I nod and sigh. I hate that she's right. I hate that she's sick.

"Feel better, okay? Did the doctor give you any medicine?"

"Antibiotics and a steroid for the nebulizer."

"Call me tomorrow and let me know how you're feeling."

We exchange good-byes and hang up.

My hand is in my hair as I try to figure out what the hell I'm going to do without an assistant.

I call Tara and ask for help.

"Sorry, babe. I have my niece's sweet sixteen in New Jersey, remember?"

The answer is, no, I don't remember, but I apologize and call the two other assistants we've used on events. They are both busy working other jobs. I call some friends, at least the few I know who might be useful. I get fierce apologies and *wish I could* and *if it were any other weekend*. Finally, I panic-call Jillian, who is in Maine, for a funeral, and practically cry as I explain what's going on.

"Shit. Samantha must be severely ill if she's canceling like this," she says on the other end of the phone. I can hear the house full of family members chattering in the background of their Kennebunkport estate.

"The girl sounded like she was three steps away from death. Tara is unavailable. Loriann, Dana, Jacqueline, Amaya, Nevaeh, Callista—"

"Callista is the least reliable person on the planet."

"I was desperate. I even asked the woman who does my nails."

"Man, you are overreaching for help on this one. Maybe there's a flight that leaves in the next half hour? I could get there by—"

"Jillian, that's insane. Don't you dare!"

"You've clearly tried every other person you know. Plus, it'll give me an excuse to run away from my family. My father has set me up with seven dates while I'm here."

"That's kinda sweet."

"I'm here for my grandmother's funeral, Melissa! My parents are certifiably insane. I'll come home."

"No. Don't. Your mom is bonkers, but you were excited to see friends during your trip, and your uncle is sick. You should spend time with them. I can do this on my own. The florist will be there, and we have the furniture delivery drivers. I can give them a few bucks to help me move things. Of all the weddings you're away for, it had to be this one. We do every event together."

"Except this one. This sucks for you, and it's a ton of work to do on your own."

"Forget about me. You need to grieve with your family."

"Keep me updated. Text if you're having a nervous breakdown."

"Sure. I'll stop mid–panic attack and give you a cordial ring."

"You got this."

We hang up, and I start my immediate squirm around the room, making sure I have everything on my list. I grab my iPad, ensuring it's fully charged, and grab a backup charger to place in my emergency kit. I count the props in the bins. I have the vendor contracts, specialty table numbers, and … I feel like I'm forgetting something.

My cell phone rings. I grab it out of my backpack and am surprised to see Will is calling.

"Hey." My voice is clipped.

"Did I call at a bad time?"

"Kind of. I'm having a small meltdown at work. My assistant is dying, not literally, but enough to call out sick. Everyone I know is unavailable to fill her spot, so I'm scrambling." I spin around and spot the closet in my office when a mental bulb goes off in my head. "My suitcase! That's the thing I almost forgot."

"You bring a suitcase to weddings?"

"This bad boy is my most precious work possession. It has every emergency item I could need when in a bind. As I'll be decorating a wedding with one hundred guests by myself, I'd say I'll be in a few binds today."

I roll the suitcase over my toe and yelp. I might even release an expletive or two.

"What kind of help do you need?" Will asks.

Hobbling on one foot, I pull the suitcase toward the stairs. "An assistant. A second set of hands. There're twelve tables that have to be dressed, vendors that need to be met, furniture to be delivered, lighting to be set, plus whatever *oh shit* moments that arise as we dress the room. Honestly, this is a three-man job. Jillian was going to work today since she had helped me plan the logistics for the setup. Now, she's in Maine for a family thing, and we only booked the one assistant without a backup planned. If you ask me, that was a big mistake, but I digress."

Lugging the suitcase down the stairs, I continue, "I thought it was fine. I mean, I have everything planned. I'm crazy organized, but now, I'm wondering if I'm just plain crazy because I'm about to go to this event solo. Planes run on autopilot, but you need a pilot at the helm. What if the pilot passes out and the autopilot fails and you need to land the damn thing? There has to be a copilot around to grab the wheel and get everyone to land safely."

Will chuckles on the other end.

"I'm sorry, what about this is funny?"

He doesn't let the amused tone in his voice subside. "Your analogy."

"Pardon me for being frazzled. I can't talk right now. I have to get these bins to the truck and to the venue, or I'll never get this event ready for the first-look pictures at five o'clock." I open the back of the Lavish Events truck and hoist the suitcase inside.

"What do I need to wear?"

My breath is a bit winded. "Wear for what? And why are you calling?"

"I was calling to set up a time to come by and practice with Hunter. I hadn't heard from you."

"Yeah, sorry. It's been a long week." I leave the back of the truck open and start walking back upstairs.

"Looks like I called at the right time. You said you called everyone you know, but you forgot one person."

I nearly trip and right myself. "You?"

"I don't work Saturday nights, so all I need to know is what to wear."

"Something simple. Black. Dressy. Not sweats or anything. Or jeans. Oh God, no, wait. You can't help me. This is something for someone who knows how to decorate."

"Was every person you called a decorator?"

"Well ... no. Even still, you work Friday nights, and you haven't slept and—"

"Melissa?" His voice is so soothing, like a weighted blanket on a cold day.

I actually stop my frantic moving and listen.

LOVE ... IT'S COMPLICATED

"I have to shower, but I can meet you at the mansion in an hour. Are you okay with getting whatever you need there?"

"Yes."

"See you there."

He hangs up before I can tell him this is ridiculous. It is, and yet it's not. He's a physically capable human being. At least, as capable as my nail girl. The jitters in my belly are pushed aside because, well, there's no time to overthink this one.

I text Jillian and then ignore her incessant calls because I have to get my things downstairs and into the truck.

I've designed many weddings before. I shouldn't be this nervous to arrive at a venue. My vendors are all confirmed and on their way. I have checked in with the bride and groom, and my assistant is on his way.

My assistant ...

I have to turn the air on in my truck.

I'm at the mansion, and I have the bins in the center of the dance floor. The florist is unloading the centerpieces, and the cleaning crew is vacuuming. The bride has checked into the adjacent hotel and is enjoying champagne while she awaits the hair and makeup team to arrive. The groom is at a nearby golf course for eighteen holes with his dad and brother. This means my countdown clock has begun.

The gold crushed linens have already been placed on the tables by the catering hall manager, so I unfold the table runners and start placing them. The tables are eight feet long, which makes it hard to get the runners flat and aligned. I'm angling my body in an awkward position, trying to straighten out one side without disturbing the other, when the runner is suddenly pulled from the other side.

I look up, and I'm done for.

Black shirt. Black dress pants. Tan skin. Killer smile.

Will's hair is still moist from his shower and combed back in an elegant way, making him look like a movie star. He's stunning—aside from the quizzical look on his brow.

"I thought you said no sweats." His eyes roam up and down my body and the black ponte pants and V-neck shirt I have on.

"These aren't sweats."

"They look like yoga pants. They're ... tight."

"I assure you, they're dress pants. Well, dressy-ish pants."

"Stretch pants."

"Dress pants."

"Leggings," he says as he walks over to where I'm standing. "Paired with sneakers. Your rules are one-sided."

I wave him off and grab the next runner from the bin. "I had a lot of things to carry in. This is a flexible yet appropriate outfit. I'll put a dress on after the setup. First, we have to do the tables because there will be mass deliveries starting in an hour, plus the ceremony room that needs to be put together, and the clock is already—"

"Melissa." His voice is gravelly as his hand sweeps hair that flew out of my ponytail and in front of my face. He tucks it behind my ear and gently rubs my earlobe. Smoldering eyes level with mine as he leans in a touch closer. "Do you have any of those sketches you showed me at your house for this event?"

I nod. His thumb is working on me like sensual Valium.

"Show me all your detailed drawings and layouts. I know you, and you are prepared for this with or without me. Since I'm here, all you need to know is, I got you."

He removes his thumb and looks down at me. I take a deep breath, rub my hands on my pants, and shake off the unnerved feelings of a few moments ago.

"Since you're here, you can help with the tables."

"Yes, ma'am." He grins, and I scowl. "What? You're my boss. Seems appropriate to use a title of respect even if she's wearing pajama pants."

Steady and on target, we get to work. The color scheme of the tables is gold, hot pink, and a deep purple. Candelabras are on each table with candles made to drip romantically from the wick. The florist starts setting two low, yet large floral arrangements beside the candelabras in the same vibrant colors as the table linens. I place moss between each element to give the tables a meadow-like feel.

When my delivery truck arrives with the twelve-foot artificial wisteria trees, Will and I quickly lift one off the truck together and place the weeping wisteria in the room. There are eight in total, which are then decorated with hanging lanterns with battery-operated candles inside.

A lighting crew has been brought in to make the room glow with lights placed on the floor, shooting upward, and a spotlight lights up the floor with the monogram to create a feeling of seduction and magic that even Shakespeare would be proud of.

When the second delivery crew comes, I help them with bringing in the giant mirror that will serve as the seating chart and

LOVE ... IT'S COMPLICATED

set up the lounge area, which has become very popular among our clients. It's a place for guests to gather with those who aren't at their table and gives a chic club vibe.

With the mirror engraved and the lounge set to perfection, I grab my stepladder and head to the atrium in the front of the mansion, where the ceremony will be held.

I stand by the door and watch as Will directs the delivery crew and catering hall staff. My iPad is in his hand, and he's referring to it with great detail. An altar is up, chairs arranged, gold podium placed, and there's even a space where the cellist will perform the wedding music. He's even gathered my bin of flameless candles and set them up and down the aisle atop garlands of wisteria.

Will looks up from where he is by the altar. His lips part as his chest rises, like he just remembered to breathe after being busy for so long. Hazel eyes glisten as he sees me walking toward him.

"Glad you're here. I tried to set up as much as I could, but unfortunately, I don't know how to make this"—he motions to the metal arch that's over the altar and down to the sketch—"into this."

With a smile, I grab the bin of tulle that is sitting by one of the chairs. "That's my specialty."

I open my stepladder and climb to the top. Will hands me a spool of tulle and a box of twinkle lights. Taking my time, I weave the soft fabric and lights onto the rod with small clips. We move around the arch, quietly synchronized. Every once in a while, I break my concentration from the fabric and look down at him. Most times, he has a look of impressed amazement on his face. Another time, I catch him looking at my ass.

Both instances make me smile.

I'm amazed at how easy it is to work with Will. He's not a bulldozer when it comes to setting things up. No task is beneath him. Even when I ask him to hand me branch after branch of wisteria, he does so without complaint.

With the mansion set up for a magical, woodsy wedding ceremony and reception, I make my way to the restroom to change into my dress. It's a simple black spaghetti strap dress that I pair with comfortable flats. I style my hair and do my makeup in a professional yet glamorous way. I want to blend in with the wedding so as not to ruin any pictures, should I accidentally get caught in one. As per the contract, I will stay until after the ceremony to ensure the reception is perfect when the bride and groom enter for their first dance. Then, I'll return at the end of the night to break down the room.

I exit the restroom, and Will is walking with one of my crates.

"Wow," he says, his hands full, yet he stops in his tracks at the sight of me. "You clean up nice."

"That expression always confuses me. Was I dirty before?"

A wicked gleam appears in his eyes. "Not touching that one. I want to make a joke, but since you're my boss, saying it out loud might get me fired."

I laugh. "Then, you'd better keep your jokes to yourself, mister." I place my bag on a crate. "I'm going upstairs to get the bridal party. Can you put the rest of the bins in the truck?"

"Yes, ma'am."

For the next hour, I walk the bride thorough the venue and show her the finished product. She gushes and almost ruins her makeup. I stand her in the lobby and bring the photographer to do a first-look session. The groom waits at the altar as the bride enters. When he turns around, his face has everyone in the room tearing up. I offer Will a tissue, which he refuses with a grunt and then takes it when he thinks I'm not looking.

While the bridal party takes pictures, Will grabs my hand and insists it's our job to make sure the photo booth is running properly by getting our pictures taken in the most ridiculous poses—me putting him in a headlock, two of us with pouty faces, and him making a muscle and me looking unimpressed.

"One nice one. For the kids," he insists.

With his hands on my waist, he takes his place behind me. I'm about to crack a joke about how we look like a prom photo gone wrong when he adjusts himself so he's holding me with both hands, pulling me close, intimate. I rest my head against his chest and become lost in the scent of him and my eyes flutter as the picture is taken.

"I blinked."

He looks at the preview screen. "You look like you're a mixture of sniffing me and falling asleep."

"Shut up, Bronson, and give me your best smolder."

I hit retake, and the picture we take is frame-worthy.

The ceremony is about to begin when I notice the bride's train is wrinkled in the back. It's not my job as a designer, but I'd be a terrible wedding specialist if I didn't fix the matter. At the same time, a waiter mentions the band has moved the cake table because it was in the way of an amplifier. Not only is the cake table part of the decor, but it's also holding a three-thousand-dollar designer cake on it.

My heart races at the two small emergencies happening.

Will places a hand on my arm. "Where's the steamer?"

"In the suitcase of tricks, but that's a menial task. Just bring the suitcase upstairs. I'll be up there in a few."

After some painful negotiations with the wedding band, I've settled the floor plan issue and rush to the bridal suite to rescue Will. To my surprise, he is on his knee, carefully steaming the bride's dress with the assistance of her bridesmaids, who hold up the fabric for him. He's telling them about how his brother-in-law spilled red wine on his sister's wedding dress.

"That wasn't even the worst part of the day. That was when the groom thought it would be funny to say *I don't* instead of saying *I do*."

"And she still married him?" one of the bridesmaids asks.

"Nine years and four kids later, and they're really happy. And he hasn't changed a bit." He grins and continues his tales as he slowly steams the dress so perfectly that you would think he worked at the dry cleaners.

The wedding is only delayed by fifteen minutes. Will and I stand in the back of the atrium as the couple exchanges their wedding vows. I take some video from my phone to post on social media. I might even get a couple of Will because, well, everyone loves some eye candy.

By the time the bride and groom have their first dance, I'm exhausted and in need of fresh air, which I find on the cobblestone path of the mansion's courtyard. The stars are luminous with the dark evening sky clear of clouds on this cool autumn night.

I run my hands over my arms and inhale the country air.

"You're cold," Will says from the doorway.

"Wasn't expecting the temperature to drop so much."

"Here," he says, taking a step toward me. He doesn't have a coat to offer. All he has are his hands, which are large, warm, and soothing as he places them on my arms, rubbing them up and down to warm me.

"Thank you."

"I'd take the shirt off my back and wrap you in it, but I don't think the wedding guests would approve."

"There might be a bridesmaid or two who wouldn't mind. I caught a few stares headed your way."

"They were looking at how freakishly strong you are." He squeezes on my bicep and feels the muscle beneath. "You put the delivery crew to shame with how easily you could shift those heavy trees around."

"Tell that to my dad. He says I'm weak."

"You are definitely not weak. I'd like to see you throw a punch."

He moves his hands to my shoulders and starts to rub. I let out a moan as his thumbs find a knot in my back and work it out.

"Keep those hands moving the way they are, and I'll save you from having to find out. Damn, do you have magic hands or what?" I drop my head forward.

I feel his chest vibrate against my back with the rumble of a groan.

"You're amazing, you know that? This night, the event, it really is something, Melissa. I knew wedding designers existed, but I didn't know it was an art. You're very talented."

I'm glad my back is to him so he can't see me blush. "That's nice to hear. Not everyone feels the same way."

"Validation should only be given by the one who is seeking it."

"Confucius says?" I bemuse.

"Will Bronson says."

"Pretty deep."

His hands continue working, this time lower down my back. "When you work in a profession that fluctuates from everyone loving you to hating you, it's important to keep your pride in check and your priorities in order."

I look over my shoulder. "The criticism and praise go hand in hand."

"Even on the days I question my decision, I just remind myself why I joined the force in the first place."

"To protect people."

"The early retirement and pension package," he deadpans, and I spin around with a quizzical, surprised look on my face. He smiles. "Yes, Melissa, I always wanted to catch the bad guys. I know you don't think I'm a good guy, but I strive to be."

I nod, knowing that as much as I question his actions when we first met, he has been pretty admirable since. "Do you ever get scared?"

"I'd be a fool if I didn't. The way I see it, we're on earth for a finite amount of time. If we give up every time something scares us or doesn't go our way, we'd miss out on a lot of opportunities. You can't get time back. You do, however, have unlimited chances."

"No one ever wants a wasted life, and yet we spend so much time-wasting hours on meaningless moments. I've spent nights agonizing over thoughts, actions, and words said that have no bearing on my tomorrow."

"The only validation that counts is your own, Melissa. Your work is an art."

With a glance through the windows into the wedding venue, I see the room ornate with trees, candles, and swoony mood lighting. "I am really good at what I do."

I grin and look up. He has a small piece of purple fuzz on his shirt. I pick it off and blow it away into the air.

"You're impressive, Bronson. Who knew you were so astute?"

A luminous smile graces his face. "I know I just said you only need validation from yourself, but hearing that coming from you just did a lot for my ego."

I laugh and shiver again. His hands find my arms again, and I look away.

The hedges and topiaries around the courtyard are perfectly manicured. They're interesting objects, so pristine. All they need to do is be left alone for a week too long, and they unravel, everyone seeing them for the unruly messes they are. Except tonight. In this moment, they are shaped to perfection, not a branch discolored or out of form.

Sometimes, I feel like a hedge. Put together on the outside, but if I neglect to care for myself, I'll unravel into an overgrown, frightened mess.

Inside, the band plays a slow song. We might be on the other side of the panes, but the hauntingly beautiful melody of a piano serenades the courtyard. The lead singer croons into the microphone as the percussions gently build.

I take a step closer to Will.

"You know, I can't explain how thankful I am for what you did today. You're always coming to my rescue."

"Not too long ago, I thought you hated me."

"I did. Mostly, I hated myself. But I don't want to be mad at you anymore. What happened between us was stupid. I shouldn't have thrown myself at you."

"Are you confessing you did indeed throw yourself at me that night at Lone Tavern?"

I lay a hand on his chest to push him away. "Enough with you and your interrogations."

I'm laughing, and then I'm not because my hand is still on his chest. His heart is beating a million miles a second against my palm. His chest, as he breathes heavily, presses against my lifeline. I feel that push down to the soles of my feet, pulsating and pounding with a fierce need.

I'm pretty sure it matches my own.

Will's hand runs down my arm, straight down to my fingertips. The soft, feathery touch sends a quiver up my body and down my front. I curl my stomach in as I look up at him. Those gorgeous hazel eyes are brooding in the moonlight. My lips part for air.

"Is it unprofessional if we share a dance out here?" His voice is a husky whisper.

"Yes," I breathe.

His hand glides along the small of my back. He takes my hand with his other as his lips bow down to my ear. "Good."

My back arches.

Our hips touch.

My insides flutter.

We dance under the moonlight. He spins me slowly, and I'm right back in his arms, smiling.

Hours ago, I would never have envisioned myself dancing in a courtyard and smiling. I was in a panic, and he came to the rescue.

He makes me laugh, and think, and grin. Above all else, I like the way he makes me feel. Even when I'm at my worst, he has this way of calming me. He's like a joint after a crazy workweek. I'm relaxed and dizzy, all at once. My problems still exist, yet they don't matter. Not in this moment. Not with this man.

I shouldn't feel this way. He was someone else's when we met. He's not mine in any way now. We're friends, but he's not really my *friend*. I have plenty of those. What exactly he is … I'm not sure. He says we're two people who came into each other's life at the right time. Maybe he's right.

LOVE ... IT'S COMPLICATED

I think I'm starting to figure that out.
The song ends, and we stop our dance. Our bodies are pressed against one another. My hands around his neck, his gripping my hips. His breathing is thick against my temple. My lips are near the base of his neck, inhaling the salt I can taste on my tongue without taking a lick. My eyes flutter up, and I know I shouldn't have done that. Will is staring down at me ... brooding down at me.

His gaze flicks to my mouth. Those hazel orbs dilate. For a man who has no interest in devouring me, his famished eyes say otherwise.

I lift my fingers and place them on his lips. They're lush, soft, and oh-so warm. I don't know what possessed me to touch him this way, but now that I am, I can't stop.

His eyes close at the touch, and he sighs against my skin.

When his lips brush against my forehead, I groan, imagining them lowering down my face and taking over my mouth.

My hand traces the granite cut of his jaw and the cleft in his chin. I trail down his throat, over his Adam's apple, and leave my hand resting on his heart that's strumming like a wild horse in the forest.

I'm startled by the thick feel of his erection, pushing against the cotton of his pants. Women are supposed to pretend they don't notice these things. Not me. Instead, I press my belly against it and let the wanton sense of Bronson intoxication wash over me.

When his eyes open again, they're savage.

His head lowers, our lips inches apart.

I grip his shirt. Firm hands caress my torso.

My breath hitches, and I run my tongue over my bottom lip. If he were to kiss me right now, I'd let him. I'd hate myself in the morning, but in this very moment, I'd shed my clothes in a courtyard and give myself to him.

And then he vibrates.

Literally, Will is vibrating.

I look down at where the vibration is coming from. It's his crotch. Well, of all the magical things, now, I know he has a vibrating crotch.

He steps back from me and takes out his phone. Kent's name is across the screen. He hits Ignore, but with his phone in his hand, he looks at the screen with more interest and starts swiping.

"I have a bunch of text messages," he says, sweeping over one in particular. "Tara's looking for you. Where's your phone?"

I swallow, confused. "It's in my bag. You brought it to the truck."

"We have to go."

"Tara's knows I'm at a wedding. What does she want?"

He puts his phone to his ear and takes my hand, pulling me rather forcefully around the building, past the service entrance and to the staff parking lot.

"Where are we going?" I ask as he weaves us toward his truck.

"The hospital."

"What? Why?"

He stops for a mere second and looks me straight in the eyes. "Hunter's been in an accident."

fifteen

THE FLICKER OF THE fluorescent light overhead is pulsating to the beat of my pacing.

Hunter. Accident. Emergency room.

Thanks to Will, we were able to get a police escort from the mansion all the way to Valor County Hospital, cutting the travel time in half. I couldn't breathe, let alone think properly, as we zoomed down the interstate, each mile marker passing at an impossibly slow speed in my mind.

Get there faster. Drive faster!

I said a few prayers to my mom. Chants to my mama for my baby. I know she's not a saint or miracle worker, but she's up there somewhere, and our boy needs angels on his side.

I call my dad. He said Maisie drove Izzy to his house, and they're having cocoa while they wait for news. Izzy won't get on the phone. Dad says she's shaken up and won't speak.

Tara was able to fill me in on the few details she knew.

Hunter was in an accident outside of Tyler's house. He was rushed to the hospital by ambulance. Tyler tried my cell, but I wasn't answering. He then called Tara, who called Kent … and now, here I am with my shaking hands in my hair, waiting for someone to let me see my son.

Will walks over to me with his phone in his hand. "I spoke to the officer on the scene. Hunter was riding an ATV on Greenwood Place when a car made an illegal turn without stopping at the stop sign. Hunter was riding in the middle of the street when the driver slammed into him. He was wearing his helmet, but he hit his head hard when he was knocked off the vehicle."

"Oh my God!" I cry out. "Was he responsive? Bleeding? Broken bones? Where was Tyler?"

"He was responsive when he got in the ambulance."

"What about when he got *out* of the ambulance?"

Will shakes his head and clenches his jaw, as that's all the information he has at the moment.

The doors to the emergency room are locked. With quick steps, I walk to the reception desk I've been to three times in the same number of minutes, slamming my palms on the counter.

"I need to see my son!"

The nurse appears not pleased to see me standing here again.

"We are at full capacity tonight, so you're gonna have to bear with me while I try to locate your son. It's possible he has been taken in for testing," a nurse tries to explain as calmly as possible from her desk in the emergency room.

"You don't lose a five-year-old in a hospital!"

The woman flinches at my curt response.

I grip the edge of the desk and lean over it. "Open that computer again. Type in Hunter Landish. Brown hair, brown eyes, A positive blood type. He was riding an ATV because his father, who is the biggest imbecile on the planet, decided to be Parent of the Year and put a five-year-old on a death trap. He could have bought the kid a cotton candy machine or a trampoline, but, no, he went for the one thing I'd said no to because instead of anyone making him the bad guy for destroying his family, he has to go over the top and do extravagant things in order to own his kids' affection. My son is back there on a gurney somewhere. Find where he is and tell me in three seconds, or I'm marching myself through those doors, and you're gonna have to carry me out if you don't like it!"

Will places a hand on my shoulder, gently pulling me back. His demeanor is far calmer than my erratic one. "Let me see what I can do."

I put my foot down hard. "I'm not leaving this spot right here."

LOVE ... IT'S COMPLICATED

He nods, running a hand down my arm and turning to the nurse. He takes his wallet out of his back pocket and shows his badge. "Bronson. Valor County Police. I understand the protocol, and you are doing a great job. Is there any way I can walk back there and see if I can get eyes on the boy?"

She looks at me out of the side of her eye and then back to Will. My foot is making a rapping sound on the linoleum floor. Will looks down at my foot and raises his brows. I stop, earning me a smirk from him as he looks back at the nurse. He's putting on a mixture of serious cop and sympathetic man.

There's a gentle nod from the nurse. "We're short-staffed and out of beds. It's all hands-on deck back there. It says here he was checked in with his father, so he's not alone. If you just give me a few minutes, I can find out where he is. As I said, he's probably been brought in for testing."

While she lifts the phone, I cross my arms and bite my nail. "I can't just stand here, Will. I need to see Hunter."

There's a scurry of people who walk into the emergency room. A group of about sixteen people come barreling in, looking in the same shape as I am—worried, exhausted, needing answers. They push their way to the desk, forcing Will to close his arms around me and pull me to the side.

The room is packed. Every seat is occupied. Many have their cell phones plugged into the wall, clearly planning on being here for a while. I look around and see people stretched out across chairs, visibly in pain, and a few sleeping on the floor, as if they don't need to check in, like they just need a place to spend the night.

"This is common for a Saturday night," Will says, walking me toward a wall near the vending machines.

The television is playing prime-time cable news. I turn my head away from it and press my forehead against the buttons on Will's black shirt.

"Come," he says, lowering his hand to my back and moving me toward the exit doors.

I step away from him, refusing to leave the building, but he places his other hand in mine and escorts me outside of the building. The cold rush of air hits me in the face. I think I'd be freezing if my adrenaline wasn't pumping quarts of hot blood through my anxious veins.

Will hooks a quick left, walking along the sidewalk until we're at the ambulance bay. Three ambulances are parked outside, all with their engines running.

A doctor is standing by the door, talking to an EMT. A patient on a gurney is nearby. Will holds up his badge even though no one seems to be paying attention, and we walk inside. He escorts me through a waiting area of sorts and down the hallway. There are beds along the walls, presumably people who aren't able to get into a room. Moans from a man have me looking over in one direction until a woman's scream has me swiveling in the opposite.

"Hunter won't be here. Pediatrics is in the back," Will explains as we make a left.

"I haven't been here in years. Not since my mom was admitted after her final collapse. She fell all the time in the end. We'd help her up, and most times, she'd make a joke about it. That last time, she couldn't get up, even with our help. That's when we knew she was nearing the end. She stayed for three days. I hate this place."

His hand squeezes mine tighter.

There's a set of double doors at the end of the hallway. One side opens, and Tyler appears with his head down, looking at his phone and cursing.

I call out his name. He looks up and stops, his shoulders dropping as he takes a step back in slow motion, appearing relieved to see me.

"I've been trying to call you, but there's no fucking reception in this place." His voice is laced with anger and annoyance. Then, he looks down at our joined hands. "Who are you?"

Will doesn't get a chance to answer because my fist rises and hits Tyler in the chest.

"You jerk! What were you thinking, letting our son ride a goddamn ATV in the dark?!"

Tyler holds his arms up but doesn't fight me off as I slam my fists into him, as if he were the punching bag at the gym. My hair is falling wildly in front of my face as I pound and pummel him in the chest and forearms. Will pulls me off Tyler and holds me back just as a nurse comes running toward us.

"Who let you back here? You have to leave this area immediately!" she announces with her arms spread out to keep Tyler and me apart. It's for naught as Will has me in a bear hug, and Tyler is standing rigid against the wall.

"Our son is getting a CT scan," Tyler explains as he rubs his chest where my knuckles just landed. He turns to me as he explains, "I was going to the waiting room to call you. You can't get a damn signal in this place."

"I told you explicitly, no ATVs, but you refused to listen, you selfish prick!"

The nurse doesn't seem to care for my outburst. "Enough of this! I'm going to call security."

"No need. He's a cop," I spew.

"You are?" Tyler asks in keen interest. "Wait, you look familiar."

I narrow my eyes at Tyler. "Who lets their five-year-old ride an ATV in the dark?"

Tyler has the nerve to curve his brows, as if remorseful. "It's not what you think. It's a little-kid one. It's not even gas-powered. It only goes five miles per hour. He was on it all day, and I ran inside for five minutes. If the idiot driver had yielded at the damn stop sign ..." Tyler's fist goes to his mouth, and his eyes, now that I'm looking at them, are red, swollen, and filled with the fear of a father who has been in the emergency room with his son. "I didn't hear the accident. I heard Izzy. She screamed so loud. I went into panic mode when I heard her. I thought she was being kidnapped. When I got outside, Izzy was at Hunter's side. She's so brave, that girl. So fucking brave. She was talking to Hunter, telling him to stay awake. I knelt beside him and went to take his helmet off, but she told me not to. Said she saw something on TV about causing more harm when you try to help."

"Smart girl," Will says.

Tyler nods. "I called the ambulance and told Maisie to bring Izzy to your dad's. I didn't ..." He pauses, his hands on his hips as he looks down at the ground. "I didn't know what was going to happen. I still don't know what is going to happen. I didn't want her here in case—"

An audible gasp escapes my lips. I cover my mouth and frown in my hands, devastated for my baby. "Is he going to be okay?"

"He was talking to me in the ambulance and when we got here, but he's a little loopy. Maybe a concussion. He might have broken his wrist."

"Broken?" Since Will won't let me hit Tyler, I use Will's arms to lift my body and start to kick my ex-husband, forcing him to move backward and Will to use his full force to hold me closer, like a bull before a rodeo.

"This behavior is uncalled for!" The nurse looks frazzled.

"If you want to stay back here, you need to relax. You have to decide what's more important—hurting Tyler or seeing Hunter." Will's words are like ice to my heated rage.

Tyler runs his hand behind his neck and looks down at his phone. There're a slew of text messages coming in now that he seems to be getting service. He ignores them.

"You can't worry like that. I've seen a lot of accidents, and if you say Hunter was talking, is still talking, that's a good sign," Will explains.

The lines on Tyler's forehead are deep as he looks up at me and Will. "Who are you again?"

The double doors at the end of the hallway open. A bed is pushed out. Lying in it is a little boy with chubby cheeks and a love of magic.

"Hunter," I cry out, forcing Will to release me and let me run to my boy.

"Mommy!" he calls out, raspy and not as boisterous as my baby boy usually is. I'm down the hallway so fast, hovering over the side and hugging my boy and showering him with kisses as best as I can.

I do a full assessment of him. All limbs are accounted for, but I'm careful not to touch him too aggressively. He's in a hospital gown. His arm is black and blue with some road rash on it. His eyes have dark circles, which I assume is from exhaustion and crying.

I start crying again. Salty tears fall down my chin. "I'm so happy you're okay. Mommy was so worried. I'm sorry I wasn't with you."

"I wanted you," he says with a whimper.

"I know, sweetie. I know you did."

"Hi, Melissa."

Behind Hunter's bed is a hospital worker. I look at him, confused how he knows me, and I'm positive the voice who said my name was female. Then, I realize the greeting came from behind the worker. There's a woman in designer jeans, a cashmere sweater, and long, flowing, perfectly blown-out hair.

I do a slow, dramatic spin toward Tyler. My chin is down as I glare at him. "Maisie's here?"

He has the nerve to look at me like I'm insane for asking. "She was with me when the accident happened. I rode the ambulance with

LOVE ... IT'S COMPLICATED

Hunter while Maisie brought Izzy to your dad's and then met us here."

I squint my eyes closed. "Let me get this straight. I had to sneak back here, but Maisie's been rolling Hunter around like a candy striper?"

A doctor in a white lab coat appears from the door Maisie, Hunter, and the worker just came out of. He has a clipboard and a smile—that is, until she sees me, Will, Tyler, Maisie, Hunter, the nurse, and hospital worker standing out here in the hallway.

"Is there an issue?" the doctor asks the two nurses.

"We're on our way to room 720," the hospital worker says.

"These five seem to be having a reunion of sorts," the nurse states, unamused.

"Why was she back there?" I'm pointing to Maisie and asking the doctor.

The doctor seems perplexed. "Parents are allowed to accompany minors in the hospital."

"She's not the mother," I deadpan.

"Who's the father?" the nurse asks, now more interested in the dynamic of our group than her need to scurry us out of here.

"I am." Tyler raises a hand.

"Who are you?" she asks Will, to which Tyler follows with an exasperated, "Yes, who the hell are you?"

"William is my friend," I explain.

Tyler takes in our all-black ensembles, me in a dress and Will in a button-down. "Were you on a date?"

"Melissa needed an assistant for a wedding tonight, so I helped out," Will answers.

"I thought you were a cop?" the nurse asks, confused.

"I am," Will says at the same time as I explain, "He is."

Maisie lifts a finger toward Will. "I remember you. You came to my salon for the hair color card. Your hair looks really nice, Melissa."

Tyler scowls. "This guy went to your salon for what?"

"A hair color card," Maisie, Will, and I say in unison.

"What the hell is that?" Tyler asks incredulously.

The nurse looks to Maisie. "If you're not the mom, then why were you with the boy?"

I raise my hands in exasperation because that's a really great question.

I'm about to go into a long soliloquy about the dynamics of our family—because that's what I'm good at—when a small voice chimes in from below us.

"That's my dad. That's my mom. This is Maisie, Dad's girlfriend, who makes really good French toast, and this is Will. He's a cop who was once shot and is helping me put on a magic show."

Well, he left out a few adjectives and angsty past-tense descriptions, but Hunter's synopsis of our crew is very accurate.

The doctor steps forward and takes center stage in our little family show. "While this visitor count is well over the hospital limit, I am happy to see Hunter is recalling his facts. The CT scan was unremarkable, which means there is no indication of a brain bleed or swelling. As for the wrist, it appears to be a hairline fracture. If you ask me, this young man has an angel over his shoulder."

For the first time in an hour, I smile.

"Now that you have good news, I am going to say this one time. Please, if you are not the biological parents of the child, you need to leave." The nurse is firm yet kind.

The doctor walks down the hallway, and Hunter groans because he wants to go home too.

Will walks over to Hunter and gives him a pound. "You gave everyone a good scare tonight. Next time, stick to the sidewalks."

Hunter looks down at his wrist in a makeshift splint. "Does this mean we can't levitate?"

Will's lip rises. "This means we can levitate even higher. You worry about getting better first, okay?" Will turns to me, his steps closing the distance, as if he doesn't want Tyler to hear what he's about to say. "I'll wait for you in the lobby."

"No. You've done so much today. You are officially off duty."

"You don't have a car, remember?"

I forgot I left it at the office and took the Lavish Events truck to the mansion with all of our things. "The wedding! I have to get back there and break everything down."

"Don't you worry about it. I have plenty of guys I can call to move everything."

"I can't—"

"I've got this," he states firmly.

I nod at his authoritative stare. It's disarming and has me looking to the side.

Tyler doesn't seem too keen on Will's take-charge attitude. The line on his forehead is deeper than the Grand Canyon.

"Every time I think I've got ahold on one aspect of my life, another implodes."

"Take care of Hunter. I'll check in on you tomorrow." Will places a soft kiss on my forehead, and it sends a calming warmth down my body.

Maisie walks over to Hunter. "I'm so happy you're okay, Hunty." Then, she places a hand on Tyler's arm. "I'll wait in the car and follow you back."

"No need," Tyler says to her. "I'm going to bring Hunter and Melissa home. I'll see you back at the house."

Maisie's eyes dart to the side. "Absolutely. Take care of your son. I'll wait up."

She leans forward and gives him a kiss on the lips. It's the first time I've seen them intimate. The other times we've been together, they've never so much as held hands in front of me.

Their action doesn't bother me like I thought it would. I'm confused by this, yet I shake it off.

"Looks like I'm going home with Tyler," I explain to Will. "I think Hunter will like having Mom and Dad dote on him a little."

The tense lift of Will's chin is pointed in Tyler's direction. "Call me if you have any problems."

I roll my eyes. "The man's harmless."

"That's true, but you're not." Will winks and then walks down the hall.

As Will and Maisie head out of the hospital, Tyler and I stand in the hallway with our son. I look down to see we each have a hand on one of his shoulders.

"Can we go home now?"

Tyler runs his hand over Hunter's head. "Yeah, let's go home."

It's two more hours until we get Hunter seen by another doctor. A pediatric orthopedist takes a look at his wrist and gives him a cast. We opted to just have it done there instead of going tomorrow. It's already late, so what's another hour?

After, the pediatrician has to review the charts and schedules a follow-up visit for Monday.

By the time we walk in the front door of my dad's house, Hunter is fast asleep, and Tyler is carrying him into the house.

As they climb the stairs, Dad is coming down.

"How's he doing?" His tone is one of a concerned grandpa and not the ornery kind he uses at this hour when he's waiting for me to come home.

"He's okay. Gave us a good scare, but he's all right."

Dad thumbs up toward the staircase. "You'd better check on your daughter. She's still up. Been worried sick about her brother. Doesn't say much, but there's a hole in her comforter the size of Montana from the threads she's been picking at it. I told her he's fine, but she wanted to wait until you got home to see for herself."

I head up the stairs and follow the soft light coming from the bottom of Isabella's doorway. I knock as I enter the room.

As soon as she sees me, she sits up. I fall to the mattress and hug my little girl.

"Hunter's in his bed. Sleeping. He has a cast on his wrist. Other than that, he's fine."

Izzy nods, and her hands release the comforter she was holding. Dad was right. She tore this thing to shreds.

"It was so scary, Mom. Hunter wasn't supposed to be in the street, but he didn't listen. I yelled at him, but he just kept on driving."

"Keeping your brother safe is your responsibility, but it's not your job. That's what Dad was supposed to do." I run a hand over her strawberry-blonde hair and relax the muscles tightening on her head. "Dad told me you were very brave."

"He did?" She seems surprised.

"Yes. Will agreed how smart you were to tend to Hunter the way you did."

Her knotted fingers relax as she takes in that information. She's only eleven, and yet her manners make her seem so much older, like she has the world on her shoulders. I want to lift that weight for her so badly. If she'd just allow it.

"He was on his way to his mother's house for Sunday dinner when she called and asked him to pick up a gallon of milk."

I pull the comforter up to her chin. "Who was, honey?"

"Will. The day he was shot."

I still. Will hasn't told me the story yet, and last time we broached the subject, Izzy didn't think it was her story to tell. Something clearly changed her mind tonight, so I listen.

"There were people in the store when he walked in. A couple standing near the register. Another two in the back. He said he knew immediately that something was off. The cashier had his hands on the counter, planted firmly and unmoving. That's when he saw the gun. It was being pointed at the couple and the cashier."

I take a deep, shaking breath. I have so many questions, but I don't ask.

"He said he didn't think; he just helped. He didn't have a gun on him, but he reacted because if he didn't, these innocent people could die. That's what I did tonight with Hunter. I just reacted. When Will told me his story, I thought, *Wow, this guy is a hero*. He put others before himself. Now, after tonight, I'm wondering if, well, maybe I'm a hero too."

"You are, my beautiful girl. You are very much a hero. Without you, who knows what could have happened to Hunter."

"Maybe I can be more. A doctor or a police officer. Someone who is there when people are hurt." Her voice is soft and pensive.

I rub my thumb along her cheek. "You'd make an amazing hero. Whatever you choose, Isabella Landish, you are destined for great things. I hope you know that."

She shrugs, and I see the side of Izzy she's been showing us for over a year now. The one who doesn't quite believe in herself. The one who doesn't believe in anyone around her.

She yawns as I kiss her head and turn off her light, then rub her back as she falls asleep. My girl is out in minutes.

I plan on sleeping in Hunter's room tonight, nervous he might be in pain in the middle of the night and to make sure he's alive since the doctors said there is a possible concussion. As I enter his room, I'm surprised to see someone else had the same plan.

Tyler is curled up in Hunter's bed. He's holding his son, his head pressed against Hunter's. The two of them are facing one another with Hunter's wrist carefully lying across his chest.

Tyler is in his clothes with his shoes kicked off on the floor. I take a throw blanket from the closet and lay it gently over the father and son. Tyler is many things I can't stand, but he's always been a good father.

sixteen

My custody agreement has been hard on my heart yet makes it easy for me to work weekends, knowing the kids are with their father. I try not to think about how Maisie is playing mommy to my kids while using my waffle iron.

The robe has since been burned on a drunken Saturday night when Tara and I decided we were the sisters from *Practical Magic* and did a ceremony of witchcraft in the backyard firepit, cursing Tyler's manhood. It ended with my father breaking the extinguisher out at one o'clock in the morning to put out the fire … and then dousing us into sobriety.

When I woke the next morning, the house smelled like wet wood, I had a printout of my mug shot we got off the Valor County Police Department website taped to the refrigerator, and I vaguely remembered Tara convincing me to respond to an email promotion about ordering new checkbooks and sending a box to Tyler's house. I'm pretty sure I ordered personalized checks for my ex featuring my face as the background.

Reminder: I need to stop spending my wallowing weekends with Tara.

I get home after a particularly long day of work, and the smell of brownies wafts through the kitchen. There's Lizzo playing from the device in the kitchen and a cake on the counter that's as lopsided as the bun on the baker's head.

I put my tote bag on the kitchen table. "I asked if you could pick up the kids from school and hang with them for a few, not open a bakery." I motion to the confections laid out on the counter—cupcakes, a cake, and a trifle.

She smooths pink icing on the tilted cake and tosses the rubber spatula in the sink. "No biggie. You know I love to bake, and it's no fun, doing it for one."

"Things not going well with Kent?" I bemuse.

"No, and I'm so damn sexually frustrated that I might explode." Her eyes widen as she practically collapses against the counter dramatically.

I laugh and lift a pink-frosted cupcake. "Baking away your feelings?"

She rolls her body along the counter and grabs a cupcake, peeling away the wrapper. "It's either that or I'm going to mount that walking sex on a stick you have in the den."

My hand flies to my chest as I look at her with a raised brow and a frown of disgust. I look toward the entrance to the den and then back at her since the only man in this house is my father. If she thought I had a problem with him dating Anna, I'd die a very early death if my best friend went to bed with my ... *dad*.

Just then, a deep, loud laugh sounds from the den. It's a laugh I've become very familiar with over the last few weeks. A laugh that rings my bell on varying days, depending on his schedule. True to his word, Will has been meeting with Hunter to work on the school talent show, which is happening this weekend.

My hand slams into my forehead. "I forgot Will was coming over tonight."

"I'm so excited I got a chance to see."

"See what? Him teaching Hunter how to levitate?"

She almost drops her cupcake as she declares, "The hot-as-heck police officer who has been arresting my friend's heart."

"All right, Miss Romance Obsessed. No one's heart is in play around here. The man has been very kind to my son, and we happen to get along well. If memory serves me, you thought he deserved to have his balls cut off not too long ago."

The oven timer goes off. Tara grabs potholders and takes out a tray of brownies and places them on the stove.

Tara might be an awesome baker, but she's made a mess of the kitchen. Dirty bowls and spoons create a mound in the kitchen sink.

LOVE ... IT'S COMPLICATED

The countertops are full of crumbs, egg and milk splatter, and open ingredient packages.

"Brownies!" Hunter flies into the kitchen with his Avengers cape flowing horizontally and his casted arm in the air.

I scoop him up before he's able to get the brownies and place a ton of kisses on his neck, making him giggle.

"Brownies?" I say between kisses. "I think you meant, *Mommy, you're home! I love you and missed you. I haven't seen you all day!*"

He laughs as my hands tickle his sides. "I love brownies!"

"And I love you!" I put him down on the ground and then playfully spank his butt as he rushes over to Tara to be served a brownie. "Wait. You haven't eaten dinner yet. Daddy's gonna be here soon to pick you up."

His eyes light up. "Oh yeah. He's making macaroni and cheese tonight. It's so good. He uses three cheeses now and puts bacon on the top! It's my most favorite food in the whole wide world."

Tara cuts a hearty slice and hands him a plate. "Have a brownie, kid. If Dad says anything, let him know Aunt Tara spoiled your dinner."

I raise my brows at her, but there's no need to scold an adult. Besides, it's better when she misbehaves around the kids. I have to stand my ground and show a good example.

"Hunter said there's brownies?" Will walks into the kitchen.

Sliding my hands in the back pockets of my jeans, I puff out my chest. "Tara made enough confections for an army. Help yourself."

"I'm a sucker for a cupcake."

Tara's eyes roam over his torso, which happens to be clad in a tight-fitting long-sleeved shirt. "I bet you are."

I hip-check her while offering a napkin to wipe the proverbial drool from her mouth.

Will takes a cupcake out of the tin and peels back the wrapper. He leans against the counter and savors his delicacy while I savor him. His Adam's apple bobs in a masculine tease. Really, he makes eating a cupcake a freaking art, including a slow licking of his lips, followed by the sucking of a fingertip. It's the sweetest gesture a middle finger ever did make.

I grab a napkin for myself as well.

Hunter cleans the gooey chocolate on his mouth with his forearm. "Aunt Tara is a great baker. She bakes when she has boy trouble."

Will nearly chokes on his cake. "Problems with Kent?"

"He hasn't tasted my cupcakes yet."

This time, Will does choke. He is in a coughing fit that has Tara pounding on his back with an eye roll as he regains his composure. She might even leave a lingering hand on his back to assess the physique.

She looks at me and mouths, *Wow*.

Hunter looks up at Tara. "You made a lot of cupcakes. You should take him a tray. You know, the boy who won't eat your cupcakes. I bet if you made him try one, he'd love it."

I laugh out loud and then pull my cute kid to me and kiss him on the head. "Go upstairs and clean up and tell Izzy to come down and talk to me before Dad picks you up for the weekend."

I ruffle his hair before he runs upstairs, singing at the top of his lungs.

Tara places her hands on her hips and gives Will an intense staredown. "I'm not one for spilling the tea, but I'm getting a little confused. Your boy acts like he's very interested. Calls every night. Sends sweet texts during the day. We've been on a bunch of dates. But he's slow to—"

"PG, please. Kids are in the house," I remind as I grab a spray bottle and clean the counters.

She quirks a brow. "Put the beater in the bowl, if you know what I mean?"

Will glances at me, and I shrug.

He wipes his hands on a napkin and tosses it in the open trash can. "Well, Kent is a gentleman. I'd guess, if he's taking his time, it's because he really likes you."

"Sounds like you're trying to spare my feelings," she says.

He crosses his arms and looks down at his sock-clad feet on the polished floor. "When a man is really interested in a woman, he doesn't want to fuck it up, so he takes it slow."

"I get slow, but maybe he could take a nibble. That wouldn't be so bad," she suggests.

"Not all men are purely out for … cake. Going slow sets the pace for intimacy and connection."

"Damn, you are smooth," she muses. "Do you mean to tell me you could spend evenings with a woman you're attracted to and who … baked all day for you—and I'm not talking a store-bought mix; I'm talking beautiful, made-from-scratch cupcakes with cherries on top—put it all on a serving platter, and you wouldn't take a bite?"

Will's eyes glance in my direction. A wave of nervous energy zings through my body. I move to the sink and start cleaning the dishes.

He lifts his chin. "I could wait forever if that meant I still got to hang out with her in the kitchen. Plus, when I finally do get to savor it, I bet it'd be the best damn meal I'd ever have in my entire life."

My insides growl.

I suddenly feel famished.

"The only way you'll know is if you just ask him," Will states.

She throws her hands up in the air. "Aren't you his friend? Can't you just tell me what he talks about?"

"This isn't high school. Men, at least my friends and me, don't sit around and talk about our relationships. If we did, I probably wouldn't have been in one I didn't belong in for so long. I'm meeting Kent for a drink later. Why don't you join us?"

I glance over my shoulder. "Don't you work tonight?"

Tara gives me a stare like it's amusing to her that I know Will's schedule. I don't know a ton about Will, but over the past three weeks since Hunter's accident, he's been over as many times to work on the show and stays for a while to chat.

As per Dad's suggestion, I haven't asked Will to stay for dinner again. It's intense enough, having him work with Hunter. I don't want to have them build this incredible bond, and then the man ghosts him after the talent show and breaks his heart.

Right now, I see him like a teacher. All kids have teachers they connect with, and that ends after the class. This is magic class, plus some conversation at the end with Mom. After the show, Will won't have a reason to be around anymore.

"I worked last weekend for a friend who needed the night off, so we traded. Plus, it'll be nice to be in bed before midnight. I'm gonna be in a big show tomorrow."

"It's sweet that he's taking this show so seriously," Tara quips.

I smile. "A huge part of me questions whether he actually wants to do this or feels roped into it because of a cute kid in a wrist cast."

Will ignores us and continues, "Come to Lone Tavern. I know, I know, Melissa, it's not your favorite bar, but I promise you, they have amazing burgers, the beer's always cold, and the music is really good. I even have it on good authority that they now serve Whispering Angel Rosé."

"How do you know that?" I place a clean pan on the counter.

"Because I asked them to," he says with a smile as he pushes off the counter. "Come out and listen to some music with me."

Music.

I remember that music and the strong hand around my neck as he dipped me in the sexiest reverse choke hold ever. I shake my head because there is no way I can go to that bar with this man. It will lead to dancing, and so far, I am two for two in dancing experiences with Will that have led to me losing all control over my thoughts and body. I become possessed by the Will voodoo. It's been weeks since he's unleashed that damn smolder, and I'm very happy, staying doused from the flames that are William Bronson.

Before I can answer, Tara is jumping up and down. "Lone Tavern. I love that place."

"You're not concerned about crashing his boys' night? Maybe even appearing a bit desperate?" I ask.

Will scoffs. "You're a terrible fairy god-homie."

"What's that?" Tara asks, and I laugh with a bashful smile that he remembered our banter from that first night at Lone Tavern.

Will motions toward Tara's phone. "Text Kent and ask him if he wants to go to Lone. I bet a stiff drink that he responds in thirty seconds with a yes."

While Tara does as Will suggested, he moves to the sink and takes one of the dishes I just washed from my hand, grabs a towel, and starts to dry it. His hip presses up against mine, and the hair on his arm tickles my skin. I drop the bowl I was cleaning and have to bury my hand into the soapy water, looking for the bowl … and my composure.

Maybe I should start baking with Tara.

Her phone pings, and she lets out a guffaw. "Looks like I owe you a stiff drink, Officer Bronson."

"I like my whiskey neat."

She laughs and points a finger at him. "I like you. You're certainly proving your worth."

Will pauses mid-dry and tilts his head. "Thank you?"

Lifting her purse from the stool on the island, Tara swings around and then blows me a kiss. "Okay. I'm going home to get ready for our double date. Melissa, I'll be by at nine to pick you up."

I blink up at her, but she's out of the kitchen, chanting good-byes to my kids before she's out the door like a tornado of black-haired, blue-eyed energy.

"Did she just say double date?"

Will takes the cup out of my hands—hands that seem to have frozen in place.

"She did say double."

The room is suddenly very, very quiet... aside from Lizzo singing about getting ready for love in the background.

"A double date implies it's a date. But it's not a date."

He purses his lips with a slow, knowing nod. "It's not a date, but it's a double."

I look up at him in question. "What does that mean?"

With the dishes now cleaned, he turns the faucet off, dries his hands on a towel, and tosses it on the counter. "Guess we'll see."

He winks and walks out of the room, taking my nerves with him.

"Hey, Mom. Hunter said you wanted to see me." Izzy walks past Will, high-fives him in the doorway, and comes into the room.

I take my internal question and shelve it for later. First, I have to be a mom.

But, seriously, *what's a double?*

seventeen

"WHISKEY. NEAT," WILL SAYS as he places a bottle of Old Grand-Dad Bourbon Whiskey on the table.

"She bought you a bottle?" I muse from my seat in the far corner of the bar.

"Tara paid for my drink, and then I bought this from the bar."

"Bottles are crazy overpriced when you buy them at restaurants and bars. I know cops are paid handsomely, but you seem to live a lavish lifestyle. My expensive haircut and now a bottle of whiskey you probably paid ten times the normal amount for. I'm sure you have bills. A car. A mortgage. Do you have a mortgage? That's a bit presumptuous of me to ask. Forget that question."

Will chuckles as he opens the bottle. "We've spent how many evenings together, talking about bullshit in your kitchen, and tonight, you're nervous?"

"Three evenings, to be exact, and I'm not nervous. Why would you say that?" I ask like this is a ridiculous notion.

He pours whiskey into the two lowball glasses he walked over from the bar. It's not a lot. The liquid fills maybe an inch.

"You ramble when you're nervous. I've always found it cute as hell. And, yes, I have a mortgage."

"My rambling is not cute. And I don't ramble. I overspeak. There's a difference. And I'm not nervous. What's there to be nervous about? Tara and Kent have been glued to one another since we got here, and you and I are just hanging out, enjoying some whiskey and conversation, like we have many times already, whether it be in my home, a venue—"

"A jail cell." Will slides my glass over to me, and I take a look at the amber liquid with a scowl.

"You don't have to drink it," he says. "I told you I'd get you a rosé."

I wave a hand in the air. "No, no. I want to try whiskey, so I'm gonna give it a whirl and put some hair on my chest."

His gives a devilish smirk as he leans back in his seat, graceful yet masculine.

"Cheers," he says as he raises his glass to his lips.

I lift mine in the air and take a sip. It's smoky, malty, and bitter compared to my sweet wine preference.

I must be making a face because he asks, "No good?"

"I'm okay. I think it's one of those drinks I need to settle into after a few sips."

For the next hour, I drink slowly while Will and I talk about our week. It's ridiculous he thought I was nervous around him when we've fallen into a comfortable relationship. I love hearing his work stories. Many of them have me laughing, to the point I want to cry. Even the horrible nights and dangerous situations, he seems to find a way to lighten them into a story.

In turn, I always have something to tell him about an erratic bride, another wedding shenanigan, or a story about the kids. No matter what I say, he always seems interested, like the tale I'm telling him is what he's waited all week to hear.

There's a lull in our conversation, so I take a look around the room for Tara and Kent. They're currently on the dance floor, getting their country on. I know for a fact that Tara hates country music, so she must really like Kent if she's out there, learning a line dance, which looks like a honky-tonk version of the Electric Slide.

"She's in a fit of giggles out there, so there must be something going right," I say, motioning toward our friends. "I hope Kent turns out be a winner. Despite her bravado, Tara is sensitive. She's also incredibly resilient."

"I can tell there's a story."

"She was left at the altar."

Will's eyes widen. "You mean, literally at the altar or before the date was even set, like …" His voice trails off.

"She was in a white dress and having her pictures taken when the groom called and apologized because he got cold feet."

"That's horrible."

"It was. First, she bawled her eyes out. Next, she got angry. Like *champagne flute breaking* angry. Made a few rage-filled phone calls and was moments away from purchasing a billboard along the highway to display her ex-fiancé's face and the words *lying scumbag coward*.

"Then … something happened. She did the most peculiar thing. She had her brother walk down to the ceremony and let everyone know that while the wedding was called off, the party was still on. It was like a switch had gone off in her mind. From distraught to delirious. According to Tara, why waste a seventy-thousand-dollar wedding on an asshole who didn't even have the decency to call off their happily ever after in person?

"So … we partied. Well, most of us. The groom's immediate family knew better than to stay. She got rip-roaring drunk, danced in her dream wedding gown, and had a blast until we dragged her drunk ass home at two in the morning. She's been searching for that new Mr. Right ever since."

"I have a newfound respect for your friend. Which means I'm gonna get mine to make sure he treats her well. Kent's different. He's shy, which is why he turned to online dating. Helps to fast-forward past the awkward pickup line in a bar."

He lifts the bottle, asking if I'd like a refill. I tap my glass as a yes.

"You've been friends long?"

"I met Kent when I joined the Valor Country Police Department. He trained me. How about you and Tara?"

"We met in middle school. She heard a rumor about me and decided, instead of spreading it, she was going to ask me if it was true. It wasn't, and that simple question was the start of a lifelong friendship."

"What was the rumor?"

"That I wore boys' underwear to school. It was started by Amanda Presley."

"And how did you get back at Amanda Presley?"

I feign insult. "What makes you think we—fine, we glued three pairs of my dad's boxers to her locker. It was harmless."

He laughs and takes a drink. Moisture on his bottom lip glistens under the lights. I look back at the dance floor.

The music changes to a slower tune. Couples find one another in a scene reminiscent of the first time Will and I were here. My fingers swipe the tender skin of my neck, and my skin burns beneath.

"Want to dance?"

I look at him and give an abrupt, "No."

He mouths the word *no* and nods his head with a furrowed brow. He leans forward with his elbows the table. "Then, let's play a game."

"Drinking games and I don't go well together."

"Good thing you're with the man who has the key to the cell." He holds his glass to his mouth as he smiles.

"Funny."

"Not a drinking game. Just a game. An eye for an eye. I tell you one detail about my life; you give me one of yours."

"This is fun?"

"For me, yes." He winks with his arms folded on the table, leaning and giving me his complete attention. His mannerisms are so charming; they're like a suction cup to my heart, pulling me across the table and into his lap—metaphorically, of course.

"Fine then. I'll go first," I state, to which he agrees. "What's the situation with Allison? Is your family still not talking to you?"

A sigh falls from his lips. "It's getting better. My mom invited me back to Sunday dinner. My family tried talking me into calling the wedding back on, but I made my decision, and they're starting to respect that. I have five siblings, four of whom are married and gave my parents eleven grandchildren. They won't rest until they know I'm happily married and have a kid on the way. It's how they measure success. That's not a bad thing, but they have to realize I might not be marriage material. For thirty years, I have done everything by the book. I'm a good son, a great brother, and the best damn uncle on the planet. And if being those three things is enough for me for now, then it has to be enough for them."

I nod. "Your friends?"

He sways his head, like this isn't as easy as the situation with his family. "The good ones, like Kent and Genevieve, they're solid. Everyone else ... I think when Allison meets the right man and has a family, they'll see how it all worked out for the best. I'm just going to have to wait for time to heal this one."

LOVE ... IT'S COMPLICATED

"When Tyler and I split, we each lost friends. As for time showing me everything will work out for the best, I think I'm starting to see that."

"We just need to wait and let fate do her thing." He clicks glasses with me, and we take a sip. "My turn."

"Nope. You didn't finish answering my question. Allison."

He lowers his chin and looks up at me. "You really want to talk about this?"

"Yep."

With his glass set on the table, he spins it around slowly as he speaks. "She went from calling every day, to which I picked up and talked as long as she wanted and answered all of her questions. Her calls stopped two weeks ago."

"Do you miss her?"

"No," he answers easily and then seems upset by that. "Do you miss Tyler?"

"That's a loaded question."

His eyes are set on the glass spinning in his hands. He stops, gives a slow nod, and then lifts the glass, finishing his drink. "Well then, let's get drunk."

Will pours us each another glass. I'm happy he's keeping the pours incredibly short, but I'm also aware I'm on my third drink of the night.

"What is one of the weirdest things you did as a teenager?" I ask.

"Dyed my hair blond to look like Justin Bieber to impress a girl." He speaks louder over the music that has picked up tempo from the ballad that was playing before. It's now his turn to ask a question. "What did you love about growing up in Newbury?"

"The arcade on Main Street. I still have the high score in the Terminator game."

"You're MJ? I've been trying to beat that score with my nephew!"

"Not as a dangerous with a gun as you thought." We clink glasses. "Last show you binge-watched?"

"*The Watcher*. You?"

"*Yellowstone*."

"Into cowboys?" he asks with a devilish grin.

"Who isn't?"

"Good to know."

He winks, and I gulp. Winky Will is cute. It's second to smoldering Will.

"If there were an Olympic sport for everyday activities, what would you win a gold medal for? You can't say wedding designing or being a mom."

"Crafting. Where is your perfect vacation?"

"Fly fishing in Smith River in Montana."

"You? Fly fishing?" My cheek falls to my hand as I gaze at him in interest. "You learn something new every day. Have you been to Smith River before?"

"Once, with my brother Jack. It's the prettiest freestone river in the west. It's so popular that you have to win a lottery to fish in it. Seriously. Thousands of people apply for a permit, and we won. We went trout fishing between the canyons. It was fun and quiet. Just you and the majesty of the mountains, your thoughts free as you listen to the birds and the wind whistling over the river. At night, we ate our catch, and it was the best damn trout I've ever had my life."

"Sounds perfect."

"Nearly perfect. If I go back, you should come."

I nearly spit out my whiskey. "Me and fly fishing? I'd talk so much that I'd scare the fish away."

"What vacation do you want?"

"Spa retreat. Tara and Jillian treated me to one this summer, and it was heaven."

"Maybe you could have a spa day while I fished, and we'd meet back at the cabin."

I lift my glass in an air cheers. "Now, that, my friend, is something I can agree to. Okay, my turn." I lean into the table, my thoughts pensive. "Are you really good at magic, or are you pretending?"

"You'll find out soon." Those words are spoken so nonchalantly, and yet there's a gleam in his eyes, a teasing glint that makes me feel like there's more to that comment—words laced like they have so much promise. So much desire.

Will must sense the flush I'm feeling beneath my skin because his eyes narrow. He's already leaning forward, but a small motion makes it feel like he's closed the space exponentially.

He places his hand near mine. Our fingers brush, and it's like this heated force field being shot from the smallest part of his body into mine. I don't move my hand. If I do, I might do something rash,

LOVE ... IT'S COMPLICATED

like run my fingers over his lips—those soft lips, which are so pouty and lush. I want to kiss him. I always want to kiss him.

"What's the best thing that's happened to you this month?" I ask him out of turn.

"You." His answer is quick, and I nearly forget to swallow my drink. My heart speeds up, and I nearly don't hear his next question. "Why won't you dance with me?"

"It's dangerous."

"Is being with me such a bad thing?" he asks with his hazel eyes smoldering. It's the gaze of an incredibly sexy villain of a man.

"For me, yeah," I state honestly. "Besides, I'm not your type, remember?"

"You're not."

Will moves his hand closer to mine. I'm startled by it and look up. His eyes are like a wildfire in the western forests, tearing down everything in its path as it scorches earth.

"No. You're not my type. Unpredictable is an understatement," he says. "You're loud, a wild card. You overthink and pace ... a lot. Your sarcasm is your only defense, and you only let your guard down when you're with your friends or your kids. There's a good chance you're already stringing together every word I'm saying and getting ready to question me, as if I have an ulterior motive. And you'll never trust another man again."

"Well, you're not incorrect ..."

"You're insecure, which is crazy because you're this successful, talented, amazing mother who is quite possibly the most beautiful woman I have ever seen in my entire life. You're also the funniest woman I've ever met. You have this quirkiness I'm drawn to, but not as much as I am to your mouth. I want to kiss you like a dying man in the desert needs a drink."

His eyes are scorched with an anger I've never seen from him before. It's a determined anger. A lustful anger.

I bite my lip and let him continue.

"When you kissed me in the parking lot, I did kiss you back. I'd have been a fool not to. That kiss was ... fuck, I stay up at night, thinking about what it would be like to put my mouth on yours again. To put my mouth ..." His voice trails off, as do my thoughts.

I have no doubt this man's mouth all over my body would be the ultimate undoing.

"I won't try to kiss you though," he says. "That's your call. While I know what I so desperately want, I also know what I need. Right now, I'm content with having you in my life just as we are."

I fight the urge to kiss him and punch him in the face. "Goddamn it, Bronson. You're not supposed to say things like that."

"This is my truth. I won't ever lie to you."

"I've heard that before."

"Not from me."

My breath is shaky as it escapes my lips. It's his conviction. The fact that he says what he feels and with this earnest quality that makes you believe he'd die before breaking your trust.

I turn back to the dance floor. Kent and Tara are making out like teenagers at a rave. The sexual explosion happening on the dance floor matches the tension being felt at the back corner table.

I let out a small laugh. "I think our friends are safely headed to the bedroom."

"Mission accomplished then."

My sarcastic laugh is followed by my quick finish of my drink. It was hard to swallow earlier, but now, it goes down like water. This is what happens when you adapt. You numb yourself to bitterness.

"Melissa." His voice is mellow and somewhat melancholy, calling my attention.

I shake my head and look down at the whiskey glass in front of me. It's nearly empty because, despite my initial protests, I keep coming back for a sip of the drink I never thought I'd like.

He twists the cap back onto the bottle. "If you plan on driving Tara's car home, we should slow down."

He's right. We should slow down. And not just because Tara is probably going home with Kent, but also because the more alone time I spend with Will, the deeper I fall. My parachute tore long ago. There's only a hard landing in this girl's future.

"Will, I'm sorry. It's just—"

"I know, Melissa. Trust me, I know."

eighteen

"MOM, OVER HERE!" IZZY calls me over to the sixteenth row of Newbury Elementary's auditorium. She has her ticket in hand, waving it in the air, near her seat at her brother's talent show performance.

I look behind me to make sure Dad hasn't gotten lost in the crowd.

"Everyone's acting like we're going to a Broadway performance, not a damn talent show." He moves his shoulder out of the way of an obscenely large bouquet a parent has brought.

"Should I have brought him flowers?"

He snickers. "We gave him something better."

Dad is beyond clever with his gift to Hunter. He made him a wooden magic wand, sanded and polished in a crisp black to look professional on tonight's stage. It's longer than the kid ones you find in stores.

"Best grandpa ever," I quip, to which Dad nods in modest agreement as we reach our row.

"Melissa. Gavin," Tyler stands and greets us. Maisie follows suit. They're wearing coordinating camel-colored outfits. So trendy. So bland.

We exchange polite handshakes. Well, I do. Dad just stands there and stretches out his neck.

In order for Izzy and me to get to our seats, Tyler and Maisie have to push back into their seats to make way for us. This is always so uncomfortable. If I walk in with my front to them, our faces will be uncomfortably close. If I give them my back, I'll be rubbing my ass into them. I choose the ass side and suck my stomach in to be as far away from touching them as possible.

I make Izzy change seats with me so she's next to her father. As we do so, I see Dad is still standing in the aisle with his hands in front, not saying a word. Tyler and Maisie are still standing as well, pressed awkwardly against their seats. Maisie takes the hint first and moves out of the aisle. Tyler looks like a boy being scolded as he, too, moves out of the aisle and makes room for my father to walk in. Izzy and I go to exit as well, but Dad tells us to stay and does the shimmy-in-front method to get to the seat next to me.

"Mom, can I get popcorn for the show?" Izzy asks as a kid comes down the aisle, selling Ziplock bags of treats.

I'm about to take out money for her, but Tyler is already calling over the kid and handing over a ten-dollar bill for five bags of popcorn.

I take the bags from Tyler, one of which I keep on my lap. I know there is no way Dad will accept anything from him.

"Izzy, did you see who's in the row three rows in front of us?" Maisie asks in a hushed tone, and Izzy looks at me.

"Maisie asked you a question," I tell her, assuming she didn't hear.

"Oh." Izzy looks down at her popcorn and plays with a kernel until it smashes in her fingers. "Yeah."

I look around a few rows in front of us and don't see anyone we know. "Who's here, sweetie?"

"No one."

Tyler laughs. "That's right. My daughter is too young to have a crush. You have to wait until you're sixteen."

This makes me laugh. "We were dating at fifteen, Tyler."

"Exactly," he and Dad both bemoan the same time.

I cross my legs and lean into Izzy. "Hey. You have a crush?"

She slinks down in her seat and hides under her sweater, like a turtle afraid to come out of its shell. "Mom! God. You're all so embarrassing. No … I don't like anyone. Dad and Maisie were just asking me questions at dinner, and they read into it. That's all."

LOVE ... IT'S COMPLICATED

Tyler doesn't seem fazed by Izzy's comments. Maisie, on the other hand, drops her posture in defeat. *I wonder how much Maisie and Izzy really do talk.*

The show begins, and we sit through the standard elementary school show openings of the pledge, a song, and then a long speech by the principal, followed by the head of the arts department. It's thirty minutes before the show actually starts.

Four "bands" and three dancers perform before it's Hunter's turn. Dad shifts in his seat, anxious to see his grandson. Tyler, Maisie, and I are amused by the kids.

Even Izzy looks at me a few times and says, "They're not bad," or, "That kid was really good."

"Thank you, Erol and the Bandits, for that awesome rendition of 'Thunder'! Now, for our next performance, we have a magical treat for you. Kindergartener Hunter Landish and his partner, Officer William Bronson of the Valor County Police Department, will perform a magical levitation!"

We clap as the head of the arts department heads offstage and wait a few moments before the curtain opens. From what I understand, their magic show comes with props that Will was bringing from his house. I've seen some of them over the past few weeks, but I have yet to see the performance. Hunter was adamant it remain a surprise and would only let Izzy be their practice audience.

"The cop is going onstage with him? I thought they were just practicing together?" Tyler looks at the program booklet, confused.

Izzy explains, "Hunter needs a lot of help, especially with his cast on. Will's got him covered though."

Will walks out onstage, and butterflies take over my chest. He's wearing a tuxedo and a top hat, carrying a small speaker and placing it onstage. He hits a button on his phone, and theatrical music plays.

"Welcome, everyone. My name is Officer William Bronson, and it is my honor to introduce you to the great Huntino!"

Smoke pours from a fog machine I didn't realize was onstage, filling up most of the space. Hunter appears out of the fog with his hands up in the air theatrically.

The audience cheers at the handsomest five-year-old in a tuxedo with tails and a top hat, holding a magic wand.

"Thank you, and welcome to the Great Levitation. For my first trick, I will make this card float in the air." He holds up a playing card and shows the audience.

He makes a great show of proving to the audience that the card is ordinary. Before he starts, he turns around and shows Will the card. Will fiddles with Hunter's hands for a minute while the music plays. When Hunter is ready, he turns around and magically makes the card float in the air between his hands.

It's visually quite impressive, although I'm pretty sure he has an invisible string or something to make that happen. Still, the crowd cheers and whistles, making Hunter smile.

"For my next trick, I will levitate off the ground, standing up."

Will takes out a small blanket and hands it to Hunter, covering the front of his body with the blanket. Hunter looks down and gets himself in place. When he's ready, he lifts the blanket off the floor, and when he does, his feet rise with the blanket, and Hunter appears to be levitating.

The cheering starts again but milder this time. Clearly, this crowd needs to be wowed in order to form a commotion.

When that trick is done, Will places the sheet back while Hunter addresses the crowd. "And now, for my most dangerous trick, I will levitate while lying down!"

Will changes the music to one of intensity. The fog machine goes on again, and Hunter walks to center stage. When the fog has subsided, Will is behind him. The two start their trick with hoops in their hands. They're painted gold—something they asked me to do last week. They choreographed a short dance and make some cheesy poses for the crowd as they prove their hoops are solid. It's like a vaudeville act with the two tuxedo-clad gents acting goofy and showing off for the audience. This routine earns a big applause—most, I presume, is from the women. If you didn't know better, you'd think the duo were father and son.

Tyler shifts, uncomfortable in his seat, with a clenched jaw.

"Now, for the big trick!" Izzy grips the edge of her seat.

Hunter says some magic words and suddenly falls over Will's arm until he's horizontal in both of Will's hands. Slowly, Hunter starts to rise, and Will's hands slowly move away from him. In a fascinating feat in magic, Hunter is floating midair, eyes closed and stiff as a board. Will takes his hand and moves it under Hunter to prove there are no strings. He then takes the hoops and waves them over and around Hunter's body to show Hunter is levitating with magic.

The crowd goes wild.

People stand and cheer. Whistles and calls of amazement come from the parents and kids alike. It's an amazing trick, and I can't for the life of me figure out how they pulled it off.

I look over at Izzy in question.

She lifts a shoulder. "I'll never tell."

I smile and then look at Dad. He's a hard one to impress, and in this moment, I can see he's both mesmerized by Hunter and proud of his grandson.

Will lowers Hunter just as slowly as he raised him. Hunter falls back into Will's arms, and he stands Hunter right side up. When he's done, he takes a bow.

I'm out of my seat and clapping like a maniac. Hunter is the happiest I've ever seen him. As he takes a bow, Will is by his side, arms urging the crowd to cheer on the kid magician.

While I'm ecstatic for my son, I find myself enthralled by the man beside him.

Will. This wonderful, caring, man. He spent weeks, dedicating his time to a boy he just met and helping him put on this incredible performance. Hunter's own father wouldn't give his passion for magic the time of day, but Will came to the rescue tenfold.

The show ends shortly after. Tyler and Maisie are out and down the aisle before anyone else. By the time Dad, Izzy, and I get to the parent pickup area, they are already hugging Hunter and showering him with congratulations.

"My man!" Tyler lifts Hunter in the air, his hat falling off his head. "You were awesome!"

"I was!" Hunter beams and hugs his dad so tight that Tyler's face reddens from the lack of blood flow. "Will taught me everything! He's my best friend."

Tyler slowly pulls away. "Bud, he's a grown man who helped you with magic. He's not your best friend."

"Pretty close. We bond. Like men do."

Hunter is finishing that sentence as Will rounds the corner from backstage, wheeling a crate with the equipment they used in their performance. He's still dressed to the nines, except the top button of his shirt and his tie are undone, hanging loosely around his neck. Maisie does a double take when she sees him, probably because he looks absolutely delectable. I blame the tie. It's giving him a total swoony effect.

I shoot my invisible daggers at her up-and-down of Will. *Down, girl. You can't have this one too.*

Izzy gives Will a high-five. "You guys were awesome. It was even better than your practice."

Will, as modest as ever, gives a curt smile and thanks Izzy. "We couldn't have done it without your pointers."

"I'm not impressed by much, but for the life of me, I can't figure out how you got that kid in the air. I'm gonna start looking up how to do that," Dad states.

Will takes my dad's offered handshake and accepts his accolades as well. "Maybe I'll show you how to get Melissa up in the air. You can wow your buddies over at the diner."

"Good luck getting Melissa to do a trick like that. She's afraid of heights," Tyler adds with a sarcastic gleam.

"I think I can manage being five feet off the ground. I can fly in a plane; I can handle a small levitation," I quip.

"Yeah, right. Remember that tree house in your neighbor's backyard, the one we used to sneak into when we were teenagers and make out? I could get you up, but you would cry the whole way down."

Tyler thinks his story is amusing when, in actuality, it's awkward. Bringing up teenage rendezvous in front of the kids, my dad, even his new girlfriend leaves an uncomfortable sting in the air. It's like if you move, you'll combust, so we just stand still and look around, hoping for someone to say something more prolific.

"Hunter, I had an awesome time working with you. Thank you for letting me be part of your show," Will says kindly to my son.

Hunter moves away from Tyler and wraps his arms around Will.

"You're the best, Will. When I grow up, I want to be just like you."

The words are like a tug to my already-bursting heart after what the two of them did tonight. Will kneels down and hugs Hunter—really hugs him. It's tense and frightening. All that fear I had of Hunter growing close to Will has just come to the forefront of my brain. They've bonded, and there's no going back without heartache.

"What's a grown man doing, spending so much time with a kid?"

"Tyler," I admonish him as Maisie nudges him in the arm for his rudeness.

LOVE ... IT'S COMPLICATED

"What? No one's going to question why this guy put on a penguin suit and dedicated his time to putting on a magic show with a little kid he doesn't know? Unless he's working his magic in other ways," Tyler continues, but Maisie steps in front of him and takes Hunter's hand.

I jut my face out at Tyler and give him the mom eyes even though he's not my child. "Don't be crude, Tyler."

"Don't be so gullible, Lyss."

"Come on, kids. Let's go take a walk." Maisie places a hand on Izzy's shoulder and guides the kids away from us.

For the first time in two years, I'm grateful for her presence.

Will elongates his six-foot-two frame and looks down at Tyler. "What do you mean by that?"

"I don't like you being alone with my son." Tyler squares his blazer-clad shoulders, trying to make himself appear as large, if not as tall, as Will.

"What's your reason?" Will asks coolly.

"Your relationship isn't normal. What do you do when you're together? Because if you're not sleeping with his mother than you have some other motive in mind."

With a fierce step, Will gets closer to Tyler in a challenging manner. "Watch your mouth."

I look around at the lobby filled with parents hugging children and handing over bouquets of flowers. Luckily, no one can see the pissing match of testosterone taking place right now.

Tyler lifts an accusatory finger. "You have a problem with me protecting my son?"

"No. It's the only intelligent thing I've heard you say. My problem is with the way you talk about Melissa."

"You don't know the history we have, so why don't you mind your business and let me talk to my wife?" Tyler goes to move around Will, but the officer blocks him with his body, looking down with a steel-cut gaze that causes me to gasp at its severity.

"She's not yours."

Tyler blinks a few times, as if realizing what he said. *Wife.* The rapid spin of his body, presumably to look for Maisie, is followed by a quick sigh-like curse from his lips.

Despite his cool composure, Will's fist curls at his side. I place my hand over his to relax him. Tyler's eyes follow the motion. This pissed off yet slightly defeated quality he bears right now is unnerving.

"Before I let anyone around my kids, I want to know everything about them. Maybe I should take you back to court and—"

"That's enough, Tyler." Dad takes purposeful steps forward, forcing Will and me to take a step back. "If you're saying my daughter is mishandling Hunter's safety, then you're saying the same for me. I'm home when they do their magic. It's odd at best, sure, but William's devoted a good amount of his free time to make sure your son did the show he wanted. Yes, he's your son, which is why, since you weren't the first one to do this nonsense with him, you should be thanking the man for stepping in. I dressed up as goddamn Colonel Sanders for Halloween one year because this one wanted to be a chicken."

My head nods at the memory. "This is true. I was an adorable chicken."

"Before you question what goes on in my house, I want you to think about what goes on in yours. Last I heard, you had my grandson in the hospital with his head in a halo and his wrist in a cast." Despite the rise in his voice, his stature remains steady.

Dad puts his hand on Tyler's shoulder and levels his eyes with him. With a softer tone, Dad gives one final warning. "Walk away. You know how to do that. Just walk away."

Tyler nods. In many ways, Tyler will always be the young boy seeking Dad's approval. The thick swallow in his throat and widening of his stance are from a man who is trying to regain his footing in a troubling situation. "I'm taking the kids home with me tonight. It's still my weekend."

"I want to say good-bye to them."

He buttons his blazer and squares his shoulders. "You have five minutes because we're out of here."

I turn to Will and Dad, letting them know I'll be right back, then follow Tyler through the lobby.

Most of the people have left now, about a quarter of them remaining, milling about. Hunter, Izzy, and Maisie are talking with the principal. When Tyler and I get to them, we are inundated with comments on how wonderful the performance was. Every time the principal brings up Will's name, Tyler's jaw clenches, but Hunter's smile broadens. As the conversation wraps up, I give my kids hugs and let them know I'll see them tomorrow.

LOVE ... IT'S COMPLICATED

By the time I get back from saying good-bye to the kids, Dad is the only one standing in the lobby where I left him. "Where's Will?"

"He left."

"Oh." My back softens, as if deflated. I wrap my scarf around my neck and frown.

Dad fiddles with the buttons of his coat as we walk toward the exit. I shuffle my feet across the pavement of the parking lot, kicking tiny pebbles away. It's cold tonight, far chillier than it has been this season.

Tonight was fun. Awesome actually. Yet why do I feel like a kid who had her hot chocolate with whipped cream and a cherry on top taken away before she got to take a sip?

Dad takes a cap out of his pocket and places it on his head.

"He's a good man, that William. I think he's growing on me."

The side of my face rises with an *I told you so* smile. "Proved you wrong. Looks like he actually does do magic. No one could have pulled that off unless they knew what they were doing."

He lets out a harrumph sound. "I'm also right too. That man likes you. A lot."

"Dad." I dismiss his assumption.

"Don't make this weird," he commands with a stop.

I turn to him, standing in the parking lot. He's not one for making a scene or getting involved in other people's business unless it's mine. Tonight, it looks like he's going two for two.

"Your generation, they always talk about soul mates, as if there's this one person in the world you're meant to be with. I don't know if I agree with that. I believe in love—big and small. If you're fortunate enough to find that big love, you hold on to it, and you ride the wave until the clock runs out and one of you is left behind. We don't talk about Mom that often because, let's face it, neither of us is emotionally capable of handling the amount of grief we've been feeling. She was my big love, and she left."

"Well, that's oddly morbid. If you were going for a *pick me up* speech, this is not it."

"What I'm getting at is, you're far younger than me, yet you act like there's no hope. That's not right for a wonderful young woman to be handling this burden for so long. Everyone expects me to spend my final years walking around in sorrow. I'm supposed to wear my grief like a cloak and shield myself from everything and everyone. Now, I don't know about you, but that sounds horrible.

Anna might not turn out to be a big love like your mother, but she's a small love, and I'm willing to take a chance on that even if it never grows bigger. She's fun, and I like being with her."

My grimace is washed all over my face, I'm sure. The reaction is not because I don't want him to talk about Anna. It's because what he's saying is true.

"You have many more years left. I'm not saying go off and date every man in Newbury. You'll give me a heart attack despite how in shape I might be. However, if there's a chance you can find a big love out there, a true love that you want to hold on to and ride the wave until the bitter end, take the chance. It's out there for you, kid. In fact, it might be closer than you think."

Dad's words hit me harder that the cold wind blowing through the parking lot.

A man is the last thing I need in my life and the furthest thing from what I'll allow. But I'm not dead inside, so while I don't need someone, there's still this huge part of me that wants it.

I rub my cheeks and look up at my father—my handsome father, who has been my saving grace these last two years, whether he knows it or not. "Jeez, Dad, where did that huge romantic speech come from?"

He narrows his eyes. "I said not to make it weird."

"I'm not. That was really beautiful."

"I'm done with you."

He takes his keys out of his pocket and hits the unlock button. I follow behind with my hands in my pockets and feet scurrying.

"I'm not lying. I want to write it down and etch it onto a quilt."

"Good night, Melissa." He opens his driver's door.

"Hey, Dad?"

He stops and then rises, peering at me over the roof of his car. "Yes?"

"I love you."

A small smile appears on his face as he shakes his head and then goes back to a grimace. "Don't be creeping in the house in the middle of the night. I'd like to get some sleep this weekend."

I give him a salute. "Don't wait up."

nineteen

MY FIST RISES TO knock on the large oak door of a one-floor Craftsman-style ranch with wood beams, shaker-style shingles, and an American Flag hanging from a post. As I look back at the well-manicured lawn, I shouldn't be surprised that Will has a home with charming curb appeal.

The lights are on inside, so I knock again and hug my coat around my body. I'm sure he's running surveillance through the doorbell camera, so I give a wave and hold up the bottle of whiskey I brought as a peace offering.

He opens the door slowly.

The first time I met the man, he was wearing an officer's uniform, and I could swear that was what made him sexy. Then, it was the damn boots and the black clothes with movie-star hair, all fabricated in this delicious *William Bronson cleans up well* package.

Despite my disbelief that the man would be as sexy, his intense gaze nearly as powerful, if he were wearing pajama pants and a hoodie, I am, in this moment, proven wrong. So very, very wrong.

Plaid pajama pants, a white T-shirt, and a navy hoodie, unzipped to showcase said T-shirt, which fits him like a freaking glove.

My eyes trickle down to his bare feet, and my hands rise in utter annoyance.

"Even your feet are sexy," I declare as I brush past him and walk into his house.

He stares at me with a tilted head when he closes the front door. "My feet?"

Unraveling the scarf on my neck, I toss it to him, and he catches it haphazardly. "Yes, your feet. They're as hot as the rest of you, and it's really unfair. If I don't get a pedicure every month, I look like Wolverine."

There's a mirror in the hallway. My cheeks are red, my face flush, and the hair on my head is flying up in random directions, thanks to the wind that picked up when I got out of the car. I pat my hair down with the pads of my fingers and try to look a modicum as good as I did when I showed up for the talent show.

"You came here to tell me about my feet?"

The bottle of whiskey is in my hand as I turn toward him. He's curious, yet the way he's leaning back on his heels with his hands crossed over his chest, he appears slightly amused.

"No, I came here to give you this." I hand him the bottle, and he takes it, looking at the label of the same whiskey we drank last night at Lone Tavern.

"Thank you?" His appreciation comes out as a question. "Was this all you came here for?"

"Maybe."

Will gives an amused flicker of an eyebrow. "Maybe," he repeats and lowers his gaze to mine, probing me to finish my sentence.

I play with the buttons of my jacket. This was easier when I drove here on autopilot and adrenaline.

"You left before I was able to say thank you. Thank you for being an amazing friend to me. For not only being *my* knight in shining armor, but also for what you did for my son. Man, you freaking levitated him off the ground—and I need you to tell me how you did that because, well, talk about a party trick. And not just the show—although it was cute, and you looked adorable in a tux, by the way—but also the attention you gave Hunter these past few weeks. That was amazing, Will. You're so amazing, and I don't tell you enough. Probably because we've only known each other for a second, but it's a second too long for me to tell you that. I also owe you a fierce apology because my ex is an ass."

"You don't owe me an apology."

LOVE ... IT'S COMPLICATED

"I do because I brought him into your life. Which is why, while you didn't have to defend me tonight, I am so grateful that you did. That was really ..." I bite my lip, thinking of all things I could say. *Kind. Brave. Masculine ... sexy as hell.* "Amazing."

"You said that already. I don't disagree. I am pretty amazing."

I raise a shoulder in agreement and roll my eyes. "It was the best adjective I could think of."

"Astonishing," he quips with a grin.

I squint my eyes, wondering where he's going with this. With a squeeze of his shoulders, he seems to be thinking.

"Astounding. Staggering. Awe-inspiring."

"Okay. I see what you're doing there."

"Bewildering."

"Conceited," I retort.

"Startling. Stupendous."

"Yes, stupid. You're such an idiot." My light giggle betrays me.

"Stunning."

"Okay, we already know you're good-looking."

"Enthralled."

"By what?"

"You."

That simple word nearly knocks me on my ass. I have to metaphorically hold myself up against the wall before falling.

My mouth is dry as I exhale slowly and regroup my wits. "I thought you were deranged when it came to me."

"Melissa, there aren't enough words in the dictionary to describe how I feel when I'm around you."

Perplexing. It's another word for him that has my chest rising and my stomach tightening as he saunters toward me and places the bottle on the entryway table. With long, deft fingers, he undoes the buttons of my coat, one by one. I watch his large hands as they undress me of my jacket. My brain is woozy from the scent of vanilla, hot-blooded man, and ... garlic?

There's a thick smell of garlic sautéing in olive oil wafting through the house. "Are you making dinner?"

"Speaking of amazing, I make a mouthwatering Bolognese that is almost done. Since you're here and you brought the drinks, why don't you stay for the food?"

As his hand slides into mine, warm and all-encompassing, I follow him down the hall, kicking my shoes off and leaving them near the entryway.

Will's home is comfortable. Cream-colored walls, wood furniture, and a hint of green accented throughout, including a large sectional sofa. His kitchen is a small galley type with dark wood cabinets on all sides and a bright white stone countertop. Our hands release when we enter, and he goes to the stove, stirring his sauce and raising the heat.

I stand here, unsure of what to do with myself.

Will shrugs off his sweatshirt and tosses it on the counter. The muscles in his back protrude—husky and ripped. I haven't marveled enough at how well built this broad-shouldered man is. Probably because he's always wearing thick clothing. He opens a cabinet and takes out a wineglass as I pull on the neck of my sweater, clearly warm from the working kitchen.

Will takes a bottle of wine out of the refrigerator.

I eye it quizzically. "Whispering Angel Rosé."

"I bought it after your first arrest. Figured if it was potent enough to land you in my cell, then it was worth trying. Been saving it for a special occasion."

He passes me the bottle, thumbing over to the drawer where I can find the corkscrew. Two glasses are poured, and I walk them over to where he's standing.

Unlike Tara and her haphazard baking setup, Will is neat and organized. He only takes out what he needs and puts away the rest. The counters are spotless; you'd never know someone was cooking in here.

"Here you go." I hand him a glass.

He turns his body toward me—tall and imposing against my now-shortened height, thanks to only being in my socks—and takes it. Our fingers brush. I think about that zing you hear about in romance movies, when two people touch and this current of electricity is felt deep within their bones. I don't get that when I touch Will. No, this is better. His touch is warm and soft, as simple as the brush might be. It's soothing.

We each take a sip, and I lean against the counter, waiting for his approval.

His full mouth purses. "It's crisp. Fruity. Definitely not whiskey."

"Can't even be compared."

His Adam's apple is a magnet for my eyes as he drinks again, and I watch it bob with the action.

"Not my type, but it might just be exactly what I need." I do my own swallow and place the glass on the countertop before it accidentally slips from my hand. "Bolognese is really meant for red wine."

"Says who?"

"Every cooking show ever. I believe Merlot would be the wiser pairing."

His glass is placed on the counter, and he leans into me. "Well, I hate Merlot. I'd rather have what I want than swallow a drink I just can't stand."

"You want the rosé?" My question comes out timid and maybe a touch squeaky.

That lean of his draws him closer until his mouth is mere inches from my ear. "I want to drink every last damn drop."

I'm not thick enough to not realize we're no longer talking about wine.

I clear my throat. "So, um ... I thought Bolognese sauces took, like, four hours to make."

"I started this afternoon, let it cool while we were gone, and now, I'm ready to devour it."

"Wow, that's, um ... quite the commitment for a meal."

"The best things in life are worth the wait."

I take a long swig of my drink until the glass is empty. The food analogies are going to my head, and now, I'm wondering if I'm so hard up for this man that I'm imagining it all.

Will chuckles as he turns to a lower cabinet and takes out a large pot. He fills it with water and moves it over to the stove, turning on the flame.

His glance at me comes with an amused grin. "You're flushed."

"It's hot in here."

"Not touching that one."

"What? No witty comeback?"

"You're not ready for it."

"Try me," I dare and instantly regret it or welcome it. Verdict's out as he turns to me fully, his body angled to mine.

For some reason, the way he's looking at me—really looking me, as if it were the first time—has my coy smile falling.

"When I was cooking before, I was in a sweatshirt because there's a draft that creeps under that wall over there. As soon as you walked in, I couldn't stand being in it. When you walk in a room, the temperature rises. My palms are slick, and my whole damn body feels like an inferno. I swear it's your eyes. They're ice blue but with flecks of amber that make them appear alive, like a flame that dances and flickers. Or maybe it's your candy lips, cherry-stained and beckoning me to lean in and press my lips against them. They make me burn. I want to kiss that mouth because I know how sweet it tastes. It makes me think of how sweet the rest of you will taste."

His words pierce through my core. I wasn't prepared for his honesty. It's heady, and my brain fizzles, as if I drank too much wine yet I only had a sip.

While these words should make me nervous, they do the opposite. They make me feel … euphoric. Isn't this what I've wanted for myself? Isn't this why I've placed myself in this man's company again and again despite the red flags waving around me, telling me it's not right?

I never set out to find a man, but I've always wanted something more. Something big.

Big love.

I want to laugh and have good conversation over whiskey, to dance in courtyards, and to feel that shiver, that feminine quake that was reawakened in me the moment I met Officer William Bronson in a cold cell, late on a Friday.

There are so many reasons why I shouldn't be with him. God, there are so many, and yet I cast them aside.

His palm is splayed out on the counter, not too far from my own. Sliding my hand over, I watch as my pinkie gracefully settles next to his, lightly brushing against his skin. It's the simplest of touches, and yet the mere connection sends shock waves from my heart straight into his eyes, which look at me with burning desire.

His hazel orbs blaze as I move my hand over his slowly—so damn slowly—and I run my hand up his forearm, taking in every corded muscle that appears though his clenched form.

He's holding himself back, steady and strong, looking at me for intent.

"I won't kiss you," he breathes.

LOVE ... IT'S COMPLICATED

My hand continues its journey up his bicep, and I roll it over his shoulder, sliding down his chest. His heart beats faster and faster as I close the gap between us.

We've been here before. Body to body, breath upon breath. This is the point of retreat that we've done many times before.

My lashes flutter up to his, and what I find leaves me on edge. The heated smolder of a man in lust. His deep, molten inner sexuality, shooting through his eyes into one undeniably sexy stare. I've been hypnotized by this look for months, and while I thought it was his natural look, I realize now that it was always for me.

My hands roam over his body, my eyes seeking permission to pursue. His deep, rapid breaths tell me to proceed.

Like a woman with no sight, I let my hands travel over Will's torso in order to feel my way. Every ripple and taut muscle, strong yet lean beneath my fingertips. I could splatter my hands with paint and re-create every divot on a canvas. That's how familiar he feels.

Breathing deeply, he remains standing, astonished by the brazen motions of the woman before him, taking liberties with his body.

It's not just his body I want.

It's his mind and his thoughtful stories. His mouth and the words he says to make me smile. The way he smiles when we're together. It's his hands and how they carry my burdens. And his heart that welcomes every important piece of mine into his.

I want this man. Mind, body, and soul. It might not be right, but I'll be damned if anyone tells me it's wrong.

"Melissa," he croons as his gaze steadies on my tongue licking my bottom lip. He closes his eyes, and it feels like a curse. "I won't kiss you, but if you kiss me and then pull back in regret, I won't be able to recover."

"If I kiss you, I'd better mean it then?"

His eyes open, and his sharp stare is like an arrow piercing through my heart and anchoring itself there.

"You'd better swear your next fifty years on it."

I lift on my toes and place my lips on his. The seconds our lips touch, he groans, and it's like a sigh of relief and expectation, all at once.

There is no coaxing involved as Will's mouth opens in anticipation, instantly sliding his tongue against mine and moving in sync.

His hands cup my face and weave into my hair, pulling my head closer. I do the same to his hips, urging him to fill the space between us until our bodies are pressed together so tightly that we can't tell where one begins and the other ends.

We've only kissed once before, yet the way our tongues and lips dance together, it feels like we've been dancing for an eternity. I savor the sweet and tangy taste of the wine on his tongue as his hand moves down to my jaw, angling my face so he can move his kisses from my mouth to my cheek, my jaw, my neck, my clavicle. My skin is overtaken by this man, sending shivers throughout my body. I roll my head back and let out a moan.

"Sweet Melissa, I've craved this kiss for too long," he growls against my neck as his lips move back to reclaim my mouth.

To have a man crave your kisses the way he does is invigorating. I let the rush roll over me as my butt hits the counter and his hands lower to my hips, lifting me up onto the granite.

His steel erection, uncontrolled by the loose fabric of his pajamas, settles between my open legs. I roll my hips against the delectable bulge as I wrap my legs around him.

Strong hands are in my hair, on my face, my shoulders. Will is touching me in desperation. I suppose I'm doing that as well. With free rein to finally grasp at one another, we paw and pet like animals.

The thought makes me giggle, and he breaks our kiss to find out why. I want to share my thoughts, but when I see the glisten on his lips, his dilated pupils, and the raging fire burning in his glare, my giggle subsides and is replaced by intense desire.

Will must sense my seriousness because he takes a step back. With a glance, I take in his cock straining through the fabric of his pants. He shows no remorse for his obvious attraction. Instead, his gaze is steady on mine.

The air in the room is thick, sizzling with heated lust and desperation. My panting breaths cause my chest to rise. Without Will, the draft cools me, and I can feel my nipples hardening beneath my blouse.

With nimble fingers, I undo my buttons, one by one. Will's eyes follow my hands as I slide my shirt off my shoulders. I arch my back and unsnap my bra, letting it fall to the floor along with my blouse.

His fist rises to his mouth as he takes me in, feasting over every inch of my breasts as he bites down, holding himself back.

LOVE ... IT'S COMPLICATED

My fingers roll over my collarbone. "Say something, Will, because I'm sitting here with no top on and you're way over there, and now, I'm starting to get nervous you're having second thoughts."

His gaze flicks to mine. "Nervous? Fuck yeah, I am. But not because I don't want to touch you."

I raise a brow and look to the side.

"Then, why aren't your hands all over me right now?"

"I'm afraid if I do, I'll come in my pants like a damn fifteen-year-old."

William Bronson—sexy, smoldering man—has no idea how he can make me feel like the most wanton, sexiest woman on the planet with his honesty.

I bite the inside of my cheek. "Can you come more than once in a night?"

His smirk answers before he does. "Easily."

"Then, I'm going to need that mouth on these nipples right now."

"Yes, ma'am," he croons, closing the distance between us, but not before stopping at the stove and turning off the burners.

When he comes to me, his lips don't move to my swollen breasts, but are on my lips, his tongue stroking against me in fierce, promising licks. His hands are on my hips, guiding my legs around him and lifting me off the counter.

"I liked your kitchen." I pout as he carries me into the living room. "It was a lot of fun there."

"You'll like my couch more." He settles himself onto the couch with me straddling him.

No sooner are we on the couch than we're kissing again, his hands tugging at my hair, my fingers grasping at his shirt. He holds my hair back as he runs his tongue down my throat, stopping for a moment on my clavicle, swiping a circle in the tender spot, and then caressing down to my breasts.

I hiss out loud, relieved at the touch.

His mouth wraps around a nipple, and the pulse of electricity, fire, and heat are overwhelming. His tongue flicks and sucks, moving in vicious circles. He runs a thumb over the other one, tugging at the elongated nipple and then switching his mouth and hand to give equal pleasure to both sides. The sensations are too much. I grip his head, lean back, and pray to the gods of second base.

On instinct, my hips rock, rubbing my clit against his crotch, desperate for any friction I can get inside my jeans.

"Fuck, you're trying to kill me," he growls against my breast, yet he seems to be in no hurry.

This man can make a meal out of my chest, kissing every inch of skin, putting me in a frenzy, and then licking and slightly biting my nipples to send me over the edge.

He's right. I like this couch a lot more than the kitchen.

Desperate for the feel of his skin, I grip his shirt and move it up his body. Will leans back for a moment to shed himself of the tee.

As soon as he does, I gasp.

On his chest, just below his shoulder, is a scar. It's dark and raw, the sign of a bullet that went through a hero who risked his life for others.

I want to touch it, but not with my hands. I crawl down Will's body until my lips are level with the scar, and I kiss it.

As my tongue glides over the wound, he lets out a groan. I follow it with an exploration of his chest, something I've felt yet never tasted. My nose tickles as it passes through the hair on his chest. I kiss every inch of torso, stalling when my mouth reaches the happy trail of his stomach and the deep V that heads down into his pants and the erection that brushes against my neck.

With my mouth so close, I stare at him, open my mouth, and run it over the thin fabric of his bottoms and the thick steel of his erection beneath. Up and down, I tease him, taking in how well-endowed he is and wondering what it will feel like in my mouth. My tongue darts out, and I place a long stroke on his shaft. I taste cotton and feel the pulsating of his member as it bobs with pleasurable shocks.

"Are you trying to kill me?" he asks with bated breath.

"A little." I'm coy as I sit up on my knees, down on the floor, and stare at him.

He's glorious. Shirtless with a gorgeous physique that could rival the Greeks and Romans combined. He's panting, erect, and looking at me with a look of lust the sights I've never seen on a man.

Before my hands can unravel his pants, he grabs my hands and forces me to stand. Will sits up and kisses my belly. He undoes the button on my jeans and delicately unravels them down my legs. When all I'm left in is my panties, I save him the ask and glide them down my legs, showcasing myself.

His hands lay on my hips as he pulls me close and stares up into my eyes. "You're so beautiful, Melissa."

I smile. "I was just thinking that about you. But you already know that because I tell you all the time that you're hot."

"Don't deflect." His words are stern. "I'm loving on you right now, and you're not accepting it, so let's try this again." He takes a breath, places a kiss on my belly, and then looks up at me. "You're beautiful, Melissa."

I swallow and have to take a deep breath to hold back my emotions.

He kisses me again, this time slower.

"You're powerful."

His tongue glides over my core.

"Strong."

His nose is in the tiny hairs as his mouth kisses the folds.

"Brilliant."

He swipes his tongue, and it hits my clit, making me shiver.

"Phenomenal."

He sucks gently, and I quake.

His mouth is replaced by fingers, which move slowly, delicately as they run over my clit. His other hand rises to my breasts, caressing me until my knees are wobbly. When he slides two fingers inside me, I curse like a sailor.

"That's my girl. I need to taste you."

He guides my knees onto the couch. I think he wants me on his lap or to lie down on the couch, but I'm stunned when he stays in place, grabs my waist, and lifts me up until I'm straddling his face.

His mouth claims my vagina fully, and I gasp, grasping above the couch and praying I don't fall off the damn thing as he sucks and flicks and eats me the fuck out.

My knees are climbing on his shoulders and the top of the couch as he laps at me, holding my body in place with a hand on my ass and another inside me, pumping his fingers.

The hallway mirror is far away, but I'm able to see a glimpse of us in the reflection. William, large and powerful on the couch, with me naked and riding his face. The sight of us together turns me on, and I watch as his hips strain to stay in place as they move in the rhythm of a man gyrating in anticipation.

I feel the early waves of an orgasm building.

It's been years since I've felt this, and it's frightening. Each time he groans against my core, as if what he's doing is the biggest turn-on of his life, the waves come in stronger and closer.

My body rocks against him, and I sit up, almost standing, and thank Tara and her intense kick boxing classes for good core strength. Not needing the couch to hold me up, I stare down at him and meet the eyes of a man who is claiming me with his hands, mouth, and freaking soul. Instead of fearing this wave, I ride it. Oh, do I ride it.

Will feels it, too, because he kicks up his game. His tongue stronger, his lips with more suction, and his hands moving like they were born to elicit every ounce of pleasure from my body.

The sight of him up close, mixed with the overwhelming sensations, is too much to bear. I cry out as my orgasm builds and slashes inside of me. I feel like I'm levitating to the ceiling as I shout out his name in praises.

His hands release me, and I'm pulled down onto his lap. He kisses me. I taste my orgasm on his lips and soak it in because these lips just gave me the high of a lifetime.

"Please tell me you have a condom in this place," I ask between kisses.

He doesn't answer. Instead, he lifts me again and carries my *limp from pleasure yet still aroused* body into his bedroom. I'm placed on the bed, and I watch as he walks over to his dresser and takes out a condom, tossing it on the bed beside me.

Sitting up on my knees, I move toward him and take off the rest of the clothes left between us—his. Fully naked and fully erect, Will stands before me, and I can't help the urge to slide my hand over the well-endowed package and then follow it with my mouth.

Silk over granite … that's what he tastes like in my mouth. I bob and move over the engorged head of his penis and down the shaft, sliding my tongue over the pleasure vain and listening to him moan. I know he can't last too long, and I am desperate to feel him inside me, so I sit back on my heels and look at his cock, ready and glistening.

Will takes the condom and tears it open with his teeth. I'm enamored as he covers himself with it and then moves back to the bed, and rests my head on the pillow. He settles his hips between my thighs and kisses me long and lovingly.

I wasn't expecting this kind of kiss.

LOVE ... IT'S COMPLICATED

I wasn't expecting tonight.

It's been full of feelings and emotions, even when no words are spoken.

As he slides himself into me, the greatest unspoken words are shared.

With every pump of his hips, he tells me we've always been more than friends.

With the raise of my hips, I let him know I've wanted him for so long.

With the caress of my face, he tells me I'm exactly who he wants to be with.

And as we cry out in pleasure, panting and pleading, shouting out each other's names, I let him know it's possible I just might be falling in love with him.

twenty

I'M AWAKENED BY A warm, strong hand rubbing up and down my back with the perfect amount of tranquil ease and ache-reducing pleasure. I hum like a kitten into my pillow.

"Did you just purr?" Will's husky morning voice croons as his hand stills.

"Shh. Still sleeping. Keep rubbing."

Shimmying my hips toward his hand, I urge him to keep up the motion. I'm bone-tired, thankfully due to an evening of incredible, sporadic sex.

Yes, I, Melissa Jones, went to bed with a man. I'm shocked. Not that it's a man. I happen to be very fond of the gender. I'm stunned that I took the leap right into Will's bed.

The thing that really perplexes me is that I'm good with it. Especially when he rubs his large hands over my shoulder blades and down to the small of my back. It feels good; even the back of my head tingles.

His hand glides up the sides of my torso, grazing the rim of my breast. I curl my arm in to fight the tickle.

"Watch the side boob."

His hand roams south and comes back up, once again caressing the tender flesh. "It's my hand. I can place it where I want."

"And it's my side boob."

With a swift roll of my body, he flips me over so I'm lying on my back as he hovers over me. Even in the morning, he looks absolutely delectable—tousled hair and ruggedly handsome with the light shadow of a beard. His mouth lowers to the side of my breast and places an open-mouthed kiss on the spot in question.

"As long as you're in this bed, it's mine."

The kiss leaves me ticklish and curling to the side. He rolls over with me, coaxing my skin with his fingers and mouth until I'm laughing in surrender.

He spoons me, kissing my temple. "I love waking up with you in my bed."

"I can't imagine a man not enjoying waking up with any naked woman under his covers."

"You're not just any woman, Melissa," his husky voice breathes against my hair, making my heart stall for a second.

I exhale sharply and roll over, forcing him onto his back, and curl into the nook of his arm and chest. My leg glides over his hips, and I hold him as my fingers play in the hair on his chest, exposed from the blankets.

Tracing his scar and the raised edges, I'm reminded of how recent this actually happened.

"Why don't you bring it up?" I ask and hear his chest rumble with the question. "You were shot in the chest months ago, and yet you walk around like you never experienced this incredibly traumatic event."

There's a pause after my question. His fingers brush my forearm that's on his chest. He likes doing this. Rubbing me. Touching me. I still my hand on his scar and let the hardened skin graze my palm.

"When it happened, it was all anyone wanted to talk about. I have five brothers and sisters, an unrelenting mother, and a father who is as involved as any parent could possibly be. I had eight people constantly checking in on me. Visiting, doting, caring. Allison was at my side literally every second of every day. That doesn't include the counseling I got in the hospital and outpatient through work. My captain, my partner ... trust me, it was brought up. I spoke about it. A lot. Right down to the day I returned to work to a party and a report in the paper about how heroic I was."

I nod against his chest, wondering if that's resentment I hear in his voice.

LOVE ... IT'S COMPLICATED

He leans his cheek against the top of my head. "Do you want to?" he asks, and I raise my head slightly. "Do you have questions?"

"Izzy told me your story. It's sweet how she didn't want to share the details you had shared with her, but you made an impression. When Hunter had his accident, she compared herself to you, heroic and brave. I never asked because I'd read about it in the paper. I just feel insensitive that I haven't made this huge deal and fawned over you."

"People do heroic things every day. Some birth babies, and others get shot in the chest."

"Sounds like someone's deflecting. Didn't I get in trouble for doing that last night?"

He laughs lightly, making his chest vibrate. "I believe you were rewarded for that."

"Tomato, tomahto." I move myself so my head and hands are on his stomach, looking up at him. "Spill it, Bronson. What's on your chest other than this sexy-as-hell scar?"

He lifts a brow. "You think it's sexy?"

"Deflecting again."

He sighs and lays a hand on my head, stroking my hair.

See, he loves to touch me.

"Mostly, I feel heroic. I took a fucking bullet to save strangers in a convenience store, unarmed, and attacked the son of a bitch with my bare hands. Not only did I take a bullet to the chest, but I survived and came back like a bull. The doctors, nurses ... no one could get over my recovery. I know what happened was a big deal. What never gets mentioned was when I took the gun from his hands, I shot him back, and then I lay there to die. It took seven minutes for the ambulance to get there, but I swear it felt like seven lifetimes. Heaven, hell, I should haves, and promises to God. It can fuck with your head if you dwell on it too much. I don't want to be the guy who always thinks about how he almost died. I want to be the one who lives. I want to make love to a beautiful woman, and then I want to make her brunch because after she fell asleep, I had to put my Bolognese, uneaten, in the refrigerator. I also happen to make killer waffles, and I love an egg white omelet."

His ultimate deflection is something I should scold him on, but I won't because, as he said, he'd rather talk about living than dying, and I get that. Plus, he just spoke some pretty sexy words to me that cannot go unnoticed.

"You brunch?" I actually bite my lip because the thought of William and I naked, brunching in his bed, sounds amazing. *Okay, he didn't mention the bed or nakedness, but I'm sure it was implied.*

"Baby, you've never brunched until you've brunched with me ... naked and in my bed."

I giggle. Damn, this man and I are on the same wavelength.

This could be good ... or so very, very bad.

After an incredible afternoon of brunching with Will, I drive home a little before the kids are supposed to return with Tyler. I showered with Will, so my hair is pinned up in a wet bun as I walk through the front door. I hear the sound of Dad's electrical saw from his wood workshop. I drop my bag on the kitchen counter and get a start on dinner, which happens to be leftover Bolognese because Will and I only had a small amount during our brunch and he insisted I bring home the rest for Dad and the kids.

Brunch.

I'm a woman who loves the meal, but Will certainly made a meal out of it. As promised, he ate waffles, eggs, spaghetti Bolognese, and ... me in bed. My eyes roll as I think of that and the awesomely spicy Bloody Marys he made before we showered together, lathering each other up. Talking, kissing, laughing ... *loving.*

Tyler's car door slams outside, and I walk to the door. Hunter is the first up the stairs. I get my usual hug, kiss, and request to snuggle with me before he goes to bed.

Izzy is right behind him, giving me an extra squeeze, which surprises me.

"How was your night?" I ask her, running my hands over her head and looking at her tired eyes.

"We ordered pizza and watched a movie."

"Did you sleep?"

"Yeah. Dad and I were up late, talking."

"That's a good thing."

She shrugs with a sideways smile and walks past me into the kitchen. Hunter is already unloading his backpack of magic tricks that he brought with him to the show yesterday.

LOVE ... IT'S COMPLICATED

Tyler is slow to come up the stairs. There's something about the way his steps seem heavy and his face sallow that has me standing and waiting for him at the top.

"I got new checkbooks in the mail."

I tilt my head at him, wondering why he's sharing this information.

"When we got back last night, there was a box on my doorstep." He reaches into his back pocket and produces a checkbook.

I take it from his hand. It's as flat as could be, unused and the pages yet to be turned. I flip over the top white sheet and see the personalized photo check. My hand flies to my mouth as I fight back the mixed feelings of laughter and mortification.

The check features a picture of me with my nose scrunched and giving the middle finger. It was taken the night Tara and I burned the robe in my backyard and then ordered personalized checks for Tyler. I completely forgot about this.

"Use them in good health." I hand them back to him and grin and laugh.

He fights his own smile of annoyance. "You and Tara have done some dumb shit over the years, but this"—he pauses as if it pains him to say it—"is really funny."

The sun has gone down already, so I cross my arms for warmth.

He notices and gestures toward the door. "I should let you get back inside. I just wanted to apologize for my behavior last night. I'm serious about not having just anyone spending time with our kids, but the way I went about it was uncalled for. Izzy and I talked last night, and I get it. I embarrassed her, and I apologized. Hunter too. He's easier to please, but Izzy, she's growing up to be a young woman, and she has so many feelings."

"Yeah, that'll happen to a girl."

"I want to fix my relationship with her. With you. We're a family, and up until last year, we were able to coexist in the same house and have this family life without being a family."

"Ty, we lived in the same house because I was advised not to abandon the home or I could lose the rights to it, and you refused to rent an apartment, so you slept in the guest room. Then, you had an affair with Maisie and started staying with her. By the way, how's cohabitating going? For the record, you never asked me my permission to have her live in the same home as my children, yet you love to tell me who I can and can't have in mine."

193

He sighs. "Maisie hasn't moved in yet. We're taking it slow."

I narrow my eyes at him because there's something he's not telling me about that situation, but I don't care enough to pry it out of him. "I'm glad you and Izzy had a heart-to-heart."

"She doesn't talk much, but when she does, it's like a butterfly spreading its wings for the first time. I don't want her to get into her teen years and be bitter because of us. I spoke to the therapist you texted me, and I think it's a good fit to try. I can set that up for her if you need."

"It's okay. I'll schedule it. Maybe a Thursday. I'll drop her off, and you can take her to dinner after?" I suggest.

"I'd love that." He smiles, and then it falls as his eyes trail from my wet head down to my blouse. "Isn't that what you wore last night?"

I hug my arms tighter around me to hide the shirt I've been wearing for two days in a row, and then I realize I don't care what Tyler thinks. "It is."

"Was it laundry day?"

"Nope. All caught up as of Friday."

He nods with the understanding. His eyes flick to the open front door, and the smell of sauce comes out from inside. "You're about to have dinner?"

"That's what people do in the evening."

"You have company?"

I scrunch my nose. "No."

"Do you guys want some? I'd love to stay and finish what I started with Izzy. Show her I'm here for her. Show her I'm here for you."

"Me?"

"Yeah, Lyss. We're a family. I'd like to come in for a few minutes. See the kids' rooms. Share in this new part of their life. Show the kids that we can be a family without being together."

"Ty, I don't think—"

"Come on in, Dad!" Izzy is standing by the doorway, my father behind her.

She's beaming like an eleven-year-old who is inviting her father into her new home for the first time since she moved in, and he's grimacing like a man who is about to let his ex-son-in-law inside for the first time in two years.

LOVE ... IT'S COMPLICATED

Tyler walks past me and over to Izzy, grabbing her by the shoulders and walking inside.

He gives my dad a respectful nod. "Mr. Jones."

Dad merely lifts his chin and watches Tyler head in with Izzy and listens as Hunter squeals with delight that his daddy is staying for dinner.

I turn around and walk into the foyer, closing the door and looking at my dad's displeased frown.

"I don't want to hear it," I warn him.

He harrumphs. "Next time, change your shirt. He would have been halfway home by now."

My shoulders fall. I hate it when he's right.

twenty-one

THE NEXT TWO WEEKS continue on with little fanfare. I work, spend my free hours with the kids, and when they're with Tyler on the weekends, I sneak in some time with Will. Even though I have two full kid-free days, I work weekends, and he has a rotating schedule. Still, it's nice because we can go slow with this new relationship.

Today, I'm at the office, doing inventory with Jillian. Tara stopped by because she really needs some girl talk.

"I ended things with Kent."

Tara's announcement has Jillian and me pausing mid–inventory counting.

"Oh no. You really liked him," Jillian states with her hand over her cashmere chest.

"Is it the intimacy thing?" I ask.

"Yeah. I mean, it's weird that we haven't gone to bed with each other, but that's not the problem. The issue is, I only want to go to bed with him because it's some natural next step that I think we're supposed to take. I like Kent, but do I really like him? Am I settling?"

"He seems like a great guy. Maybe he's religious?" Jillian suggests, to which Tara shakes her head from the desk chair she's currently draped in, her long tendrils swaying as she rocks back and forth.

"It's been three months. He's a really great guy, but I wonder if I actually like him or if I like the idea of him."

Jillian hands me a final votive to place on the shelf. "You're a wise woman to not settle. Trust me, it's better to do things on your own terms."

Tara sits up. "The difference between the three of us is, I don't know if kids are in my future. It's never been something I've desired. Jillian, you're still young as far as biological clocks go. Why didn't you want to wait until meeting a man before having a baby?"

Jillian lifts a shoulder as she grabs a box from the other side of the room. "I don't want a man who is going to be my provider and protector. I can do that on my own. I have this idea in my head on what a man should be, and I refuse to settle for anything less. Maybe we're more alike than you think."

Tara's bangle bracelets jingle as she points a hand. "No. I give men a chance. You are a wall."

Jillian shifts her hip. "I was raised by parents who were in a marriage of convenience and made a vow to myself that I'd never go that route. But kids? That's always been a given, and I didn't want to wait a single day longer to start my life as a mom. Ainsley brings me more love than I could have ever imagined."

Tara holds a pointed finger in the air as she contemplates Jillian's words. "Someday, Ainsley will leave you for college and start her own life, and you'll be left alone."

I take a paper from by clipboard, wad it up, and toss it at Tara's head. "Way to be a Debbie Downer."

She picks it up off her lap and tosses it back at me. "I'm just being honest."

"You're kinda right," I agree, logging in the number of votives on my chart. "With kids, you give everything and pray you're doing a decent enough job that they'll grow up with a limited number of things to bitch about you to their shrink. Unless you're me and you make a ton of mistakes before they even hit their teens."

"Stop that. Your kids are awesome. Tyler screwed up, and you're doing everything to give them normalcy," Jillian states firmly as she lifts vases from the next box. "You could have raked him through the mud in court. You used a mediation attorney instead of spending thousands of dollars on multiple high-priced divorce lawyers."

LOVE ... IT'S COMPLICATED

"Maybe we can offer un-wedding design services. If it doesn't work out, I'll tell them how to get a divorce without losing their life savings."

"And I'll help them get knocked up without a partner!"

Tara's knee-high-boot-clad legs hit the ground with a thump. "You two are the worst wedding designer and event planning team ever!" she yelps as Jillian and I high-five each other like our ridiculous business plan is real. It's not, obviously, but sometimes, you need humor to cover up the pain.

Tara's right. For women who put their hearts and souls into creating amazing weddings, we certainly have an interesting outlook on relationships.

I place my clipboard down and walk over to Tara's chair, spinning it to face me, and grab her attention. "All kidding aside, you do what you know is the best for you. Don't ever settle, but don't chase a fantasy either. If Tyler hadn't left and I hadn't gone through the mess of my two-year-long divorce, here's the advice I would have given you."

I pause a moment and think about the advice because I wasn't truly planning on giving any ... so here it goes.

"Look for a man who is your partner. Someone you'd be honored to have by your side, even on the days he's driving you absolutely insane. Just make sure he's a good man because romances fade in and out. On the days where it dims, you need to be able to tolerate him just enough to make it to when it's glowing again. Because it will glow, and on those days, you'll be so happy you pushed through the dark because in his light is the most radiant place to be."

"Romances aren't supposed to dim," Jillian says from the corner.

I stand and walk back to my place by the shelf.

"I think they do as we grow up. Even us, three women in their thirties, are growing up. I don't know about you, but I still feel like a confused teenager at times, and I'm raising two of them. No matter how old we are, we grow and change. Jobs, interests, friends, everything around us evolves, as do we, and you have to hope your partner evolves when you do. The romance dims as you learn how to reconnect with the evolved version of your partner. In that moment, it ignites."

Tara's brows are curved in a deep V as she looks at me like it's the first time she's heard me speak in years. "You know, you say a lot of stupid shit, but that was by far one of the smartest things I've ever heard you say."

"Yeah, I'm even a little impressed myself." I rub my chest and make sure I'm not having a heart attack or something.

Jillian's mouth drops. "I'm a love skeptic, and I think you even hit me in the feels with that one."

I grin at her. "I know we don't talk about it a lot, but whoever that guy was years ago who made you believe true love wasn't real was a fool. And you're a greater fool for believing it."

"Yeah, Jillian," Tara chimes in. "There's nothing to lose by giving it a shot. Like you said, you already have your daughter. That's all the love you need."

She nods, seemingly unsure. "Maybe. I'm still a work in progress, I suppose. And for the record, he didn't make me believe true love wasn't real. In fact, with him, it was so tangible that I was almost afraid of it." She shakes her red hair and holds a hand up, as if all this talk is silly. "Okay, this room is getting very emotional."

Tara scoffs. "I like the effect Officer Bronson is having on Melissa. She's all swoony these days."

Jillian's lips smash as she walks over to a third box. "I hate to say it, but Melissa does have a certain glow about her."

"It's nothing serious." I open the box Jillian brought over and hear them snicker. "What?"

"It's been two weeks since you banged on his door with a bottle of whiskey," Jillian starts, to which Tara adds, "And banged the hot cop."

While Will and I have a little something going on, I've been hesitant to talk to the girls about him. All they know is I stayed the night. No additional details given. "You think you know me so well."

"You smile at your phone while you're in public," Tara says.

"You started wearing makeup again and not on workdays," Jillian adds.

"You whistle."

"You sigh."

The two of them seem to have quite the list of things that I've been doing lately. Okay, so maybe I have been adding some extra mascara on a random Tuesday.

LOVE ... IT'S COMPLICATED

"Will and I've been spending time together, and it's ... nice," I state with a sigh and quickly regret it. *I hate when they're right.*

The two of them look at each other with mixed faces of disappointment and confusion.

Tara falls back into her seat and looks at me with a tilted head. "We both know, for you to be going down this road with Will and to even be talking about marriage in such a romantic light, it has to be something more than ... nice."

Give them something more? Even if I wanted to tell my two best friends exactly what it is between Will and me, I wouldn't be able to explain it.

With a clearing of my throat, I tuck my hair behind my ear. "Okay, so you know how Will is easy on the eyes? He's easy on everything. We laugh when we're together, and we have this awesome banter. He's kind and generous with his time. I just ... we're just ... it's nice."

I turn away from them and unload the box at my feet. Aside from the glass hitting the shelf, the room is so silent.

I stand and run a hand through my hair. "Listen, I'm treading lightly. He works four twelve-hour shifts a week, plus overtime. I work weekends and have kids. There's not a ton of time to devote to this. Jillian and I also discussed how damaging this could be to Lavish Events if word gets out I'm dating a former prospective client. Plus, I don't want the kids knowing. Hunter already grew too attached to Will while working on their magic show. If this thing with Will doesn't work out, I don't want them to get hurt."

"Sounds to me like you're a chickenshit," Tara challenges.

"I'm not—"

My words are interrupted by my phone ringing. I feel a large smile grace my face and then quickly remove it just to prove my friends wrong.

"Hi," I answer the phone.

"What are your plans tonight?" Will asks, and just the sound of his voice has been biting my lip.

"Izzy has therapy, so Tyler is taking Hunter to the Lego Store, and then the three of them are having dinner in Newbury."

"So, you're free?" he asks with a laugh, and I reciprocate, putting a hand on my forehead when I realize that my children's agenda is not always mine. "Have dinner with me."

"On your workday?"

"I'm leaving work at three because I worked a double and am now mandated by our great state to take a rest. Before I go to sleep for the next twelve hours, I want to see my girl."

My cheeks warm, so I bow my head, covering it with my hair to hide from my friends and their stares. "That sounds like a great idea. They leave my house at five. I'll text you when I'm leaving the house."

"Can't wait."

I hang up and slide my phone into my back pocket. As I spin back to my friends, I see they're still in the places they were before I took my call. Tara, lounged in her chair with a Cheshire cat smile on her face. Jillian in her auburn hair, dark-eyed glory, seeming pensive in the corner.

The two are too silent.

"What?" I challenge them.

"Well, I do declare, Melissa Jones. I believe you have fallen in love." Tara swivels full circle in the chair, and Jillian gazes at me with a worried expression.

Nice.

twenty-two

FIVE O'CLOCK APPROACHES quickly. I get the kids from school, rush through their homework, and then hop in the shower to get ready for my date with Will. I suppose this is my first date with him. We've shared meals and drinks, but we've yet to go to a restaurant together. When I told the girls it's not the easiest to arrange time together, I meant it. Which is why tonight's impromptu evening is exciting.

I slip on a long-sleeved jersey dress and pair it with stockings and knee-high boots. We could be going to a diner for all I know, but I want to put on something pretty. Not just for Will. For me.

I'm fluffing out my hair when the doorbell rings.

"Izzy, answer the door for your father," I call down so I can take an extra second to put on some mascara and lip gloss.

As I descend the stairs, Tyler is standing in the foyer with the kids. His eyes flicker up to me as I come downstairs, doing a double take, like one would with a girl coming down in her prom dress for the first time. I feel like a song by The La's should be playing in the background.

"Is your dad home?" he asks as I step onto the tiles.

I raise a brow at him while fixing the clasp on my bracelet that didn't seem to catch when I did it upstairs. "No. He's out with Anna."

Izzy grabs her coat from the catch-all ottoman near the front door. "Wow, Mom. You said Anna's name without making a face. Good progress. Maybe I should start seeing *your* shrink."

"I'm not seeing a shrink, and neither are you. Your *therapist* is very nice. You're going to love her."

I have a tough time getting the damn clasp to hook, so I take the bracelet off, replace it on my wrist, and try again.

"Here, let me." Tyler closes the space between us and grabs the bracelet without my asking.

"Thanks." I stare at him with a raised brow, watching as he carefully locks my bracelet in place. "Why did you ask about my dad?"

"The front door. You never let the kids answer it. I was surprised."

"I was just finishing up with something upstairs. You guys ready to go?" I ask them because Izzy's appointment is in fifteen minutes.

"Do we have to go?" Hunter asks as he comes into the foyer with a cape around his neck and a top hat on. It's surprising since he's usually so excited, practically leaping out the door to go with his dad. "My stummy hurts."

Hunter calls his belly his stummy when it hurts. It's an adorable mix of tummy and stomachache.

I drop to a knee and place a hand on the back of his neck. "Let me take a look at you. You were okay a few minutes ago."

"I think it was the bag of popcorn I ate."

"When did you eat popcorn? You knew Daddy was coming to take you to dinner." I stand and place my hands on my hips.

Izzy chimes in from her place near the front door, "He was hungry, so I made him a bag. You were in the shower."

Tyler's mouth twists. "Were you too distracted that our kids were cooking for themselves and stuffing themselves sick?"

I mentally flip him the bird. "A microwave is not dangerous. Izzy even knows how to use a stove."

While Tyler looks at Izzy to confirm she can indeed boil a pot of water and make popcorn and various other things eleven-year-olds are learning how to do, I place a hand on Hunter's cheek and listen to him groan.

"I think I'm going to throw up," he mutters into my hand, and my eyes close.

LOVE ... IT'S COMPLICATED

I don't want to kick my *sick to his stomach* kid out of my house so I can go to dinner with the man I'm dating, but ... I really want to kick my kid out of the house. I'm a monster.

"Do you want to stay home with me?" I ask my boy, and he nods while looking so down.

"Yes, but I really wanted to go out with Daddy tonight."

I put my arm around his shoulders. "No, baby, I think you need to rest just in case it's not the popcorn. I'll put on some jammies, and we'll snuggle on the couch."

"I'd like that, Mommy. The inside of my cast is itchy." He shoves his fingers inside the cast and starts to tug at the skin.

"I'll grab Chinese."

Tyler's offer has me blinking at him in utter confusion.

"I mean, it's no Lin Chun, but Izzy's therapist is on Main Street near that restaurant your mom liked. Hunter, you get on pajamas, and we'll have dinner together. As a family."

With a hand on my neck, I look back at Tyler and shake my head. "I don't think that's the best idea."

"What's the problem?"

"It could be confusing for the kids."

"They're not gonna think we're getting back together."

"You staying for dinner again is not a good idea."

"Of course it is!" Izzy nearly shouts.

We look to her, and she's standing there ... smiling. Not just smiling. She's beaming. The kid who's shrugged her way through life this year is looking like the kid she once was, jolly and excited for her dad to have dinner in her house.

"You want Dad to stay for dinner?"

"Yes! We haven't had a family dinner in forever. We'll have egg rolls, and then we can play *Family Feud*. Mom loves that game. Tell Dad how much you love watching *Family Feud* reels. I've caught her so many times the last few weeks."

I look at Tyler. My smile is closed as I shrug. "I do like the game show."

"Daddy's staying?" Hunter perks up with a goofy grin of his own. "This is so cool!"

Tyler slaps his hands together. "Excellent! I'll get the food, and we'll have a family game night. See you in a little bit."

Tyler opens the door, and he and Izzy start down the stairs. Hunter is already on his way up to change while I call down to Tyler.

"You never asked what I wanted to eat!"

He stops momentarily at his car and smiles. "After nearly twenty years, I think I know how to order for you, Lyss."

I slam the front door and chew on my nail.

Damn it! It feels like a mini tornado just came and swiped through my fun plans and swooped them up into the atmosphere.

I'm annoyed at Tyler, and then I get annoyed at myself because, really, this is about Hunter's stomachache. Tyler totally bulldozed the situation, and I let him. Why did I let him? Because Izzy smiled. My girl, my world, lit up like Christmas morning, and I'm a sucker for my kids.

Resigned to my new night in, I grab my cell phone from my purse and head upstairs, sliding my boots off as I climb the stairs. Will's line rings, and when I hear the croon of his voice, the kind that's looking forward to enjoying a meal with a woman, I instantly feel deflated.

"Are you leaving your house now?"

I close the door to my room and fall to my bed, and it squeaks because that's what old beds do. Anyone else would have probably upgraded, but it was mine, and my mom bought it, and I'm nostalgic, so there's that.

"I'm bailing on you. Hunter has a stomachache, so he couldn't go to dinner, so now dinner's coming to me. I'm so sorry. Like, I'm crazy, utterly upset because I wanted to see you tonight, and I know I'm not the easiest person to make plans with, but life gets in the way, and you were so sweet when you called earlier—"

"Melissa, it's okay. I'd be lying if I said I wasn't disappointed, but I understand. And I'm not the easiest person to make plans with either. I work a ton and sleep like a bear. We'll figure out a routine. It's okay."

"I'd ask how an amazing man like yourself is still single, but I know the answer to that."

He chuckles. "Same to you, babe. For what it's worth, I'm glad for it."

My hand falls to my lips and runs along my smile. "Me too," I say surprisingly. I think this is the first time I haven't looked at my single status and felt so alone.

"Mommy!" I hear Hunter call from his room.

"I have to run. I'd say I'll try you later, but you need to sleep. Call me tomorrow when you're on your way to work?"

"Will do, beautiful. Good night."

"Dream of me. Sexy dreams only. Make sure I'm looking extra amazing."

"As always."

I listen to his laugh as we say our good-byes and hang up. I'd sit and sigh for a little, but Hunter calls again, and I'm up and in his bedroom just in time to watch him throw up into an old sand pail.

Motherhood is awesome.

Hunter is feeling better by the time Tyler and Izzy come home. He doesn't want to eat, but we ask him to have some broth just to get something in his stomach. Izzy is rambling on about a project she is working on for her science class, and Tyler's giving her pointers on how she could make it better. It's odd, having Tyler here. Last time, it was for twenty minutes. Dad was here too. I was so focused on his disdain that Tyler's presence went by the wayside.

Tonight though is different.

Just the four of us breaking egg rolls and reading fortune cookies, talking about our day, is … weird. We did this many times at the old house. Even during the two years of Tyler and I quasi-cohabitating while we tried to figure out what our future as a divorced couple would look like, everything felt strained with a smile. We pretended for the kids, yet it was still the home we shared. Having him in my parents' house feels natural and forced at the same time.

My phone buzzes with a text.

You have five minutes?

Yes. You want me to call?

Walk outside.

"Excuse me a minute."

No one seems to care that I'm stepping away from the table. I head toward the front door and look out the side window. I don't see anyone outside. There are lights on the street, seemingly from a car at the neighbor's.

I grab my coat and walk outside and head down the stairs. As I get to the bottom of the steps, I see Will's truck parked along the curb. He's exiting the driver's side as I walk around. He's wearing sweats and a Valor County sweatshirt. The door is still open as he stands on the driver's side and pulls me close. His hands grip my face, his fingers roaming over the skin of my cheek, pulling me in for a sensual, desperate kiss.

I fall into his embrace, our lips dancing and moving along with one another. A deep, guttural sound escapes his lips, and I moan, realizing just how much I missed being held by this man.

His hands are still on my face as they weave into my hair. His forehead rests against mine, and our smiles touch.

"I told you I needed to see my girl before I went to bed," he breathes.

A jolt runs up my body and lands on my heart. "Bronson, you are a bona fide romantic. As Shakespearean as your name."

"Doesn't everyone die in those plays?"

"Yea. Bad analogy. Still, I love romantic Will."

His chest rises with a quick exhale. I lean over and kiss him again, making out with him in the street like a teenager who has to park a few houses down from her parents' house. The sense of déjà vu is frightening. There's even classic rock playing on Will's radio.

"The neighbor's house?" I ask between kisses.

He lays his lips on the skin of my neck. A chill travels down my spine.

"I know you're not ready for the kids to know you're dating a younger man. It is quite scandalous. I didn't want them to see me."

"How thoughtful of you." I grab his ass and give it a squeeze.

"God, I love when you objectify me. When will I see you again?"

"I'm booked Friday and Saturday with weddings, but I'm free Sunday. You want to come over? This way, I can sleep in, and we won't lose any time while I drive back and forth to Castleton. I can objectify you in many ways before Tyler brings the kids back."

"Absolutely. Now, go inside before I decide to throw you in the bed of my truck and haul you back to my house. I don't think your father would be pleased if I kidnapped his grown daughter."

He slaps me playfully on the ass. I step away, and he turns his head, his attention on the car parked in front of my parents' house.

"Why is Tyler's car here?"

I look at the Benz seated on my street, pretending it belongs there. "Remember I told you dinner was coming to me? Tyler and Izzy picked up food on their way home from her appointment."

"You didn't mention Tyler."

"Well, he's not here for my pleasure. The kids are ecstatic. Trust me when I tell you, I don't want the man in my house. He just decided to take over my evening like a bat out of hell, and now, I have to go inside and play Steve Harvey while pretending he didn't leave me, divorced and—"

"Come here." He holds out his hand, and I take it, letting his warmth draw me close. "You don't have to explain. I'm not jealous."

I drop my jaw and place a splayed hand over my chest, feigning insult. "Not even a little?"

"I'm pissed he gets to have dinner with you, but I'm not jealous because I think he's going to win you over in any way."

"How can you be so sure?" I challenge playfully.

He runs a hand over my hair and plays with the ends. "Because one of us left you brassy and the other made you blonde."

A slow, sexy groan crawls up from deep in my belly. "Man, do you know how to sweet-talk a woman." Leaning forward, I give him a final quick kiss and step away. "I have to get inside. My five minutes are up."

"Night, babe."

I rush down the sidewalk. I'm an adult woman and a sexually renewed one at that. That is, until I stand on the front path of my childhood home and see the dining room curtain pulled back, and suddenly, I feel like a sullen teenager about to get in trouble with my ex-husband for sneaking into my own house when he wasn't even invited over.

twenty-three

As I roll over in bed, my bones are sore, and my body feels used and abused.

I sit up in complete darkness until I realize I'm wearing one of those furry sleep masks. I put it on when I got in last night at three in the morning after working a dream wedding with an extensive breakdown. Jillian and I had crawled out of the venue, along with the two assistants we had hired for the day, and vowed to sleep for the next twenty-four hours.

I lift my mask and see the bright Sunday sunshine pouring through my window, so I put the mask back on and crash back to my bed. I'm about to fall back asleep when the aroma of coffee and the crackling sounds of a sizzling pan pique my interest.

Sitting up, I lift the mask again and look at the time. It's ten in the morning. Dad should be at the gym for his workout and swim. After which he goes to the diner for breakfast with his friends, and then he plays billiards until two, at which time he'll come home for a nap, play the piano, and then start a Sunday sauce for the kids to enjoy when they get home from Tyler's. Got to love a man with a routine.

Confused by what could have kept Dad from his morning, I use the bathroom, brush my teeth, groan at my haggard appearance, and then saunter downstairs. When I get to the kitchen, I'm shocked by the sight in front of me.

Will is in my kitchen. White T-shirt, whisk, and moving about in all his brawny glory.

He's drinking from a coffee cup while flipping pancakes and listening to Harry Styles on the Bluetooth. His head shakes while he dances, and my heart is a freaking earthquake at the sight of him being here.

As well as utterly perplexed.

"I thought I was the one with the penchant for breaking and entering?"

Will looks up, and there's the smolder. If I didn't love this house so much, I'd worry he was going to torch it to the ground with the way he's staring at me.

I lean back in wonder. I'm wearing my cappuccino pajama bottoms and his oversize sweatshirt, and I still have a sleep mask on my head like a headband. One would think I was wearing a sexy cocktail dress with fishnets and stilettos with the way his eyes darken, threatening to turn me into a melted puddle of tired goo.

"Morning." He puts his cup down and removes the pancakes from the pan, plating them and sliding it onto the countertop. "Your dad let me in before he left. He told me not to wake you until after ten or you'd bite my head off and suggested the best way to do so was by putting on the coffeepot. When I told him I brought pancakes, he called me wise, told me I was a good man, and suggested I not do anything tawdry in his house while he was gone."

I tilt my head. "You've been here since seven?"

"I was excited to start my Sunday." His grin warms my belly. "I like you in my sweatshirt."

"I'd be lying if I said I haven't worn it every day since you gave it to me in the jail cell."

He bites his lip as I walk over to the counter-height chair and take a seat. The pancake is perfectly golden, and he even added a sprinkle of powdered sugar. When he slides two pieces of bacon on my plate, I moan.

"You know how to woo a woman. If you hadn't already gotten into my pants, this would be the way."

"All this time, I was wasting my energy on hair salons and magic shows," he teases.

"Are you ever going to show me how to levitate?"

"A master never reveals his secrets."

I narrow my eyes at him and take a bite of the pancake. "Damn, that's good. You're lucky you're a good cook, or I'd kick you out for not teaching me how to get my ass off the ground." He laughs deeply, and I point my fork at him. "No jokes."

He takes the pan off the burner and walks it to the sink. "I definitely have some ways to get your ass off the ground."

I take another bite and then lift the bacon, examining how thick and delicious it looks. "If you're just using me for the sex, you'd better think twice. I'm not that kind of girl. Oh, who am I kidding? I'm totally using you for your body. Although your ability to cook is quickly becoming my favorite thing about you." With a bite of the bacon, I close my eyes and savor it. Man, I love me some bacon.

As I'm chewing and loving on my food, I realize he's still standing by the sink. The pan is now clean, and he's just standing there, staring at me.

I lift a napkin and wipe my mouth. Then, I realize I still have the damn mask on my head. I slide it off, but he's looking me with this crinkle around his eyes and a soft haze, like he's looking at me for the first time.

"What?" I finally ask.

"You're beautiful."

The blood rushes into my cheeks. A river of shivers swooshes across my body, and I let out a shaky breath. How two simple words can cause me to clench and shake at the same time is beyond me.

My hand is in my messy hair, and I want to make a comment about how ridiculous I look—the mascara that I'm sure is still on my face despite washing it last night, paired with my blotchy skin, and poor choice of sleepwear. I'm about to point out all of it, but I don't.

There's this magnetic way he's staring at me, like his eyes are glued to my every feature, enraptured. If I think the man can't clearly see what's in front of him, then I'm more insane than my attire.

"You mean that," I state.

His piercing eyes are magnified, as if longing for me. "I do."

My body temperature rises, the sweatshirt I'm wearing feeling too warm. I need to shower.

Taking my plate, I walk around the island and bring it to the sink. Will steps to the side. I run the water over the plate and leave it there, then turn around.

My chest rises as my breasts push against the cotton, suddenly feeling very sensitive. Everything about me is sensitive. Even my feelings. His honesty makes it easy for me to be vulnerable.

"Your words disarm me, Will. I'm not prepared for it. I'm crazy about you. It's exciting and frightening. So very, very frightening to my vulnerable heart."

He places a hand on my head and rubs a tender circle over my cheek. "There're only two things you don't use your sarcasm as a defense for. When you're being a mom and when you're designing."

"It's a control thing."

"When you're at work, you have this confidence about you. Even if you're unsure, you just go with it. With your kids, there's so much love there that you know what to do. Now, for the first time, I see it with us. Is it possible Melissa Jones has decided to give in and just ... be?"

I lean back to look into his face, which is virile, full of vigor and sexual potency.

"That would mean I'd have to surrender my complete control to you."

His thumb runs over my lips. "I'd settle for an ounce because when it comes to you, I have zero."

This gorgeous, sexy, talented man has me completely disarmed. If he hasn't noticed that, it's because I've done a terrible job of showing him. My hand rises to his chest, and I feel the pulse beneath it. I move my fingers over where I know his scar is. One that made him a hero and a victim. One that had him feeling like he didn't have a choice before he took his choices back.

William Bronson is my shot in the chest. The one that has the chance to harm me. To heal me. To love me.

"Take it," I breathe.

He kisses me.

My hands rise to his shoulders to steady myself.

The feverish rush of his kiss is smoking. Our tongues slide against one another with pressure and force. I'm being pulled into his body, exactly where I want to be.

He moves south, placing a soft kiss on the skin of my jaw, sending a wave of pleasure down my body. I grab his head and rake my fingers through his thick hair as his mouth lowers to my neck, his teeth placing little nips that race tiny jolts to my core.

LOVE ... IT'S COMPLICATED

My fists grip the counter as he lifts my sweatshirt. With no bra on, my breasts spring free, the cool morning air making my nipples pucker and tighten.

A gravelly groan exits his lips as his eyes widen at the sight, like a man starving for a taste.

And taste he does.

Heated lips are wrapped around my breast, flicking at the erect bud and sucking on the skin, leaving hickeys I'll be keeping as souvenirs. I want to grab him, touch him, undress him ... but this is all for him to seize. My head rolls back as he does things to me, and I can now confirm Will is a breast man who knows what he's doing—and thank the good Lord for that.

He slides my bottoms down and roams over the curve of my butt.

"I love that you sleep commando." His gravelly tone is muted as he falls to his knees.

His hands grip my waist as he makes a meal of kissing every inch of my skin. My legs are bare, spread and vibrating in anticipation, and he's still too far north, whispering sweet nothings against my flesh.

"Your body is a marvel. It's a shame it's ever covered. Every inch is a masterpiece, each curve like fine silk. I could touch you all day and never get enough."

The coaxing pressure of his thick tongue glides down my lower belly, and I lift my hips, desperate for something more.

"I thought my dad said not to do anything tawdry in the house."

He rises and curls his fingers around my neck, forcing me to look up at him as he takes my lower lip and bites it, slowly pulling back and then returning for a heat-blistering kiss.

"Baby, nothing about what we're about to do is cheap."

Will looks over the countertop, where I slung my face mask. "Turn around," he demands.

I do so, and I'm surprised when he takes my hands and binds them with the mask. They're no steel cuffs, but his handiwork is rather impressive.

Completely naked and bound in my kitchen, I tense with need.

"What if my father comes home early?"

"I deadbolted all the doors. We'll have a minute before he unlocks everything."

"Assumed we'd have kitchen sex?"

"An officer is always aware of his surroundings and anticipates every outcome."

Will's hands are on my breasts and hips as he kisses down my back. I melt into affection and quicken with need, surrendering to his all-consuming touch as he turns me around, takes a knee, lifts my leg over his shoulder, and feasts on me in the kitchen.

"William," I cry out, calling him by his Christian name as I praise at the altar of William Bronson.

"So fucking sweet," he growls against my core. "And you're all mine."

Eyes rolling back. Skin prickling with heat. Hands desperate to move and touch and play … they're bound, and I lose myself in what he's doing to my core. His fingers run along the seam of my pussy, and my knees buckle as I moan loudly and drop my head forward, addicted to the sight of this beautiful man.

On his knees.

Worshipping me.

Right here, out in the open of my kitchen.

My orgasm builds, climbing higher inside my body, and I begin to shake like a volcano about to burst. The force of his hands and tongue creates a pressure that builds from deep within me. I can't hold on much longer.

"I love the way your body quivers when you're about to come."

Will sucks my clit once more, and I'm done for. My orgasm erupts, sending shock waves through my body.

"Fucking heaven," he drawls as he licks me once more and savors every drop of my arousal.

He lowers my leg and brings me to a full standing position, but I'm useless and weak. He hoists me up so my legs wrap around his waist, and I have to balance myself with my core since my hands are still bound.

Will places me on the kitchen table. I look down and see the oak that was sanded by my father.

"Not here," I say.

He looks down at me, his brow furrowed.

"My dad made this table for my mom. Feels sacrilegious. Plus, my kids eat here."

With a nod, he stands, and the arousal in his jeans is powerful.

"I plan to fuck you, and when I do, I'm not stopping for a very, very long time. So, where can I do so that's safe from sacrilege?"

LOVE ... IT'S COMPLICATED

I look around—couch, ottoman, dining room, Hunter's toy chest—and can't find anywhere that's not off-limits.

With one quick swoop, he places me over his shoulder, caveman-style.

"Will!" I yelp as he walks into the kitchen, bends down to grab my sweatshirt and pajama pants off the tiled floor, and then heads toward the stairs. "Where are we going?"

"Your bed."

"Second door on the left."

When we get to my room, he places me down gently, and the weight makes the bed creak. He unbinds my hands, and I'm surprised by the action.

"Wrought iron." He seems pleased with my childhood bed. "We can definitely play in here."

I scoot up the bed and wonder just what kind of *play* Will has in mind.

"New rule. If you're giving me control, then you're giving it on your own. I'm not taking it. Grab the headboard. If you let go, you lose."

"What do you win?"

"I get to take you dancing again. Country music only. May even force you into a line dance."

I groan. "If I win you have to work another wedding with me."

"That's not a punishment at all, baby. Hell, I crave time with you." He winks and reaches behind him to remove his shirt. His body, ripped and brawny, is on display. His tattoo, Saint Michael, blazing in glory, ignites on his bicep. It's as beautiful as the first time I saw it. I was in a bar, attracted to this man then and even more so now. My fingers itch to touch the inked skin. Itch to cling to this man ... but I can't.

"I love your tattoo."

"I love the way you look when you're staring at it. Your lips part, and those blue eyes widen. It takes everything in me not to touch you. For so long, I was yearning to kiss this perfect mouth of yours."

If he only knew the thoughts that raced through my mind all these months. I've been mentally drooling over this man since the moment I met him.

"You can kiss me now. All you want."

He smiles and leans in to slide that silken tongue into my mouth in a soul claiming kiss. "Happiest man alive."

I lean back on the bed and grip the wrought iron rails of my youth.

Will slides his hand into his back pocket, takes out a condom, and lays his wallet on the bedside table. As he rises to remove his jeans, I lean up a little. My eyes don't leave his until his clothes fall to the floor.

Will's body is gorgeous, right down to the large, thick erection he's grabbing. It's thick and veined. Flawless in proportion to the rest of his body. My mouth salivates as he runs his hand over the engorged tip. It's glistening with precum that he spreads over the throbbing head with his thumb. I'm full from the pancakes, yet starving for a taste of him. I clench the metal bars firmly to keep from launching myself across the bed and feasting on every delicious inch of Will.

When he's fully sheathed, he stands tall and looks down at me with smoky eyes.

Then, he slides the mask over my eyes.

The bed dips as Will kneels on it. It's only a full, so no matter where he moves, I can feel him and even sense the swipe in the air as he positions himself above me. My legs spread, and I moan at the heaviness of his cock brushing against my wet center.

"On your stomach." His commanding tone beckons. His voice is hoarse, almost a groan. It reminds me of the one he used the night we met—the police officer waiting in the shadows.

His hands are on my hips, flipping me over. Like a good girl, I oblige.

In Will fashion, he starts from the beginning. My neck, down my spine, and thighs … all loved by his mouth and tongue. He doesn't pick up where he left off downstairs. He revels in the joy of the foreplay process, and it drives me insane.

Deft hands knead my skin until it prickles.

A firm chest rubs against my back, the friction scintillating.

A thick cock tempts my ass as it slides up and down.

It's just a tease because he drops down low and lifts my hips off the sheet, level with his face. He runs a tongue up the swell of my ass and I jolt, ready for anything he's about to give me.

Two fingers slide into me, and I moan. Will begins a steady rhythm as his mouth kisses and then bites my ass. I yelp out in pleasure and pain combined.

"Baby, you're drenched." With each word he pumps deeper with his fingers, curving them to hit the most sensitive spot. I bite the pillowcase and then exhale an audible groan in pleasure.

His fingers glide out of my wetness and circle my clit, forcing me to cry out his name while gyrating my hips. My breasts swell as his free hand takes one of my nipples and tugs firm, yet gently. The sensation in the darkness of the blindfold is too arousing, too pleasing, for my body to take.

His fingers work inside me again and I'm taken from a new angle that has me panting as heavily as before. I want to touch and kiss and suck every last inch of him. My hips are bucking, my legs widening. My core is clenching tightly as I grasp at the bars and scrape my nails against the metal. The burning desire for this man to bring me to release is so blistering that it's painful.

My arms are sore from the way I've been thrashing about and holding tight. Still, I keep a grip on the metal because that's what my officer commanded me to do.

Then, he grips the inside of my knees to hoist me up and slams into me from behind. I see stars inside the dark mask as he pumps and grinds, eliciting another orgasm to build. His hands are everywhere—my thighs, my stomach, my nipples ... tugging just enough to hurt so bad that it's good.

I can barely contain myself, circling my hips to match his thrusts. Will's fingers dig into the sides of my hips, holding me still and sending me into a whirlwind of pleasure that has my hips rising off the bed and body weightless. My hands nearly bleed from how hard they're gripping the rails.

If I ever doubted the man could levitate me, I was sorely mistaken. He can make me fucking fly.

The pillow beneath me muffles my screams and chants of his name and praises to God for making such a remarkable specimen. You'd think I'd be spent, but I'm the opposite. My body is zinging with excitement, raging for more of Will.

I can't get enough.

I'm addicted.

Will leans back, so I roll over, unsure of where he is.

The mask lifts from my eyes, and I'm rewarded with the most gorgeous sight I've ever seen.

William Bronson in his smoldering glory.

That simmer in his eyes is softer, glowing hazel as he brushes hair off my forehead and places a soft kiss on my lips.

"You can let go now." He places a hand on my arm and gently guides it off the rod and then the next. "I want to make love to you now."

I smile. "You don't have to ask. This is your moment to take."

"I don't want to take from you, Melissa. I want everything you're willing to give."

I brush a finger over his lips. So lush and warm. Lips that feel like home.

"I'm yours," I whisper.

He kneels, strapping and naked, sheathed in protection and staring at me lovingly. I take his hand and guide him back down to me.

My head is resting on a mountain of pillows, yet it's nothing compared to the comfort I feel when he enters me again.

I lean up and kiss him.

Our mouths never release as he pumps into me slowly, sending my head into a dizzying haze of lust and love.

His left hand grabs my right, and we clasp each other tight, like we'd die if we ever let go. Our other free hands roam and touch.

I rest mine on his dewy skin and feel the muscles clench with every pulse of his body.

He grips my hip and pulls my body even closer to his. I can't tell where he begins or I end.

His movements are slow.

Our hearts are fast.

Two people on the cusp of pleasure and, quite possibly, forever.

"I chose you," Will breathes into my lips.

My eyes flutter up to him as I drink in his words and his desire.

"When you kissed me in the parking lot, I knew in that moment that you were the woman I wanted to be with."

My brows furrow because the words are wrong, but as a tear gently rolls down my cheek, I know I can't hide it. "I wanted it to be me."

"I didn't want to leave you that night." His arms shake lightly, as if he's holding himself back. His eyes close. "Fuck. What is this between us? I'm addicted to you, Melissa."

I grab his face and will him to open his eyes. He does.

"Two people who happen to be in each other's life at just the right time, remember?"

"The right fucking time."

My breaths are ragged, and my body is quickening again. "Don't hold back, Will. Give me everything."

And with that, my man unleashes it all. Every ounce of want, frustration, desire, and carnal need is shared in my bed. It creaks and hums in all its tawdry glory. And I'm certain neither this bed nor I will ever be the same.

twenty-four

My head is nestled on a very warm chest, except there is an excessive banging that's definitely not coming from the heart of the man whose chest I'm lying on. I sit up in a groggy haze, place my hand on my temple, and look around my bedroom. To my right is a sleeping Bronson, looking devilishly handsome in his white-sheet-clad glory. I, myself, am sans clothing and surprised we both fell asleep. I guess I'm still tired from last night.

Bang, bang, bang.

The sound is not coming from my head. It's pulsing from downstairs. The front door foyer, to be exact. I look over at the clock and see it's two in the afternoon. I walk over to the window, and there, on the street before me, is a familiar Mercedes.

"Shit!" I rush over to the floor and grab my cappuccino bottoms and sweatshirt that Will carefully dropped when we came up here. I slide them on and close my door before rushing down the stairs and letting my children in the house.

"What took you so long?!" Izzy pushes in with an eye roll and sarcastic attitude. Her strawberry-blonde hair is in a high ponytail, and she seems extra exasperated for her eleven-year-old self.

"I thought you'd never let us in the house!" Hunter wraps his arms around me.

I lean down to kiss his head.

"We didn't think you were home, but Daddy saw your car outside and said you had to be here. Where's Will?"

I run my hand through his hair and over his face. "How do you know Will is here?"

"His truck's outside." Hunter runs into the living room, presumably to see Will.

I glance upstairs nervously. I don't want my children seeing a naked man in my bed. My nerves are quickly elevated when I turn back to the front door threshold and am visually slammed by a very disturbed, very annoyed-looking Tyler Landish.

"You've got to be fucking kidding me," he says with complete disdain that has me tilting my head at him and squinting my eyes. "Just rolling out of bed, I see."

"You brought the kids home four hours early. I was asleep upstairs. Why are you here? Is everything okay?" I take Hunter's backpack and Mr. Snuggles from him.

"If there's a man upstairs in your bed, I do not want my children in this house."

Tyler walks inside with a shopping bag in his hand, but I place my hand on his chest to keep him from stepping farther.

"You are not allowed to snoop in this home, just as I'm not allowed in yours." *I should know. I have the phantom cuff marks on my wrists to prove it.*

The upstairs door to my bedroom opens, and I close my eyes, silently hoping he will stay up there, but from the heavy footsteps walking down, I know Will is, in fact, coming downstairs. Tyler looks from me and up to the staircase with a mouth that's pinched, and his hands are clenched.

Will comes down to the foyer and takes a step directly behind me. I do a quick glance to see he's in his jeans, tee, socks, shoes, and all. Even his hair is perfectly combed. He places his protective hands on my arms and secures me with a gentle rub of his thumbs.

"Everything okay here?" Will asks gruffly.

"Yes," I say to Will, but I'm looking at Tyler. "Tyler and the kids came home early to …" I stumble, confused. "Why are you here?"

"Why are you sleeping in?" Tyler folds his arms across his barrel chest.

"I took a nap because I worked until three in the morning, not that it's any of your business." I say, annoyed, because it isn't any of his business, and yet, in a weird way, it kind of is.

"The kids wanted to surprise you."

"They succeeded. I'm thrilled they're home. You can leave now."

"Actually, they asked me to stay. Izzy remembered this morning that she has a history presentation tomorrow, and she needed a special kind of poster board. We traveled all the way to Castleton to get it." Tyler holds up a brown bag with the thick poster board inside. "She said she has plenty of art supplies."

"She also has about ten art kits at your house," I deadpan.

"I wasn't driving another forty-five minutes from Castleton, all the way back to Greenwood Village, and then back here for drop-off. We figured we'd do the project here to save time," he says and just stands here, staring at me and looking over at Will, as if wondering when he's leaving.

I glower back at him because I refuse to ask Will to leave.

"I'll be in the kitchen. Do you want to order in? The kids and I haven't eaten since breakfast." Tyler smirks and brushes past us and walks toward the kitchen.

Hunter and Izzy squeal, and their happiness to have their father here both eats at my heart and feeds it.

Will steps around me, his hand still tenderly holding on to my arm. "Melissa, can I have a word with you outside?"

With a nod, I grab a jacket to follow Will outside onto the front porch and close the door.

He shoves his hands forcefully into his coat pockets. I lean forward and zipper his coat because he's looking at me as if staying warm out here in the cold is not a clear concern for him. When I'm done zipping the teeth of the zipper up his chest, I look at him and smile, and then it falls because he is not smiling … at all.

"What the hell is Tyler doing?"

"He brought my children home. Did you forget he is indeed the father of Hunter and Isabella?"

"He's here, playing house." His jowl is protruding out of his skin. "I would tell him to go to hell, but it's not my place yet, and I'm waiting for you to look at him and tell him to go the fuck home."

"Tyler is a pompous asshole, but this *hanging out at our house* appears to be a new thing the kids want to do with him. I'm not thrilled about it, and I have to get Tyler to make it stop. He's like a stray cat that you feed once, and it's back on your doorstep."

"It's your house. Kick him out."

"It's my father's house."

"Then, have *him* kick Tyler out."

"It's my children's home too. They planned this with their father today, and I've done everything I can to make them realize this is their home through and through. If I kick Tyler out, I'm the bad guy."

Will pinches the bridge of his nose. He lowers his hand and looks back at me with a severe stare. "Melissa, I wanted to spend the day with you. I didn't come over here for a quickie and a nap."

"I wasn't expecting my children to come home early." I look at him with equal exasperation and wonder why he is not understanding that I have zero control over my children being here. "Frankly, Will, I thought you were cool with the fact that I have children. Why are you behaving as if their presence is ruining your day?"

"I love your children. The problem is, I don't want Tyler spending the evening with you when it was *my* plan to spend the evening with you. If that meant having pasta with your kids or making papier-mâché army men for a history project, then that'd be great. Instead, the man who gave you up is inside the house, and the man who desperately wants to be with you, in every way, is standing outside in the cold."

"For the record, you brought us outside."

"You know what I mean!" His tone rises, and I know I've struck a nerve. The smolder I love has cooled completely and is replaced with an icy glare. "I can't go back in there. Not with him here."

"Will, look, I am really sorry, but … *dammit* … if I go in there and tell the kids that I want Tyler to go because you're staying, they're going to hate me for kicking their dad out and hate you for taking his place. This is why I don't want to tell them about us. Not yet. Divorce is messy, and mine is no neater than anyone else's."

His Adam's apple bobs as he swallows fiercely. "He gets to stay, and I have to leave?"

I run my hand through my hair and pull at the scalp because he has every single right to be upset about the situation right now, but I still have to look at him in his beautiful, kind, caring face, and say, "For now, yes."

Will starts to turn, his body tight and clearly distraught by this conversation.

LOVE ... IT'S COMPLICATED

I grab the lapels of his coat and pull him back, inching up on my toes. "I'll make it up to you."

I place a kiss on his lips. He fights me for just a moment until he returns it and sinks into me in that way that he does when we connect.

Hands, lips ... even our feet are practically on top of one another.

"Tomorrow? You're off, and I'll take a huge, tremendous break in my day. Let me treat you to a fancy lunch and show my man a good time on a Monday morning-slash-afternoon because I have to get my kids from school."

He glances down at me under hooded eyes and long lashes, not happy with today's situation, but seemingly pleased with the promise of tomorrow.

"Fine. Under one condition." He pauses and waits for my full attention, which I am giving him with batted lashes. "You have to tell Tyler how serious we are, and you have to talk to him about his expectations of what my presence in your life is going to look like."

"What is that exactly?"

He leans in so our foreheads are touching, gripping my hips, and I soak in every bit of breath he takes. "He'll be seeing me a lot, and so will his children because I plan on being around for a very, very long time."

My heart feels like it's grown ten times too big. Problem with hearts when they swell is, they feel like they might explode. I have to rub my chest to shrink my heart back down so it's not a fragile size. Nope, doesn't matter. It's still totally shatterable.

"I'll try."

Will's departure downstairs seems sullen as he makes his way to his truck. I watch his car roll down the street, and my hand lingers on my lips that were kissed many times by him today.

When I go inside, I prepare for the onslaught of fake happy family and the incessant questions from Tyler, and I wonder why the hell Tyler seems to be wanting to come around so often lately.

Odds are, I won't get the answer to any of it.

twenty-five

THE HISTORY PROJECT WITH Tyler and the kids turned into a Hunter magic show. Having Tyler over wasn't unbearable. For once, he took interest in Hunter's magic kit and even looked up how to do a hidden coin trick. He even offered to help Izzy study while I took Hunter upstairs for his bath.

Dad locked himself in the garage workshop because he couldn't handle seeing Tyler's face in his home. There are now two men who despise my ex-husband's presence in my kitchen. When I went to talk to Tyler about it, he was already gone. Izzy said Maisie had called, and he rushed off.

I called Will before I went to bed, but it was brief because I was still exhausted.

So, here we are on Monday as I get my shit together. I stop by the office and drop off bins and start cleaning and itemizing. Jillian and I check in with the delivery drivers and one of our assistants to make sure all the props were placed back in the storage unit. Jillian has to take Ainsley to a doctor's appointment, and I'm set to meet Will at a restaurant in Greenwood Village at noon.

It's a cold, crisp morning, yet the sun pours down, warming the day. I have my coat on, yet it's open, and I walk down the cobblestone sidewalks to the restaurant. I'm a few minutes early. My phone is in my hand, and I'm checking the weather for the rest of the week when I hear an angry squeal. It's high-pitched, surprised, and very close. Looking up, I come face-to-face with a woman I haven't thought about in a while.

Allison Lalayne.

Yes, the woman who Will was engaged to when we first kissed is standing on the sidewalk, glaring at me with hardened brown eyes and a scowl on her face that is anything but the happy bride turned sad ex-bride I met weeks ago.

"Hey," I say to her and start to walk faster because the look on her face is making my heart speed up in an uncomfortable way.

"You bitch!" Her words have me halting my feet and clenching my eyes and ears closed.

I turn around very slowly and face her. Allison is wearing a pastel-blue peacoat. It's a sweet-looking color for a very irate-looking woman. There's a large iced coffee in her hand that she's clenching as if it were a sword.

"Excuse me?" I say even though I heard her. Loud and clear.

Her face softens just a touch before settling back to her pissed off pout. She takes a step forward. "I've thought what I would say to you, and now, here you are, and all I want to say is … you're a home-wrecker!"

"Allison, please understand—"

"I haven't been able to look at my social media because everything makes me so sad, especially your posts because you were supposed to be my wedding designer. Then, I started feeling more like myself, so I went on and saw your post from a wedding you did. You made *A Midsummer Night's Dream* event. There was a video, and … I don't understand. Why was Will with you at that wedding?"

My social media.

Why was I an idiot who didn't think she'd see it? I mentally berate myself as I hold up my hands to explain. "My assistant was sick, and he offered to help."

Allison looks down at her heels and shakes her head. Her eyes flicker, like there're a million thoughts running through her head. "My friends saw you with him at a table at Lone Tavern. They said he was having drinks with a woman, and they sent me a picture of you two together. I didn't want to believe it was you, but then I saw Instagram, and he was with *you*. Will called off the wedding after our brunch. It was you. You stole my fiancé!"

"That's not correct."

LOVE ... IT'S COMPLICATED

"You two met, and he left me. You saw him at brunch and wanted him, which is why you started talking about how horrible marriage was. You wanted him to break up with me. When he did, you swooped in and started hanging out with him."

My ears boil red as steam pours out of them. "That's not how it happened at all."

"You stole my fiancé!"

"It was just drinks at the bar!" I defend. "And, yes, fine, I might have kissed him first, but that was before I knew he was engaged. He didn't know I was going to kiss him, and he pushed me away. It was a shove really and a very embarrassing one for me. The next day, we saw each other at brunch, and I was shocked and mortified, and the entire situation was shit, especially when he ran into me at Target, but I sent him away. Then, I was in his cell, and we made a truce, and it was never meant to be anything but a simple kind of friendship."

Now, it's more. So much more.

As soon as the words are out of my mouth, I instantly regret them. I always knew my diarrhea of the mouth would outdo me. Today is definitely the day. Stupid mouth.

"Allison, this is a conversation for you and Will. I shouldn't be involved in any of this."

I start to move, but she keeps following me down the sidewalk. I ignore the curious glances of passersby. The virtual scarlet letter on my back, blaring in neon red for all to see. Seriously, it's like a bad Demi Moore movie out here.

"You're too old. He'll never settle down with you."

"You're right." I lift my hand in agreement. *She's right. He could go for a much younger girl with boobs that don't sag.*

"You're not even pretty."

"I'm haggard." *Okay, so I was feeling pretty this morning but I'm not about to argue with her about it.*

"Your ass is huge."

"Way too fucking big." *Geez, she's really hitting below the belt, no pun intended.*

"Don't you have kids? I've seen them on your Instagram. Your daughter never smiles and your son is a brat. Will would never be able to stand them."

Okay, so my vanity might not be that important to me, but there is a line that gets crossed when my children are brought into a conversation. I spin around. "My kids are fucking awesome. Will loves my kids, and they love him back."

In the blink of an eye, her momentary mean demeanor is back to the distraught and troubled one of a woman deserted.

Tears stream down her face as she clenches her chest and coils in.

"He was supposed to love *my* children."

This …

This is the moment my entire existence is shrunk into a mere pebble below her patent leather heels. She was supposed to be the mother of Will's child. Her future with the man of her dreams wasn't the only thing ripped from her. Her plans of being a mother, having a family of her own, were torn from beneath her fingertips' grasp.

I feel that pain from deep in my core.

My heart drops. Nausea bubbles from within me.

Allison is steadfast on her feet and growing more upset with the passing seconds.

"I can't believe someone whose husband left her for another woman would steal someone else's man. I know your story," she spits. "You planned my cousin's wedding, so I asked around. Your husband left you for your hairdresser. You were kicked out of your own home and had to go live with your widowed father in Newbury. Your kids left their school, and you lost your life. Everyone in Greenwood Village knows it. I felt sorry for you, but now … I despise you. You're no better than the woman who betrayed you. You took a love that belonged to me. It wasn't yours to take, and for that, I hope you rot in hell!"

I grip my stomach and feel the wound of her words. I've been sliced by the knife of truth, and it stings.

"Allison, please. Let me explain."

"Just wait until I blast on every wedding blog there is that Lavish Events is a man-stealing whore industry. They'll plan your wedding and steal your groom."

My bravado sinks with her comment. Jillian's nightmare of our business being tarnished came to life in that one sentence.

"Let's talk about this. I'm a cretin. A horrible, villainous woman. What Will and I did or didn't do has nothing to do with my business. It's not solely mine. Jillian Hathaway is a gem of a woman. A single mother of a beautiful little girl. Don't destroy her business."

Her steps get closer to me as her finger is out in a vicious point. "Why would I worry about your business when my life is ruined? You stole my husband!"

"He wasn't your husband."

"He was my everything! If he didn't meet you, none of this would've happened!" she yelps. In one swift motion, she lifts the lid off her cup, and her iced coffee is thrown at me.

Like an avalanche of overpriced coffee, I am drenched from head to navel. Face, sweater, coat, ... all soaked in dark brown liquid.

I gasp as the ice drips down my neck and into my cleavage. My phone that was in my hands a moment ago is now on the ground, the glass shattered, making the picture on the screen unrecognizable.

Kneeling down, I grab my phone and try to swipe the screen with no luck. I'm now cold, wet, and phoneless ... oh, and I've been publicly decried a home-wrecker too.

Allison looks stunned by her actions. She backs up onto the curb and then takes off down the street. A woman standing nearby offers me a tissue. I refuse it because what I really need is a hose and a lobotomy.

"Melissa." My name is called from across the street by a woman's voice I know well. "Are you okay? That girl just attacked you with the largest coffee I've ever seen!"

As if my morning couldn't get more dizzying, Maisie Mirlicourtois is walking toward me with her hands full of shopping bags and wearing head to toe vegan leather. Oh, and her hair looks freaking awesome.

"Come in the salon. We could stop in there and blow-dry you off. We'll even wash your hair."

She's staring at me like I'm a wounded puppy who just got hit by a car. I feel like one actually. I'd rather hobble my way home than go back with her to her salon of adultery.

"I need to get out of here."

I start to move, nearly tripping over the plastic cup and straw stranded by its owner. Its pastel wearing, coffee throwing owner. My hands are outstretched because I'm cold and stunned. Stunned because of what Allison did and stunned by the fact that the words she said were true.

I am a home-wrecker.

I'm staring at the woman who wrecked my home.

Hot tears build behind my eyes, but I widen them in hopes of holding the tears in. I refuse to cry in public, and more importantly, I will never cry in front of Maisie.

I turn around and start running back toward my office, where my car is parked. I need to get out of here. I have to get in my car and go home and decompress from the onslaught of truth that just assaulted me.

"Melissa! Wait. Where are you going?" Maisie shouts out, and I ignore her.

By the time I get to my car, I'm crying with tears streaming down my cheeks. I start to drive, my hands shaking, aimlessly heading around Greenwood Village, and then hit the highway. Two years' worth of hot remorse comes out of my body in a loud sob.

I know the pain that was just pelted at me by Allison Lalayne because I'd felt it too.

Hell, I still feel it on a daily basis.

I loved Tyler Landish, and he left me for the love of another woman. I don't care how mentally strong you are; you never get over that shit.

"I chose you."

Will's words from yesterday pierce my ears.

"When you kissed me in the parking lot, I knew in that moment that you were the woman I wanted to be with."

If I hadn't launched myself at Will, would he really have left Allison, like he claimed he was going to? He says it was inevitable, but I know better than that. I destroyed their happily ever after.

Will is no better a man than Tyler.

I'm just as evil as Maisie.

I once told Tyler it was his fault for putting himself in a position to love another. Will did the same. He saw me at the bar, and he flirted with me. I know I'm not crazy when I say he gave me bedroom eyes and danced with me the way no taken man should ever dance with another woman. Just the thought of Will now dancing with someone else like that has my palms twitching. I'd be livid. I'd be heartbroken. I'd die.

Allison should be upset. She should be absolutely devastated. She has every right to attack me on a sidewalk, armed with an iced coffee and vicious rhetoric.

I'd do the same.

In fact, I did.

LOVE ... IT'S COMPLICATED

A long time ago.

I marched myself into Maisie's salon with my fist in the air and my words curling through the packed salon. She looked like she wanted to cry as I called her a slut. I also told her she was a shit stylist. I threw a hairbrush at her, like a total psychopath, and stormed out.

"Fuck!" I yell in my car when I reach a stoplight and bang my hands on the steering wheel so hard that my palms feel tingly and numb.

How life has come full circle is beyond me. It's so messed up, and there's no way for me to clean this mess.

The worst part is, I'm pretty sure, somewhere along the way, I fell in love with William Bronson.

When Tyler left, I never thought I'd love again. I'd invested my whole world in him, and when he left, he took a chunk of my confidence with him. I felt like second-best. A downgrade. A discard. In fact, I felt like that long before he left.

I drive down to Castleton and past the bare trees that look over the mountaintops. I think about how happy I was when I was just a teen, driving these roads for the first time. Tara and Tyler were in tow, and we'd sing at the tops of our lungs while weaving down the valley.

When I reach Newbury, I'm on the familiar roads Tyler and I would take on long evenings when Izzy wouldn't sleep. She loved the car, so we'd pile in, listening to the radio, and lull our little girl to sleep. Hunter always liked the stroller. I drive past the woods where we went for hikes with Izzy's hand in Tyler's and Hunter in an infant carrier on my chest.

As the kids got bigger, the park was our usual haunt. Tyler wasn't around as much during those days, so it would be me and the kids walking around the neighborhood for hours. I went from a crazy teen to a stressed-out mom in a heartbeat. Those first few years of each of their lives, I was so invested and exhausted. I had little of myself to give to my husband.

Then, Mom got sick. I spent most of my days with her at doctor's appointments and pushing her wheelchair around town so she could get fresh air. I didn't see Tyler for almost a year because I was with my mom so much. We knew her days were finite, and I wanted to spend as many as I could with her.

When he told our marriage counselor that I let the marriage go, he was right. I chose our children's early days and then my mother's final ones over ours.

When she died, I was a shell of who I used to be. Overweight, depressed, and drowning in the humdrum of being a stay-at-home mother of two. My job as a wedding designer was falling by the wayside until Jillian offered me a job, and I slowly started to get back into living again. Tara had me at the gym, and I was feeling like myself once more.

When Tyler asked for a separation, I asked him to try to make it work. We stayed at the house and went through the motions of being a family without really being a couple.

When he told me he had fallen in love with another woman and wanted a divorce, I nearly died.

Growing up, you have this vision of what your life will look like. Everyone tells you that you can't control the future, yet no one expects the worst to happen. Death, divorce, and depression were not in the cards. I started this life with a full house. As I played my hand, the cards I had been dealt just got shittier and shittier.

Finally, I met Will. The part of me that had been abandoned was loved again. Long before we became lovers, he started rebuilding me from the inside out by being my friend. He built me up. No longer second-best, I was the upgrade. My entire being felt valued again, and it was liberating. I became myself again. No, I became this amazing newer version of myself, and she was awesome.

I did so at the cost of another woman's happiness.

The thought tarnishes every good feeling I have.

My *woe is me* sobfest is still going strong as I pull up to my parents' house an hour later. I need to change and make a few phone calls, yet I'm shook by the sight before me. A Mercedes and a truck, both I know well, are parked in front.

While I want to cry in a corner, I have to pull up my pantyhose and march my ass inside because my ex-husband and boyfriend are alone. This can't be good.

twenty-six

"Where have you been?" Tyler is on me as soon as I walk through the front door.

I toss my coat and bag on the table by the front door and look at my ex in utter disbelief. "You should be at work, not in my home."

Will walks into the foyer from the kitchen. He looks handsome with his hair combed back, like a man who got himself ready for a date. "You didn't show up for lunch."

My hand flies to my head, and I close my eyes in mortification. "I forgot. I'm sorry."

"You forgot?" He's looking like a puppy, sad he was forgotten yet ferocious he was … forgotten.

Tyler ignores the look of remorse I'm giving Will and intercedes. "We've been calling your phone for the last hour. Izzy was at school, sick. They called me after they couldn't get ahold of you, so I left the office to get her. Come here to find Romeo on the porch, all panicked that you didn't arrive for your date. Maisie said you were accosted by some woman." His dark eyes do a once-over of my attire, which is now dry but covered in a brownish-beige stain. I'm pretty sure my makeup is streaked down my face from crying. "You look like shit."

"Thanks, asshole," I say to Tyler, then turn to Will. "I ran into Allison. Oh my God, she is so upset. Correction: she is destroyed and has every right to be."

Will holds his cell phone up and confirms. "She called, and that's when I started looking for you. Why didn't you pick up my calls?"

"She threw her coffee on me, and I dropped my phone. It's broken." I hold up my own phone to show just how shattered the screen is.

"Why is a woman throwing coffee on you?" Tyler asks with his arms crossed, then turns to Will, who has a furrowed brow as he holds my phone and looks at Tyler. "Were you dating someone when you two got together?"

"I was engaged," Will states with conviction, and I internally cringe.

Tyler, on the other hand, finds this amusing. "The hero cop who my kids think does no wrong left his fiancée for my ex-wife." His smug demeanor is even more crude as he looks at us with pure enjoyment. He raises a fist to his mouth to hide his obvious smile. "I knew you were a smug son of a bitch the day I met you. Wait. I remember now. You were there the night Melissa got arrested. You walked her out to me in the lobby. Do you have a habit of picking up women from jail cells often? Easy lay."

Will takes two quick steps toward Tyler, his fist raised in the air and aimed for Tyler's face. Will's face is stern, jaw clenched and face reddening. "Watch your mouth, Landish!"

I thrust my body in front of Will and push him back. The veins of his arms are protruding through the skin.

"Please, Will, stop!" I shout loudly.

Izzy comes rushing from her room and stands at the top of the stairs. I look up at her. She's already in her pajamas and holding a tissue to her nose. Will doesn't seem to notice her as his focus zeroes in on Tyler.

"Don't you dare speak about Melissa that way," Will states to Tyler, eyes focused and threatening.

"Will! Don't hurt my dad!" Izzy yelps, and Will throws a cautious eye her way.

His body looks like he's been punched in the gut with the way she's looking at him. Not as the hero she saw him as before. Now, he's the man with his fist up to her father's cheek.

LOVE ... IT'S COMPLICATED

"You're gonna pretend to be self-righteous now?" Tyler threatens. "You're not worthy of being around my children, and you're certainly not worthy of dating my ex-wife."

"Mom, you're dating Will?" Izzy asks from the top of the stairs, and I nod. "I thought you were dating Dad?" Izzy's question comes out as a cry.

"I am definitely not dating your father. Why would you think that?"

"Because Dad said you two were going to work things out. He said we're forever a family." There's a desperate wish to her words, and it pours down the foyer and straight to my heart.

I glare at Tyler. "When did you say that?"

"Fuck." Tyler looks at me with a shift of his feet and his hand rubbing the back of his neck. His grievance with Will forgotten, he looks up at Izzy. "Sweetie, you misunderstood."

"You two suck! I hate you guys so much!" Izzy storms back to her room and slams the door.

The three of us flinch from our spots in the foyer at the sound that makes the house shake. Tyler rushes up the stairs to talk to Izzy.

I turn to Will. "You should go."

Apprehensively, Will looks upstairs and then back to me. "I'm getting used to being the guy who is always told to leave."

"Will, that's not what is happening right now."

He grabs his jacket and opens the front door. He starts down the front steps, and I follow him down without my coat, hugging myself to fight off the cold.

"Will, I just ... I'm sorry."

He pauses when he reaches the bottom and shakes his head. "It's okay. I need to get away from Tyler before I say something I'm going to regret. Izzy's freaking out, and I know Allison must have messed you up mentally. You need a minute."

"A minute? I need a year!" I exclaim. I take a step back and do a slow spin as I hold my face and catch my breath. "When I saw Allison today ... she's not okay. You think she's fine, but she's absolutely, utterly destroyed by us. She threw a large coffee at me. That is not the action of a woman who's *fine*. She's putting my whole company on blast, stating, *Don't book these women to plan your wedding, or they'll steal your groom and your heart.* You know what? She's right, Will. You said you chose me. I both loved hearing those words and dreaded every one. You promised it wasn't about me, but you confessed that you chose me, and I can't un-love that!"

His hands fly to his head, and he holds the top and looks up at the sky, as if searching for the answers. "Fine. Yes, I chose you. What does that make me? A man who ends a relationship with a great girl he didn't love to see if maybe, possibly, this incredible woman—who hates him, by the way—would even talk to him. This is about *my* choices, not yours. I chose you. I'd do it again even if it meant you were drenched in coffee every day for the rest of your life because I'm selfish. Fuck, I'm crazy about you, Melissa. I have been since you kissed me. Thirty years. I've kissed a lot of women, but never someone I can't stop thinking about. Someone who makes me fucking happy just to see even if it's for fifteen minutes in her kitchen after a long day. Someone who I would race down a goddamn aisle to be with because I'm that excited to spend the rest of my life with her."

I grip my gut and hunch over. "This is too much, too fast. I'm just getting my life together. My business is finally taking off. Jillian is depending on me. My daughter is falling apart, my son is becoming too amendable, and no matter how hard I try, I can't ever move past the fact that I made you leave another woman."

"You opened my eyes."

"Who knows your eyes won't open up even wider with the next girl who comes into your life?"

The severe cut of his jaw hardens. He takes a step forward and points toward the house. "Do you think because that asshole inside betrayed your vows, cheated on you, and left you that I'd do the same thing? This is different, Melissa. What Allison and I had was a mistake that I ended before it went too far. What I'm offering you is more. *So* much more. I've never felt this before. With anyone. Not with Allison, not with any girlfriend I had in college or high school. Never." He runs his hands through his hair and down the back of his head, gripping his neck and then holding his arms out in a plea.

I turn around and walk a few feet away from him, breathing hard and clenching my chest. "I have kids and a business that's about to crash and burn."

"Those are excuses. I might be coming off way too strong here, but I'm not wasting time. I don't want to take your kids' time or wreck your business. I just want to be with you." He closes the space between us and stops at my back. I can feel the heat of him near, but he's not touching me. "Do you trust me?"

My eyes close at the feel of his heart, pulsating against my back, desperate for an answer.

I want to say yes.

I should.

I can't.

"Melissa, please." His commanding tone is a plea. "I burn for you."

He's right. The fire between us has burned too far, too fast, and everything around us is imploding. Our love is like a spark in the forest. It warms you until it rages on and burns everything in its path.

My silence appears to be answer enough.

"I can't keep chasing you, Melissa. I've laid my heart on the table. This is me. I've vowed to never hurt you, and yet you destroy me because you will never trust me, not because of anything I've done, but because you will forever compare me to your ex-husband. I love you. I'll say it again because I'm not ashamed. I love you. Sadly, that's not enough."

"Will ..." I gasp. My breath is hard to catch.

"Good-bye, Melissa."

He walks away from me. My tears are hot and heavy down my cheeks. I turn around just in time to see him get in his truck.

For the second time today, I feel like shit. Will is gone all too fast, and a huge chunk of my heart has been crushed under the weight of his tires. I fall against the door and sob into my forearm, wondering how I could have felt so alive and crushed in the same afternoon.

Inside, I glance in the mirror in the bathroom and look at my haggard self. A bath and a long winter nap is in order, but I have a damaged eleven-year-old who needs to be consoled, an ex who needs to be put in his place, and a business that needs to be salvaged.

I look upstairs and don't see a shadow. I hear a sound in the living room, so I walk in to find Tyler seated by himself. His head is between his knees.

"Is Izzy down here?" I ask him.

"No. I left her upstairs. She hates me."

"That makes two of us."

He lifts his head, his expression distraught, not the pompous stance he had just fifteen minutes ago. "Lyss, I need to talk to you—"

"If I had a dime for all the people who needed to talk to me today, I'd have ... fifty cents. Forget that. You can wait. Trust me when I say, I have a million things to shout at you, and none of them are kind. First, I need to talk to Izzy. She's sick, and clearly, she's upset."

"This is all my fault."

I stop in my tracks and laugh at his admission of guilt. "If you hadn't played the family man two years too late, then she wouldn't have thought we were getting back together."

"I didn't mean to give that impression."

"Come on, Tyler. You can't be that daft. You went from choosing another woman over our marriage to suddenly coming over for family dinners and playing happy daddy. Of course she was going to get the wrong impression. She's a kid. She wants her parents back together, and you dangled it in front of her like a carrot to a horse. And what was that comment she made about you saying we were going to work things out?"

"I never said that!" He comes off defensive. "Crap, maybe I did. I meant I wanted to put our family back together. Fix the mistakes we made."

"*We* didn't make a mistake, Tyler. You're the one who gave up on us."

"You gave up on us first, Lyss. You gave up on me."

"I didn't give up on you. I gave up on myself."

I wasn't prepared for all of this honesty in one day, but since I'm opening up, I might as well let it all free—my emotion and my tears. *Fuck it.*

"I loved you, Ty. I loved you so much that I stayed in that house for far too long, probably hoping that you'd change your mind. Since I was fifteen, you were the only man I'd ever wanted. I went against my family to be with you. I gave my youth to be the wife and mother you wanted me to be. Every day I was with you, I might not have been the best wife, but I swear my heart belonged to you, Tyler Landish. So, don't you ever say I gave up on us because in my darkest days, your love was the only thing that kept me going."

His dark eyes soften. "I loved you too, Melissa. That's why it was so hard to have you pull away."

LOVE ... IT'S COMPLICATED

My chin is wet from tears that have started to fall down my cheeks. His words are like a vise squeezing around my neck. "Step back and take those words with you."

His rubs his neck and looks around. "I'm an asshole."

"You certainly are." I wipe my face and take a breath of false composure. "It's the past now. There's no need to relive it."

"Is it?"

My palm rises in defense of my heart. "I need to go see my daughter."

Upstairs, I look in Izzy's room. She's not in there, nor is she in the bathroom. I look in my room, assuming she's lying in my bed, which she often does when she's sick. My bed is perfectly made, and my bathroom is empty. I look in Hunter's room, then my father's before heading back to Izzy's. I look in her closet and even under her bed.

"Izzy?" I call over and over again.

Tyler calls from downstairs, "She's not up there?"

"No. Did she come down when you were in the den?"

"I didn't hear her. I'll check the garage."

I walk down the stairs and head to the basement. It's an unfinished cellar with boxes from my move from the old house and a ping-pong table. She's not here.

Running upstairs, I see Tyler looking exasperated. "Where the hell did she go?"

"I don't know. You were here with her," I explain.

His eyes travel to the back kitchen door and then to the foyer. "You were outside with your boyfriend. Did you see her walk out the front door?"

"Of course not! You were in the den. Did you see her walk out the kitchen side door?"

There's no time to argue. Tyler and I search the house again, switching rooms and double-checking where the other came from. We walk around the house and even look in our cars.

Izzy is nowhere to be found.

This isn't right.

As my search for her becomes desperate, I say her name louder. "Izzy!"

A pause and long look at her bedroom window, open with access to the front porch roof and the trellis that winds down to the front lawn, has both our faces and bodies dropping in utter disbelief and despair.

I shudder.

Our daughter ran away.

twenty-seven

My feet are loud on the pavement as I run down the block, calling out her name. She couldn't have gone far. I wasn't outside with Will that long, and Tyler was upstairs, talking to her before coming downstairs. Then, our fight began.

I circle the block and get back to the house just in time to see Tyler, sweaty and panting with red-cheeked desperation, round the next corner. Tyler texts Tara to pick Hunter up from school and then my father to let him know what happened. Then he calls the police, and there's a patrol car outside my house in moments.

"Strawberry-blonde hair, blue eyes. Average height and weight. She had on pajamas, and her hair was tied up." I give him a description while handing him a picture of Izzy.

"She probably went to her friend's house, ma'am-," one of the officers who arrived states and then asks for her cell phone information and if the Find My Phone option is on.

"She doesn't have one," I tell him and watch his brows curl.

"You have an eleven-year-old without a phone? How did you manage that?" he replies with a smirk.

"Good parenting. Now, what do we do now?" Tyler has his hands on his hips.

The officer takes out a pad and pen. "I'm gonna need the names and numbers of her friends. Most runaways head to a friend's house.

You need to start a text exchange with the other mothers to have everyone keep a lookout for your daughter."

Tyler shakes his head and explains, "Izzy doesn't have any friends in a ten-mile radius. They're all in Greenwood Village, and that's too far for her to get on foot, especially since she's only been gone about half an hour."

"You never know. Children can be resourceful. Had a runaway last month walking the median on the highway."

My legs are shaking as I think of Izzy walking on the death trap that is our interstate. Tyler and I are quickly on our phones—cell phone for him, house phone for me—calling the parents of Izzy's old friends, explaining the situation and asking them to talk to their daughters and keep an eye out for her.

Tara walks into the foyer with Hunter. They're both in their winter coats and hats.

I grab Hunter and give him a thousand kisses.

He cries into my shoulder. "Is Izzy gonna be okay?"

"Yes, sweetie. We're doing everything we can to find her."

"Have you tried the school? I thought about it on the drive over. It's a familiar place for her. Maybe she's hiding in the library like I used to when I wanted to ditch class. I'll head back there," Tara offers, and Hunter chimes in, "I want to come. I can show you all the places I've seen her on campus. It's really big. You'll get lost, and they probably won't let you in after hours since you don't have a kid who goes there."

"Wow, buddy. That's really smart." I give him a kiss on the head and try to act like I'm not freaking out internally.

Tara looks at me for approval, and I nod, allowing it since he might need something to do to keep him distracted. They leave just as Jillian pulls up with Ainsley in tow. She is clutching her three-year-old's hand as she runs to the house.

"Any word?" Her green eyes flit in worry.

"No," I state with a fright that is threatening to pour out of my eyes. "I don't want to think the worst. She's only been gone a short while. Maybe she ran away in a fit of preteen dramatics but will come back when she realizes there's nowhere to go." I grab my coat. "Can you and Ainsley stay at the house and call Tyler's phone if she comes home? I'm going back out on foot. She couldn't have gone far. I just want to find her before it gets dark. I don't even know if she has a jacket on."

LOVE ... IT'S COMPLICATED

The coat Izzy's been wearing this season is in the foyer. If she is wearing another, I can't for the life of me think of what it is.

"Why would she run off?" the officer asks. We all shrug and shake our heads. "Is there marital strife?"

"We're divorced," Tyler explains, sliding his hand in his pocket and rubbing his forehead. "I think she was hoping we'd get back together."

"Wonder why," I say and then close my eyes, annoyed at myself for being so childish with him when there are more important things to focus on.

Will's car pulls up to my house. He bolts out of the driver's door and runs up the stairs.

Of course, the man who I'm pretty sure just broke up with me is back here the second he heard my family is in trouble. I give him the eye that lets him know I'm scared. The kind that's probably frantic and wide-eyed. I want to run to him, have him hold me and tell me everything will be okay. I lost that right.

His eyes turn down as he pulls the officer to the side within earshot. "Officer Bronson. Valor County Police Department. We're putting an APB out," Will announces.

The second officer on the scene holds his arm up and shakes his head. "That's unnecessary this early. The child hasn't been gone an hour."

"What's an APB?" Tyler asks, and the responding officer seems annoyed.

"It's a police broadcast, alerting all law enforcement personnel in the area to look out for her. We haven't even checked with all her friends and the usual places she might have gone. The kid is eleven and knows the neighborhood. She's probably hiding out nearby. Maybe she's doing this for attention from your divorce."

In an act that surprises me, Will leans into the officer. The sharp lines of his face are granite as he clenches his jaw and lifts a finger to his face. "This isn't just some kid. She's not the type to run away for attention, and even if she did, we are pulling out all the stops on bringing her home safe and sound before the sun goes down. Put out the fucking APB on Isabella Landish now."

"Do you know this family personally?" the officer asks.

"Just make it happen," he declares, forcefully.

The officer takes a step back. "Fine. I'll go to the car and call it in."

If my head wasn't spinning a million miles an hour, thinking about where my daughter could be, I'd take a minute to think about Will and how good he is to my family and what a shit I was to him just an hour ago. I can't let my mind wander there because I need to get back out and look for Izzy.

"Ainsley and I will stay here," Jillian states, now holding her child in her arms.

I give her a hug and then head out the door. Will and Tyler follow.

"What's the plan?" Tyler asks as we walk down the stairs.

Will gives him orders. "Call Maisie and have her keep an eye on the house. I know it's far, but it's possible she went to your home. If it's the divorce that has her upset, she might be on her way back to what felt normal to her."

"Maisie already closed her shop, and every employee is out, looking for Izzy. She's a wreck. Once she heard the police were involved, she said her hands were shaking, and she couldn't work even if she wanted to."

I hug my arms around me and feel my brows furrow. "Do you really think Iz would try to get back to Tyler's? Why not just tell him she wanted to go there when she was home?" My questions come out with pauses between each word.

"I'm thinking off the cuff. The library, movie theater, her favorite pizza place … it's all a possibility," he adds and pulls his keys from his pocket. "I'm going to drive down all pedestrian roads from here to Greenwood Village. The ABP will cover all of Valor County."

"Let them know she's sick. She came home with a stomachache from school. She might be in distress," I add and take a deep breath and start walking down the sidewalk. "I'm heading out to the woods. I don't think she'd venture in there alone, but it's the next logical place, and if she's lost, then I need to find her within the next hour."

Tyler is quick at my feet. "I'm coming too."

I push back on the idea. "You should go look somewhere else. Maybe she's walking the streets."

Will takes a step forward and interrupts, "Tyler's right. He should go with you. It's not safe for you to be in the woods alone. Search parties are better in pairs. Plus, you don't have a phone. You can't be out there alone and without contact."

Tyler nods his head to Will in a thankful, albeit surprised way.

LOVE ... IT'S COMPLICATED

"Take flashlights and keep the phone locator on," Will commands, and we follow his instructions.

We take off in pairs. Dad and Anna stay on Main Street, hoping Izzy shows up in one of the stores. Tara and Hunter are at the school while Will travels the highway. Tyler and I climb over fallen trees and walk around mounds of prickly bushes as we feel the sun setting at our backs and the clock running out.

We call out our daughter's name and listen as the sound echoes against the trees. We walk for what feels like an eternity, shouting for her and listening for any sign of footsteps and look down for clues.

"I think she heard you yelling in the living room. That's why she left," Tyler surmises, and I cast him an evil glare.

"This was a culmination of two years of heartache for her. I've tried so hard to act like everything is going to be okay, that this new life is a good one, and then you tried to act like the past never happened. We moved on, and you pulled us all back into the past."

"Stop acting like you have it all together. You've been acting rash, getting arrested. Breaking into the salon. If it wasn't to get back at me, then I don't know what—"

"I was sick of everything being taken away, including my fucking hair." I turn to him and nearly fall over a prickly bush. I right myself and get my bearings while he just stands there with his phone in his hand and a perplexed look on his face. "I broke into the salon because, for once, I was taking back what was mine. I wanted a part of my life back. My mother left me, and then you left, and it's taken me a long time to heal a fraction of the hole that was left. Hell, I can't even hold a decent conversation with my father's girlfriend because it's just a reminder that we're all replaceable."

"You're not replaceable. Not in any way. In fact, you're really hard to forget." He shines his flashlight on my legs, creating a halo around us. "I know my actions don't show it, but you are still one of the most important people in my life."

I turn away from him and run my hands over my head, looking up to the trees and their bare branches that show through the dusk. His words are like a vise that squeezes around my neck. A year ago—heck, six months ago—I might have welcomed this conversation. Today, I can't even catch my breath.

"What is going on with you? You fell in love with another woman, and lately, you're acting like ... it almost feels like ... like you want to get back together, and I know you don't."

He grips his neck and lets out a growl in frustration. As he lowers his hand, he holds out his arm in explanation. "I love Maisie. I know you hate hearing that, but I do. She's about to move in, and everyone is talking about marriage. I hadn't thought about the fact that she might want children until we were at dinner, and she saw a baby, and she melted. All of a sudden, I realized that I was about to do it all over again—get married, have kids. The cycle is going to continue, and all I've been thinking about is ... I already did that. I had that. No, I *have* that. I had a wife and children and bills, and fights, and memories, and I gave that all away. It was selfish. I disrupted my children's lives all so I could do it all over again with someone else, and ..." He sighs, looking at me with downcast eyes. "It makes me wonder if I threw away our family for the right reasons. I've been thinking about it a lot, and I'm sorry, Lyss. I'm so damn sorry."

That vise around me is squeezing so tight that I lose my breath. Every woman who has ever been wronged wants to hear the words my ex-husband just spoke to me.

Validation though groveling is good for the ego.

As for my heart, it's no secret that I still love Tyler Landish.

I wipe my cheek and cross my arms, taking a shaky breath as I stare at him. That boyish charm he once had still peeks through the masculine demeanor he adapted as he aged. Sheer bravado is overshadowed by the vulnerable posture of a man.

It's the same man who held my hand and kissed my head as our babes were born. The man who rubbed my feet when we watched our favorite shows after the kids went to bed. The man who helped the kids make me breakfast in bed on Mother's Day and sang my favorite songs when he was in the shower because he knew it made me laugh.

I love Tyler Landish. The problem is, the Tyler Landish I love doesn't exist anymore.

"You're scared," I state, and he looks up with a crease in his forehead. "I can imagine how the thought of starting over at thirty-four years old is frightening, but it's not so crazy. A lot of people get married for the first time in their thirties and have kids close to forty. We just did everything so young. We were defiant, which is probably where Izzy gets it from. And we were in love. Blissfully so. We were also very lucky that the teenagers we were grew up to be adults who still wanted to be with one another. High school Tyler and Melissa were different than college Tyler and Melissa and so very different from the parents we became in our twenties. Marriage isn't about putting in the work to love one another. It's about still liking the person your spouse is growing up to be. And we never stop growing up. Hell, I'm still as lost as I was twenty years ago. I'm even sleeping in my parents' house and getting reprimanded by my father, but that's a different story."

Tyler shrugs in agreement. "Your dad always has been a hard nut to crack."

I nod and then exhale. "It wasn't right of me to fall apart on you the way I did without knowing how to pick up the pieces. And it wasn't fair to me when you threw them away. When you walked away from our family, you grew to be a man I couldn't love even if I tried. That love is gone. Same for you. The old version of me is someone I can't pretend to be anymore. I've changed. I'm pretty sure it's for the better, but this version of me is not for you. That's why you walked away."

He pinches the bridge of his nose, and he looks down. As he looks up, it's with a small, sad smile. "You know what's the worst part about knowing someone since you were a kid?"

"That they know everything about you. Yeah. Tell me about it. Sucks, doesn't it?"

"You're right. I'm scared. I love Maisie. She's who I want to be with. I don't ever want the kids to think I love anything more than them."

"You won't, Ty. Just promise if you move on with Maisie, you won't give up on her. Our children need to know a good marriage exists."

I give him a moment and start to walk again, calling out for Izzy, and he soon follows. Our flashlights are both on as we travel deeper into the woods. With the sun nearly down, it's freezing, and I can't help the chattering in my teeth—both from cold and from nerves. When we see the lights of the highway just beyond the pines, my stomach drops.

The light from the highway guides us to the edge of the woods, and we circle back, walking to the house on a new path. We use

Tyler's phone navigation to see where we are in the woods. His battery is dying quickly.

We shout out Izzy's name again and listen as the sounds of silence answer us back. The fear of my child being alone in the woods is crippling. I start to cry as I think of the many horrible things that could possibly happen to her out here in the cold, dark night—the horrific, frightening things that could happen to a child, period. With a shiver, I curl my arms around myself.

It's been three hours since Izzy climbed out her bedroom window. My feelings are going from intense worry to sheer panic.

This can't be happening in real life.

"This is too much. I don't know where she could have gone. By now, someone should have found her, heard from her ... anything!"

He places a hand on my shoulder. "We won't stop until we find her. I promise."

I nod and pull back the sniffle and tears.

As the night creeps, getting darker, so do my thoughts, and now, I'm angry I'm in the middle of the goddamn woods when I could be in my car or in the streets or literally anywhere else but here.

My heart is pounding, and I'm starting to feel nauseous when Tyler's phone chimes for the hundredth time tonight.

"It's Will. He found her!" he gasps and stops to read the text again.

"Is she okay? Where is she?" I ask, desperate for the answer.

His feet start to run as the need to get out of here and to our daughter is imminent. "The place we used to make out."

"The car?" I'm right behind him.

"No. The tree house."

twenty-eight

My parents' house is flooded with light and filled with people. We burst through the front door, looking for our girl. Dad is in the foyer, grabbing my arms and rubbing them assuredly.

"Izzy's okay. She's out in that death trap, but she's okay."

"Did you see her?" Tears of relief burst from my face as I hug my father because no matter how old you get, you still need a hug from your dad.

"Will brought her a coat and a blanket, but she won't come down yet. He's standing guard outside while she takes her time going through whatever the hell it is that kid is going through right now." He looks at my appearance and down to my coat and sweater. "What do you have all over you?"

"Coffee," I explain. "Long story. Crazy, long story. I'll share it tomorrow."

I let out a shaky breath as I turn to Tyler. He's holding Hunter, who has his head buried in Tyler's shoulder. Maisie has her hand on Hunter's back, rubbing it in a tender motion. Her face is puffy. She looks worn, like a woman who's been sick with worry over a missing preteen.

Tyler might be scared and questioning his choices, but of all the women my ex-husband could have fallen in love with, even if it was when he was still married to me, it might as well be someone who actually loves his kids. And who knows good hair. That can't hurt.

I look over to Maisie. "Thank you for closing your shop early and looking for Izzy."

Maisie creases her brow. "She means the world to me. I'm so happy she's been here the whole time."

Anna, Dad's girlfriend, and the recent bane of my existence is standing on the other side of the room, serving coffee to Tara, Jillian, Kent, and some of my father's friends who must have joined the search.

I walk over to Anna and do the same as I did with Maisie. "Thank you for your help tonight."

Anna accepts my appreciation with a gentle smile. "Anything for your family. A child missing from home is frightening. I can't imagine what you must have felt tonight. I'm happy she's home. So, you want something warm to drink?"

"I'm good." I look to Tyler, who is now at my back. "Let's go get our girl."

We walk out the back door and over to the neighbor's tree house.

"What's the plan of attack?" he asks. "Scream at her for being an idiot or love on her like we just spent the last few hours searching for her like the panicked parents we are?"

"A little bit of both," I muse. "I wish parenting came with a manual."

"One for marriage wouldn't have been bad either."

I shake my head as we walk toward the ladder. Will is here with a thermos and standing out in the cold. He's wearing a thick black parka jacket and his boots. I love those damn boots.

Tyler shakes Will's hand. It's an odd show of respect, especially since Tyler's been a total dick to Will the last few times he's seen him.

"Thank you for watching over her and for taking care of business earlier with that other officer."

Will shakes Tyler's hand back. "Just doing my job. I was on my second trip back from Greenwood Village when I remembered you talking about a tree house you used to sneak into. When I got back to the house, I asked Jillian about it. Imagine my surprise when I found a very scared, very cold Isabella was trapped up there. The ladder broke, so she couldn't get down. I found your father's ladder in the garage."

He points to a metal ladder, stretched out some twelve feet off the ground. It looks like more of a death trap than the old tree house, but I have to get my baby.

"Will, I'm ..." I pause. There are so many things I want to say, but my gaze flicks up to the tree house and the little girl who is cold and scared.

He rests a hand on my cheek, rubbing a small circle with his glove and then tucking hair behind me ear. "It's okay, Melissa. Go to your daughter. The officers on duty will be here to take a final statement to close out the night and then help you down."

"You won't be here when I come down?" My heart drops a little.

Tyler is standing beside me, clearly eavesdropping on the conversation. I couldn't care less, as my focus is on Will.

"No. My work here is done. You have a family to tend to, and they are the most important thing. Here." He holds out the thermos. "This is for you."

I take the thermos from him and frown at the sweet gesture.

Tyler's hand clutches my shoulder as he moves me toward the ladder. "Come on, Lyss. I'll hold that while you climb up."

With one hand in front of the other and one shaky foot after the next, I climb the ladder. The tree house is bright. Will must have given Izzy a flashlight. She's huddled in the corner of the tree house with a large blanket wrapped around her and a thermos in her hand. Her face is red and tearstained.

"Mommy!" she cries.

I fall to my knees, grabbing her, holding her, kissing her. Tyler comes barreling behind me and takes a place next to Izzy and does the same as me.

Looks like we're going for option number two—loving on her like the panic-stricken parents we are.

"I can't believe you ran away like that. Do you know how sick with worry we were?" I state as I hold her and cry and laugh and scowl. "Isabella Landish, don't you ever do anything like that again. No matter how mad you are at me or Daddy or the world, don't ever leave home."

She cries into my chest and then looks up at me and Tyler. He rubs her tears from her cheeks and kisses her head.

"I love you. *We* love you, Izzy. We love you so much. Don't do that to us again," he pleads.

She speaks through staggered breaths, her lips trembling. "I was so angry." Her words are hard to hear as she fights through the gasps.

Tyler rubs her head, and I pat her back and shush her to calm.

"I want our family back together. I want to live in our old house and go to my old school."

"Iz, if this is about the house and school, you know you can live with me."

"Tyler!" I admonish.

I know Izzy's going through something, but he can't blanket a statement like that to her.

"I want to live with Mommy. Why can't you two be normal?" She grips Tyler's shirt and looks up at him with a frown that cascades down her face. "I hate you so much for cheating on Mommy with Maisie. You don't talk about it, but I know what happened. I hate you, Mom, for always pretending everything's normal. It's not fucking normal!"

Tyler looks like he's been punched in the gut. I understand the feeling. I also note Izzy's appropriate use of the F-word, which, by look on Tyler's face, neither of us is going to address right now.

He gently removes Izzy from the tight grasp she has around him and moves back so she can see his face. "Iz, this is all my fault. Everything. From breaking up with Mom to giving you false hope that we could be a family again. I love your mom, and I have since I was fifteen years old. We fell out of love with each other, and there's no going back. If we did, we'd be pretending, and that's not fair to you."

"I was happy when you were pretending. When you were separated but living together before the divorce ... I was okay with that."

He gives a sad smile. "I don't want you to grow up thinking it's okay for a man to hurt you the way I did your mother, and you take him back to pretend to be happy. You deserve so much more than that. While I'd love to be a family again—because coming home every day to you and Hunter is the thing I miss most in this world—I can't do that to you."

She looks over at me for confirmation.

I nod.

LOVE ... IT'S COMPLICATED

"He's right. Daddy and I had our hard times, yet I wouldn't change a thing. Our love brought us you. Being your parents is the greatest joy in the world, and there is no pretending with that. As for our family? Well, I just walked through a room full of people who were very scared tonight. Scared because they love you. Hunter, Grandpa, Tara, Jillian, Ainsley, Maisie ... even Anna was out with Grandpa."

"Will was here too," she adds. "He brought me cocoa."

I run a hand down her hair, look over at the travel mug Tyler placed on the floor, and smile. "Our family might have broken up, but it got put together bigger and stronger. Dad and I might not be married anymore, but we're still family. We're your family, and we're going to love you ... at least until we're old and gray and you have to choose which one of us you're going to take in and which you're going to leave in a home. In which case, I hope it's your father because he did break up the family and all."

"Lyss ..." Tyler scolds, and Izzy laughs.

"Don't worry, guys. I'll take you both in. You don't stand a chance with Hunter. He'll probably be roaming with the traveling circus."

Tyler and I laugh in agreement. Our girl has her sense of humor back.

With a ragged breath, I brace myself as I ask, "Do you really want to go to your old school? I selfishly want you with me, but I can't afford to live in Greenwood Village, so if you want, I'm okay with you living with Dad, if that's what will make you happy."

Izzy's eyes clench closed. She looks like she's going to cry again. "No, Mom. I don't want to leave you."

Tyler leans in. "I'll do a better job of letting you out on the weekends to be with your friends. Maybe we can get you back on the soccer team. I'll use my address, and you can play with your friends this spring."

Her head bobs with agreement. "I'd like that a lot."

"That's a start. Izzy, you have to talk to us. Even when you think it's going to make Daddy or me upset, we'd rather have your honesty than you get so upset that you run away. We might be nice right now because we were scared, but we're also incredibly angry with you. Running off was a dangerous thing to do."

She sits up, brushes the last of her tears from her face, and starts breathing normally again. "I'm sorry. I was so mad, and I didn't know where to go. Then, the ladder fell, and I was scared, yet I didn't want anyone to find me, so I didn't say anything, even when I heard Grandpa yell for me. I hope he's not mad."

"Oh ... he'll be mad. But that's part of his charm," I tease.

Izzy looks at Tyler. "Do you want me to be honest? Like Mom said?"

"Absolutely, kiddo. I can handle it."

"I think Will's a really cool guy," she says, and Tyler's eyes close, like it's the last thing he wanted to hear. She turns to me. "I like Maisie a lot. I tried so hard not to, but she's really easy to talk to, and I can tell her things, like who I have a crush on—"

"You have a crush?" I ask excitedly, but she cuts me off.

"Without you getting all annoying," she finishes, and I frown.

Call me selfish, but I want to be the person she goes to when she likes someone.

"For the record, I'm not a fan of you wanting to tell her things, but"—I grab her hand and give it a squeeze—"I'm really glad you have an adult in your life you feel comfortable talking to. That's really important for a young woman. Please know that takes a lot of inner strength for me to utter those words. This doesn't mean I'm ready to go on bonding trips with her or anything." Turning to Tyler, I roll my eyes and declare, "If you were going to be with someone other than me, I'm glad you didn't *downgrade*. Let's be honest. There're very few people who are as amazing as I am."

Tyler laughs and pulls a now smiling Izzy into his chest. "Melissa, you are without a doubt irreplaceable. As is my Isabella. You two are still my world. I hope you know that. And Hunter. Can't forget my boy."

"Nah, we can forget him for a moment," Izzy jokes, and we all sit up, smiling. "Dad, are you going to marry Maisie?"

With a glance to me, he asks her, "Would you be okay with that?"

She inhales deep and then replies, "Yeah. If I can't have the family I want, I kind of like what Mom said about our new one being bigger and better. Maybe I'll get a new brother or sister."

Tyler looks like he's about to pass out by her comment, and knowing what he just declared to me earlier this evening about his fears of starting over, I place a hand on his shoulder and turn to Izzy.

"Let's give Dad a chance to think this out one step at a time. Maybe Maisie moving in is step one."

LOVE ... IT'S COMPLICATED

He coughs and says, "Good idea."

"I'm ready to go home now," she declares.

I kiss her hand. "Me too."

Tyler nods. "I'll go first and hold the ladder."

The three of us depart the old tree house. We let Izzy go down second, so I can watch her from the top as he assists her down below. When I hit the ground, Tyler hands me my thermos back. I look to see if Will is still here. My heart drops when I see he left, as he said he would.

I take a sip, and the heat does nothing to warm me fully.

The house is filled when we get back and starts to clear out once everyone sees Izzy. Hugs are given, good-byes are said, even by Tyler, who realizes he has to find his place in our new life and staying in this house is not where he's meant to be. He leaves with a promise of seeing Izzy during the week.

As I tuck my kids in bed, I look around at the house. My parents' house. The place I grew up and where my children will now grow up. I moved in here, hoping to give my children familiarity and hope. Hope for a good life, a positive future, and all the love that comes with living with family. I always kept the idea of moving out on my own in the back of my mind, but the truth is, I like it here. This is the house that raised me. It's where my best and some of my worst memories are. With every creak of my bed or echo of the wooden stairs, I hear the sounds of my childhood and the whispers of my future. It's where my mother's past is held and my father's next days are spent. It's where the new me was found, and I'm forever comforted with knowing this is home.

I walk downstairs to see Dad and Anna having a cup of tea. At my entrance, Anna starts to get up, but I motion for her to sit.

"Stay awhile," I tell her.

Even Dad seems taken aback by my action.

Grabbing a bottle of water from the fridge, I head to the foyer. "Don't stay up too late, you crazy kids."

With a kiss to the sky and a prayer to my mother, I head up and feel ... okay ... about our new, growing family. I've been trying to keep it closed for so long, and I kept hurting everyone around me, even myself. While I want to fix this final piece of my life, I'm worried I've ruined it for good.

Tyler has Maisie, Dad has Anna, Tara is still looking, and Jillian is refusing the notion.

Love … it's complicated.

Sometimes, we find it when we least expect it. Oftentimes, we go searching, and it's the luck of the draw on if it works out. I've been in love twice in my life. Once to a boy when I didn't even know what love was. Another to a man whose love is so real I'm petrified.

There's no secret formula. Even I know you can't count the success of a relationship based on the positive outcomes. Shit happens. Fights are had. People make mistakes. It's how we choose to forgive, learn, and move on that has the relationship growing.

William Bronson is a good man. Too good for me in many ways. I know he didn't set out to fall in love with me. That just happened. I just wish I knew if I was woman enough to let my insecurities go in order to love again.

twenty-nine

WILLIAM

Life or death.

It's a term you hear often when you're a man of the law.

A woman is trapped beneath a car after an accident.

A man has his expensive watch stolen while out to dinner on Main Street.

Both are life-or-death situations, according to the calls that come in.

What serves as one person's trauma is another man's cakewalk. You don't know what constitutes such an event until you're in one.

Being shot in the chest isn't painful. I felt my flesh absorb the shock waves of the bullet piercing my skin, and there was this intense vibration at the entry point. You ignore it because there's a rush of adrenaline coursing through your veins, and you hardly feel a thing. That's how I was able to rush the attacker and wrestle the gun from him. I'll never forget the look on his face—absolute shock that he'd pulled the trigger, mixed with horror that I was charging at him. I grabbed the gun and shot him center mass.

I remember one of the hostages in the store, a man who had been clutching on to his wife when the burglary was happening. He was standing by the register, still holding his wife. As soon as I hit the floor, he grabbed the gun from my hand, and he held me. Lying on the floor, in the arms of a stranger, with a hole in my chest, waiting for the ambulance to arrive, every fear and emotion crept in as I struggled to breathe, not knowing whether I was going to live or die. That part … it can fuck with you if you let it.

Death never scared me until I saw the blood on his hand. My own blood was pouring from my body. Heaven and hell became real. In seconds, I was looking forward to it and fearing it.

Will it hurt?
Where will I go?
Dear God, please don't let me never see my mother again.
Every life choice was questioned.
If I had more time, would I do this?
Why did I waste so much time on that?
And for fuck's sake, why is my last breath going to be in this goddamn dirty convenience store?

Then, I woke up after surgery. My family was by my bedside, and Allison was sobbing, and suddenly, every promise I'd made to live came rushing back. Many of the choices I made after that were because of a bargain with God. It took me a while to realize I'd also promised I'd live my life to the fullest.

That was my life-or-death moment. It made me appreciate just how beautiful each breath you take was.

Then, Melissa kissed me.

A kiss should never constitute as a life-or-death moment, but in mere seconds, when Melissa Jones threw herself at me in the parking lot of Lone Tavern, I died and came back to life for the second time in the same year.

I'd never set to fall in love with her.

I remember the night we met, she was in the holding cell, and I was questioning her before her release. She was going wild child, a frantic mess. Pacing, rambling … and absolutely beautiful. It's rare you find a woman with her icy-blue eyes, porcelain skin, and fierce demeanor, packed into this petite frame. She had fire in her and a zest that was addictive to watch.

I almost didn't let her go home with her ex that night. I could see in her eyes that she was hurting. Hell, she was having a damn nervous breakdown after what he did to her. Yet she looked at me with conviction and pleaded her case: even though she was divorced, that man was still her family. There was something about the selflessness and honor of family that pulled me to her.

She walked out the door of the station, yet she never left my mind. I thought about what she had said all day. Hell, I thought about her damn lips and the way she had smiled this crooked grin when she was being humorously critical of herself and the way her teeth had grazed her bottom lip when she was lost in thought. It was cute as fuck.

I was so wrapped up in thinking about her that Kent suggested we go out for a drink to get my head together. I didn't tell him why I was out of it. He just knew because that's the kind of friends I have. We don't have to share our feelings to know when one of us needs a few beers to decompress.

I still can't believe the woman who was the reason I needed a drink was standing in front of me.

Melissa was there. I couldn't decide if it was fate or the Devil tempting me to see if I was worthy of going to heaven. Like the curious son of a bitch I am, I had to talk to her, get to know her. I hoped she was crazy, so I could get her off my brain, but she was funny as hell. When we danced, she completely surrendered herself. It was so damn sexy, and I knew the night needed to end.

Then, she kissed me and ... *fuck.*

She tasted like sin, and her lips were as soft as cotton candy.

She even let out this little moan that traveled from her lips straight to my groin.

My world went into a complete spiral after that kiss. Pushing her away was the greatest act of willpower I've ever shown.

By the time she drove out of the parking lot, I was gone for her.

I'd already known I couldn't marry Allison, but after meeting Melissa, I couldn't wait any longer. How could a man feel not just attracted to another woman, but also literally addicted to her. I felt like, in that moment, a lasso was tied around us, and we were bound to one another, whether I ever saw Melissa Jones again or not.

My shock the next day when I saw her at brunch only paled to the feeling of remorse I had for both her and Allison. I was about to break one woman's heart, and I was pretty sure I'd shattered the other.

Breaking up with Allison was one of the hardest things I'd ever had to do. She's a good woman. Too good for the likes of me. Still, I couldn't marry her, and watching her fall into a puddle of tears was painful.

After that, I went from being the hero who everyone doted on to the scum who had destroyed everything. My phone didn't stop ringing for three days. Friends, family—mine and hers—telling me how wrong I was to let a great girl like Allison go. I couldn't disagree. I was cursed at, had doors slammed in my face, and pleaded with to "do the right thing."

I didn't fight it. They were right. A man who broke his vow was hardly a man. Men are the oath keepers, protectors, the ones who provide, and yet here I was, tearing down a family.

"I am beyond disappointed in you, William," my mother said as she gripped the edge of her kitchen sink. "The Lalaynes are family to us. Allison is like a daughter now. How could you call off your wedding?"

"I don't love her, Mom. Not the way she's supposed to be loved. Not the way Dad loves you."

She turned to face me and gave a disappointed look. "If you think marriage is all love and flowers, then you're wrong. Maybe your father and I did a poor job of showing you the strife. There are plenty of hard times, and you just have to work through it."

"Maybe in five, ten, twenty years down the road, but not before we're even on our honeymoon. Allison and I never fight. It's not about our compatibility. I don't feel that rush when I'm with her."

"What do you know about a rush? You sound like one of the vulgar novels your sister reads."

"I know it because I've felt it with another woman."

My mother kicked me out of the house after that. That was the hardest part of the situation. My mother, the person who I'd thought of when I was lying on a store floor, bleeding out and dying, was so disgusted by me that she didn't talk to me for three weeks. It was the longest twenty-one days of my life.

When the whole world goes silent on you because they just can't stand to hear your voice … it's worse than the scolding.

That pain was only relieved by the two chance encounters I had with Melissa. I swear I wasn't stalking her when I saw her at Target. I wasn't prepared. No big speech or awesome declaration of my convictions was planned. It was just me, like a jerk, walking her bags

LOVE ... IT'S COMPLICATED

to the car with her kids staring at me and thinking about how this was my one chance to talk to her. I botched the whole thing up. She stormed out of that parking lot and left me in parking row D, feeling like a complete ass, wondering if I'd ever see her again.

Valor County isn't that big, but for a woman I'd never seen before in my life to land in my jail cell, it was like the gods were pushing us together. I wasn't messing this up again.

I was a fool to think I hadn't already, yet each time I found myself in her company—every banter back and forth, every heated exchange that almost went too far, and every easy conversation—that lasso was pulled even tighter, squeezing so hard that I damn near suffocated.

For my heart, it was a life-or-death situation.

Maybe that's what a soul mate is. Someone you connect with on a level that's unexplainable. A person your heart continues to find, even when you aren't looking.

I didn't set out to fall in love with Melissa Jones, but I can tell you the exact moment I stopped denying it was happening.

"What you working on?"

From the look on Melissa's face, I'd startled her from where she was working at the kitchen table. I had seen her sitting there, and she looked busy, but I couldn't just walk out and not say hi.

"Done already? You really don't have to perform in the show. I mean it. I can fake an illness for you. I'd pretend you broke a bone, but if a kid can perform with a fracture, then so could you."

It was a weekday, and Hunter and I had just finished one of his levitation lessons before the talent show. He had gone into the den while Izzy escaped to her room.

"I'm happy to fill in for you. I mean, my kid wants to perform, so I'll make it happen."

"You know how to levitate?"

"No, but I can YouTube pretty much anything. I once tried my hand at whittling. I nearly lost a thumb."

"Whittling, as in shaping wood?"

"I thought I could make awesome crafts for weddings, but Dad and I decided we'd leave the woodworking to him."

I smiled in agreement. She had this ridiculous bun on the top of her head that looked like it was about to topple over, and she was wearing my sweatshirt. It was the first time I'd seen it on her since I had given it to her in the jail cell. It looked way too big, yet it was absolutely perfect. I liked the way she looked in my shirt. I liked it so much that I wouldn't comment on it, for fear she'd try to give it back.

"You need help?" I gestured to the table of glass balls and boxes of ribbon, glitter, and tiny beads. It was a craft table that would have made my nieces scream with excitement.

"Not really, but I wouldn't mind the company if you have time to kill before work." She gestured to the seat, and I sat down. "I'm making wishing ornaments for a wedding. I'm filling them with beads of the wedding colors, and each guest will be given a piece of paper to write their wish and place inside. They bring it home and hang it on their tree. It's a wedding favor."

"May I?" I asked, and she handed me an empty clear bulb.

"Make as many as you'd like. I have plenty if you want to make them for your nieces and nephews. These are special markers you can write with. My hand is cramping from writing one hundred sixty names today."

I took her hand in mine, flipping it over to expose the palm. It wasn't the first time I'd grabbed her hand, so she didn't find it odd as I pressed my thumb up and down her lifeline and massaged her hand.

She let out a groan and dropped her head. "That feels magical."

"You should see what I can do with a back."

"I'm imagining many things, Officer Bronson, and feeling this good from a hand massage shouldn't be legal."

I chuckled. "If this is what gets you going from a palm touch, I can't imagine what you do when you go out on an actual date."

It was a loaded comment. I could imagine what she'd be like. How she'd fall apart in my arms as I touched her in all the places. Couldn't blame me. I was a hot-blooded man, and she was a beautiful woman.

I also knew there was a strong possibility she'd be in another man's arms someday. We were in this place where we were friends, yet I felt like we could be more if she'd just let her guard down. It was possible she never would. I was okay with that. I had to be. She wasn't mine.

She took her hand back, and I opened a small bin and found Ziplock bags of beads and charms that were different than the ones on the table. While we talked about our week and then took turns asking each other Family Feud fast-money questions we looked up on our phone, we filled our ornaments. It was easy to talk to Melissa. From the first time I had spoken to her, I had seen the openness in her.

Our banter and conversation flowed like no other. Even when she was holding back, I could see her tells. The way she twisted her mouth when she wanted to ask a question. Her eyes would widen when she was lost in thought,

LOVE ... IT'S COMPLICATED

which I found she did whenever she touched me. And then there was the humor, the sarcastic wit she used to protect herself from getting emotional. She might not be as easy for others to read, but for me, she was an open book.

"Having a hard time over there with your chubby boy fingers?" she teased as I dropped a few beads on the table.

"They're called masculine man hands."

"Is that what you tell your ego?"

"Part of my daily mantra. Followed by how large my feet are."

Her eyes gazed down, not able to look at my shoes, but based on the smirk on her face, I had a feeling she wanted to. Melissa enjoyed ogling me. Didn't bother me one bit.

I held up my finished product, forcing her gaze back on me, and showed it to her.

"That's beautiful, Will. You know, you really have a knack for this wedding designing thing. The colors are perfect."

"Good." I leaned forward with a grin. "It's for you. Figured blue was your favorite color. You wear it a lot."

"Wow. That's really sweet."

The pinkish hue that curled up her cheeks was enough for me to know she liked it. I wondered if Melissa had received gifts, even simple trinkets that were hand-crafted.

"I even love the flowers you put inside. Roses are my favorite. Cliché, I know, but it's the truth."

"I would have guessed wildflowers."

"You're not incorrect. Wildflowers are beautiful, but ... my mom. She was the rose lover. She always thought they were classic, sturdy, and beautiful, no matter the season. That's why they're my favorite. Because they were hers."

"You have a lot of love for your mother."

"Yeah." She gave a wistful sigh. "I miss her tremendously."

A pen was lying on the table. I picked it up and handed it to her. "Now, you have to make a wish."

She took the pen and looked at the wishing paper for a few moments. Her hair fell in front of her face as she looked down and wrote. It must have been something good because she rolled it up quickly, curled it into a scroll, and slid it into the ornament. She reapplied the top and added a ribbon. Holding it in front of her, she grinned and looked inside the bulb and the charms that glistened in the light.

With one of the fancy pens, I took it back and wrote in the best handwriting I could—Melissa's Wish.

"There. One complete wishing ornament." I handed it back to her.

She smiled and stared at the beads and metal charms inside. Her teeth grazed her bottom lip as she looked from the ornament and back to me with a glistening grin.

"Cat got your tongue?" I pried.

"I got you something today, but then I ... never mind."

"I love presents."

"It's not what you think."

"I'm not thinking anything since you're not giving it to me."

"Fine. Wait here. And don't laugh."

While she went toward the foyer, I picked up the ornament and admired my handiwork. It wasn't too bad, not that placing beads in a hole was hard. My chicken-scratch handwriting was nothing compared to her artistic penmanship, but it looked nice enough.

Peering inside, I noticed the paper had unraveled, enough for me to see the ink. My name on the paper caught my eye, and I moved the ornament so I could read the unfurling paper inside.

I wish that Will finds his happily ever after.

I knew you weren't supposed to know another person's wish, but I did, and there was no turning back.

Melissa had one wish and she gave it to me.

She was back in a flash. In her hands was a bouquet of flowers.

"Okay, I know this is super cheesy, but I was at a florist with a couple, picking out wedding centerpieces, and I put this one together. It was so pretty that I had to take it home, so I bought it, and as I was driving home, I thought, I should give these to Will. I mean, men never get flowers, and that's a sin because flowers are beautiful, and everyone loves getting flowers. I bet even men do. So, here are your flowers. Do you like them? They're dumb. Yeah, I shouldn't have gotten you flowers I'll take them back—"

"Melissa." I said her name once, deeply and forcefully.

It calmed her out of her ramble. She looked up at me with wide, blinking eyes.

"I love them."

I meant it, and yet ... I meant more.

My heart was racing like a goddamn mountain lion, and my palms were starting to sweat.

She was standing there, beautiful, nervous, vulnerable, and cute as hell.

LOVE ... IT'S COMPLICATED

Her hair was still in her face, this time falling in front of her eye. I curled the rogue hair around my finger and tucked it behind her ear. As she looked up at me with those intimidating eyes, I was done for.

I didn't just love the flowers. I loved that this woman had one wish and given it to me. I loved that she had bought me flowers and then was so nervous to hand them over. I loved that she thought of other people and was a good friend, an amazing mother, a loyal daughter, and that with every passing day, I was becoming more attached to her.

Then, something crazy happened.

In that moment, just looking at her—arresting, wedding designing Melissa Jones with the messy bun, wearing an oversize sweatshirt—my body relaxed. I wasn't pulsing or head spinning or wired like a race car engine revving. In fact, looking at her with her teeth skimming her bottom lip and fingers rubbing together as she waited for me to say more, I felt calm.

I felt like I was home.

I knew it wasn't like, or lust, or mere attraction to this woman.

I was in love with her.

Life-altering, death-defying in love with Melissa Jones.

It wasn't going to be easy.

When you date a single mom, you thrive on the moments. Her time is precious, and you fight for her last five minutes, but when it comes down to you or her children, the kids always win. There are no dinners out on a whim or trips away for no reason. You can't drop in on her whenever you want and take her up against the refrigerator on a Tuesday night. Her time is precious, and you should be honored she's giving it to you.

I knew life was complicated for Melissa, and I hoped we could make it work. I never imagined, at the end of the day, she just couldn't trust that I was the man for her.

How it went from amazing to fucked up so fast is beyond me.

It's been a few weeks since Isabella went missing and was found in the tree house. I left Melissa that night and hoped she'd call. My phone's been silent. Like a preteen boy waiting for the hottest girl in school to ring him, I look at my cell phone screen at least ten times a day, wondering if she's texted. When I said I couldn't keep chasing her, I meant it. It didn't mean I didn't hope she'd come around this time.

Now, I wonder, *If she did, would it even matter?*

As I walk around my house, I see the mementos of her scattered around. A hair tie she left on my nightstand, a bottle of whiskey she brought to my house, and the photo we took at the wedding. They all serve as reminders of the whirlwind that was us. Tonight, I open the top of the bottle and pour a glass.

I'm sitting on my couch when my doorbell rings. I look at my phone because, like I said, I'm an idiot who is waiting for her to come around. To my surprise, not only is Melissa not at my door, but it's another woman who has been plaguing my heart the last few months.

I open the door and furrow my brows. "Mom. What are you doing here?"

"Can't a mother visit her son whenever she wants?" She hands me her purse, walks inside, and then throws her coat on the coatrack.

I close the door, follow her inside, and place her purse on a table. "You can, but it's peculiar since you've never done so before, and you haven't been speaking to me exactly."

"Don't be so dramatic. I spoke to you at your nephew's birthday party. And at Thanksgiving."

"*Please ask the man who broke up with a very nice girl to pass the mashed potatoes* is not exactly talking to me."

She hits me gently on the arm. "You're always so sarcastic. I've made peace with the fact that you called off the wedding."

With her arms out, she looks at me, confused. I raise a brow at her.

"Are you going to offer me a drink? William, you are not the best host."

I walk into the kitchen and grab a glass. My mother likes iced tea, so I pour her a glass without asking what she wants. Back in the living room, I hand it to her, where she's seated on the couch. She's looking at the picture of me and Melissa, where we're making crazy faces at the camera.

"Is that the woman?"

I simply nod.

She picks up the photo and stares at it. "She's pretty. I like her hair. I wrestled some information out of Genevieve. Heard she was a good girl. Mom. Has two children. A terrible scoundrel of an ex. Made quite a name for herself in the wedding industry."

"You've been snooping."

LOVE ... IT'S COMPLICATED

"I've been concerned. Is she also why you haven't left this house in weeks, except to go to work?"

"Why would you assume that?"

"Your siblings talk. Apparently, you've been a bit of a homebody lately. You need to shave. Your face is too handsome to walk around looking like a homeless man. You want to talk about what's going on in your life?"

"I don't think you want to hear about it."

She puts the photo down, leans forward, and places a hand on my knee. "William, I might not like everything you have to say, but don't you dare assume I don't want to hear it all. You're my son, and I love you. At the end of the day, I want you to be happy. From the look on your face, the whiskey in your glass, and the fact that you're home alone on your night off, I know you're not happy."

She's right. I'm not.

I take a seat on the couch and grab my glass, take a drink, and then look down at the floor. "I messed up. It started months ago. I shouldn't have been with Allison as long as I was. I couldn't break up with her after she lost the baby. I should have done it as soon as I got out of the hospital. Because of that, I broke her heart, and I gave Melissa, a great woman who I should be with, a reason to believe that I'm the kind of man who walks away."

I take another drink. The liquor's burn is the only thing that numbs the ache in my chest. "Allison loved me more than I really understood. I destroyed her and believed her when she said she was fine. It took a lot of understanding on my part to see what my staying too long did."

"Look at me. I mean it. Look at me." Her tone is severe. The woman who scolded me in my youth has that similar fierceness in her eyes. "William, you are not the only one to blame. When Allison was pregnant, we asked you to do what was right, and you fulfilled that wish. You stepped up and proposed to a woman who I now know you did not love. You have always been the good one. Of all your brothers and sisters, I never had to worry about you. That's why I didn't realize you were so unhappy. When you were in the hospital and we didn't know if you were going to live, I prayed to God, asked him to save my son. My hero. My son of honor and value. I would have given anything—and I mean, anything—to save your life. I can't believe I was so cruel to you so soon after."

"You didn't know what was going on."

"I should have listened better. I would have understood why you walked away when you did. You said you met another woman, and it all sounded so scandalous."

"It wasn't. I swear. Melissa appeared one day, and over the past few months, she has become the most important thing in my life. I pushed my way into her family which is something I know she's protective of. I bonded with her kids and now I've walked away from them. I walked away from her. On top of that, I almost ruined her business. Allison was one click away from virtually blasting Melissa's wedding planning and design company she runs with her friend. I knew Melissa was concerned how our relationship would impact her business. That took a lot of pleading on my part. A lot of explaining my actions to Allison. I had to help her understand. We had fun, but the two of us together, we're not meant for forever. Allison finally gave up. She said she couldn't ruin another woman's business when Melissa's only fault was loving a man who wasn't worth the dirt beneath her shoes."

"Allison's a better woman that me. I would have blasted you in every newspaper from here to California."

"She's a good girl."

"But she's not who you love."

I shake my head.

Mom leans back in her seat and tilts her head, assessing me with her eyes. "What do you like about Melissa?"

"What do I *like*? Where do I start?"

"With the simple things."

"That she has this amazing artistic ability to create. Whether it's something small like a crafted favor, or an altar with fabric and lights, she can make beautiful and meaningful things. I like that she wears pajamas with coffee cups on them. She doesn't care if she's decked out in a full face of makeup, or wearing yoga pants, in order to leave the house. She's comfortable in her skin. I like how she talks with her hands when she gets very excited, or how she crosses her arms when she's defensive. Her teeth skim her bottom lip when she looks at me for too long. I bet she doesn't know she does either of those things. She rambles. A lot. Always when she's nervous or uncomfortable. She makes me laugh. She makes me happy."

Mom folds her hands on her lap and asks, "Do you love her?"

"Yes." It's an easy answer.

"Even though she doesn't trust you?"

LOVE ... IT'S COMPLICATED

I lift a brow at her. "How do you know that?"

"I told you. I have my ways."

I roll my eyes and groan. "She doesn't trust me. I understand why she didn't at first, but the fact she still doesn't, hurts. I'd spend my entire life showing her I'm worthy of every last ounce of her trust if she'd give it."

"As your mother, I don't like to see you feeling this down about a woman so I have to know something. Do you trust her?" she asks. I furrow my brows so she explains further. "Do you trust Melissa with your heart?"

With a light laugh, I lean forward. "Mom, this is going to sound melodramatic, but here goes. Being shot in the chest was easier than walking away from her. I don't trust her with my heart at all because she's the only one who can break it. That said, I'd risk it. Over and over again. Man, I need to stop drinking."

She smiles and looks down at her phone, where she seems to be typing. "Well then, this is quite a shame then."

Before she can finish her sentence, my doorbell rings. I get up and walk to the door. When I open it, it's with complete confusion.

What the hell is going on?

thirty

WILLIAM

"Bronson. William."

When I opened my front door to see Kent in his sergeant uniform with a car outside with the lights shining and a pair of handcuffs in his hand, I was floored.

I asked a thousand questions as he read me my rights and hauled me into the backseat of the car like a common criminal.

My charge: breaking and entering into Genevieve's salon, Illusion Salon and Spa.

It's all ridiculous. I hoped to get answers, but Kent wouldn't speak to me aside from reading me my rights. He was silent on the drive to the precinct. I had my picture taken and then was hauled into the cell.

I've been sitting here for ten minutes, my arms now free of cuffs and my head going crazy with wondering why the hell I'm in here. My mother should arrive any minute. As I was arrested, she was stunned silent. I'm sure she was calling my father as I was driven away. I was hoping this was some sort of prank, but with each step, it keeps on feeling more real.

When I hear my name being called from the other side of the room, I know this isn't a prank. This is something … more.

How do I know that? It's the voice. Sultry with a touch of nerves, Melissa's tone as she says my name has me standing from the bench and walking over to the bars.

It's hard to see her at first. The lighting in this room sucks, and she's cast in an odd shadow, yet from the silhouette of her body, the womanly curves let me know that it is, in fact, my Melissa.

"Did you have me fake arrested?" I ask her in utter disbelief.

She walks forward, and I have to pause. She's wearing those leggings that hug her body, the kind she wore when we were setting up the wedding. Her eyes sparkle against the silk top she's wearing, and her long blonde hair is flowing down her shoulders.

"I did," she says as she walks up to the bars and stares at me. Her gaze stops at my boots, and she pauses for a moment.

"Care to share?"

She closes her eyes and bites her lips, then shakes her head for a beat. "Sorry. Momentarily distracted."

"Is it possible you could be distracted with me standing on the other side of these bars?"

"No," she says, and I repeat her, trying to figure out what the hell is going through her head. "You have to stay there because I have a lot of things to say, and I don't want you … distracting me."

"You could have called."

"Seriously, Will? Can you just let me do this?"

"Then, explain what this is—"

"It's a grand gesture!" she yells in that excited way only she can with her arms outstretched and her eyes wild. "Damn it. You really know how to take the romance out of a situation. When I asked Kent for help, he seemed reluctant, but I had to explain how dire the situation was. Yes, I understand this isn't the most romantic setting, but it's where we met … and, well, I just thought you needed to be here, behind those bars, for what I'm about to say."

I lean back on my heels. "What do you want to say?"

"You scare me. Everything about you. You're this handsome hero cop who is too perfect in so many ways. You have the potential to hurt me like no other. This heart of mine, it's been broken before, but you … you have this power to shatter it into a million pieces." She curls her arms around herself, and her teeth chatter. "Shoot. I forgot how cold it is in here."

LOVE ... IT'S COMPLICATED

I take my sweatshirt off and hand it to her, leaving me in a T-shirt.

"I can't. You're gonna freeze," she says.

"Put it on, Melissa," I command. While she slides it over her head, I ask, "You were saying something about my heart-shattering power."

Seeming warmer, she folds her arms across her body. "For a long time, I didn't think I was good enough. I thought if one man could leave me, fall in love with another, then I wasn't worthy. It made me feel powerless. I wanted to take control of my life back, and I asserted that control by keeping you at arm's length. Even when I had you, I was so careful to let you fully in because I knew when I did, I'd be yours in a way I'd never let anyone else have me. I'd felt too much loss in my life by people I love. I couldn't take that again."

I slide my hands in my jeans pockets and take a deep breath. "Melissa, I can tell you I'll never hurt you a million times a day, but until you believe it, it doesn't matter what I say."

"I know. It's a hard lesson I'm trying to learn. Tara and Jillian have been awesome as they let me cry on their shoulders and then vent during our workouts. Even my dad has been on Team Will, telling me I need to take a chance on our small because it has a potential to be big."

I'm trying to follow along, but I know with Melissa, sometimes, it's best to just let her ramble.

"I started seeing a therapist," she says, and she's piqued my interest. "It's only been a few sessions, but it feels good to deep-dive into my issues. And, yes, I am publicly declaring that I have issues. No jokes."

"I'd never," I swear. "I think it's great you're working on yourself."

"I always felt like unless my kids were good, my business was established, and my life was all together, I couldn't move on even if I did find the answer to feeling worthy enough to do so. You know what I found out? My life is never going to be completely together. It's a complicated mess, but it's my mess, and I love it."

She gives a small smile, mostly to herself, and then she looks back at me.

"Will, I know what we have is different from what each of us had with any past relationship. This is unique to us. It's real to us. I shouldn't have brought our pasts into our future. You stormed into my life, all sexy and brooding and cute as hell with my kids, completely reliable in any situation, and funny, and cool, and you made me fall in love with you despite how hard I'd tried to fight it. And I had. I'd fought it good, but you and your damn smolder just came in and burned me down to the ground."

Her words make my heart skip. Yes, my man heart actually skips a fucking beat. I grip my chest and take a step closer to the bars.

"You love me?"

She looks at me like I have a thousand heads. "Yes, Will! I am so damn crazy in love with you that it hurts. I'm pretty sure I have been since I met you in this very cell and you had me smiling over what was said in barber chairs. I started falling for you so easily; it was difficult, keeping those feelings at bay. I couldn't deny it because the second you walked away, I felt like a piece of me went with you. Why else do you think I had you arrested and placed in a cell?"

"Because you're crazy." She growls at me, so I add, "And in love with me, I see."

"Yes. I wanted to tell you that. That's it. I'm sorry. I love you."

"That's all?"

She swallows. "Yes."

"Thank you."

The deep V that forms in her forehead is mirrored by the pout she gives. "You're welcome."

She stands there, hugging herself and looking down. My response to her declaration doesn't appear to be what she wanted to hear.

I call her attention. "You can let me out now."

She looks up and blinks a few times.

"You know locking someone up who isn't actually convicted of a crime is illegal," I explain.

"Oh. Right."

She fumbles for the keys, and that reminds me that I have to give Kent shit for this stunt. I'm sure the guys are all laughing at my mug shot, which I'm now realizing they took for the fun of it.

When the door is unlocked, I take a step out and take the keys from her, placing them in my pocket. We're standing by the open door, face-to-face. Her eyes are looking down; mine are looking at the perfect slope of her nose and the cheeks that are pink from the cold.

"Thank you," I say to her.

"For what? Having you placed in a cell for no reason and then opening the door for you?"

"Exactly," I say, closing the gap between us, forcing her to look up at me.

I look at her—really look at her with every fiber of my being—and wipe a tear that's fallen down her cheek.

I grip her waist and pull her into me—a move that has her lips parting and her chest rising.

"Because now, I can hold you when I say, I love you. I told you once if you were going to kiss me, you'd better bet the next fifty years on it, and I meant it. I'm all in, Melissa. And I love you so fucking much that I don't want to live another day without you."

I kiss her. My mouth crashes into her, and I caress the one woman who has captured my heart, mind, body, and my whole damn soul. Her hands quickly wrap around my neck, and we kiss like if we don't, we'll never breathe again.

Our pasts are messy.

Our present is complicated.

And the future is so fucking beautiful.

As we break from our kiss, our foreheads touch as we let our heartbeats simmer.

I look at her with a squint. "Are you the reason my mother came to see me today?"

She bites her lip. "I saw her at Genevieve's salon. I couldn't keep my mouth shut. I had to tell her how amazing you were. How hurt you must be. And how crazy I was about you."

"She knew you were getting me arrested?"

She smiles. "Me? This was her idea. She told me if I was really in love with her son and if I had any plans of being her daughter-in-law in the future, I had to stop acting like a child and make a grand gesture that showed I meant it."

"That sounds like my mom. That daughter-in-law part doesn't seem to scare you. You know what that means for my family?"

"Will, I wouldn't dream of thinking about a future with you that didn't include trying to make you a father."

I lift her chin and speak against her mouth. "Marriage or more kids ... whatever life brings us, I'll be a happy man, just having you, Hunter, and Isabella in my life."

"You really mean that, don't you?"

"Yes. And more importantly, I don't want to forget our pasts. They're ours, and they make each of us strong. They make our love invincible. You hear me?"

"I do." She looks up at me like I might melt. "Damn, do you give a good smolder."

"You think that's good? Wait until you see what I have in store for you when we get home."

"I can't wait. I'm ready for the next fifty years to begin."

epilogue

MELISSA

"I CAN'T BELIEVE WILL'S moving in with you and the kids!" Tara exclaims as she nearly spills her drink at our table at Lone Tavern.

"I'm so confused about this entire living situation. It's probably because you have an incredibly supportive parent, and mine suck," Jillian adds.

I sway my head, understanding exactly how our story sounds to anyone on the outside. I wave my hand in the air as I explain, "Will suggested we take the next step and move in together. I was incredibly hesitant, as you know."

Jillian looks over at Tara. "Melissa was a mess for the entire week. I had to take the colored pencils away from her because every time she sketched out a wedding, it would have a pros and cons list of whether or not she should move in with Will. And for the record, the pros list was incredibly long."

Moving in with Will is definitely a pro. Over the past six months, he's been the most dedicated boyfriend and a huge support to Isabella and Hunter. We managed to figure out a way to spend time together without interfering in our careers or my time with the kids.

As it turns out, the kids love having Will over, and I love our lazy afternoons when the kids are in school or at Tyler's, and we can sneak away for some much-needed intimacy.

"What are the cons?" Tara wants to know.

"Just one." I suck on my straw.

I wasn't worried about how the kids would feel about Will living with us. In fact, the conversation started when Hunter suggested it. Will spends an exorbitant amount of time at our house, but never sleeps over. I stay at his place on the weekends, and we're both there when the kids get dropped off by Tyler on Sundays. Izzy even chimed in that it would be nice to have Will cook dinners for us regularly since he was far better in the kitchen than I was. I tried not to take offense to that. And since Maisie has officially moved in with Tyler while they plan their winter wedding—*no, I am not designing it. Thank goodness!*—it doesn't seem odd to the kids that we're increasing our family to this big, wonderful, complicated mess of love.

Tara nods in understanding. "I bet it was your dad."

I laugh with a sigh. "Dad would have an issue if it were anyone else. The men who spend time around his grandchildren is a serious matter for Gavin Jones. But he and Will … they've developed quite a relationship over the past few months. Will is a man my father respects greatly, which doesn't come easily, and Will finds my father quite comical even though the man's not trying to be funny." I look over at my dad at the bar, standing at the bar and talking to Will over a glass of whiskey. "My dad's actually the one who came up with the living arrangement. Will is moving into my parents' house with me and the kids while Dad is going to Will's house."

"Then, what was the holdup?"

"Me." I shrug. "I moved back to a home that reminded me of my youth, reminded my children of my mother, and was a giant hug. I know it sounds crazy, but I'm very attached to that house. It's my home and a place that built me not just once, but twice."

Jillian takes a long swig of her drink. "So different from how I grew up. I couldn't wait to run away from my parents' place. In fact, when they head to Maine for the summer, I feel like I can finally breathe."

"Funny. You need yours to leave, and I want mine to stay. Those two are on yet another cruise. I swear they should just sell their house and be one of those couples who lives aboard cruise ships," Tara quips.

LOVE ... IT'S COMPLICATED

"They have singles cruises. You should go on one," Jillian suggests, to which Tara bounces on her butt and nearly knocks over her glass.

"Let's go together. Two girls on a trip of a lifetime!"

"No, thank you. I'm good, being home. Plus, I have no one to watch Ainsley for that long. My parents are good for a few hours here and there and the occasional sleepover. Long trips are out of the question."

"I'll watch her," I offer, trying to push my single friend to get out into the word and find love. I wish she'd take a chance on someone. Just once.

She tugs at her collar and bites her lip. "Maybe. I'll think about it." She gives Tara a stern look. "No promises. Don't go booking anything."

Tara already has her phone out and appears to be scrolling the internet, I'm sure looking at singles cruises. When Jillian raises her brows, Tara looks like she's been caught with her hand in the cookie jar.

Jillian leans forward. "So, how is this situation working? Is your dad buying Will's house?"

I shake my head. "My dad has an odd sense of duty, if you will. In his words, the house is going to belong to me anyway, so I might as well have it now. He offered to live in Will's house—for free, of course, since Dad has paid off his mortgage and refuses to acquire a bill. Will was happy to shake hands on that deal. He'd never accept a penny from my father anyway."

"When is all this happening?" Tara asks.

I look over at the bar, where Will is laughing with my dad. He must sense I'm staring because he looks over with that effervescent smolder. He takes my breath away from across the room.

"It pretty much already has. Will helped my father move his personal belongings over to Will's house, and vice versa. Over the next few weeks, we have to get the woodworking station into the new garage. We already have the gym in one of the extra bedrooms."

"Looks like your dad can have his bachelor pad over there." Tara winks, and I groan.

Dad and Anna have been spending more time together around me. While there will forever be an uncomfortable pit way down deep in my belly at the fact that my dad is with someone who's not my mom, I know he has no choice since Mom's not here. Just because your great love passes away doesn't mean you spend the rest of your life without companionship. And for my dad, I hope the love he has with Anna is enough to keep him to his final days. It makes me happy that he's content and well cared for.

Same for me. I understand Will and I haven't been together long, but ... when you know, you know.

While I might not have been single long, I have been by myself for years. Tyler and I gave up long ago. I might have lived in that home, but pretending isn't real. Being with Will, the good, the bad, the easy, and the hard ... it's my real.

My therapist would be proud if she heard my inner monologue. We chat over zoom once a week and it's really helping. I used to be one of those women who never thought she needed therapy because I had friends to talk to. Amazing friends who listened, gave advice when needed, and are a fantastic support system. Turns out, burning robes and bitching about my ex-husband over a bottle of wine wasn't the only therapy I needed. A professional helped me dig deeper to really tackle my abandonment issues stemming from the worst two years of my life.

I have to thank Izzy for recommending I go.

One night, I sat in bed crying when I thought the kids were asleep. At that point, I had known Allison wasn't going to blast our business because she had called Jillian and told her. I believe the exact quote was, *"While I wish gonorrhea on Melissa, I want you to know I respect you as a woman and business owner and that is the only reason why I am not putting your company through social media hell."* Jillian was relieved and I was a bit surprised by the fact Allison and I are more alike than I thought as I once wished a severe case of herpes on Maisie.

No, this particular night, I'd been wallowing over missing Will. Izzy came into my room and hugged me. She didn't ask any questions. She combed my hair with her fingers the way I do for her. I quickly morphed into my everything-is-fine mantra, asked what was bothering her that she had still been up, and then snuggled her until she went to sleep. The next day, Izzy suggested I talk to someone the way she does. I'd knew I'd be a hypocrite to say no so I agreed out of principle.

After one session I loved it.

I mean, I do love to talk and having an open forum where I can dish about everything and anything is a total win. Plus, it's more

LOVE ... IT'S COMPLICATED

confidential than a barber shop or salon chair. The therapist can't unload my secrets and I can confess to anything without judgement.

I also cried. A lot.

I laughed. I pondered. I surprised myself.

I grew over the next few weeks. It was enough for me to pull my head out of my ass and give a great man a chance to love me. To love him back.

Months later, I wouldn't dream of giving up my therapy sessions. There will always be as scar left by Tyler's betrayal. There's no magic potion to remove it. Instead of trying to cover it up, I wear it proudly as a reminder of the strong, single mother I am. It helps me love Will in a new and deeper way.

Damn, I'm getting melancholy in my old age.

I snap back to reality and look around the room.

Tonight's dance floor at Lone Tavern is a packed. The place is not filled with young coeds, half-dressed in cowboy attire. No, tonight is all about Sergeant William Bronson.

My handsome officer is sauntering across the room in his smoldering glory over to where I'm seated with my girls.

As he approaches, he places his arm around the small of my back and pulls me up, kissing my cheek and looking at me with such adoration that it's like he hasn't seen me in days when, in fact, we came here together.

"What are you doing over here? You're the man of the hour. You should be mingling with your friends and family."

He whispers, "Why would I want to hang out with them when my favorite person in the world is over here?"

I playfully slap him on the chest. "It's been a year since you were shot. Everyone is here to celebrate your heroism and promotion. Go play nice with the family." I lean in and whisper so no one can hear me, "Don't worry; the actual celebration has been planned for you tonight when the kids go back to Tyler's."

"Handcuffs?"

"And the baton." I lean up and place a chaste kiss on his lips and shimmy out of his hold, but not before he grabs my hand and pulls me toward him and places the sexiest, most arousing kiss on my lips.

"Will!" I admonish even though I love when he treats me like this—like I'm the most important thing in the room and what he can't live without. "Your mother is staring."

"Good. If she didn't like it, she shouldn't have helped you get me arrested."

"She and I have an understanding now. When you get out of line, we know where to put you."

"Up until last year, I'd never been in trouble in my life."

"So I've heard. Such a Boy Scout."

I smile and then let him lead me toward the dance floor. The music is playing a similar country tune to those we danced to last year. The kind where he leads my body in a sultry dance and my heart into a trance.

We don't dance like that tonight. Instead, the friends and family who came out to celebrate Will join us. His parents and siblings, nieces and nephews—yes, the Bronson clan is huge. His friends, who have stuck with him. Men and women he works with, and my small family, including Jillian and Tara. They all take to the floor.

Hunter, who long ago got his cast off, does a terrible rendition of the Worm while Izzy shakes her head, her eyes rolling, and then laughs. Dad takes her hand and twirls her, showing her how to do a proper dance, as Gavin Jones doesn't mess around on the dance floor.

As Will pulls me in, I fall into his embrace, as I have been since the very first time I threw myself at him in the parking lot of this very bar.

I love William Bronson as much today as I did the first time I declared it, but not as much as I will tomorrow and the day after that.

It's not just his kisses.

I found my big love.

The kind that will stay until we're old and gray and one of us leaves first.

And if by chance, in ten to fifteen years down the road, it doesn't work out, I've settled into the fact that I'm so blissfully happy right now that I wouldn't change a thing.

Love … it's complicated, sure.

It's also beautiful, amazing, and what I can't live without.

Read the extended epilogue at
https://dl.bookfunnel.com/ss9073f3pg

Melissa and Will have a big announcement
to make in their bonus scenes!

If you enjoyed *Love … It's Complicated*, you might want to check out these best-selling novels by Jeannine Colette.

A REALLY BAD IDEA

JUST TEN SECONDS

Books by Jeannine Colette

ABANDON COLLECTION

Pure Abandon
Reckless Abandon
Wild Abandon
True Abandon
Sinful Abandon

STAND-ALONES

A Really Bad Idea
Just Ten Seconds
Wrecked
Body of Trust

SEXTON BROTHERS

Austin
Bryce
Tanner
Layover Lover

FALLING FOR THE STARS

Naughty Neighbor
Charming Co-Worker
Rebel Roommate
Arrogant Officer
Bastard Bartender
Loyal Lawyer
Heartbroken Hero

acknowledgments

I ONCE HAD A year that sucked. My mom's advice was, "Write."

"Write what?"

"Write what you know."

I didn't know it at the time, but that was the beginning of my self-publishing career. My mother's encouragement was the motivation I needed to take a chance on myself. She read each word and shared every social media post with pride. She was the driving force behind my every motion, and when she died, I couldn't move. I never believed in writer's block until I found myself at a metaphorical roadblock in my mind, unable to get the creative forces in drive. Grief was now in the driver's seat, and I didn't know how to hit the gas.

Over the next twelve months, I learned to navigate this world without the most amazing woman I'd ever met by my side. Sure, she had flaws, but even her flaws were perfect to me. I had to kick grief to the side and take control of my emotional vehicle again. (I don't know where all the car analogies are coming from, but let's roll with it.)

In order to move on, I surrounded myself with amazing women who, while they could never replace my mother, each filled the void in ways I never imagined. To Nanci Weaver, Gwenn Monopoli, Kathy Curro, Dina Pedula, Maria Giuffre, Lynn Distefano, Michelle Worden, Jessica Hertzberg, Jill Meister, Dana Bellini, Nicole Lancelotti, Tara McCormick, Nickie Parsons, Shannon Rinelli, Loriann Kelly, and Jillianne Tejani. Your friendships, simple conversations, and small actions combined have done the world to fill the enormous gap left in my heart, and now, only a small hole remains—a hole I never wish to fill because it's a reminder of her. Thank you for being you.

To Marissa Jones, who is a true champion of a friend. I've never met anyone who selflessly cheers on others to succeed the way you do. To Lauren Costa, for your excitement with my words, for pushing me to get back to work, and for being my narrator guru.

To my grandmother, Marilyn Thompson. A woman I've used as a muse too many times to count because she is so fabulous a character in real life. We are blessed to have one another, and I cherish having you by my side every day and more so over these past two years. I love you.

Now that I've cried my way through my acknowledgments, let's get down to business!

Autumn Hull of Wordsmith Publicity. You stuck by my side, even when I had no words, no motivation, and completely dropped the ball on promotion. Not only are you an amazing publicist, but your dedication as a friend is unparalleled. Thank you for not giving up on me.

Jill Meister of Meister Innovations. A best friend and now media guru. You held my hand through the hardest parts of the past two years—both personally and professionally. Thank you for helping me shine.

Lauren Runow. My co-author and bestie from the westie. I still don't know how I'd manage this industry without you.

LOVE ... IT'S COMPLICATED

Wilmari Carrasquillo-Delgado, my alpha forever. The woman who has seen my words evolve since 2015. Thank you for your friendship, commitment ... and for recommending books that are so damn good that they consume me and I don't get my own work done! Just kidding. Keep the recs coming!

Thank you to my betas—Lucy Berson, Cattigan Dawes, Jennifer Castiglia, Amy Dietz, Penny Stone, Maria Black, Nadine Killian, Amanda, Christine Armstrong, Sandra Godinho, Nicole Westmoreland, Terri Osborn, Paramita Patra, and Erika Van Eck. Your insights were perfect!

A HUGE shout-out to the team that makes the physical book look absolutely perfect. Sarah Hansen of Okay Creations, for the most beautiful covers ever! Jovana Shirley of Unforeseen Editing, for making my words make sense with your editing and flawless interior design. Virginia Tesey Carey and Courtney DeLollis, for proofreading this work with expert precision.

Above all, my love to my husband, who told me on our tenth wedding anniversary that I needed to write a love story about a divorced single mother. ;) Thank you for being my favorite beta reader.

And to my three children, who have now taken a love for writing themselves. Yes, now, Mommy can help you write your children's books. I promise!

about the author

JEANNINE COLETTE IS THE author of the Abandon Collection—a series of stand-alone novels featuring dynamic heroines who have to abandon their reality in order to discover themselves ... and love along the way. Each book features a new couple, an exciting new city, and a rose of a different color.

A graduate of Wagner College and the New York Film Academy, Jeannine went on to become a Segment Producer for television shows on CBS and NBC. She left the television industry to focus on her children and pursue a full-time writing career.

She lives in New York with her husband, the three tiny people she adores more than life itself, and a rescue pup named Wrigley.

Jeannine and her family are active supporters of The March of Dimes and Strivright The Auditory-Oral School of New York.

www.jeanninecolette.com

Printed in Great Britain
by Amazon